THE MAN
WHO WOULD BE
GOD

THE MAN WHO WOULD BE GOD

SATAN'S FINAL REBELLION

PHIL ARMS

HighWay
A division of Anomalos Publishing House
Crane

HighWay
A division of Anomalos Publishing House, Crane 65633

Printed in the United States of America

09 1

ISBN-10: 0982211988 (paper)
EAN-13: 9780982211984 (paper)

A CIP catalog record for this book is available from the Library of Congress.

Cover illustration and design by Steve Warner

Author photo courtesy of Charles Foster Photography, © 2008

INTRODUCTION

Many historians attempt to make a distinction between secular and religious history. However, all history, in its final analysis, is spiritual and plays out against the backdrop of biblical truth.

The worldview that allows for secular realities and current events to be interpreted in the revealing light of the scriptures may be new to some, but this is the perspective from which all believers should understand their world. All things past, present and future are ultimately a reaction to "It is written." Simply put, history mirrors the universal conflict between righteousness and unrighteousness, a conflict that one day will end. On that Day, both the writers and makers of history will kneel at the reality that all things in human history point to the Savior, Christ, King of Kings and Lord of Lords.

Until that Day the world will increasingly feel the "birth pains" that all creation is currently experiencing in anticipation of its redemption and restoration. The raging spiritual war will dramatically intensify until "all things" surrender and in humble submission bow to Christ the Lord.

But before that Day, the prophets foretell of an Antichrist, a powerful, charming but evil dictatorial leader who appears during a time of worldwide desperation and deprivation and provides a chaotic world with hope. His coming will not be the result of a gentle, bloodless coup or an antiseptic political evolution. It will be accomplished and accompanied by brutality and bloodshed on a scale far greater than that depicted in this book. This remarkable individual with supernatural diplomatic skill will dazzle a desperate generation and will bring peace to a world staggering on the precipice of anarchy and annihilation. Hence, he will be lauded as history's greatest peacebroker.

The Antichrist, the one nonfictional personality portrayed in this book, according to the prophets, will come to power in a dead-to-truth world, and most will flock to this remarkable man. But they will be drawn to his warmth and light only to be destroyed by his fire.

The prophets do not attempt to sugarcoat or downplay the violence and the horror that accompanies these events, though I have attempted in telling the tale to modify both in deference to the reader.

Using the actual biblically prophesied timeline as a plumb line, this fictional account occurs just as "the man of sin" begins his conspiratorial assent to become an all-powerful world ruler. The story answers the oft-posed question by many students of prophecy who read of his meteoric rise to power and ask, "How could this happen?"

Having spent the last 35 years as a biblical preacher, teacher and researcher, I have tenaciously endeavored to remain true to both the tenets of the faith and the basic eschatological facts revealed in the Word of God. For Christians, books such as this stimulate faith in God's prophetic Word and encourages anticipation of that "Blessed Hope."

For those without Christ, books such as this, accompanied by the godly witness left by raptured believers, will be among the few pointers to Truth for those trapped in the tribulation holocaust. It will help those unbelievers understand what is happening to their world and why and what to do to escape "the wrath to come."

Giving thanks unto the Father, who has made us fit to be partakers of the inheritance of the saints in light, Who has delivered us from the power of darkness and has translated us into the Kingdom of His dear Son, in Whom we have redemption through His blood, even the forgiveness of sin...For by Him were all things created, that are in heaven and that are in earth, visible and invisible, whether they be thrones, or dominions, or principalities or powers—all things were created by Him, and He is before all things and by Him all things consist. (Colossians 1:12–14 and 16–17)

PROLOGUE

40 YEARS PRIOR

The river ran swift and cold with the melting glacial waters and thawing snows from further up the Alps. After rushing down the slopes, the frigid waters slowed as they reached the valley. There, the pretty Swiss village of Cherwith sat snuggled between the jagged, snow-covered peaks surrounding it. The late afternoon was gray with low clouds that hid the towering mountaintops.

Like so many other picturesque little villages that adorn the Swiss Alps, Cherwith was enchanting in its quaint Alpine simplicity. The hills surrounding were dotted with centuries-old chalets and small dairy farms. Each had its own bell-laden Jerseys lazily grazing on the rich spring turf and mountain wildflowers. Their bells would signal their every move toward greener grass.

Aged villas fronted the two-lane, main road that wound through the sleepy village. Intermingled with these antiquated masterpieces of architectural design were later-built weathered homesteads comfortably nestled together. Two and three stories high, each house displayed a burst of color radiating from the overflowing flower troughs that highlighted every window and dormer.

Along the main street were small souvenir shops offering clocks, woodcarvings, and jewelry to the passing tourists. A popular pub elbowed its way between the numerous small-town businesses.

Halfway through the village, a small country road intersected with the main road, creating a four-way stop. On each side of this smaller crossroad for less than a kilometer each way sat additional homes, an attractive mountain hotel, a tavern, and a cheese shop. The most distinguished building housed the canon bakery that saturated the village air every morning with the aroma of fresh-baked breads and pastries.

Just across the street from the popular bakery, an old chalet served as the local hospital. It contained only four rooms for the infirm whose minor needs might require an overnight stay. All the more seriously injured or ill had to be ambulanced to a larger town 50 kilometers away.

The hospital was, in truth, little more than a clinic. The personnel consisted of two volunteer nurses, both in semi-retirement. They only came in when absolutely necessary. The elderly Dr. Corday, who should have retired 20 years earlier, was the only other part-time volunteer at the facility.

As the night fell, Dr. Corday was, once again, called in to attend a very pregnant young woman who, in his aged opinion, thought she was the first woman in the universe to face childbirth. Both nurses were preoccupied elsewhere and the old doctor would handle the birth himself.

Three hours earlier, the young mother-to-be had been brought in on a horse-drawn hay wagon from further up in the hills where births were usually handled by local midwives. The old man who drove the wagon had acted strangely frightened and very much in a hurry. The man had helped the girl waddle into the clinic, then he thrust a stack of money into Dr. Corday's hand and hastily left without saying a word. Now, in the later stages of a very hard labor, the woman had volunteered no information about her background or family history.

As the elderly physician rummaged around the ill-kept birthing room preparing for the inevitable, he had no idea nor could he have ever imagined the significance of the historic event about to take place in his tiny clinic. Nor could the gracious old doctor have known that this assist would be the final act of his long-distinguished career, and would bring his life to a terrifying end.

ONE

At 30,000 feet, the earth slipping by below resembled a patchwork quilt with various-sized squares, each with its own shade of brown and green. The small bodies of water reflecting the sun's rays looked like diamonds sprinkled on the canvas, and the rivers appeared as shiny silver ribbons. At this altitude, the earth took on a serene peacefulness that was hardly the reality on the surface below.

Such were the thoughts of Captain Eric Holder as he pondered the view from his pilot's side window. Thoughts that were abruptly interrupted as his headphones sprang to life and crackled with urgent sounds from the real world around him.

"Air Force One, this is French Departure Control. Please descend to 10,000 feet. Upon arrival at one zero thousand, contact Italian approach on 127.43."

Captain Holder, shaken out of his daydream, compressed the comm button on his yoke and responded, "French departure…understand. Air Force One is cleared to descend to 10,000 where we contact Italian approach on 127.43. Thank you and good day."

The French controller acknowledged in heavily accented English, "And to you, sir…Departure out."

Just as Captain Holder finished programming the newly assigned altitude into the 747's autopilot, he heard the cabin door open. Glancing over his shoulder, he saw his co-pilot, 1st Officer Jerry Saples, returning from a short break.

As the 1st Officer twisted his 6'2" frame to squeeze into his cramped co-pilot's seat, Captain Holder asked, "Did you enjoy your break, Saples?"

Saples snorted as he adjusted the headphones back into position, "Yeah right, if you call a four-and-a-half minute trip to the head a break."

Noticing the change in the plane's attitude, the co-pilot continued, "And since you have obviously already set us up for our descent, that means we are now in Italian air space and probably about 30 minutes from touchdown. So shouldn't you inform our distinguished host and his guests to wipe the sleep from their eyes, down their mouthwash, and prepare for another one of Captain Holder's three-point landings?"

Holder, sometimes annoyed, but most times amused by his co-pilot's jocular banter, smiled. "I tell you what, Saples. Since you're all chipper after 12 hours in-flight and are clearly bright-eyed and bushy-tailed, why don't you give 'em the good news. Then be a good boy and get the figures on weights, fuel on board and numbers of pax."

Smiling broadly, co-pilot Saples gave a mock salute, "Aye, Aye el' Captain. Consider it done."

With that said, Saples reached forward and flipped a toggle switch on his control panel that activated the speakers throughout the 747. Then in his most relaxed, bass pilot's voice, he said, "Good morning ladies and gentlemen. This is 1st Officer Saples reminding you of the eight-hour time change at our destination. It is now 3:29 p.m. in Rome, where we will be landing in approximately 30 minutes. Upon touchdown, all of our honored guests will be briefed by administrative personnel concerning de-boarding protocol. At that time, they will also provide each of you with an updated presidential schedule for our stay in Rome. The President of the United States of America, along with the staff and flight crew of Air Force One, thank you for flying with us on the safest and most secure aircraft in the world."

With the autopilot controlling the descent from 30,000 to 10,000 feet, and with his co-pilot back in the right seat, Captain Holder relaxed. Once again, as he gazed out his side window to take in the meticulously manicured Italian terrain below, his thoughts turned to his family.

At 52, after almost 30 years as a military pilot, the captain was ready for a change. He contemplated his last conversation with Sarah, his wife of 28 years and the love of his life. Both of them had agreed that it was time for Eric to retire from active duty.

They also agreed that their two boys, 11-year-old Brett and 13-year-old David, most definitely needed their dad at this special stage in their lives. He and Sarah had put off having children for almost 15 years in order to accommodate their careers. Now, both felt it was time to accommodate their children.

Flying F-16s in the Kosovo conflict and during Gulf War I had merited Eric two Distinguished Flying Crosses. Over his career as an Air Force pilot, he had received a dozen other meritorious awards, not only as a fighter pilot but also as an instructor. But all the medals in the world could never replace the time he had already lost by constantly being away from his family.

Ten years ago, he had been ready to pull out. His 20 years were up, but the Force had bonused-up and talked him into becoming Chief Flight Instructor for young F-16 pilots. As it turned out, the job consumed nights and days, leaving very little down time for family.

Then seven years ago, Eric had been offered the prestigious, high-frills chief pilot position on Air Force One. He headed one of the four teams responsible for flying the President of the United States anywhere in the world, anytime he wanted to go.

But now the demands of the job were once again robbing him of the time that he longed to spend with Sarah and the boys. He was tired of missing his sons' baseball, football, soccer and basketball games. He was tired of making promises to his boys that the next weekend they would all go camping, fishing, or hunting, only to have to cancel because duty called.

Sarah's job as assistant editor for a high-profile women's magazine could now be handled completely from their home. Just before Eric had left on this trip, the couple had decided that his pension and retirement, combined with her salary and their substantial savings, would get them by quite comfortably. Thus, they had determined that he would submit his resignation when he returned. He couldn't wait to see his sons' eyes light up when he told them that from now on he wouldn't miss any more of their sports activities or family outings.

Only yesterday, Eric had talked to his 32-year-old co-pilot about priorities. He had told Saples how, if he had an opportunity to do it all again, things would be different.

Saples and his wife had been married only five years and just had their first child six months ago. Since then, Saples had spoken frequently of his desire to spend more time with his wife and new son. Eric had counseled him not to wait until the boy started shaving to get to know him.

"Captain?" Saple's voice in his headphones broke into Eric's thoughts.

"Yes, what is it, Saples?"

"Sir," responded the co-pilot as he handed Eric the BlackBerry with data, "here are the numbers, weights, ratios, pax numbers, et cetera that you requested."

"Thank you, Saples," responded Eric, "I will look them over now. Advise me when we reach 10,000."

"Yes, sir."

It had taken three weeks longer than he had initially planned, but Fazul Abdullah, with Allah's help and Al-Qaeda's blessing, had made it happen. He still was not certain just who was orchestrating and financing the operation that he was on the verge of accomplishing. But he knew whoever was behind it was acting as the arm of Allah and was well connected with Jihadist leadership.

Security in Rome today was tight and even though Fazul had checked and rechecked to see if there was any surveillance on his tail, he was still skittish. He had just parked the second car he had used today and was now in the third, a 12–year-old, tan Mercedes van. Still, he knew he must remain vigilant. He could only hope the others were being as careful as he.

Recognizing his destination, he slowed the van and turned into the parking lot behind a long line of warehouses. They were to rendezvous here, out of sight of the traffic passing in front of the warehouse complex. Fazul maneuvered the van into a parking space facing the back of the warehouses.

The location was less than a mile from the checkpoint and eastern gate entrance to Da Vinci International Airport. As he put the van in park, Fazul looked at his watch, which had been synchronized to the second with that of his team. He noticed he was two full minutes ahead of schedule.

Fazul rolled down his window and nervously lit a cigarette. He tried to make himself relax, to no avail. He was nervous, excited and hyped. This was hardly his first mission in the holy war, but without doubt it was the most ambitious—and if successful, would be the most memorable. Fazul had fought on the front lines of Jihad's ongoing battles against the Great Satan long enough to know that there is a big difference between dreaming of glory and actually achieving it.

As he counted off the seconds, sweat poured from his face. His fingers nervously pounded out a rhythm on the steering wheel. No sooner than he had decided to check his watch again, he saw a black BMW sedan pull into the lot and roll into the space right next to him. Seconds later, a yellow, stretch city cab slowly entered the lot and parked by the BMW.

He knew the automobiles contained three men each. But no one, including Fazul, exited.

They sat. They waited.

Exactly two minutes later, an American-made Humvee slowly rolled into the parking lot and stopped. The greenish camo paint job and the decals on its sides, front and back left no doubt that it belonged to the Special Security Forces responsible for the Da Vinci International Airport. The Humvees whose decals sported the bright blue security force logo on a white background were now a common sight all over Rome, but especially so near the airport. The troops they carried intimidated everyone who served in all the other police and security agencies of Rome. Most in the other agencies felt that these specially-trained troopers needed a stronger civil authority to govern their actions. But when it came to airport security, especially this week, few were griping about their strong-arm tactics.

The Humvee had stopped and was just sitting there with its motor running as though it was studying Fazul and his entourage. Then it slowly rolled forward—straight toward Fazul's group of three automobiles.

Fazul, as well as occupants in the cab and the Bemer, sat frozen in place. Fazul had not turned his head to follow the Humvee's slow progress but he could now hear the crunch of the gravel under its tires as it eased up behind him and stopped, blocking any possible escape route. Then, almost simultaneously, the drivers and occupants of all four vehicles opened their doors to exit.

The driver of the Humvee stepped out first, dressed in the spit-and-polish security uniform that intimidated so many. Completing the uniform was the red beret on his head and the 40-caliber Beretta strapped to his waist. In his left hand he carried an AK-47–103 with a full clip. On his left shirt pocket was an embossed clip-on ID tag with the officer's name, rank and unit emblem.

As Fazul stepped out of his van, he moved toward the security officer. When he was close enough, both men reached out for the other, embraced, and kissed each other's cheeks with the traditional Middle Eastern greeting. Fazul then pushed himself back, leaving his hands on the shoulders of this friend, and spoke.

"Amer, may Allah be praised. Your timing is perfect."

Fazul turned to address the rest of the men who had climbed out of their automobiles. At first glance he was taken aback. He knew they were all to be dressed in the same security uniforms as Amer, but still, the authenticity of the disguises momentarily startled him.

Pleased with what he saw, Fazul spoke to the tallest of them, saying, "Sa'eed, load everyone in the Humvee. Use only the two back bench seats."

As the group moved toward the Humvee, Fazul turned again to Amer, asking, "Is everything in place? Has anyone encountered any problem or setbacks?"

"Everything and everyone is in place and not so much as a whisper of resistance has surfaced. But," Amer rushed to add, "we must hurry, Fazul. Our target is just under a half an hour out."

Fazul smiled large, patted Amer on the back, and said, "Then get in and we will go avenge Allah, may his name be blessed."

As Amer slid behind the wheel, Fazul jogged around to the passenger side, opened the door, and got in. With a backward glance, he saw all six of his commandos. They were quiet, game-faced and pumped, ready to inflict pain on the infidels. They had repeatedly gone over every detail of this mission for weeks. They were prepared for any contingency. Each of these men owned this mission. Each was prepared to die as a martyr if it was necessary to guarantee success.

As the Humvee lurched forward and made a 180-degree turn to exit the parking lot, Fazul turned to face the front. Buckling his seat belt, he said, "Now we will make the infidels cry a river of tears."

Air Force One is hardly just another Boeing 747. The aircraft and its twin are specially modified and uniquely configured to meet the needs of the world's most powerful man.

Over six stories high at the cockpit and longer than a city block, both of the 747s that serve as AF1 have been radically redesigned. The planes are divided into a three-level floor plan.

The top level is fronted by the cockpit and flight deck. Just aft of that is a small galley and lounge that butts up against the most high-tech airborne mobile communications center on earth. Behind this center is a stairway leading down to the second level.

Turning right at the bottom of the stairs will lead to a hallway which, if followed, goes into a full lounge and bar area. At the back of the lounge still another stairway leads down to level three.

However, it is on level two that the president's office is located. Going to the left at the bottom of the first stairwell leads to the Secret Service-guarded door of the Chief Executive. Upon opening the door, to the left sits a beautiful, solid cherry desk. On top of the desk are a bank of phones, a computer terminal, and various personal effects. Just in front of the desk are two leather-bound lounge chairs for guests. Beyond those is a long walnut table with seating for up to 12 people. Still further back is a door leading into a fully equipped medical station, and aft of that is another lounge with a staircase down to level three. The president's bedroom suite and personal facilities occupy much of level three.

Today, the president's office on level two was bustling with the brisk exchange between the president and a few of his cabinet members.

Secretary of State Nathan Whittle was saying, "Mr. President, if I may be so bold, this trip is not about policy. It is about politics. And you, sir, cannot run the risk of being perceived as dancing to the tune of these European maestros."

Having said that, the Secretary of State, satisfied that he had made his point, leaned back in his chair and took a deep breath.

After a moment of silence that seemed to last an eternity, the president said, "Mr. Secretary, I assure you, I'm a terrible dancer, especially to European-conducted overtures. That not withstanding, I invited you three men to accompany me on this three-day diplomatic jaunt in order to tell you what I believe is really going on behind all the hype of this Euro dog-and-pony show.

"Later this evening when all the formalities are completed, we will again meet in strict privacy. After you hear what I have got to tell you, then we can put our heads together and rewrite the tune we are being asked to dance to."

The slight presidential rebuke of his Secretary of State quieted the outspoken secretary. But the rest of what the president had just said piqued the curiosity of everyone there.

Secretary of Defense Leonard Chatwell and director of the National Security Agency William Bird had served this president in one staff position or another since he had been elected governor of Oklahoma 15 years earlier. Both men and Secretary of State Nathan Whittle had been a part of President Mathew Dillon Carr's inner circle since then-Governor Carr had run for the Senate. All three men had made substantial career and financial sacrifices in order to serve this man through two senatorial terms and a tough presidential campaign.

These men knew Dillon Carr well enough to understand that when he had finally listened to all the debates and weighed the facts, his assessments were rarely wrong. They also knew that once he had made a decision, he was as tenacious as a bulldog in seeing it implemented. They knew his heart, and along with millions of other Americans, were stirred to action and sacrifice by his passion and his vision for his country. In the short three years since being elected, Dillon Carr had become the most loved and respected president since Ronald Reagan.

But he was not without opposition. The partisan politicians on the opposite end of the political spectrum mocked what they considered the one-dimensional naïveté of this administration's worldview and foreign policy. They were unabashed globalists who were convinced that the United States must be willing to sacrifice its superpower status in order to bring about what they called "a more equitable sharing of the world's power and wealth." These men were firm in their belief that America was living in a New World, and that in order for America to walk hand in hand with other nations toward prosperity and peace, certain concessions needed to be made. They preached that the era of America's self-centered, force-our-will-on-the-world attitude must end.

President Carr knew that America must retain its military supremacy, as well as its economic advantages, in order to protect the Nation's sovereignty. On that he would not compromise.

"Now," the president continued, "as you know, this conference in Rome is designed to pressure us to move toward moderating our resistance to Euro-Asian expansionism. The European Union, in an effort to appear conciliatory and more global, has been cooperating with this new International Federation of Nations. In a remarkably short period, the IFN has courted and won approval from 85 percent of the member countries of the United Nations.

"This meeting in Rome is, in totality, the brainchild of IFN leadership. They hope to pressure the United States and the other few national holdouts to join their global party.

"The pressure on us is not just from the internationalists. Our own domestic *opposition* is in bed with the IFN. And the national media is painting this administration as narrow-minded, war-mongering and imperialistic.

"Secretary Whittle, you're right in saying this conference is not about simple policy. But neither is it about mere politics. In truth, at the risk of sounding a bit melodramatic, it is about the viability and survival of our nation as we know it."

After a brief silence, Secretary Whipple spoke, "Mr. President, please accept my apology for my earlier outburst. It's just that I was unsure if you could see the wizard behind the curtain in this charade."

"I assure you Nate," replied the president, "while you have spent the last four weeks overseas lobbying the Saudis and the Chinese on this matter, I've been finding out more than you can imagine about the 'wizard' behind all this. Men, I am not going into Rome with my eyes closed; nor am I unaware of the ramifications of these efforts."

"Sir," the Secretary of Defense said, "if I may. I, too, have spent countless hours studying this so-called Federation's goals for the military arm they are proposing. In its final analysis, their plan far exceeds anything ever proposed by the E.U. Frankly, sir, it's frightening."

"I am aware of that, Mr. Secretary," answered the president. "I have thoroughly studied your very comprehensive report. I have also gone over and over the National Security Agency's reviews, as well as the exhaustive CIA analysis. I have combed through the two private sector studies we commissioned as well. And I must tell you, everyone concludes the same thing, and that is, hell should freeze solid before we yield on a single point to the IFN."

"Mr. President," a reluctant Secretary of State spoke, "one of the most damaging salvoes we have suffered comes from your own Vice President, Jordan Hunt."

The president leaned back in his chair, let out a deep breath, and said, "I know it, Nathan. That's what I get for listening to party leaders during the campaign who convinced me we had to have Hunt's state to win. So he ended up on the ticket. Still, we didn't even carry his state in the general. Bad move on my part. He's been wimpy and a coward on every policy effort we've championed. It's a sure bet that someone, somewhere, is pulling his strings."

The president closed the notebook holding the meeting's agenda and said, "Secretary Whittle, we have very little time, so just hit the highlights regarding the hot spots and then after tonight's festivities we'll all meet again and I'll tell you a chilling piece of intel we've stumbled onto. I have a feeling it's all connected to the matters at hand. After you hear it, we will nail down a solid response to these guys."

"Yes, sir," responded the Secretary of State as he opened a large black notebook containing his briefing material.

The beautiful blue-green waters of the Tirreno Sea gently lapped at the sandy beach of Italy's west coast. Watching it on this clear warm day was almost hypnotic. Four kilometers due east sat Rome's Da Vinci International Airport. But it was here, near the water, where Yousef Awal and his two brothers in arms lay in wait.

Yousef, now 35 years old was, in his opinion, born to be a freedom fighter, a defender of the faith and—when the time came—a martyr in this glorious Jihad.

Born in the West Bank town of Ramallah, he understood struggle. At only 13 years of age he had begun his training with Hamas in the occupied territories. When he turned 19, he was invited north, to Lebanon's Bekka Valley, to train and fight with Hezbollah. There he was seduced into Al Qaeda, where he had served faithfully since.

He sat on the third-floor balcony of an abandoned beach villa, where he had a perfect view of every plane heading for Da Vinci Airport from the west. The closest other villa was over a half kilometer to the north. Additionally, the public beach along this stretch had been declared off-limits to beachgoers due to construction that temporarily cut off access. From where Yousef sat, it was less than 200 meters to where the incoming tide kissed the sandy brown beach.

Resting at his feet against the 36-inch-high balcony barrier sat his weapon, the American-made SK-7 shoulder-fired missile launcher. With a large enough payload to bring down any aircraft in the world, it could easily reach an altitude of 10,000 feet.

Its speed, especially if fired at close range, left very little time for evasive efforts on the part of a crew. The heat-seeking head of the missile would chase down even a moderate heat source with unforgiving rage and pin-point accuracy.

Yousef's skill with the weapon had been demonstrated on two previous occasions by his downing of American helicopters in the 1990s Mogadishu affair. Yousef was known for his killing of Blackhawks. He had also helped his leadership in 2003 bring down a Sri Lankan 747 filled with civilian passengers.

Picking up his hand-held, short-range, comm device, he pushed the button to transmit and spoke one prearranged word telling his two men to respond if they were in position and ready. Within seconds of saying "Saladine," he received the three-word confirmation, first from one and then the other, "Saladine The Great."

Several months had passed since he had been teamed up with these two men, whom Yousef did not know before then. Twenty-five year old Kamal Aziza, the short, stocky, full- bearded one, had told him that he had been a recruiter and weapons specialist for Al Qaeda in Afghanistan. Yousef felt Kamal exuded confidence. He trusted him.

Saudi-born Aris Zukarmaen, 29 years old, had fought in Afghanistan with the Taliban. He had fled when the Americans ran the Taliban out of power. Until he had been assigned to this mission, Aris had been in hiding with other Islamic extremists in Somalia. Just being around Aris gave Yousef a chill. The "Saudi Assassin," as Aris was known, reeked of hatred and vengeance. All of the men were on the top most-wanted terrorists list at NATO and in the United States. All were thirsty for the blood of infidels, but mostly for that of American devils and Zionist swine.

Each of them was armed with the same kind of SK-7 Yousef possessed. Yousef, on the villa balcony, had set up Kamal 50 meters to his left, lying on his belly between two tall sand dunes. He had placed Aris in the olive orchard 50 meters to his right.

They were all poised like cobras, ready to strike when the order was given. The deadly powerful missile from a single SK-7 left any target small odds for averting disaster. But when all three missiles were simultaneously sent on a mission, there would be no escaping the terror they delivered.

Yousef checked his watch again. He knew it was almost time for the dragon of Jihad to once again breathe the fires of justice.

TWO

Air Force One to Italian Approach."

"This is Italian Approach, Air Force One," came the response in crisp, Italian-accented English. "Welcome to Italy. We have you at 10,000 feet, heading 145 degrees. Please maintain your current altitude and heading. Expect further instructions shortly. We are pretty busy today. Thank you."

Captain Holder clicked the comm button on the top right side of this yoke confirming his receipt of instructions.

The co-pilot spoke. "I bet they're busy. Dozens of heads of state, plus all their lackeys, inbound from all over the world. Makes me glad I'm not in traffic control."

"I am glad you're not either, Saples," a jesting Holder returned. "As long as we can keep your bum sitting right there, the world of aviation is safe from your wandering mind."

"You may be right, Captain," responded Saples, "but you may not think so highly of these local boys after they've kept us up here flying circles for another hour or two, waiting for them to unclog this aerial traffic jam they created."

"Take a deep breath and relax, Saples," smiled Holder. "We carry the true Chairman of the Board. They'll give us priority very shortly. You'll see."

The Da Vinci International Security Forces Humvee carrying the driver, Fazul, and his six comrades rolled through both checkpoints with little more than a casual glance and nod from the gate guards. The special

Humvees were in and out of these checkpoints throughout the day and the hot, bored duty guards did not like to leave their comfortable chairs and air-conditioned huts just to confirm IDs of those they knew were security personnel.

Everyone in the Humvee let out a deep sigh of relief anyway as they watched the steel crossbar blocking the entrance lifted and the sleepy, nonplused guards wave them through. Even though Fazul and his team, through weeks of surveillance, already knew that lax discipline of checkpoint guards probably guaranteed easy access, their audacious deception still exposed the team to great risk.

Having cleared both checkpoints, their Humvee slowly continued toward the tower facilities 200 meters ahead of them. The single level building next to the control tower housed ground control, responsible for coordinating aircraft traffic to and from runways. It was also the building that held 30 monitor stations, each manned and responsible for aircraft approaching the airport but still at least six miles out.

Fazul and company, however, were focused on the tower, which was accessed by entering a lobby at its base and taking an elevator 10 stories to the top. The tower atop the tall structure was bowl-shaped and enclosed by thick, soundproof glass. From there, one could look out and observe the entire airport sprawling in all directions.

In the tower, six skilled controllers worked the traffic on the last six miles into the airport and directed the flights waiting to depart on the runways. Additionally, the tower contained two live observers with high-powered binoculars and a supervisor.

In order for anyone to go further than the lobby area, he or she had to have a security pass card that could open the elevator and/or the single fire escape stairwell. These pass cards, similar to a credit card, were strictly controlled and available only to tower personnel or security forces.

As the Humvee slowly pulled into one of the parking spaces outside the tower lobby, Fazul double checked his Velcro-sealed front shirt pocket to insure he still had the security pass card. It had been prearranged for the single police officer at the entrance of the lobby to simply nod them through.

As the Humvee's engine stopped, Fazul could hear his team locking and loading their AK47–103's. He checked his own, making sure the newly fitted silencer was tightly secured. Then he checked the Berretta at his waist. No sooner had he re-holstered the pistol, he caught movement in his peripheral vision outside the driver's side window. Turning his head left, he saw another security Humvee, identical to their own, pulling into the space right next to them. His heart leapt in his chest.

The quiet gasps from the back seat let Fazul know that his freedom fighters saw it as well.

"No one move, or speak," Fazul said just loud enough for his group to hear.

To the driver, Fazul said, "Amer, glance over at them, then smile and wave. Don't panic. They're just a routine patrol."

Without answering, Amer did as he was told. As he did, Fazul could see that the Humvee contained two officers. The one on the passenger side was checking something on his clipboard. The driver was lighting a cigarette while talking to his partner.

Amer's brotherly smile and slight wave had gone unacknowledged, and the one with the clipboard was studying the ID number on their door decal with a curious look on his face. He looked back again at his clipboard, then turned to speak to his driver while shaking his head in the negative.

Fazul knew now that they were about to be confronted and exposed. He spoke in a barely audible voice, "Amer, lower your window and lean back."

As Amer complied, he looked with ashen face back at Fazul, and with barely contained panic, said, "The driver is reaching for his radio mike!"

By the time Amer had spoken, Fazul had put his weapon on semi-automatic mode. The barrel was laid across the front of Amer's body, resting on the windowsill. Just as the passenger door of the newly-arrived Humvee swung open and the driver pressed his radio comm button, Fazul, with practiced skill, brought his AK-47 to shoulder where it sprang to life with two silenced puffs.

The first bullet caught the driver an inch above the right eye, just as he opened his mouth to speak into his radio. Two seconds later another bullet penetrated the exiting officer an inch above his right ear.

The driver slumped forward as though he had fallen asleep on the steering wheel. The other officer was pushed by the force of the round that smashed into the right side of his head back into his Humvee, where his body fell across his seat, leaving him half in and half out of the vehicle. The entire episode, from the moment the second Humvee pulled in, to the time when both men where felled by Fazul's silenced AK-47, took less than two minutes.

Seconds later, a voice from the back seat joyously said, "Their mothers are swine. Allah's blessing on Fazul." Five other voices mingled their quiet praises to Allah.

Fazul and Amer were still frantically scanning the area to make sure their actions had not been seen or heard. Satisfied there were no witnesses, Fazul turned his attention back to those within the Humvee. Lifting his voice a level above the praises of his men, Fazul said, "Yes, Allah be praised. Now, be silent and focus."

Turning back to Amer, still in the driver's seat, Fazul added, "Amer, get out, carefully. Put that infidel's body back into his Humvee. Lay him down so no one driving or walking by can see him. And push the driver's body over so it to is well hidden from traffic."

As Amer slid out his door to obey, Fazul turned to his men in the back seat. "On my order we will get out. When everyone is out, then we shall casually walk as a group into the lobby of this building. The entrance is just around that corner, 30 meters to our right. One policeman stands at the entrance. You need not speak to him. Simply smile, nod, and walk past him into the lobby. You each know your assignment. If a threat arises, do not hesitate to use your weapon. Now, let us go and honor the Prophet."

Less than eight minutes had elapsed since Italian approach had instructed Air Force One to hold altitude and heading.

"Air Force One, this is Italian Approach. Uh, we are stacked up high as wine casks today. We have asked four other inbound heads of state for permission to divert their support aircraft to Ciampino Airport, 30 kilometers east of Da Vinci International. It is the only way to get you on the ground within the hour. Is it possible for you to release your support to do the same?"

With a deep sigh, Captain Holder responded, "Approach, Air Force One will submit your request. Stand by."

Airport personnel around the world who facilitate AF1 flights are fully aware that a fleet of aircraft accompanies the president's 747. It is not uncommon on international flights for the presidential entourage to include up to 14 additional aircraft. Air Force One usually carries a crew of 26, which includes stewards, cooks, hostesses, tech personnel and a contingent of Secret Service employees. The plane also carries a press pool of up to 12 network and print reporters on a rotating schedule. A number of VIPs are always on board most flights, upping the passenger list to 102.

The fleet normally includes two G-5 Galaxy heavy transports, each carrying up to 50 Special Forces troops and additional White House Staff. The cargoes of the huge planes include three bullet-proof limos, a fully outfitted ambulance, and three VH60 helicopters with blades folded. On occasion, up to three C-17 cargo planes are along, carrying dozens of additional troops and still more equipment. Included in the mix are several KC-10 Air Force tankers, which in fact are modified DC10s used for in-flight refueling. An additional 747 carrying another press corps also joins the entourage. Flying with the group is an E-4 Flying Command Post. If needed, the president can run a war or national emergency from within. Without fail, two to four F-16s, fully armed, follow AF1 to its destination.

At the request of Approach, Captain Holder turned to his co-pilot. "Go back and check with Command and Control. Explain the traffic problems. They'll ask you that if they okay the diversion, how long AF1 would be without air cover. Tell them, no more than four or five minutes max and most of it on final."

"Yes, sir."

Within minutes Saples returned. He again worked to squeeze back into the co-pilot's seat and said, "Captain, C and C said our C-5s and our C-17s landed at Da Vinci half an hour ago. They were a bit ahead of us. Our fuel on board is more than enough to get us in with some to spare so we do not need to hang onto the tankers. That leaves our other 747 and the E-4, and our tankers which can all be vectored over to Ciampino. It will really tick off the media on the 747 though. And Chief said he will release our F-16s to go back home to France on your command."

"Very good," responded Holder. Keying his mike, he said, "Approach Air Force One."

"Go Ahead Air Force One."

"Yes," returned Holder, "I am told our C-5s and C-17s are already on the ground at Da Vinci. So we will be releasing everyone else in a minute, with the exception of our F-16s. We are now informing everyone else to follow your orders and vectors to Ciampino."

The response was quickly received. "Thank you much, AF1. Now let's try to get you guys down. Begin your descent to 5,000 feet and upon reaching 5,000 contact Da Vinci Tower on 132.25."

"AF1 going to 5,000. Upon arrival we will contact Tower on 132.25."

With that said, Captain Holder instructed his co-pilot, "Go ahead and inform C and C to release our F-16s as soon as we reach 5,000 feet."

"Yes, sir."

"And that's about all I've got time to cover for now, Mr. President. The rest can wait until our later meeting." Secretary of State Whittle closed his black folder and leaned back.

"If I may, sir," chimed in NSA Director Bird, "I might add, that in every single global hot spot the Secretary just mentioned and a good number of others he has not covered yet, our diplomatic, as well as our intel efforts are being frustrated by this new IFN group. They are always one step ahead of us. It's as though they are attempting to be seen as real shakers and movers."

"I know, Bill," answered the president, "and later tonight after things settle down, I'll tell you why they're doing it. You'll have trouble, as did I, believing it. But for now all of us need to get out of these blue jeans and sweat suits. We're close to landing. So you're free to go."

As they all filed out of the room, the president followed the hallway and took the stairs down to level three. Just behind him, an Army colonel followed with the "football," a large briefcase containing all nuclear launch codes. The president's Secret Service man also stayed with him.

Located at the front of level three is the president's Suite, complete with a king-size bed, closets, armoires, a mini-bar, a full shower, and bath facilities. All furniture is bolted to the aircraft frame to avoid in-flight shifting. Security protocol called for the Secret Service man to enter the suite first, followed by the president. The colonel carrying the football took up a position just outside the door.

Already peeling off his shirt as he headed for the shower, the president spoke over his shoulder to his Secret Service shadow, who was just about to step back outside the room. "Hey Mark. Stick around. Make yourself a drink while I get cleaned up."

"Uh, thank you, Mr. President. I think I will, sir. It'll make another great story to tell my grandchildren."

The president smiled, and then disappeared behind the privacy doors.

Agent Mark Spears, with the Service for 18 years, felt sure that both he and the president were safer in this suite than almost anywhere. He had studied the schematics of this room on more than one occasion. He knew the exterior walls were heavily armored with a new lightweight, but high-density steel, encased in a powerful bulletproof, gas-proof, bomb-resistant shell. The room was airtight and waterproof. Tests proved that it could absorb the force of an extreme explosive power without as much as a crack.

After mixing himself a Coke and rum at the mini-bar, Agent Spears took a seat in one of the comfortable, leather lounge chairs. Leaning over to pick up the remote to the flat screen on the wall, he let out a sigh, saying to no one, "Man, this is a great job."

The frumpy receptionist just inside the lobby entrance paid little attention to the security patrol as they sauntered in. Such walkthroughs were standard operating procedures but she always sensed a bit of irritation when they strode in, as though they should be bowed down to. In her opinion, they must have little else to do but hang around wherever they could find cold drinks and air conditioning until their shift was over. As they walked past her desk, she tried to ignore them and turned her attention back to sending the e-mail to her mother.

Amer and two other of Fazul's men stopped just inside the lobby entrance and took up their station while Fazul and the others walked straight to the lifts. With one quick swipe of the security card, the elevator doors slid open with a muffled "ding." Fazul and two of his men quietly stepped into the elevator as the remaining pair took a position outside the lift as the doors slid closed.

The guards left in place by Fazul were to make sure no one accessed the elevators or staircase while he was in the tower.

As the door of the lift closed on Fazul and his companions, he pulled a key from his pocket, inserted it in the matching key hole on the floor indicator, and turned it. He had been assured this would keep the lift stationary with doors open on the tower level until he re-entered and was ready to leave.

THREE

Carla Cavaletti's rise to the rank of tower supervisor was hardly the result of mandatory advancements because she was female. Male chauvinism dominated the Air Traffic Control Corps and she was the only female supervisor in all of Italy. For the seven years she had been employed here, she had been forced to tolerate her male co-workers' perverse remarks and sexual harassment. But she had stuck it out through all the ugly vulgarities and focused on doing a better job than her male counterparts.

Carla did not consider herself particularly attractive, though her curvaceous figure was impossible for men to ignore. Her five-foot-seven-inch, mid-size frame; shoulder-length, thick, black hair; dark brown eyes; and pouty mouth made her appear more sensuous than pretty.

As far as her lack of socializing with men off the job, she blamed her long, irregular work hours. And the Italian men in her work environment, who all saw themselves as great lovers, were either married or outright geeks. Hardly a day passed without one of them hitting on her. Though she always pretended to be disgusted, deep inside she treasured the fact that in spite of her 35 years of age, men were still attracted to her.

The secret she worked very hard to keep was how very lonely she really was.

This made her extremely vulnerable to the handsome, smooth-talking, Middle Eastern man she had "accidentally" met after work one day. They were both exiting the parking lot when she had felt a bump on the back fender of her eight-year old Jetta Volkswagen. Though the damage to the front end of his new Fiat had been far worse than the scratch on her rusted fender, the handsome stranger had fallen all over himself apologizing for his recklessness. He had demanded she allow him to pay for the repairs to her car. She had laughed, telling him, "It's nothing, really." Still, he had insisted on making some kind of restitution. After she continued to decline the offer, he had reached into his pocket, producing a large wad of bills, and begged her to take them. Still, she refused.

Finally, acting every bit the pouting little boy, he said in his exotic Middle Eastern accent, "All right, you take no money but I must insist you allow me to take you to dinner. That is, unless you are rushing home to a fat husband and six screaming children."

At that, Carla was forced to laugh. Disarmed, she said, "All right, but I have errands to run first, so…" glancing at her watch, "I'll meet you at the Piazza De Santo arena. We will choose one of those cute little outdoor cafés. But, dinner and that's all."

With that, Fazul smiled slightly, bowed his head while kissing her hand, and said, "Surely, it is the gods that have brought us together."

To which Carla responded, "It is more likely that it was your careless driving. I'll see you at 8." And they parted.

Since that night six months ago, she and Fazul had been inseparable. He had charmed his way into her life and then into her bed. Now with his talk of marriage, and babies and more, she was hopelessly in love. Without realizing it, Carla had become putty in the hands of her knight in shining armor.

With a muffled "ding," the lift that emptied into the back of the control tower room quietly slid open. Fazul and his two Jihadists silently stepped off as the doors behind them remained open. Each of them held his AK-47 at hip-level ready to fire.

As Fazul and his men quickly sized up the room, not one of the six controllers on the lower deck who sat with their backs to the intruders even looked up from his station monitor. They sat in a horseshoe arrangement, wearing their earpieces and mike sets, speaking softly to pilots of the little green crosses that appeared on their screens.

Six feet in front of the controllers, two steps led up to the slightly elevated deck from which two observers with binoculars and the shift supervisor monitored the delicate aerial ballet of aircraft, as they converged on the airport. This upper deck was surrounded 360 degrees by the thick soundproof glass through which could be seen approaches to the airport from every compass point.

Fazul could see Carla and the two observers on the top deck with their backs toward him. As Carla was speaking into the mike attached to her earpiece apparatus, she turned and saw Fazul and his two men standing in front of the open lift doors. She quickly turned her back toward them, acting as though they were not there. With that, Fazul simply nodded to his men. Both stepped up behind the six seated controllers. The Jihadist standing behind the three controllers on the right fired a burst from his weapon, shattering the consoles and screens of the three. All six controllers were so stunned by the explosions of the AK-47 they either fell back out of their chairs or jumped up screaming in fear.

Seeing the armed men, each of the controllers, who had by now all jumped to their feet, threw their hands up. The man who had just destroyed the three monitor stations quickly turned his weapon upon the three men whose screens had been blown to pieces and, without hesitation, pulled the trigger. The men fell where they stood while the three others, along with the upper deck observers, watched in terrified shock.

Fazul ordered the three remaining controllers to sit back down, promising them death if they used their communications equipment to warn anyone. They quickly complied and he ordered them to tell the approaching planes that the tower had suffered a power surge, and to maintain their altitudes and heading for a few minutes.

By then, Fazul had bounded up the three steps and at point blank range shot the two observers between the eyes.

Carla stood in wide-eyed horror. She and Fazul had planned this takeover of the tower for months, repeatedly going over every aspect of the incursion. But never had Fazul said a single word about killing any of her crew. Her assignment was to act as if under duress, and redirect the plane of the American President, forcing it to land from the west. That, Fazul had told her, would bring it to a stop at the east end of the runway where his men, acting as Italian security, would stop and board the aircraft.

Their plan would be to kidnap the American President, holding him hostage until the United States withdrew its murderous military from all Muslim countries. Fazul had promised her he would release the president unharmed as soon as the U.S. complied with his demands. After this was all over, they would flee together to his oil-rich inheritance in a secure country. There, he had promised they would live as heroes in royal splendor, hailed throughout the Muslim world.

Never could she ever have imagined the slaughter unfolding before her eyes. She turned and stared hard into the face of Fazul with a desperate look. He grabbed her arm and pulled her close. Moving close to her ear, he whispered, "Stay calm, my love. It is almost over. Then you and I will find our own paradise."

After he said it, he roughly pushed her backward, yelling, "Whore, you will do as I say or the rest of you will die!"

Their plan had included Fazul's rough treatment of her so it would appear that she had nothing to do with the episode. Keeping in character with her assigned role, Carla spat at Fazul with a look of hatred and yelled, "I will do nothing you ask unless you promise not to kill any more of my people."

The three remaining controllers were shocked, but pleased with their boss's show of courage.

Fazul, without hesitation, backhanded Carla across the mouth, screaming, "Witch, you die first unless you do as I say. Now!"

Carla took the powerful blow knowing it was necessary to maintain her cover. Tasting the salty blood trickle into her mouth, Carla wiped her chin with the back of her hand, sneered, and asked, "And what is it you want?"

Fazul jerked the Berretta from his belt clip and stuck it to Carla's head. Holding her tightly by her arm, he opened his mouth to speak when the intercom speakers came to life. Carla had turned the speakers on when Fazul first appeared so he would know when Air Force One, acting on instructions from approach, contacted the tower.

"Air Force One to Da Vinci Tower. We are at 5,000 feet, 10 miles northwest on a southerly heading of 180 degrees."

Carla turned her head to see the radar screen flashing AF1's position.

Fazul pushed the barrel up hard under Carla's chin and growled, "Okay. These are the instructions you will convey to Mr. Air Force One." He handed her a small piece of paper from his shirt pocket.

She took it even though she already knew what it said, but she also knew the ruse must continue. She jerked her head free from the barrel of the pistol, and through gritted teeth, growled, "I need my chin free if you expect me to speak."

Fazul relaxed his grip, and with his gun waving in front of her face, yelled, "Do it!"

Keying her mike, Carla spoke. "Air Force One, DaVinci Tower has you northwest over the water. Slow to two-two-five knots and descend to 1500. In 11 miles, that is one-one miles, you will intercept radial 090. As soon as you do, you will be seven miles west of the threshold. You're number one for runway nine right. Our brand new ILS will bring you home. Welcome to Rome."

The response was immediate. "Air Force One, slowing to 225 knots and descending to 1500. Turning left on the 090 radial in 11 miles, for landing on runway nine right. Keep the lasagna warm. AF1 out."

Fazul sneered and whispered, "Oh, it will be warm. I assure you that."

Yousef and his two backups had been on location, keeping a low profile for over 10 hours. He knew his men were as hot, sore and hungry as he. Just as he began to feel sorry for himself, the cheap, throw-away cell phone stuck in his pants pocket began chirping. His exhaustion was quickly replaced by an adrenalin rush as he fumbled to remove the phone from his pocket.

Trying to calm himself, he knew that only one man on earth had the cell number. Yousef answered with the prearranged code phrase, "The Scorpion's stinger is poised." To which the voice on the other end, replied, "The eagle arrives in three to five. Strike a blow for Allah."

Fazul pushed the button to end his call.

He turned back and saw his two men standing behind the three remaining controllers on the bottom deck. With a simple nod of his head toward the two Jihadists he conveyed, "Now. Do it."

In an instant, the two AK-47s spit their death into the heads of the three controllers.

Carla was aghast and screamed, "No!" as the gunfire began. When the weapons grew silent she turned her tear-stained face toward Fazul. "Fazul, why…?"

But, before she could finish her question, Fazul grabbed her, drew her close, and placed a lingering kiss on her mouth. As he felt her tension released, he pulled back to stare into her eyes and tenderly said, "My love, didn't I promise you paradise?"

Carla reached up and pushed a lock of hair on his forehead aside. She looked lovingly into Fazul's soothing eyes, but before she could answer his question with the soft "yes" he knew was coming, Fazul raised his pistol, placed it against her temple and pulled the trigger.

Carla's dead body slumped against him. He took a step back, allowing her to fall next to the dead already littering the floor. Fazul looked down at her face, saw her eyes were wide with surprise, and said, "And to paradise you shall go."

The voice of one of Fazul's men broke the silence. "Fazul. We must go. Quickly." Fazul finally looked up, waved his pistol toward the lift, and ran with his men into its open doors.

As the doors slid closed, only three minutes had passed since he and his men had entered the lobby.

Waiting for the president to get ready, Agent Spears had slowly nursed his Coke and rum while watching CNN on the suite's flat screen. He was not used to a lot of downtime on presidential duty, and if his boss saw him now he knew he would be canned. "But," he silently rationalized, "I'm only following orders from the Chief!" His guilt trip was interrupted when he heard the president calling his name from behind the closed door of the bathroom.

Agent Spears jumped up so fast he spilt his drink all over his pants and the carpet. Cursing under his breath, he moved toward the president's voice and answered, "Mr. President, I'm here. Is everything okay?"

He heard a chuckle and then the president's voice from behind the closed door, "Would you mind looking in the closet next to the television and bring me the brown suit bag hanging in front?"

"Yes sir, Mr. President. Just one minute." Spears moved back across the room. Looking in the closet, he grabbed the brown suit bag, scampered back to the other side of the room and gently tapped on the door. "I have your things, Mr. President."

The door opened a few inches and the president's bare arm reached out with an open hand. The agent placed the handle in the open hand. The suit bag disappeared behind the door. Spears heard a muted "thank you."

The president, who had already showered and shaved, pulled his shirt, tie and various amenities out of the bag. He put on everything except his suit coat and quietly opened the door. Glancing out, he saw Agent Spears watching CNN's report on the Rome Conference, with his back to the president.

"Anything of import on the news, Spears?"

Embarrassed that the Chief had caught him glaring at television, the agent stammered, "Oh no...no, sir...I mean you probably know everything they do and a whole lot more."

The president smiled and started putting on his tie. "We're in trouble if I don't. Incidentally, on the way in a while ago, I laid my 'keeper' on the nightstand by the bed. Would you be so kind as to bring it in here, Spears?"

The "keeper," as the president called it, was a small device less than one inch by one inch, and no thicker than a quarter, that Presidents carry on their bodies 24 hours a day. It works on the same principle as a GPS transmitter by sending out a signal on a secure frequency that is picked up by a series of satellites connected to the NSA and a myriad of other surveillance resources whose job is to keep tabs on the physical location of the president around the clock.

No president could leave home without it.

Agent Spears retrieved it and was handing it to his Chief Executive just as Air Force One went into its turn onto final approach. It was enough of a turn to catch the agent off balance just as he was letting go of the device over the president's open hand. Spears stumbled and dropped the small device to the floor; he and the president watched it roll under the armoire against the wall.

"Mr. President," the agent stammered, "I'm very sorry. I'll get something and dig it out, sir."

Amused, the president said, "Remind me not to let you carry the football, Spears."

The agent, who had returned with a plastic coat hanger, began crawling around on the floor trying to find the keeper.

Their eyes were locked on the tiny speck that had appeared in the western sky. With each passing second, the speck grew larger. Right after receiving Fazul's call, Yousef had called Kamal and Aris telling them to prepare for the kill. All three assassins had rechecked their weapons and had started positioning themselves to fire.

Kamal, hunkered down in the sand dunes, knelt on his left knee and pulled the SK-7 onto his right shoulder. Looking through the special optics of his weapon's sights, he was ready to fire. Aris and Yousef both stood with feet planted but slightly spread. They were now focusing and clearing the SK-7s. All three men had now visually acquired their target and were ready to lock on their guidance.

Aris, in the olive grove, was to fire first, followed by the release of Kamal's missile. Lastly, Yousef would send his arrow of death to strike a blow for all Islam.

The SK-7 launchers possessed upgraded targeting capabilities. The guidance array automatically compensated for unsteady operators. The missile itself was heat-seeking with a distance measuring device. It tracked the heat source, automatically adjusting the trajectory, allowing for windage, drift and evasive action on the part of the target.

As Air Force One turned onto final, all SK-7s were homed in on its engine's heat signatures. When the aircraft was five kilometers from the airport and less than two kilometers from the Jihadists, they planned to fire.

Just as Air Force One's onboard distance measuring device read five kilometers to Da Vinci, Aris set off his weapon. Two seconds later, Kamal released his. Five seconds after that, Yousef followed suit while yelling, "Allah Ak Bar!" The powerful "whoosh" told him his missile had cleared the launcher and begun its run to the target.

"Uh, sir," co-pilot Saples started to tell his captain that they had just been locked onto but before he could get it out the shrill audio alarms began blaring through their headsets.

Command and Control aft of the flight deck simultaneously registered the warning. The young lieutenant at the monitors reacted about as quickly as humanly possible. Pushing the button opening the comm circuits to the flight deck and all relevant personnel, he spoke, "We, uh, oh God, no…we have two…no we've got three missiles inbound and locked on…initiating onboard defense procedures…uh…recommend immediate evasive action."

Six heat flares were rapidly released from the plane's undercarriage, hopefully to draw heat-seeking warheads away from the huge engines. But by the time the countermeasures had been deployed, the incoming ordnance was only seconds away.

Captain Holder had no time to respond to any of this verbally. His next moves were instinctive. Knowing flares were already in the air, he reached for his throttles, shoving them to the stops in an effort to gain power and altitude. Simultaneously, he executed an extreme right upward turn. But Air Force One is no F-16 and regardless of what the Captain did now, it was too late and he knew it.

Suddenly Captain Eric Holder, husband of Sarah and father of two beautiful sons, Brett and David, began to sense everything in slow motion. He could now see the white trails of the three inbounds coming straight toward him. They were like the fingers on a great hand reaching out to embrace him and carry him to God. He knew now that he would never share those special times with his wife and boys.

The first missile took the bait and chased one of the flares off to the left.

By then, every passenger and crew member on board, most of whom had been seated and belted in for landing, were being jerked around like rag dolls as the plane surged, then jerked up and to the right. Overhead compartments opened violently, spilling their loads on those below. Oxygen masks rained from above, adding to the fear and confusion. The screams of frightened passengers filled the cabin.

The president rarely regarded the nuisance of a seat belt warning except on take off and just seconds before wheels on the ground. His habit did not stand him well on this occasion. Just before it all started, he had been standing in front of his restroom mirror adjusting his tie while Agent Spears was still down on all fours looking for the "keeper" he had dropped. Both men were left very vulnerable. The abrupt change in the plane's speed combined with the radical right upward turn threw the president off balance and to his right, out of the small lavatory. From there he stumbled over Agent Spears. Both of them rolled across the floor in a tangled heap.

It was then that Kamal's missile, which was the second one fired, just seconds away from slamming into the 747's giant left engine, missed its mark by inches. Not to be denied its destiny, the missile, fractions of a second later, caught the back left undercarriage and exploded with a ferocity that shook Air Force One. That fiery explosion created a larger and hotter signature for the third missile. Like a hard-charging, great white shark smelling blood, it slammed with full authority into the already burning underside. The second hit took out all the plane's computers, as well as the pilot's ability to work all control surfaces via the cockpit. The concussion froze the elevators, vertical stabilizers, ailerons and flaps. It knocked out fuel feeds, which immediately shut down all engines.

The second explosion peeled off the exterior skin of the fuselage located behind the left wing to the tail section. Five rows of passenger seats along with their occupants were blown out of a gaping hole on the left side. In the back of the second-level passenger section, a flash fire created a dozen human torches.

Air Force One was now a floating, burning death trap. The aircraft was in a slow glide towards the water with the nose down by 15 degrees. In the passenger sections that were not yet in flames, poisonous gases and smoke were filling the cabins. People were dying.

Yousef, Kamal and Aris stood staring in awe at their handiwork.

The aircraft came down while still a mile from the Italian beach. The nose hit first, at a slight angle but with enough force to crush the cockpit and the command and control section just aft of it like an eggshell. As the plane came to a stop, the 747's tail section was held high out of the water for a few seconds. When it broke, it left only the ugly rear stump of the plane's fuselage hanging just above the waters of the gentle sea.

The left wing, almost torn free at the fuselage, hung down in the ocean waters. The water this close to shore was only 25 feet deep, causing the tip of the sagging wing to dig into the sandy bottom.

"Sir!" yelled a panic-stricken approach controller. "We've got chaos in the sky over and around the airport."

Just seconds before, Superintendent Carlos Parcetti had seen the developing catastrophe. He was momentarily paralyzed with shock as he watched the seams of his normally tightly-woven aerial fabric begin to fall apart.

"Sir, we've got planes all over the sky on collision courses. What are your orders?"

Parcetti gazed in disbelief at his master monitors that reflected mass confusion in the tower's control zone. Finally, the superintendent yelled to one of his assistants standing next to him, "Get the idiotic tower on the phone, now! The problem's in their airspace."

Another ashen-faced controller ran to the superintendent. "Sir, we have repeatedly tried to raise the tower! They will not respond."

Parcetti, raising the volume of his voice considerably, yelled, "Then get somebody up there now and find out what the devil's going on!"

At that command, still another staffer just returning from an effort to reach the tower came running up. Gasping for air, he said, "Sir, the main lifts are not functional. The power boxes have somehow been blown, and no one up there is responding to calls on the phones, tower radios, hand-helds or computers."

"Well, then," the barely-in-control Parcetti growled. "Get someone off their butts and climb the freaking stairs of the fire escape, you moron."

"Yes, sir, but we've already got a team working their way up the stairwell. As soon as they reach the tower they'll report the status."

Before Parcetti could respond, the voice of yet another controller, still working his station in approach, came over the superintendent's headphones. "We have just lost on-screen contact with Air Force One inbound on final for runway nine."

The entire room and all 30 controllers suddenly erupted in a flurry of movement and raised voices very uncharacteristic for the normally calm atmosphere. The emergency phone lines on the superintendent's console were flashing. Controllers all over the complex were beeping him to seek guidance.

Parcetti could not believe his ears. "What do you mean, you lost Air Force One? That's not possible."

The controller repeated, "Sir, Air Force One simply vanished off the screen seconds ago. On its last contact with the tower it was vectored to 090 degrees for an approach to nine right. But at five clicks west of the threshold, it just disappeared from the screen! Sir, shouldn't we contact emergency services and search and rescue…and…."

Cutting the emotionally deteriorating controller off, Parcetti said, "I'll take care of that. You focus your entire section on contacting every plane that was under tower jurisdiction and try to unscramble that spaghetti bowl without getting anybody killed. And I don't care how high you have to stack them. You tell every pilot up there we're declaring a CAT-1 emergency."

"Yes, sir."

Parcetti forced himself to recapture his composure and regain control of the situation. He picked up a special direct line to all airport emergency response teams. He knew if the American president's plane really had gone down, from this second on every move and decision he made would be intensely scrutinized 10,000 times over and it would all be considered part of the historical record. He was determined to do this by the book.

Turning to Ben, his second in command, he said, "Benny, as soon as our boys return from the tower, get them in here. In fact, go see if you can find out what in the Sam Hill is taking them so long. *Go!*"

As he stood holding the phone, waiting for the Chief of Emergency Operations to pick up, Parcetti studied the chaos on the screens before him. Then he mumbled, "Dear God, don't let this be happening."

The downing of Air Force One resulted in the deaths of more than 100 people on board. Many of the dead were among the most powerful men and women in the world.

However, few people are aware of the multilayered security apparatus that is in place to protect the life of the President of the United States of America. Since the assassination of John Kennedy, every possible contingency imaginable had been studied. The Secret Service had vowed never to lose another Commander in Chief. Thus, the security apparatus protecting the most powerful man in the world had become redundant, almost fail-safe.

No expense had been spared in building the network of security systems that afforded any president under attack the greatest possible chance of survival. Not only was this over-the-top obsession with security apparent in places like the presidential limousines, which are more tank than automobile; it is also evident on Air Force One. If the extensive, external security of the aircraft is somehow compromised, then there are the internal security precautions built into the system.

The presidential suite on Air Force One is a multi-layered, bullet-proof, bomb-resistant cubicle built into the heavily reinforced air frame of the modified Boeing 747. It would have to take a direct hit by sizable ordnance to penetrate or collapse its walls. Such protection would, of course, be irrelevant if the aircraft, for any reason, exploded in flight. In such a case, though the cubicle might remain intact, the sheer violence of the concussion or the fall from altitude would insure the death of any occupants. It was the responsibility of the engineers and the security planners to figure out ways to protect the president in anything less than a catastrophic in-flight disintegration of the aircraft.

Not only had they created a remarkable cubicle almost impervious to penetration, but they had also modified all the interior surfaces of the suite. The ceilings and walls could literally inflate, creating heavily cushioned surfaces throughout. If sufficient shock factors are registered on built-in sensors, the walls and ceilings, much like air bags on an automobile, would automatically inflate. The entirety of the cubicle's interior would become extremely cushioned, able to absorb significant impact of the human body without causing serious harm.

The sudden power surge and quick upward turn initiated by the pilot in an effort to avoid incoming missiles had sent the president and his agent rolling across the floor.

The exploding second missile to hit Air Force One not only contributed to its slow death glide into the sea but it also caused the surfaces within the Presidential suite to inflate. The impact of the plane, while killing what few crew and passengers had survived the flaming inferno raging through much of the fuselage, violently tossed the president and Agent Spears against the walls and ceiling. Both men were seriously hurt, but due to incredible foresight and remarkable engineering, the crash had been made survivable for the two men...but just barely.

The plane's flight deck had virtually disintegrated on impact and the tail section furthest aft had broken off. The main section of the fuselage back to the Presidential suite was charred and cracked but structurally intact. The forward section was totally submerged, leaving the back remaining section with the president's suite dangling just a few feet above the water. In relatively calm seas, it would take a while for the downed plane to be torn apart and distributed to the depths by nature's forces.

Seconds after hitting the water, the smoking corpse of Air Force One wallowed in the slight swells like a lifeless whale.

FOUR

He had already been caught twice and heavily fined by the Italian game and fisheries authorities for fishing in this area. It had been declared off limits to fishing boats. But Francisco Botalli had no choice. He had to catch fish. It was the only means of survival for him and his 13-year-old grandson. Since the boy's parents had died three years prior in a horrible car accident, Francisco, as the only surviving relative, had been the sole guardian and provider for Raphael. Now, well into his 70s, the bent, but strong and sturdy Francisco, who had fished the coasts of Italy most of his life, was not about to be intimidated by those young, cocky fisheries wardens.

So, this afternoon, once again, the belligerent old fisherman with the full gray beard and silvery curls of hair had loaded his grandson and fishing gear into the 20-foot fishing skiff, cranked up the little 25 horse-power outboard, and puttered north. Arriving at the spot he sensed was ripe for a bountiful harvest, he told Raphael to drop anchor.

Francisco's practiced eye told him that they were about three-quarters of a mile off the beach, which he had heard was temporarily closed to the public due to some kind of construction. It was fine with him, as there would be no infernal lifeguards or resort personnel to ring the authorities and report him.

The old fisherman had lived in these parts since just after World War II. As a teen, he had joined the Italian underground to help fight Mussolini's fascists and Hitler's jack-booted Nazi troopers. When the Allies finally invaded Italy, he had been put to work by American GIs as a guide and scout. He was in his mid-teens when the war ended. That is when he learned to fish for a living.

But his days of captaining the big trawlers or working as a summer deck hand on the expensive yachts of tourists were long over. He was now content to fill his small nets three or four times a week and sell the catch at the dockside market. It brought in enough money to meet the most basic needs of he and Raphael, and on occasions, when a bit was left over, he had put some funds aside in hopes of sending Raphael back to school on the mainland.

As soon as Raphael tossed the anchor overboard, the bow of the boat slowly swung around, pointing into the light easterly breeze. Immediately, the boy prepped the nets while his grandfather shifted gear around in the boat to make room for them to sit comfortably.

Just as Francisco sat down, he glanced toward shore to be sure no one was watching him. He was not prepared for what he saw. Suddenly, from somewhere just behind the sandy beach, three objects streaked into the sky only seconds apart. The old man had not seen anything like it since his war years as a youth. He had no doubt that someone was firing some kind of military ordnance.

At first he panicked, thinking perhaps he had pushed the game wardens too far and now they were determined to rid themselves of him for good. But as he watched in awe, he realized the rockets, or whatever they were, were arching too high for him to be their target.

Raphael saw his grandfather staring up at the sky. He wrenched himself around to better follow Francisco's gaze and he too, witnessed the streaks cutting a wake across the blue.

"Grandpapa!" Raphael gasped. "What is it?"

"Shhh, Raphael. Let us wait and watch and we shall see." Francisco kept his eyes on the climbing missile tracks.

He heard the roar of the approaching aircraft before he actually saw it. At first, knowing the DaVinci International was very close, the sound of the approaching plane did not alarm him. But as he followed the track of the flying rockets, it occurred to him that they would shortly be competing for the same airspace into which the now-visible aircraft was moving. Before he could voice his alarm over the impending collision, the first missile veered slightly to the left and under the plane, barely missing it. He watched as the second one slammed into the back underside of the gigantic aircraft, creating a cloud of fire. "Holy Saints of the Church," mumbled the stunned fisherman as he crossed himself.

Seconds later, the third rocket flew into the fireball of the first. The resulting blast blew off pieces of the plane and spread the fire burning on the outside of the fuselage. Francisco and Raphael watched in silent awe as the big aircraft, at first, seemed to flutter. Then, trailing smoke, flames and debris, it began a slow glide toward the sea.

The burning, smoking plane was slowly moving straight towards them but it took a moment for Francisco to realize that their boat was in the path of the falling plane.

Without taking his eyes off the incoming meteor, Francisco calmly spoke. "Raphael, pull up the anchor, quickly. Quickly boy." But the old fisherman already knew there was not enough time left to pull the anchor, start the engine, and make an escape. As Raphael struggled with all his might to pull in the heavy anchor, Francisco closed his eyes and whispered a prayer, "Dear God, the boy. Let the boy live."

He opened his eyes in time to watch the airplane careen into the sea less than a quarter of a mile from where the little fishing boat bobbed on the surface of the gentle seas.

There was no place on the body of Agent Spears that did not hurt. The 37-year old Secret Service man, at 6'3" tall and 230 solid pounds, was built like an NFL linebacker. Stringent daily workouts and five mile jogs four times a week kept him in peak physical condition. Throughout the missile strikes and the subsequent crash, Spears had remained conscious, though he now felt like he had been beaten senseless, stuffed in a barrel, and rolled down Mt. Everest.

Once the plane came to a standstill, he tried to clear his head and focus. He realized he was sitting with his back against the forward wall of the Presidential Suite. The wall felt strange, kind of soft and cushioned. His first thought was that somehow he must be lying on top of the mattress from the bed. He had never been briefed about inflatable surfaces.

He noted that his feet were tilted a bit upward and that all the lighting was out. Had it not been for the sliver of sunlight slipping through the slightly ajar door of the suite, he would not have been able to see anything. The door was uphill from where he sat on the opposite side of the room.

He blinked, shook his head, and worked to regain his senses. He smelled a pungent odor and realized the room was hazy with smoke that was stinging his eyes. From his years in combat, the agent realized he smelled burning flesh.

His thoughts raced to the welfare of this president. His mind and training demanded he move now to locate President Carr.

Spears knew he was hurt and realized he would be of no help to the Commander in Chief if he, as his agent, was incapacitated. He began to slowly check the mobility of his arms, then his legs. He was able to move his limbs, which told him that they were not crushed or broken.

As he struggled to get to his feet in the tilted room, Spears felt a severe stabbing sensation under his left shoulder blade. Attempting to maintain his balance, he roared in pain as he used his right arm to reach around his back. There he touched a thin piece of metal that was deeply buried under his left shoulder blade. He grimaced as he gripped the part that remained outside his body. Then with one quick pull, he jerked the long metal shard out. It looked like a piece of molding to him, but the pain he now felt momentarily froze him in place. As he braced himself and tried to get his breath, he began to feel a warm liquid creeping down his back and onto his legs. He gently reached around and touched the warmth. Bringing his hand back around, he held it up to his eyes. It was blood, a lot of blood. It was pouring through the open wound on his back. Standing, bent over, with his hands on his knees, he forced himself to take slow, measured breaths. His training as a Navy Seal instinctively kicked in as he worked to ignore the pain and complete his mission.

He looked around the haze-filled suite in an attempt to locate President Carr. His singular responsibility, his orders, his very reason for existence, was to protect the life and well-being of the President of the United States, even if it meant forfeiting his own life. With great effort the agent kept breathing, even though, with each labored breath, he felt the excruciating stab of pain bring a new wave of agony.

Finally, he saw a pile of rubble and discarded clothing against the wall on the other side of the room. With Herculean effort, he crawled to the pile and began to feel around until he touched a foot, then a leg. On his knees, his left hand supported his weight as, with his right hand, he threw the rubble and loose laundry off the president.

"Mr. President! Mr. President!" the agent sputtered between coughs, "Sir, can you hear me?"

Spears reached to feel for the president's pulse. He found it. The president was still alive.

"Don't worry, sir, we're gonna get you out of here."

Agent Spears, still in great pain, succeeded in positioning himself behind Carr. Reaching under the president's arms, Spears drug the president's limp body as close as possible to the slightly open door of the suite. Once there, he reached for the door while still on his hands and knees and then realized he had no clue as to what terrors lay just beyond the threshold. He did know that Air Force One had been intentionally brought down and that, somehow, he and his charge had miraculously survived.

As Spears reached over and attempted to force the door open, he was able to see a clear blue sky above and water beneath. He saw enough to know they were dangling over the water, and that beyond the door, everything aft of the suite had broken off.

He tried several times using all his remaining strength to force open the door but it would not budge beyond the four-inch crack already there. He fell back exhausted, hurting and gasping for air. He knew he didn't have long before he would pass out from the loss of blood. He murmured a prayer, "God, I really need some help here."

Within seconds of the plane hitting the water, Francisco had started his outboard motor and, running wide open, headed straight for the wreckage. During the war he had witnessed a great number of bombers and fighters, Axis and Allied, go down. On most occasions there were no survivors. And though he had no idea what to expect now, he knew that being the first one on the scene could mean the difference between life and death for somebody.

As they drew near the wreckage, he could already see the bodies floating lifelessly in the water. Some were still buckled into their seats that had broken off their mounts and been thrown out of the plane's interior, but all of them were beyond help. Francisco wished that young Raphael was not there to witness such carnage. However, the possibility that they might be able to save a life trumped his concern.

The fisherman slowly maneuvered through the floating debris and charred corpses. Raphael asked, "Grandpapa…these people, are they dead? Are all of them dead?"

Francisco answered, "Raphael, try not to look at these unfortunate souls. Pray the Mother of God will have mercy on them. Just pray, my son, and help me look for anyone we may be able to help."

Francisco steered his boat down the exposed side of smoking fuselage until he reached the point where the rear section of the plane had broken off. The back section that remained hung precariously a few feet above the water. The shorn edges of the broken fuselage was a tangle of twisted conduit, steel-edged remains of the broken air frame, loose wiring, and insulation.

Francisco stopped his boat and gazed up at the broken fuselage and a partially opened door. He yelled up, "Can anybody hear me? We're here to help! Can anyone hear me?"

For a few lingering seconds, his calls were answered with silence, then somewhere from above him within the wreckage, he heard, "Help us. We're in here. But I can't get the door open. Can you hear me?"

Francisco's and Raphael's eyes met with surprise and simultaneously they yelled, "Yes, we hear you."

The old fisherman turned to his grandson. "You must crawl up the side of this wreckage to that door," he said. "Careful not to cut yourself on all those sharp edges. When you get to the top, see if you can force open that door."

Now excited, Raphael did not need to be asked twice. Scampering like a monkey up the broken fuselage, he put his fingers into the crevice of the partially open door and pulled several times with all his might, to no avail. Then he glanced at the base of the door and saw why it would not budge. A piece of metal from the airframe had bent over and was keeping the door from swinging open.

Raphael stretched out as far as he could and with his extended right leg gave the twisted piece of metal two hard kicks, whereupon it released its grip and the door swung open. Looking into the doorway, Raphael saw the relieved but very dirty face of Agent Spears looking back at him. "Way to go kid!" Spears cheered. "Now, help me get my friend out of here, okay?"

Raphael, now feeling every bit the hero, smiled. "Yes, sir." Turning back to Grandpapa below, he yelled, "I got it! There are two men. I am going to help them get out."

Agent Spear's strength was almost gone. He was working on sheer willpower and adrenaline. He screamed in agony as he hoisted the president up toward the doorway. Once there, Raphael grabbed hold of the president's arms and precariously pulled him out of the opening as Spears pushed from behind. Spears, laying on his belly and holding the president over Raphael and his grandpa below, waited until they could gently lower Carr down into the boat. The agent whispered a quick prayer of gratitude and, with his last ounce of strength, pulled himself out the door and dropped six feet into the boat.

Lying on his back next to his unconscious Commander in Chief, Spears raised his head, looked through squinted eyes at the fisherman, and said, "Thank you. Thank you. They tried to kill us." Then he simply passed out.

With two complete strangers lying unconscious in his boat, Francisco was unsure what to do. He knew that whoever had just shot down that airplane was near the beach less than a mile away. He also knew that he and Raphael had just helped some of the people the shooters intended to kill.

The fisherman quickly decided the last place he wanted to go was toward that beach. He swung his boat south and opened the throttle on his 25-horsepower Evinrude. The safest place he knew was the Isle de'Terreno, the tiny, off-the-map island that he and Raphael and a few other old fisherman called home. The outcropping was only a mile and half long and three-fourths of a mile wide. It sat a bit over four miles off the Italian mainland and was about 12 miles from the crash sight. With luck, on these relatively smooth seas, his little boat could be back to the island in about 35 minutes. Once there, he would try to get medical attention for the two men who he felt were Americans. The American soldiers in World War II had been very kind to him and his countrymen. Now, perhaps, he could return the favor. Francisco knew that America had a lot of enemies these days, though he could not understand why.

For many years he had been content to live like a hermit on his near-deserted island. He had very few friends left on the mainland, other than the fish buyer near the docks. Both he and young Raphael were happy living their isolated lives year after year without radios, televisions or the new-fangled computer machines he had heard about.

Eight minutes had passed since the moment of the plane's impact. After Francisco had traveled five miles from the crash site, he turned to look back. He watched as helicopters approached the wreckage from several directions. They, along with numerous smaller airplanes circling the skies above the downed aircraft, reminded him of a swarm of bees.

Glad to be putting more distance between him and the crash, Francisco continued all-out toward the south. The wind whipped his long gray curls about his face as he twisted the throttle harder in an effort to squeeze a few more knots out of the screaming old outboard.

FIVE

"Hello, I am Darryl Cannon and this is World Net News, bringing you the latest on the tragic downing of Air Force One, the U.S. President's plane. President Carr and a large contingent of invited guests and reporters were en route to a global peace conference to be held in Rome..." Thus began the continuing coverage of the crash of Air Force One.

With footage rolling, shot from helicopters hovering above the wrecked remains of the special 747, the anchor continued, "It has now been confirmed that the President of the United States, Mathew Dillon Carr, along with Secretary of State Nathan Whittle, the Secretary of Defense Leonard Chatwell and National Security Director William Bird, were among the 100-plus passengers aboard Air Force One when it crashed into the seas on its final approach to land at the Da Vinci International Airport.

"Authorities at the scene have now determined there are no survivors. While it is generally agreed that the downing has all the earmarks of a classic terror attack, no group at this time has come forward to claim responsibility. Authorities were quick to point out that the investigation is just beginning.

"As many of our viewers know, we have been covering this tragedy for several hours. Since the news broke earlier today that President Carr has been killed, leaders from all over the world have begun publicly expressing their heartfelt sympathies to the victims' families and to the American people. We are being told that the White House is now being swamped with calls from heads of state and governing bodies around the globe.

"However, not everyone is mourning the event. As you can see in this footage coming in from the Middle East, there are those in many Muslim-dominated countries who see the death of President Carr as reason for celebration. What you are seeing now are tens of thousands of exuberant Muslims from the West Bank in Israel, Syria, Iran, and various other countries in the region marching, chanting and dancing as they fire weapons into the air in celebration.

"Meanwhile, in cities from coast to coast across the U.S., prayer vigils have been spontaneously springing up. Now you are seeing footage from some of the largest stadiums, conference centers and public squares around our nation where hundreds of thousands of people are crowding in to pray or to simply stand in quietness among friends in a time of overwhelming grief.

"For an increasing number of prominent leaders and politicians, sorrow is already turned into outrage and calls for revenge against those behind this sordid act. Dozens of governors from various states are calling up National Guard units to be ready just in case civil unrest spins out of control. We are also being informed that the entire U.S. military has been put on its highest alert since 9/11/01. It is being called on to guard against further attacks on America or its citizens around the world.

"Stay tuned to WNN as we continue to bring you immediate updates as they happen.

"But right now, we join the rest of the world's media, live in Washington, D.C. Vice President Jordan Hunt has just been sworn in by the Chief Justice of the Supreme Court as the new President of the United States.

"President Hunt is now going to address the nation and the world, live from the Oval Office of the White House. Let's go to President Hunt."

LIVE BROADCAST FROM THE OVAL OFFICE, WASHINGTON, D.C.

Speaking: The newly sworn-in President Jordan Hunt.

"Friends and fellow Americans, it is with deep sorrow and a heavy heart that I join you in this moment of national pain. We have lost one of the most loved and effective presidents in American history. President Mathew Dillon Carr was among the brave souls who, while sacrificially serving their country, were shot down by cowardly thugs. While it is a time for prayer and a time to deal with our grief, I want to assure every American that the time will come, and it will come sooner rather than later, when the entire might of the great United States will reach out and bring justice to the heinous murderers who perpetrated this outrageous crime.

"But for now, I know millions of Americans across this nation join me in expressing our deepest condolences to First Lady Janice Carr, President Carr's wife of 30 years, and to Mathew Carr, their 23-year-old son, who only days ago graduated from Harvard.

"The First Lady was in Bangladesh with the American Red Cross helping bring attention to that nation's poor when she was informed about the death of her husband. She and son Mathew are both en route to the White House as I speak.

"Now I am going to ask you to allow me to speak to you as your new president.

"When I first stepped into the world of politics as a 21-year-old college student from Weatherford, Ohio, it was to run for a seat on our City Council. While I was more stunned than anyone else that I narrowly won that election, I immediately went to work for the people.

"Since that day, serving first as a city councilman then as an Ohio State Senator, and then as a Congressman and later, a U.S. Senator for my great state, I have attempted to serve with distinction, integrity and hard work, never forgetting those who had sent me as their representative to the nation.

"For the last three years I have worked side by side with President Carr as his Vice President, to achieve great goals that have improved the lives of millions of Americans. I never in my wildest dreams imagined that one day I would sit in this chair, behind this desk, in this office. On many occasions I have visited this magnificent old mansion we call the White House, but I never imagined that I would ever call it home.

"No Vice President wants to inherit this gigantic responsibility under these kinds of circumstances. However, our founding fathers, in their wisdom, foresaw the possibility that one day a sitting president may not, for one reason or another, be able to serve out his term. So, they provided for that contingency in our great Constitution. Therefore, less than 30 minutes ago, the Chief Justice of our Supreme Court swore me in as president of these United States of America, invoking the provisions of the 25th Amendment.

"Please know, my fellow Americans, that I, of all men, am most aware that I could never fill the shoes of a man like Mathew Dillon Carr. He was a statesman, as well as a great man. However, I can and do now promise you, the people, that I will faithfully serve, with every fiber of my being, as your president.

"Now, over the next few days as more information regarding this unimaginable tragedy becomes available, I will make sure that you get that information. You will know what is going on behind the doors of this administration, as we work with Congress to keep our nation moving toward its destiny.

"As I close tonight, I want Americans everywhere and the nations of the world to know that even in this dark hour, we stand ready and most able to respond to any further threat to this nation or its citizens. And we will not rest until we have found and judicially dealt with the criminals behind our pain. May God have mercy on their souls, for it is a certainty that we will not. Until I am able to speak to you again, I ask for your prayers and your patience. Thank you, and God bless America."

It was raining, a slow, melancholy kind of rain. It did much to add to the morose atmosphere that hung like wet sack cloth over the city of Rome.

It was 9:00 p.m. in the city upon the seven hills as the new American President addressed his nation and the world. It had been five hours since the news broke about the downing of Air Force One. The people of Rome were in shock that such an atrocity could occur near their beloved city. Even those Italians who may not have cared for President Carr's policies were still grieved by his death and the tragedy of Air Force One.

The normally bustling Roman night life was nowhere to be seen on this night. The clubs, casinos, and sidewalk cafes that usually began to fill up at this time every evening were strangely empty. The crowds on the streets, the busy, honking traffic, and the crammed sidewalks full of happy, fun-seeking locals and curious tourists were nowhere to be found.

The city was mourning, suffering the shame of its new infamous reputation. The people were indulging themselves in a kind of introspection, not unlike the people of Dallas, Texas after the 1963 assassination of President Kennedy.

But a far more cheery environment was in evidence on the 37th floor of the Grand Regency Palias in uptown Rome. It was the most luxurious and expensive hotel in all of Italy. The entire floor, including its presidential suite, had been leased to the International Federation of Nations and its enormous staff. The security, which was extensive and maintained 24/7, was extremely tight. So much so that it would make any head of state envious.

Most would not consider the two men sitting in the suite's lounge to be especially significant in the arena of world affairs, at least not yet.

"It was absolutely necessary," said the blond-haired, handsome, middle-aged man. His name was Charon Drakon Kostos.

"My dear Charon, the problem is not the act itself, but the mess that is often left in its wake." The 70-ish, immaculately groomed, sophisticated gentleman on a lounge chair sitting next to Kostos was the famous French industrialist, Maurice Dubois, whose personal wealth was staggering.

He smiled faintly, sipped his brandy, and added, "But you are quite right. It was indeed necessary. It was also necessary to quickly eliminate those fanatics who did the dirty deed."

Charon Kostos laughed. "Those types consider it a great honor to die for their god and there are thousands, no millions, just like them waiting to do their part for Jihad."

"I suppose," added the Frenchman with a chuckle, "that by now those minions are fully absorbed in the virginal pleasures of their Edenic paradise."

Kostos took another small sip of his drink. "Do you think they really believe that bunk about all those virgins just sitting around waiting for their martyred souls to arrive in paradise?"

"Oh, yes, indeed," Dubois answered. "They are true believers. Their religion is all they have ever known. They all believe and do whatever their mullahs or imams tell them to."

Kostos shook his head, "You would think that at least one of them would someday notice that their mullahs and spiritual advisors never strap on a vest full of dynamite. They simply order martyrdom for everyone else."

"Ah, is not religion a wonderful thing, Charon?" yawned Dubois.

"Humph," grunted Kostos, "a necessary evil. But one that serves our purpose. Now, if I may change the subject. Tomorrow around 4:00 p.m. here, it will be 8:00 a.m. in Washington, D.C. Be here, because that is when I will place a person-to-person call to the new President of the United States and congratulate him on his advancement. I have also rescheduled our IFN Peace Conference out of respect for the dead Americans and the crash of Air Force One."

Breaking in, Dubois asked, "Don't you think we should give this new fellow, President Hunt, a little more time to adjust to his new responsibilities?"

Kostos came back quickly. "Power is such a seductive mistress. Let's not give him time to flirt with her. I want him to be put in remembrance of his debts."

"In that case," Dubois held his glass up in a toast, "I am certain that the new leader of the free world will be delighted to hear from us. Cheers."

"Cheers, indeed!" Kostos added, "Here is to new beginnings."

Both men downed what was left in their glasses and laughed heartily.

Francisco slowly maneuvered his boat to the little wooden pier. Having secured it, he sent Raphael to their modest cabin a quarter of a mile up the slight hill, instructing him to bring the old collapsible cots. Then he was to hook up the hay wagon to the old tractor and bring them back to the pier.

When Raphael returned with the tractor and hay wagon, he saw that his grandpapa had tied a long rope to the crossbars of the now legless cots, creating stretchers. He had also backed the boat up against the embankment so that they could use the tractor to gently pull the loaded cots onto the tilted hay wagon.

Working together, Raphael and Francisco were able to get both of the injured men onto the wagon. Arriving back at their isolated little cabin, they worked very hard for over an hour, until they finally succeeded in moving both men inside.

Having slept less than three hours, President Jordan Hunt was up at 5:30 a.m., shoveling in a quick breakfast and rushing to get ready. He walked into the Oval Office at 6:15 a.m. sharp. By 7:00 a.m. he had read the voluminous recommendations for new cabinet members, prepped overnight by congressional leaders of both parties.

The positions left vacant by the deaths of the National Security Director, the Secretary of State and the Secretary of Defense would, for the time being, be filled by the undersecretaries of each department. Hunt decided he would name permanent replacements within the next three to four weeks, if necessary.

He had scheduled a meeting at 8:00 a.m. to be held in the Oval Office with the director of the CIA, and undersecretaries of the National Security Agency, the State Department and Department of Defense. Also attending would be his new Chief of Staff.

At 7:58 a.m., the new president was glancing at the agenda for his 8:00 a.m. meeting when his intercom came to life with his secretary's voice.

"Mr. President, the principals for your 8:00 a.m. are all present. I've had coffee served to them in the waiting room, and..."

Before she finished the sentence, Hunt cut her off. "Thank you, Della. You can show them in now."

"But, sir," injected the secretary, "you also have a call holding from a Mr. Charon Kostos in Rome. He convinced your Chief of Staff that it was a matter of critical importance. Do you wish to speak to him or should I send him back to the Chief?"

At the mention of the name "Kostos," the new president broke out in a cold sweat. The last thing Hunt wanted to do this morning was deal with that man. *Why*, the president wondered, *would he dare call me here?* After a moment of silence, Hunt responded. "No, I'll take the call, Della. Be so kind as to tell our coffee-drinking friends that I'll be with them in a few minutes."

"Yes, sir, Mr. President. I'll transfer his call to line one, which by the way, sir, is a secure line."

"Thank you, Della."

Hunt let the phone beep four times before taking a deep breath and picking up the receiver. "This is President Hunt," he said coldly in his most businesslike voice, attempting to convey the perception that he was extremely busy.

"Ah, Mr. President. Are you so formal with all your old friends?"

To that, Hunt testily responded, "Sir, I remind you of two things. One, you are talking to the President of the United States; and two, you must be discreet. Anyone could be listening to this conversation."

Kostos only chuckled at the bravado. "My dear old friend. Let's not be coy with each other. Both of our lines are most secure. So relax. In fact, let's start over and you work on being more civil in your tone. You can call me Charon and I will call you Jordan, just like the old days, huh?"

"You listen to me, Kostos," the president came back heatedly. "Our relationship ended years ago. And I do not want you to ever call me again!"

Lightheartedly, Charon continued, "Oh, Jordan, Jordan. I am deeply wounded by your words. Perhaps I should put you in remembrance. It was only four years ago, that is 48 months, dear Jordan. Not so long ago, huh? That is when you came crawling to me like a wet sewer rat begging for help. You had made quite a mess of your career and your life, had you not? You had met the beautiful Regina, a covert Russian agent, while you were still just a lowly Senator. All those so-called 'necessary' junkets you took to Zurich were just your cover to perpetuate your tawdry affair with the little lady."

Hunt was at the boiling point. "Shut up, Kostos. All that's in the past. You have no right to…"

"Oh, but Jordan," Charon mockingly continued, "it did not end with your lusty adultery that you hid from your darling wife, did it? While you and your lover romped in your Zurich love nest, she seduced you into compromising many of your government's best-kept secrets. You, Mr. President, are not only a dirty old man. You are a traitor, and might I add, a very stupid traitor.

"You took the dirty money the Russkies paid for your treasonous acts, a very substantial amount of money, which you lost in an orgy of gambling in Geneva while you were in a drunken stupor, a recurring problem you have hidden for a long time."

Hunt tried again to stop Kostos' review of events. "Charon, you've got to stop."

"Oh, but you did not stop, did you Mr. President? You ran up quite a little gambling debt in Las Vegas, Monte Carlo and numerous online offshore operations. So you drug your greedy carcass back to the Russkies and your little sex queen, offering greater secrets for more payoffs.

"But that's when Regina and her boyfriend began blackmailing you."

Hunt was livid at Kostos' audacity, but he knew the man held his future in his hands. He had to try to mollify Kostos, whatever it took.

"Listen, Kostos. Just get to the point. What is it that you want?"

Kostos laughed again and answered, "Oh, Jordan, I just want to remind you that it was my generosity and loving-kindness that delivered you from your own stupidity. It was I who used my influence to intervene with Russian intelligence, forcing them to back off with their threats to kill you. And it was I who eliminated that Jezebel, Regina, ending the trouble she was planning for your life. It was I who paid off your huge gambling debts and then funneled millions—illegally might I add—into your campaign coffers and your run for Vice President. Do you really think I'm just a benevolent old fool?

"And I'm thinking that, especially at this time, it would be tragic indeed, if all the sordid details of your ugly past showed up on the front page of the *New York Times*. So, Mr. President, perhaps you should try to be a bit more respectful to old friends."

Hunt, now soaked in perspiration and shaken to his core, more humbly responded, "All right, all right, Kostos. But this is something I can't deal with right now. You're no fool. You know what's happened to this country. My hands are very full right now. What is it you want from me?"

"Old friend," answered Kostos, "just to remind you who your real friends are. Now, you go ahead and take care of your business, saving the free world and all, then later, we'll talk again. So, for now, I bid you good day and goodbye."

The president, white with fear, quietly hung up the phone. His beeping intercom brought him back to the moment. "Mr. President, are you ready for your guest?"

"Uh, no, Della. Give me five more minutes, then send them in."

"Yes, sir."

The president jumped to his feet and ran to the office privy, where he lost his breakfast.

The unconscious Americans, each on their own cot, rested in the only bedroom of the tiny two-room cabin. Francisco had sent Raphael to old Antonio Cardola's hut about a mile away to ask his friend to run Raphael over to the mainland. Once there, they were to find the aged, semi-retired Dr. Minay and bring him back to the isle.

For decades, Dr. Minay had been a friend to the residents on the Isle de'Terreno. In days past, there was a thriving little fishing village on the island. The good doctor would ferry over on the weekends and treat the aged and sick. He refused any payments, telling folks that God was able to take care of him. Francisco always loaded him up with fresh fish anyway.

In the last 10 years, all the families had returned to the mainland with its schools and modern conveniences. Only four old fishermen, not including Francisco and Raphael, remained scattered about the isle. It had been many months since Dr. Minay had ferried across.

Francisco had instructed his grandson to say nothing of the two Americans to Antonio or to the doctor. He was to tell Dr. Minay to come quickly, for his grandfather was very ill. And Raphael was to send Antonio back to his own place upon arriving back on the island.

The stew Francisco had prepared bubbled on top of the old wood-burning stove, filling the cabin with a mouth-watering aroma. He had hoped his guests would awaken long enough to take a bit of nourishment, but they had not. He had been able to stop the big fellow's bleeding from the ugly, deep wound on his back. The other stranger had also remained unconscious since being pulled out of the wreckage.

Francisco had returned to the stove and was stirring the stew pot with an old wooden spoon when he heard voices approaching. Peeking through his wooden shutters, Francisco was ecstatic to see Raphael pulling at Dr. Minay's hand, helping him up the slope and onto the small porch. He rushed to the front door and flung it open just as Raphael and the doctor reached the threshold. "May mi'Lady be praised. You are here!" shouted Francisco as he embraced the old doctor.

Loosed from the bear hug, Dr. Minay stepped back, looked Francisco up and down and said, "As I live, Raphael, it appears my trip was in vain. The Almighty has raised your grandpapa from his infernal deathbed."

Francisco laughed heartily, "My dear old friend, please forgive the deception. But I have two very sick guests who have some powerful enemies on the mainland who are trying to kill them. I thought it best that no one else know of their presence. They are in desperate need of medical attention."

The elderly doctor shook his head from side to side, “Francisco, you old goat. You will never change. You are forever finding new ways to bring trouble to yourself. Come, show me your sick vagabonds.”

With that, Francisco turned and led the kind doctor into the tiny bedroom.

SIX

Tension in the Oval Office was palpable as the five arrivals took their seats on the two couches facing each other. The president's chair, still empty, was set seven feet in front of his desk, facing the couches.

None of those attending were strangers to the Oval Office. Each of them had, on occasion, been here before to participate in departmental meetings. However, no matter how often one enters this inner sanctum, the senses are overloaded with the atmospheric presence of power.

A side door entrance into the Oval Office suddenly opened and in walked the new president, Jordan Hunt. All five visitors simultaneously jumped to their feet. The president smiled, nodded to each, and as he began to sit, said, "Gentlemen, and lady, please be seated. Thank you all for coming. I know none of you have had much sleep since yesterday's tragic events. So, for brevity's sake, let me update you on our current status.

"The crash of Air Force One not only took our beloved president's life but, as you know, we also lost Secretary of State Nathan Whittle, whose chair is filled today by Undersecretary of State, James Parlay. Secretary of Defense, Leonard Chatwell, also lost, has Undersecretary of Defense Carl Bates covering his responsibilities. And the late National Security Director, William Bird, is being replaced by Deputy Director Carol Watts. You all know Mr. William Pratt, the director of the Central Intelligence Agency, who is with us today.

"My Chief of Staff here, Earl Parsons, will start us off with an update. Mr. Parsons."

"Yes, sir." Parsons, to the president's right, straightened and cleared his throat. "On the positive side, Mr. President, your prime-time speech to the world last night had a powerful impact. Polls already show that 72 percent of Americans have a favorable impression of you and express confidence in your ability to lead the country.

"And, might I add, the speech had a sedating effect on the national turmoil that was almost at the boiling point. Fifteen state governors had National Guard Units stand down. It is clear that there is a peaceful and orderly transition underway and folks seem optimistic. Still, there is a lot of pain over our loss and increasing calls for vengeance on the people and countries behind the assassination."

Hunt nodded, "And do we have any clue on how the markets will go when they open this morning?"

Chief of Staff Parsons shrugged. "Well, as you know, Mr. President, the Dow nose-dived over 22 percent by the end of yesterday. But last night's speech, along with soothing words from the Fed, will probably turn things around by noon. At least that is our hope."

"And, Mr. Parlay. What has State got for us this morning?" asked the president.

"Sir," Parlay said, "I would like to say that it is an honor to serve with you, and as far as the international scene is concerned, every NATO country, even France, is falling all over themselves to let us know they are behind us.

"And I agree that your speech last night, at least from State's point of view, was a grand slam homer.

"However, the usual hot spots remain. The Congolese Army, as we suspected, is rejecting the recent election results and is staging a coup. Darfur rebels are not only fighting UN peacekeepers who are trying to help them, but they're now fighting each other. Chaos has broken out there.

"The North Koreans are screaming like scalded monkeys over UN sanctions and are threatening to nuke South Korea.

"And you probably know, the Middle East is erupting again. It has been 10 months since Israel bombed Iran's main nuclear sights and the Islamic rabble-rousers will not let the matter die."

The Secretary paused, took a deep breath, and added, "This International Federation of Nations, headed by a Mr. Charon D. Kostos, is gaining members and backers every day. They're sending their own so-called diplomats into every hot spot on Earth claiming they have been invited in to help negotiate peace. They're really messing up our efforts."

"Thank you, Mr. Secretary," nodded the president. "We'll address the IFN later. What's the story from the Department of Defense, Mr. Bates?"

Bates was quick to respond, "Sir, we have been able to step down the military alerts globally. We remain primed but optimistic, sir."

"Very good, Mr. Secretary." The president smiled warmly, then turned to CIA Director Pratt. "How goes the search for those who assassinated our president?"

"Sir," answered an obviously exhausted director, "we have 1200 agents working this investigation in Europe alone. The Brits, French, Italians, and all our allies have volunteered their intelligence resources if we decide we need them. Sooner or later we'll nail those who did this. Our stations in the Middle East, Far East, and Asia have it as their top priority. Italian intel and Rome police have located the site from which three shoulder-mounted missiles were fired, just off the beach where eastbound planes on final for landing at Da Vinci pass right over.

"Perhaps as intriguing are the three bodies of known terrorists found in a drainage ditch less than 12 miles from that beach. Each had been shot in the head, execution style, and all three had residue all over 'em from firing missiles, or similar ordnance."

The new Secretary of State blustered, "State hasn't heard a word about these dead terrorists. We should've been briefed, Pratt."

"Do forgive me, Mr. Secretary," Pratt came back, "but this notice was given to me just as we walked into this meeting...and there's more. Recordings of the conversations between the pilots of Air Force One, Italian approach and the Da Vinci Tower indicate that Air Force One broke protocol while on final, releasing the F-16 security and going in without cover.

"Somehow, bad guys got through the fairly tight security and into that tower. When they left, nine tower personnel were dead. Security cameras caught the terrorist's faces from three separate angles. All eight were known terrorists, strangely from varying terror groups. It is a certainty that whoever's behind this is now coordinating various terror groups, getting them to work together to achieve their goals.

"And lastly, but hardly least, the eight fake security guards who took over the Da Vinci Tower to redirect the president's plane into those missiles were all found dead 20 miles from the airport."

"So let me get this straight," put in the president, "You're telling us that the terror groups listed on my copy of your briefing…Al Qaeda, Hamas, the Italian Red Brigade and others, were all participants? Strange bedfellows!"

"Yes, sir," returned Pratt. "And besides the thousand-plus suits I've already got on this thing, I am sending the best and most successful black ops agent in CIA history to Rome. The Israeli Mossad has volunteered to send its best agent to work with our man. They will find out who cooked up this bowl of spaghetti."

Hunt took a deep breath. "All right Pratt, proceed with the investigation and keep me posted. Lastly, our NSA rep, Miss Watts. I was told you have an update on the crash."

"I do, sir," smiled the pretty Afro-American whose competence in Washington was legendary. "The recovery teams and Search and Rescue people have now recovered the bodies of all passengers and crew who were aboard Air Force One. All, that is, with the exception of two. One is a missing Secret Service agent on presidential duty, Mr. Mark Spears. The second missing body is that of President Carr. His GPS keeper, however, was found in the wreckage."

"You have got to be kidding me!" gasped the president. "How can you lose a president? Especially, a deceased president? This is preposterous! Explain this to us!"

Miss Watts continued, "Mr. President, what little surveillance we had at the time on the crash location has confirmed that there were, to intel's knowledge, nobody in or near the crash site until our people, working with Italian authorities, converged on the site within minutes of the reported crash.

"You should know that we have been informed by locals in the area, as well as the National Oceanic Lab, that the currents in that area can be very strong, with 40-mile-an-hour undertows. We've run computer simulations by calculating possible currents, tides and wave action at the time of the crash and we are using those various scenarios in our ongoing search.

"Also, sir, we are told that predation in those waters, mainly from a large shark population, is at a seasonal high."

The fuming president pointed his finger at Miss Watts. "I don't care if you have to dredge the entire Mediterranean—or, for that matter, gut every shark in the ocean—you find those bodies."

Turning back to the others, the president barked, "How could this happen? Don't we have non-stop surveillance on Air Force One while it is in-flight?"

"Sir, I'd like to answer that," Director Pratt said. "We had four different satellites tasked to the flight of Air Force One. One of those was offline for reasons we don't yet know. Two others were in the process of reassignment to cover close-in during the Rome conference. The last of the four was one of our older systems that does not yet have the updated programming allowing it to see through cloud cover. And to really complicate the picture, the crew of Air Force One not only released their F-16s, but they also released the E-4s, which could've seen whatever we're missing.

"We did have a couple of new weather satellites over the area and we put up their pics and data with very distant pics from an Israeli sat, and that is how we isolated the origin of the missile signatures."

"Mr. Pratt," asked a frustrated Hunt, "are these kind of screw-ups standard operating procedures for the CIA?"

"Begging your pardon, Mr. President," responded Pratt, "but the CIA is only the investigative agent on this assignment. The Air Force Wing responsible for the security of Air Force One may be something the Chairman of the Joint Chiefs of Staff can address.

"But I can tell you this, sir, we do know that within minutes of Air Force One's demise, a 10-mile security zone went up around that site that allowed no one in or out of that area. Within 18 minutes, we had a U.S. nuclear sub, the USS Scorpion, closing on the location. They were followed by U.S. Navy Aircraft carrier the USS Reagan, and a Navy missile frigate, the USS Constellation. All those ships were on their way to conduct exercises in the Mediterranean.

"Within 11 minutes after the crash, satellites had been re-tasked and air surveillance by American and Italian planes and helicopters were eyes on the location."

The president took in a slow, deep breath. "All right. Everyone has a lot of follow-up to take care of. Do not leave me out of the loop. I'll schedule another meeting with each of you very shortly. Our priority one: Find the remains of President Carr. Number two: Find out who did this! You're dismissed."

Dr. Minay entered the small bedroom and stopped at the feet of the two cots separated by only a few feet. He went quickly to the side of the larger man, whose condition, it seemed to him, was more critical.

The old doctor had been little more than a general practitioner his entire career. Rome had been his home for most of his life, except during his years at the University of London and the four years of medical school in the United States. He had opportunities to stay in Great Britain or the United States and become a specialist or a surgeon, but his love had always been Rome and the poor of the city's lower end.

His 5'7" frame now carried a paunchy 190 pounds. His age and girth forced him to stop to catch his breath every few yards when walking. It was difficult for him to get around now that he was close to 80. However, his mind was sharp, especially for his age, and his skills were still intact.

Francisco had thoughtfully brought a short three-legged stool into the room and placed it between the cots so the doctor could sit as he examined the injured. Ignoring it at first, the physician, using his stethoscope and blood pressure monitor, checked the larger patient. With a touch to the man's forehead it was evident that the patient was running a very high fever. His heartbeat was irregular and his blood pressure erratic. The doctor gently rolled the man onto his side to check the wound Francisco had told him about.

Both men's ragged, bloody clothes had been removed by Francisco when he brought them in. He had washed them and applied a tight bandage around the wound on the big man's back.

The doctor pulled back the thin blanket covering the man and saw the blood-stained bandages over the injury. Slowly and delicately, he pulled the covering away and saw the horrible wound under the left shoulder blade. After some probing, cleaning and rewrapping the wound with fresh bandages, the doctor gave the man two injections, then carefully rolled him back over.

"Well?" asked Francisco, who had watched the doctor's every move.

The doctor sighed. "Francisco, the wound is deep. It has possibly punctured a lung and an infection has already set in. He's also lost a lot of blood. I gave him an injection of morphine to ease his pain, which will increase when he wakes again. I also gave him a shot of powerful antibiotics, but the truth is, he will be very lucky if he survives another 24 hours. His only hope is to get to a hospital on the mainland. Now, let's see how your other friend is doing. Could you bring me a few clean rags and a bowl of hot water?"

"Yes, yes, I will do so," answered the fisherman as he rushed out of the room.

The doctor picked up the lantern hanging on the wall over the patient he had just examined and moved it to a hanger just above the head of the new patient. The doctor reached to retrieve his tools and bag from beside the bed of the big fellow and then turned back to take in the face of his new charge. He froze in place when he saw the man's face in the good light. It was one of the most recognizable faces on the planet.

"This cannot be." murmured the doctor to himself.

Earlier in the day, Dr. Minay had heard of the downing of the American President's plane just off the coast of Italy. His mind raced as it attempted to piece together the puzzle of how Francisco could have possibly moved the most powerful man in the world into his hut without anyone in the world knowing about it.

Shocked into wide-eyed bewilderment, the old physician plopped himself down on the stool and stared at the President of the United States of America. He could hear Francisco humming in the kitchen as he heated the water and suddenly realized that the old fisherman had no idea who he had in his bed. And why would he? Old Francisco had no television, or even a radio, and even if he did, he had no electricity to run them. He received no newspapers or information from the outside world, nor did he care what went on beyond his own shores. The fisherman was a good, but uneducated, uninformed peasant who hadn't the slightest clue regarding the importance of his guests.

Slowly, the doctor gathered his wits and began a cursory examination. The bump on the president's head had clearly caused a concussion, the severity of which the doctor could not tell without proper equipment. The man was in a semi-comatose state that often accompanies such head trauma. The brain simply puts itself to sleep until the trauma passes or recedes. Sometimes it takes only hours for a patient to awaken. Sometimes it takes days or weeks.

All the president's vital signs were stable and fully functional. Dr. Minay felt sure he would recover. The bruising on his torso had not resulted in any broken bones, but it was going to be very painful when the man did wake up.

Dr. Minay decided not to mention to Francisco, just yet, who his unconscious guest was. As the doctor completed his examinations, Francisco re-entered the tiny room.

"Well, doctor, will he live?"

The old doctor looked into his dear friend's naive eyes. "My friend, both of us are too old to be taking up new causes and picking up old strays. Yes, he will live. The other one here…well, I cannot say.

"Both need a better doctor than I am and much more care than you or I can provide here. I've made sure they will both be quiet, rested and comfortable for a few hours. I will return as soon as I can find a larger boat, and then you can assist us in getting them to a place where they can be cared for."

"But you must listen, doctor," insisted Francisco. "Somebody attacked these men's aero-plane, trying to kill them. We must not let it be known, just yet, that they still live. By the miracle of God, I was able to barely escape the horde of helicopters and boats that converged on their downed aircraft. I, too, as well as Raphael, would be dead now if we'd waited only a minute longer to take our leave. God has entrusted the lives of these men to our care. I plead with you. Tell no one of these men other than ones you can trust with your life."

"Francisco, my entire 80-year existence has been devoted to saving people's lives. So you can relax. I promise, no one will hear of these two except those I trust with my own life.

"Now, go tell Raphael to fetch Antonio to ferry me back to the mainland. Go."

As Francisco left to find Raphael, Dr. Minay took one last look back at the American President and knew exactly what he had to do. And informing the world about his find was not a part of his plan.

SEVEN

Standing on the Piazza del Collosseo, looking up at the magnificent Roman Coliseum, made Leah feel almost insignificant. It was her first visit to the Foro Romano, though she had studied its varied history as a student at the Hebrew University in Jerusalem. And yet, standing just behind a small group of British tourists, she could not resist listening to the guide explain how this entire area, at the foot of Monte Palatino, was no more than a swamp until it was built up centuries ago.

"Now," continued the English-speaking Italian guide, "it is the oldest of Rome's forums and the virtual cradle of ancient Rome. It's the ideal place to trace life in the days of Caesar, Nero or Augustus. Please follow me."

The tour group waddled along behind their energetic male guide walking toward the Coliseum entrance. She, however, took a seat on a stone bench shaded by a small olive tree. The ancient bench, she figured, was yet another relic from Caesarian days.

Thirty years old, Leah Levy was strikingly beautiful. Few people, men or women, could resist a second or even third look at her. On this day, she wore a simple white sundress with strappy white sandals ending in two-inch heels. The cut of the dress, from her shoulders to her hips, did little to hide her figure and highlighted the giftedness of her body.

Her large, expensive sunglasses added another touch of mysterious class. Her stylish, blonde hair fluttered with the slight breeze and brought out her well-tanned complexion to near perfection. To any passerby, she was the picture of a well-to-do, Western tourist casually taking in the many sights of Rome.

She sat with her legs crossed in the typical female tradition and acted as though she was reading the brochure she had picked up about the Coliseum's long history. In truth, the eyes behind the dark glasses were scanning the open plaza in an attempt to spot the contact that her handlers had assured her would make themselves known. She didn't have to wait long.

Walking toward her was yet another tour group led by a guide who was speaking German as he pointed out various locations around the Piazzo. The group didn't stop in front of her at the spot where the previous group had. All, except one, kept walking. The one person stopped directly in front of her with his back toward her, facing the Coliseum. He snapped a quick picture with a camera that hung around his neck, then turned to face her. She noticed the man was a senior citizen, tall and well-built, though pudgy around the middle.

"Aha, there you are, my dear," chirped the elderly gentleman. "I thought I'd lost you." Having said that, he leaned over and kissed her first on her left cheek then on the right.

At first she was stunned by this imbecile's forwardness until she suddenly realized this had to be her contact. The man looked to be well into his 60s, but was dressed in a dark blue, light-weight blazer over an open-necked, white silk shirt with tan trousers. His tiny salt-and-pepper moustache added to his soft sophistication and though his eyes were hidden behind his $600 designer shades, she was sure they had a sparkle to them. All of this was topped by the perky blue beret that sat slightly to the side on his balding head.

The kindly gentlemen crooked his arm, and with a slight bow indicating she should take it, said, "So, shall we go my dear? Our cab is just around the corner and the meter is running."

With her best pretentious smile, she jumped up, grabbed his arm, and playfully said, loud enough for anyone around to hear, "I thought you'd never get here, love. I'm famished and surely you are as well, so take me someplace expensive and spoil me." With that they walked on, she following his lead. To those who may have cared to notice, he looked like any other wealthy senior citizen strolling the Piazza with his young, gold-digging girlfriend.

It took less than two minutes for them to reach the corner of Via dei Fori-Imperiali, a main corridor that winds through the Foro Romano, where a taxi driver patiently waited. The gentleman opened the back door for Leah. She stepped in, followed by the man, who closed the door with authority. He then said to the driver, "You know the drill, Leo. Let's make it quick." This time when he spoke, Leah noticed, the age was gone from his voice. Without answering, the driver pulled away from the curve with a screech of his tires and entered the stream of traffic.

They drove in silence as the cab made its way through the maze of busy Roman streets. Soon they approached the canal Fiume-Tevere that wound its snakelike course around the city. They crossed at the bridge, Ponte Amedeo, which could have led them straight into Vatican City. Instead, the driver made a sharp left on a small side street called Via Glannichello. He continued for several blocks and pulled into a driveway surrounded by dense vegetation. He followed the narrow, gravel road several hundred feet until they rounded a corner and glimpsed a quaint two-story villa tucked into a lush green setting.

Within two hours of his departure from Francisco's cabin, Dr. Minay returned with a larger boat, owned and captained by one of his two sons. The other son came along to assist. Both of the doctor's sons were well into their 40s and were strong as oxen.

The doctor finished preparing both of his patients for transport to the mainland. Though he didn't expect to run into anyone outside his family and closest confidants, still he wrapped the president's face with bandages to conceal his identity.

As his sons carried the cot with the larger, more critically injured man down to the boat, Dr. Minay sat down with Francisco and Raphael at the tiny scuffed table in their kitchenette. "Francisco and Raphael, you must listen to me well. I cannot tell you how urgent it is that you say nothing of these men to anyone—not now, not ever."

"But, Doctor," inquired the old fisherman, "where are you taking them, and why such urgency in the requests for our silence? As you know, we have informed no one but you of these two, as I fear their enemies are still about."

"Francisco," replied the doctor, "we have known each other for many, many years. But now I must ask you to trust me to do what is best with these two whom God led you to help. The well-being of more people than you could ever imagine depends on what now becomes of these men. You are right. They are in danger, far more than you know. But we have a safe place for them where they can get the medical help they so desperately need. Soon, I will return and explain more fully the significance of what you have done. But until then, I ask for your trust and for your pledge of silence should anyone inquire of these men."

Francisco nodded and promised, "You can be assured, dear friend, that we will do as you wish. But do not forget your vow to return as soon as you are able to tell us what is going on."

By this time, the sons of Dr. Minay had finished carrying the cots with both injured men to the 36–foot fishing boat owned by his youngest son. They secured the cots to the flat deck and were ready to depart as soon as their father arrived.

"Go with God," said Francisco as he bear-hugged the old doctor, "and know we pray for your success." Young Raphael shook the physician's hand and said, "Via con Dios, el doctor."

The doctor stepped out of the cabin, softly closing the door behind him.

Following their driver, Brad and Leah stepped inside the secluded villa. No one needed to tell Leah that this was a CIA safe house.

"Your room, Miss Levy, is at the end of this hall. I think you will find everything you need, including your baggage that was secreted over yesterday." The persona of their driver took on an aura of more authority as he gave directions to Brad and Leah.

"I would suggest that you use the next 50 minutes or so to rest and freshen up. You will be briefed in this room at the top of the hour. There is a fully stocked bar to your left. Feel free to make yourself at home." The driver gave a slight bow and left the room.

Brad, who had utilized this house on previous missions, knew his room was up the hall from Leah's. Without speaking a word to each other, both agents turned to their designated rooms.

Leah unpacked the few items she had in her small bag. She had learned to travel light. Having finished that task, she undressed down to her underclothes and sat down in the small chair in front of the vanity. Looking into the mirror, she sighed, reached up with both hands and removed the blonde wig. Eager to lose her false identity, she unwound the tightly wrapped pony tail, removed the bands and hairpins holding it place, and vigorously shook her head.

Her own, coal-black tresses tumbled onto her bare shoulders. Taking the jar of cleanser in front of her, she walked into the bathroom, turned on the faucet and began to scrub off the heavy makeup. Underneath it, her own naturally beautiful, olive complexion began to emerge. When she finished undoing the façade, she gazed for a moment into the mirror. Looking back at her were intensely attractive dark eyes above a slightly turned-up nose and full lips. Her high cheekbones and soft countenance worked in harmony to project an air of confidence that only complimented her captivating beauty. After a quick shower, a change into a casual, black pantsuit, and applying a small amount of powder and lip gloss, Leah returned to the living area.

Brad Fuller had not needed as long to "freshen up." As Leah entered the room, their eyes met and for a lingering moment both were stunned at the transformation the other had undergone. Brad, breaking the awkward silence, spoke first. "Miss Levy, you are indeed a woman of many faces. I do hope this is the real one."

A slight smile at his backward compliment revealed Leah's perfectly formed white teeth. Too experienced to blush, she walked to the couch and sat down. "And you, sir, are clearly not in your 60s with a balding head, pudgy stomach, and Hitlerian moustache."

Brad flashed a handsome grin, went to a chair next to her end of the couch, and took a seat. "I'm working on a touch of gin and tonic. Can I mix you a drink?"

"Mr. Fuller," Leah began, "you are most kind. However, I discovered long ago that numbing my senses with alcohol can be quite lethal in my line of work."

"Ouch," winced Brad. "Then since I find myself in Rome, I will do as the Romans do." Lifting his right hand in a jesting manner of taking an oath, he said, "'Tis my vow, that as long as we are working together, no lethal brew shall pass these lips." He reached over and set his unfinished gin and tonic on the coffee table in front of him.

Leah couldn't help but laugh, but before she could respond, Brad added, "Now, may I offer you some lemonade? There is a fresh, cool pitcher on the bar, and I for one, love lemonade." As he moved to the bar, he continued, "Incidentally, Leah—if I may call you that—please feel free to address me as Brad rather than Mr. Fuller."

Letting her guard down slightly, she smiled. "Okay…Brad. And yes, I'd love some lemonade." As he filled the two glasses, Leah mused, "Brad… Bradford Fuller. That sounds so British, and yet you're not British. You're 100-proof, full-bred, red-blooded American, aren't you?"

"Well, well," he said, as he walked back with their drinks. "Someone's done their homework. What else do you know of Brad Fuller?"

Leah responded, "Only what I've read in your files hacked from CIA and NSA computers."

"Ah," injected Brad with a feigned seriousness, "so you're confessing to hacking into classified systems. It's a felony, you know."

Leah laughed, "You know how the game is played."

"Unfortunately, you're right." surrendered Brad. "So how much did these 'files' tell you about me?"

"Hmm, let me think" she teased. "I know you were born in Charlotte, North Carolina to loving parents who worked hard as civil servants. You graduated with a political science degree from Princeton. You were recruited as an operative for the CIA until your skills became widely known. You were moved into black ops, most of which, even your classified files, do not reveal.

"I know you're 38 years old, single, with no current entanglements—though your reputation with dozens of women on many continents is notorious. You're 6'2" tall, weigh 185 pounds, and don't go to the gym nearly enough to please your supervisors. You've dark hair, blue eyes, and a mark on your posterior, left cheek...made by a small caliber pistol. Because you have the highest ratio of mission successes in the intelligence history of your country, you were chosen for this assignment. Shall I go on?"

"Oh, no, no," he said. "In fact you could've stopped just before you exposed my little scar. That said, our government also has its sources, Miss Leah Levy.

"You, dear girl, were born 30 years ago on an agricultural kibbutz at the northern end of the Sea of Galilee. After you graduated from the American equivalent of high school, you fulfilled a compulsory service in the Israeli Defense Forces. They talked you into staying on for another two years because they saw promise in your keen intellect and your uncanny ability to lead, and you thought it was because you were just another pretty face...tsk tsk.

"From the IDF you jumped out of the pan and into the fire, signing on with the Mossad, where you have had a rather remarkable 10 years, during which you were able to attend and graduate from the Hebrew University in Jerusalem."

"Very good," said Leah, with mock applause.

He continued, "Oh, that's not all. It seems you're quite a bundle of fun. You've been under deep cover in North Africa, Red China, Algeria, and Pakistan. You are a skilled marksman who packs a semi-automatic nine-mill that, obviously, you're not afraid to use.

"You've killed at least four enemy agents in various, rather bloody exchanges, and taken a bullet, as I recall, in your upper left thigh that must've left a nasty scar."

"That, Mr. Fuller," interrupted Leah, "is something you'll never have the opportunity to confirm."

"Please, it's Brad. In conclusion," he added "you are a sabra, a native-born Israeli. Sabra, of course, is a metaphor named after a spiny cactus that grows in the Judean desert. Its fruit is very prickly on the outside but sweet on the inside...as are all native Israelis."

"Don't bet, dear Brad," Leah came back, "on that 'sweet on the inside' stuff."

Before he could answer, the front door swung open and they both turned to face the two men entering the room. One was their driver; the other, Brad recognized as being the CIA station chief in Rome.

Walking over and extending his hand first to Leah, then to Brad, the Chief said, "I cannot tell you how glad we are that the two of you are here. So, let's get on with this briefing. We've very little time to make things happen."

EIGHT

At night, the White House is one of the most spectacular, awe-inspiring sights in the world. However, while from the outside it may seem that all within are at ease and sleeping, the truth is, 24 hours a day, it is a beehive of activity.

At midnight, as the Secretary of State and the director of the CIA came in through the private VIP entrance, they saw staffers everywhere, all busy doing their jobs. The president was just wrapping up another 15-hour day, and the last thing he wanted to do was meet with the Secretary of State and the CIA Director. But his Chief of Staff had said it was important, so he relented, promising only a few minutes.

As Mr. Parlay of State and CIA Director Pratt entered the Oval Office, the president's surly spirit was evident.

"Mr. President," began Secretary Parlay, "thank you for seeing us on such short notice."

The president huffed, "Get to the point men. What is it that 'just can't wait'?"

"Forgive the inconvenience, sir," continued the Secretary of State, "but in the last 72 hours there have been some intriguing international developments."

"Go on," the obviously impatient president snapped.

"Well, sir, it seems that the Chairman of the International Federation of Nations, Charon Dranko Kostos, has upstaged the U.N. diplomatic mission in the Sudan and Darfur. He has also interfered with our own State Department's efforts to mediate peace in that war-torn country. The factions, divided along ethnic and religious lines for years, have refused to stop killing each other long enough to discuss a solution. However, in a meeting lasting less than three hours between Mr. Kostos, the leaders of the besieged government and rebel factions, a peace treaty has been signed by all belligerents. For the first time in years, the roads throughout the region are open without armed guards at check points. Food, medicine and relief are now flowing into the region. All factions have agreed to lay down their arms and committed themselves to participate in a coalition government under Mr. Kostos' IFN."

At the first mention of Charon Kostos' name, the president stiffened. His reaction went unnoticed.

Making a feeble effort to show bravado, the president said, "Well, bully for this Mr. Kostos. Maybe we should nominate the man for the Nobel Peace Prize. I could've read about this over breakfast. Is that all?"

"Uh, not quite, sir." continued the Secretary.

"Then get on with it," moaned the exhausted president.

"Only hours later, an IFN delegation headed by Mr. Kostos arrived in New Delhi. After meeting with India's leaders, he and the Prime Minister of India made a historic, first-time-ever trip for an Indian leader to Islamabad, Pakistan. After a four-and-a-half-hour conference, the President of Pakistan, the Prime Minister of India and Kostos made a joint announcement. India and their oldest enemy, Pakistan, are entering into a new treaty. In it, both of these nuclear powers have agreed to resolve their differences over Kashmere. As you know, sir, since 1948 these two countries have been in a state of conflict over that entire area.

"Now Pakistan is relinquishing all claims to that area and India, besides opening its markets to Pakistani exports, has promised to pull all military personnel 100 miles away from the Pakistani border."

"Sounds like a real love fest," put in the president.

Jumping in, the director of the CIA added, "It is indeed, sir. All of that happened in a space of less than 12 hours while we've been occupied with our own crises. But there is still more, sir."

"Surely, you jest, Mr. Pratt," returned the president.

"No, sir," the Secretary came back. "Within six hours of leaving

Islamabad, Mr. Kostos and his IFN entourage were in Moscow meeting with the Duma leadership and the Russian President."

"If I may, Mr. Secretary?" chimed in the CIA Director, "We received word less than 40 minutes ago that Kostos had somehow smuggled the leaders of the Chechnian revolution into Moscow on one of his private jets. After Kostos won the hearts of the Russians, who agreed to meet with their uninvited Chechnian guests, the two groups agreed to a cease fire. To top that, Russia has agreed to cede total control of three of the five provinces the Chechnians have been demanding. Further, sir, the Chechnians have agreed to release 10 Russian soldiers they have held as POWs for more than six years. The last report I received, just as I arrived here, had both groups partying at the Kremlin and getting drunk on Russian vodka."

The gravity of what he had been told was beginning to sink in. The president asked, "What's the CIA's read on this? Surely, Mr. Pratt, all those smart Yale and Harvard boys over at Langley have thought this through."

"Mr. President," continued Pratt, "this news is almost as fresh as tomorrow's headlines. Our people are just now getting up to speed. But one thing is sure, the IFN and Mr. Kostos are going to be hailed as diplomatic Houdinis. And you can be sure that Charon Kostos is not orchestrating these near-supernatural feats out of his love for humanity."

The president, listening intently, asked, "What do you mean by that?"

"Well, Mr. President, I'm not really sure," Mr. Pratt answered, "but I do know that just before leaving for the conference in Rome, President Carr had told me—as well as the now-deceased Secretary of Defense and State, and the late National Security Director—that he had just come into some critically important intel regarding the IFN and its leadership. He was to reveal all of it to us upon arriving in Rome.

"I got called away with urgent matters and couldn't make that conference and, of course, Air Force One never made it to Rome."

"Uh, forgive me for interrupting, Will," injected Secretary Parlay, "but there is one other little matter we need to share. Mr. President, according to the last report we received, Mr. Kostos' G1 left Moscow an hour ago after filing a flight plan for Tel Aviv, Israel."

"What in God's green earth is he trying to do?" mumbled the president, more to himself than to anyone in the room.

"Sir," answered the CIA Director, "we'll all know the answer to that rather soon. Mr. Kostos has been invited to New York as soon as he completes his mission to Israel. The General Secretary of the United Nations has invited him to address the General Assembly."

The General Assembly room of the United Nations building was filled to overflowing. For over 36 hours, the world had been saturated with nonstop media coverage of the IFN's successes in some of the world's most war-torn and tension-filled regions. All other news stories, even the assassination of the American President, had been pushed off the front pages. Along with hundreds of diplomats and heads of state now attempting to find seating in the UN were thousands of reporters from all over the globe jockeying for a position to see and hear Charon Dranko Kostos.

Every broadcast and print media outlet in the world was poised to insure that the entire planet could hear the man of the hour. The crowds were far too large to be accommodated within the General Assembly auditorium, thus every main hall—from Broadway theaters to Carnegie Hall to Madison Square Gardens—had been prepared with giant video screens to provide a live feed of the event. The Times Square jumbo screen would also show the speech.

After what seemed like hours of waiting, the restless crowd rose as the General Secretary called the meeting to order. He waited for the murmur of an excited crowd to subside. Finally he spoke:

"Today, the United Nations will give ear to a man who, like many of us, has dedicated himself to the good of humankind and to the advancement of peace in our troubled world. He deserves to be heard, for in only a short time, measured in mere hours, he has succeeded in orchestrating peace in places that have known only war, death and destruction for decades. It is not necessary for me to repeat here all the great attributes and personal successes of our guest. You can simply read a paper or turn on any news program to hear that. So, without further ado, I present to you, my friend, Charon Dranko Kostos, Chairman of the IFN."

Cameras of the worldwide media outlets covering the event showed the entire General Assembly jumping to their feet and erupting with applause. Directors in control centers pushed buttons revealing the same scene being reenacted in venues all over New York. It was simultaneously being viewed all around the world.

As the crowd in the United Nations finally ended the demonstration and took their seats, Kostos, who throughout the ovation had stood at the podium with arms outstretched, spoke. "I am humbled by your kindness and the generous reception of this august body."

Again, almost as if on cue, the whole General Assembly exploded out of their seats for another two-minute ovation. Finally, Kostos raised his hands as an appeal for an end of it. "While I am honored by your enthusiasm, I want to appeal for you to hold your wonderful applause until I complete what I have to say, or else it will be a very long evening."

Rumbles of approval and shifting bodies could be heard as the crowd prepared to listen.

"I won't take long, but I must share with you what I believe I have learned about conflict, war and belligerence. Conflict is easy to perpetuate once its given permission to exist. And as any student of history can tell you, conflicts can go on so long that the combatants even lose sight of why the conflict began in the first place.

"The truth is, war is the product of human pride, often disguised as national honor. One has said all wars are money wars. But that is a fable. All wars are ultimately, in the final analysis, religious wars, forged in the furnace of bigotry, bias and intolerance. Humanity's goal in this trying hour, when the earth is but seconds from self-destruction, should be to find resolution through understanding. It would behoove us, as leaders, to begin to focus more upon our common values rather than upon our petty differences.

"The critics of co-existence have always been those who longed, at all costs, to maintain their biases, whether ethnic or cultural. However, the highest hurdle for peacemakers of all ages, be it Gandhi, Martin Luther King, or Jesus Christ, has been that of religion and religious bias." By now the entire worldwide audience was captivated by the magnetism, humility and wisdom they heard coming from Kostos. They listened, fixated.

"In the late 19th century, the oratory of one of India's wise men named Vivekananda touched his generation. He said, on one occasion, the religions of the world all share the great universal spiritual truths. People just see those truths through the eyes of their own history, culture and imagery. I happen to agree, and therefore tell you, for peace to truly reign on our diverse planet, the narrow-minded biases of religious and cultural chauvinism must come to an end."

Again, simultaneously, the entire hall erupted in a fit of applause and cheering. Only after Kostos' appeal for silence would the crowd take their seats.

"Our common goals are security and safety for our families, sufficiency for our needs, and the right to worship the God of our choice. These goals can be attained if each of us will embrace the fact that God is God regardless of what one may call him. Christians, Muslims, Jews, Buddhists, Hindus and all other religious expressions can and must acknowledge the universal commonalities of the others.

"It was Vivekananda who told the story of five blind men trying to describe an elephant. One described the trunk, which he had touched. Another described the leg, which he had touched. Still another the ear; then one, the eye, and so on. All seemed to contradict the other...until their reports were recognized to be part of the whole.

"Our world is divided by those who refuse to acknowledge the whole elephant and are clinging to their own understanding of the part they know. Ladies and gentlemen, our world can know true peace but only when we reject those who cling to and preach a God who is narrow, intolerant, unyielding, dogmatic, warlike, capricious and unjust.

"Friends, embrace the truth that God is good. He's not a tribal God who favors one group over another. What utter nonsense!

"No, I am not a theologian. I am a peace seeker and a peacemaker, a student of the human condition. I assure you, however, that we will only have peace when we surrender our minds to the process of seeking it above our personal prejudices."

The crowd could not be restrained and once again broke out in a thundering show of approval. A full five minutes passed before the speaker could conclude his remarks.

"Over 40 years ago, a group of the planet's greatest minds from all over the world gathered to produce a declaration, to lay a foundation upon which to build a world at peace. Amongst the group were great educators, lawyers, clergymen, scientists, and politicians. Their declaration bravely called for an end to the division of humanity based on religious and nationalistic grounds. They acknowledged the fact that the world was approaching a historic turning point, where to insure tranquility, peace and prosperity for all, mankind must transcend the limits placed on us by national sovereignty and theological preference in order to build a world community. They called for a system of law, based on tolerance and liberty, to be universally recognized and embraced by all and enforced by a universal government chosen by all."

The General Assembly exploded out of their seats like a keg of gun powder set off by a short fuse. The noise was thunderous. Kostos, after prolonged effort, succeeded in quieting them one last time. "To the critics and the skeptics who tell us that global peace and prosperity is unattainable, I point them to the Sudan and Darfur, where tonight war and starvation have been replaced by peace and plenty. I point them to the Russians and the Chechnians, who this very hour are embracing after decades of killing each other. I point them to India, to Pakistan, where a lifetime of war tore at their souls but now the human family has been restored and old enemies have come together to build a better world. Soon, I will point you to the war-torn, hate-filled Middle East as an example of what man can achieve if he is but willing.

"These are but the humble beginnings for the people of the world who are willing to join hands and hearts, to do the undoable and to succeed where every other generation has failed. To that end, I and the

International Federation of Nations offer you our assistance in achieving this great endeavor. And this time, we can, indeed, beat our corporate swords into plowshares and, of a truth, study war no more. Thank you and God bless you all."

The United Nations had never witnessed the kind of joyous pandemonium that filled the hall upon the closing of Kostos' speech. The celebrations poured out of the venues onto the streets of New York and continued for hours. In every corner of the globe, the words of Charon Drakon Kostos were being hailed as holy writ. Suddenly, peace was breaking out everywhere. Almost.

NINE

Ten hours after his rousing speech at the United Nations, Kostos was in his top-floor suite of the beautiful Seville Hotel in Zurich, Switzerland. He sat with his confidante, Maurice Dubois, on the grand balcony taking in the mesmerizing night beauty of the great city and its twinkling lights.

Relaxed, with a drink in hand, both men had expressed their joy and mutual satisfaction over the successes of the last few days. After a while, the celebratory banter subsided, followed by a sobering silence. Finally, Kostos said, "He's alive, you know."

Dubois lifted his drink to his lips, slowly sipped it, and asked, "You are sure?"

Kostos took in a deep breath, sighed, and added, "Yes. I'm sure. I have it from my highest authority. He is alive."

Maurice Dubois slowly nodded his head. "And so, we will simply finish the job."

Still looking upon the city below, Kostos steadily responded, "Oh, yes, indeed we shall. But send our best and be done with it."

Dubois nodded again, stood to his feet, and quietly left the suite.

Kostos sat, almost trance-like, staring at the horizon for the rest of the night.

Castel Colledora is a breathtaking 30-acre estate in the rolling green Italian countryside 50 kilometers southeast of Rome. From the mid-1600s, the cathedral had served as a Catholic church. The grand castle built next to it had housed bishops, noblemen, and various state authorities until the outbreak of World War II. At that time, Mussolini's fascist henchmen and authoritarian military closed the church and took over the castle. It was used as an officer's training facility until the Allies invaded. When the Italian forces abandoned it in their hurried retreat north, the church and castle were turned into a forward command post by the Allies. Later, it was used as a hospital for wounded British and American soldiers. At the end of hostilities, the estate was abandoned again. It became uninhabited, overgrown, and dilapidated for the next three decades. In 1975, a private consortium from the Middle East purchased the entire estate and began a massive reclamation effort.

Still today, it sits in a rural area with no close neighbors. Local authorities could have cared less about the old landmark as long as the current owners continued to pay the substantial annual taxes.

Tall trees and thick shrubbery surrounded the estate's border on all sides. Just inside that tree line stood a 10-foot chain-link fence topped with concertina barbed wire. Few cars were ever seen going in or out of the iron gated and manned entrance. Anyone venturing too close, such as a confused hiker or lovers looking for seclusion, quickly discovered security around the complex was unforgiving. If anyone came within six feet of the surrounding fence, they would feel the electrical field's warning. Touching the fence left one smarting or even unconscious for hours.

Inside the electrified border fence, every 30 yards a network of cameras sent high-grade video to a constantly monitored control room. Just beyond the camera circuit, the laser-triggered alarm systems took over. The circumference of the complex was heavily patrolled by armed guards and well-trained German Shepherds. Not so much as a squirrel or a fox could breach the boundaries without alerting the entire security force.

Within the ornate castle, every floor and room had been, with no expense spared, beautifully remodeled to reflect the grandeur of 16th-century Italian aristocracy. The furniture, tapestries, and all other décor were exclusively period-pieces.

The only exception was the extensive ultra-contemporary basement areas. Over 20,000 square feet had been converted into a high-tech, well-staffed medical and research facility. Private quarters for nurses and doctors were accompanied by a fully functional operating room, ICU unit, examination rooms, and seven private rooms for VIP patients. Only a select few, affiliated with the private consortium, had access to or even knowledge of the superior care it afforded.

It was here that, upon leaving Francisco's hut on the Isle de'Terreno, Dr. Minay had secreted the unconscious President of the United States and his ailing friend.

The private room where President Mathew Dillon Carr lay unconscious was a bit larger than the typical hospital room. These intensive care unit facilities required more space to accommodate the assortment of equipment, monitors, and screens surrounding the patient.

Three sides of the square room were windowless. The entrance was on the patient's left. Much of the wall space on that side of the room was taken up by the five-by-seven-foot two-way observation window. On the other side of the window was another room where nurses and/or doctors could monitor a patient 24 hours a day, seven days a week. From the observation room, not only could they listen to and watch the high-tech equipment monitoring every function of the ailing president's physiology, but they could hold a conference when necessary away from the patient's hearing. Only a small handful of dedicated and select staff, along with Dr. Minay and his sons, knew of the president's presence.

Doctors had by design kept the president in a state of semi-coma until the MRI readings and CAT scans showed a decrease in the brain's swelling—which, almost five days after the crash, was now beginning to subside rapidly. They began to reduce the sedatives in order to slowly bring the patient back to a state of consciousness.

Dr. Minay, who stopped by daily, stood looking at the patient through the glass of the observation room. A busy nurse flittered around the room like a hummingbird when the outer door opened and Dr. Avi Cohen entered the observation area. Dr. Cohen, one of a dozen physicians who voluntarily served this facility, was an old friend of Dr. Minay. He was an energetic, 65–year-old diagnostic surgeon, and a neurologist of note. At 5'11" he was totally bald and sported a full, gray and black beard. His specialty was head trauma, and as he entered the room the nurse stepped out, leaving the two physicians alone.

"Shalom, Avi," greeted Dr. Minay.

"And to you, Yossi" returned Dr. Cohen. "I see our charge continues his rest."

Nodding in the affirmative, Dr. Minay inquired, "And your latest prognosis is…?"

Raising his hand to stroke his beard, Dr. Cohen answered, "The latest MRI completed an hour ago shows the swelling in the brain is rapidly dissipating. The trauma to the frontal lobe could've been fatal, or at the very least, caused permanent, severe brain damage. And the truth is, Yossi, more than anything we've done here, his life was saved by the anticoagulants and blood thinners you administered when you first saw him. That act was the only thing that kept the severe hematosis from developing deadly blood clots or aneurisms. However, you know of course, had he any internal bleeding, your injections would have killed him."

"Yes, I know," replied Dr. Minay, "But be assured Avi, I only did so after I had it on very good authority to do it."

"Well," Dr. Cohen relented, "while some of our old colleagues may argue the science of your actions, no one can argue the results."

"If I may ask, Avi," Dr. Minay politely inquired, "has the Council made a decision about how much to tell him when he regains consciousness? We both know he will be killed as soon as it's known he's still alive, regardless of the security level his government provides."

Dr. Cohen considered the question as he stared out at his patient, sighed and answered, "Yes, and the Council knows it as well. They're going to take a chance and tell him everything. Then it will be left up to him to make the decision."

"I fear he may not believe us, Avi," returned Dr. Minay. "I understand he's pretty much a secularist. His disposition toward the bizarre may well be our biggest challenge."

"Yes, Yossi," sighed Dr. Cohen. "Nevertheless, it is a chance we must take. He may well be the only man on earth who can give us the time we need."

"And what of his friend's condition?" asked Yossi.

"It's too early. He's still in ICU just down the hall, and as soon as I leave here…"

But before Dr. Cohen could finish his sentence, a loud warning alarm sounded on one of the bedside monitors. Both doctors rushed into the president's room, where two nurses already stood by the patient's bed. Upon seeing the doctors, the nurses backed up to give the men access to the patient.

Studying the data being conveyed on the beeping monitor's screen, Dr. Cohen said, "Well, now, it seems our patient will soon be returning to the real world. He'll probably regain consciousness within the hour. The alarm is telling us that the strong sedatives are wearing off and the brain activity is increasing substantially. I suppose you'll stick around a bit longer, Dr. Minay. It's about to become a very interesting day."

"Dr. Cohen," smiled Yossi, "I wouldn't miss it for the world."

"That, dear Yossi," answered Dr. Cohen," is what it's all about isn't it? The world."

The briefing had not been brief. Almost two hours after he began, the CIA station chief in Rome, Will Shannon, finally wrapped it up. Most of the meeting covered details regarding the downing of Air Force One. Brad and Leah's assignment was to find out why terrorists from such diverse organizations had decided to work together on this project. Further, they were to identify who had developed the plan, organized the teams, and financed what was no doubt a very expensive endeavor.

At the conclusion of the meeting, Chief Shannon asked Brad to accompany him to his car. On the way, Shannon and Brad exchanged polite chit-chat. As the Chief's driver opened the car door, Shannon turned to his agent and, with a note of seriousness, said, "Listen, Brad, I need to tell you something very much off the record."

"And here I was thinking you brought me out here to kiss me goodbye," jested the Agent.

Ignoring the humor, the station chief continued, "You should know that our boss, and by that I mean Pratt, feels there's a lot more going on behind all this. It's something more than simple 'revenge of the terrorists.' Of course, that's exactly what the new administration doesn't want to hear. President Jordon and his cohorts want this investigation shut down quickly, and the file closed."

"And just what is it that Pratt thinks is going on?" inquired his Agent.

"Brad," sighed the Chief, "don't think me nuts, but I tend to buy into Pratt's theory..."

"And that is?" prompted Brad.

"And that is, that President Carr may well still be alive." Shannon stated conclusively.

"Well, here I was believing that I was the one going nuts," responded Brad. "Ever since I examined the wreckage of the president's plane they reassembled in that huge hangar at Da Vinci, I've had the same nagging thought."

Brad leaned against the Chief's limo and continued, "The President's Suite, where Carr was thought to have been at the time of the missile strike, had better armor and more classified safety features than an M1–tank. Anyone in that suite when the plane hit the water had a good chance of survival. It was the only area on that aircraft that showed no signs of fire and no trace of poisonous gases. Nor was there any structural failure to the airframe around that suite.

"Further, Mr. Shannon, the blood that was found in there was not that of President Carr. It was the blood of his Secret Service Agent, whose body is also missing. More importantly, they've found no dead president anywhere. And forget the shark theory. Recovery and rescue was on the scene within 10 minutes. Had sharks gone into a feeding frenzy at that crash site, you'd have had a whole lot of mutilated bodies. Yet, not one of 'em bore the marks of a shark attack."

The Chief, surprised that Brad had already reached the same conclusion, added, "That's the same line of reasoning Pratt and I followed. So, while we want to know who is really behind this attack, we also desperately want to know if President Carr is alive. If he is, we want him back. But Brad, you must work fast. Director Pratt is under extreme pressure from the top to wrap this up."

"And what of Miss Levy and the Mossad? Don't tell me I've got to work around them and keep all of this to myself," intoned Brad.

"Mossad, as you well know, is usually a step ahead of everyone. President Carr was a very close friend of the Israeli Prime Minister as well as the director of Mossad," answered Shannon. "That's why we brought in Levy. Mossad is no one's fool. They're on board and are part of the good guys on this."

Shannon reached into his inside coat pocket, pulled out a business card, and handed it to Brad. "Whatever you find, report directly to Pratt. You can catch him 24 hours a day on those secured lines. Don't tell our Rome desk anything. We need to retain deniability. And Brad, whoever's behind all of this is very nasty. Be careful."

As soon as those words were out of his mouth, Leah Levy strode up. "I hate to interrupt your boy's club, fellas, but I don't appreciate all this hush, hush, cloak-and-dagger garbage. And," she added with a cold smile, "if you're not going to let me play too, I'm gonna take my ball and go home."

"I'm very sorry, Miss Levy," Shannon said quickly, "Brad is eager to tell you everything we've just discussed. As for me, I've other business to tend to, so good day." The Chief quickly got in the back seat, closed the door, and told his driver to get him out of there.

As the Chief's car rounded the corner and rolled out of sight, Brad turned to Leah. Standing there with her arms crossed, her head tilted with a look of rebuke, she reminded him of the way his mother used to look at him when he was caught stealing cookies.

Tenderly taking her by the arm, he turned her around and began walking with her back to the house. "Why do I feel that everything I'm about to tell you, you already know?"

It was the kind of day that the Italian Minister of Tourism loved to boast about in his brochures. Temperatures in the low 70s, cloudless blue skies and white sand, beaches that meet with azure ocean waters.

The candy-apple red Porsche had the top down as Brad and Leah drove along Highway 601 that paralleled the magnificent beaches on their left. They were on their way to the little coastal village of Fiumicino, only a short distance from where Air Force One had gone down.

They had to start somewhere. What better place than the area of the crash site?

Arriving at their destination mid-morning, they parked the car and walked to a small, outdoor café overlooking the beach where they brunched on fruit, cheeses, Italian pastries and strong coffee. They had already decided to stroll along the beach frontage and make idle chatter with the friendly locals. The small shops, kiosks and cafés along the boardwalk afforded an unending supply of local folks, all potential witnesses.

Both Brad and Leah knew that a dozen police agencies and intelligence operatives had already saturated this area asking the locals a list of unending questions. But the agents also knew that while most people are sorely intimidated by men with badges and uniforms, those same people love to brag to curious tourists about how close they had been to great events. Thus, the agents became simple tourists, anxious to intermingle with the friendly natives. It would be a most productive day.

However, the last thing in the world they expected to find, they found.

TEN

A thick fog slowly swirled around him. He was tumbling head over heels through a long tunnel. Someone at the far end was calling him. "*Mr. President, can you hear me? Mr. President?*"

As a faint light at the end of the tunnel came into focus, he was suddenly aware of a severe headache. Then he heard it again. "*Mr. President. You should wake up, Mr. President.*"

The doctors saw his eyes squint, then flutter open with a groggy, confused expression.

"Where am I?" the president asked in a barely audible voice. "Who are you?"

Doctor Cohen answered, "Mr. President, I am your physician. You were in a terrible accident several days ago and you are now in a hospital recovering. How do you feel?"

"What? A hospital?" the president mumbled as he made a feeble effort to raise himself. Falling back, he reached up and grabbed his head. "Oh, my head is killing me."

"Yes, but that is a good thing, President Carr," the doctor said. "It means you're neurologically functional. This is good."

"Whoa, did you say this is good? What kind of doctor are you?" moaned the president.

"Oh, I'm a good doctor," Cohen said as he held a cup of water to the patient's lips. "Now, take a sip of this water. In a moment I'll give you something for your headache. First, I want to check your eyes. Follow my little light with your eyes." As the doctor held the patient's eyelids open, he could see the reflexes and pupils were normal.

"Very good, Mr. President. You had a lot of us worried."

"What kind of accident? I don't remember. Where?" President Carr asked, still groggy.

"Sir, I am going to tell you, but you must remain very calm. Getting too excited could cause a setback. Do you understand?"

Carr answered with a simple nod and an inquisitive look.

"Okay, then." The doctor continued, "Five days ago you were about to land in Rome for a conference when your aircraft, the Air Force One I think you call it, was hit by a missile of some sort in an effort to assassinate you."

"What!?" exclaimed the president. "Is…how are the rest of the folks…the ones on the plane, too? My cabinet members, some were with me, and also our support people, and reporters, lots of 'em and the crew…everyone okay?"

"I am very sorry, sir, but you and one other are the only two survivors." The doctor's sorrow was real.

Dumbfounded, President Carr said, "No. No. That can't be true. I don't believe you. I want to talk to someone else. You're lying. Where's my family? I want to see my family now!"

"Mr. President," Dr. Cohen pleaded, trying to settle his patient, "please try to calm yourself. I am telling you the truth. You and an Agent Spears, who is just down the hall, are the only survivors. This man, Spears, sir, saved your life."

The president just looked at the doctor with a stricken expression on his face and shook his head, "No."

The doctor took a deep breath, "Your family is just fine, sir, and you'll see them very soon."

With that, the president grabbed the doctor's coat in his right hand. "Listen to me. I am the President of the United States of America, not some weak-kneed weenie that you need to patronize. Now, I want to know—and I want to know *now*—what's going on? What are you holding back?"

Dr. Cohen felt a hand on his shoulder and looked around to see Dr. Minay. "Excuse me, Avi. Mr. President, I am Dr. Yossi Minay. I was the first physician to see you after the...the incident. Dr. Cohen here doesn't want to further upset you with too much information until you're more thoroughly examined. The truth is, the entire world thinks you're dead, and but for an incredible series of miracles you, indeed, would be. I promise you, sir, if you'll just make an effort to relax a bit, we're going to tell you everything. But already, the information we've shared with you has given your system an enormous shock and it's unwise for us to push our luck. A setback with the serious head injury you've sustained could be irreversible. So please relax. And understand this. Soon you will be back on your feet. You were, and you are, the President of the United States of America. Your family, your friends and your country are all just fine at the moment. Your return will be a cause for great celebration. But first there is some critically important information we must give you."

The president, though having settled down a bit, was still agitated, "Well, then, get on with it, Doc. I've responsibilities. Just who are you people anyway?"

"Sir, on the brink of death following an assassination attempt, you were secretly brought to this highly classified medical facility south of Rome. Our intentions were first, to save your life, and second, to insure you stay alive. We are convinced that those who want you dead are stalking you, searching for you even now. They'd love to kill you before you leave here and before you get back to your Ovaled Office."

"That's Oval Office, Doc," replied the Chief Executive. "But you still haven't told me who you guys think you are, playing Batman and Robin with my life."

Dr. Minay looked quizzically at Dr. Cohen, not understanding the reference to a "Batman and Robin."

"Yossi," Dr. Cohen spoke up, "the president refers to two fictional superheroes in American culture who go about doing good. But," turning back to address President Carr, Cohen continued, "in a very short time, sir, all your questions will be answered. I promise. Then, if you choose to leave, you may do so. And we will do all we can to support your decision."

Frustrated, the president raised his volume, "Are you guys gonna tell me who you are and what's going on, or not?"

Dr. Minay took the question as a cue for him to jump back in, "I will tell you, sir, but after I do, you must rest a bit longer. Then I will answer all of your questions without delay. Agreed?"

"Like I've a lot of choices," growled the president. "I saw your two well-armed goons over there in your little glass enclave. I suppose I'm a hostage, right?"

"No, Mr. President," responded Dr. Minay, "these men are not to keep you in. They are to keep others out, to insure your safety."

"If you say so. I guess I am feeling a bit wasted," the president said around a large yawn. "Okay. I'll agree. Compromise is the art of diplomacy. So, first you tell me exactly who you people are then." Yawning, he continued, "I'll get a little rest and you'll answer every question I've got...right?"

"First, I shall tell you who we are," Dr. Minay replied, "Dr. Cohen and I, along with the staff of this facility and a good number of others not at this facility belong to what one may call a clandestine or secret order called Sodote Shalom."

"So, pray tell," an increasingly sleepy president asked, "what in tarnation is Sodote Shalom?"

"It is, sir," Dr. Minay said, "a Hebrew term. It's most literal translation into English would be 'the Secrets of Peace.'"

"Hmmm...Sodote Shalom...good name," said the sleepy president as he strained to keep his eyes open, "Secrets of Peace?...I guess that's what everyone's trying to figure out huh...the secret?"

The president's eyes fell shut and he slept.

Dr. Minay, still looking down at the patient, spoke over his shoulder to Dr. Cohen, "Avi, you think he's okay? He just went out."

As Dr. Minay turned, he saw Dr. Cohen with a mischievous grin on his face, standing by the I.V. line running into the president's arm. He was holding an empty syringe.

"You didn't?"

"Yossi, he's too fussy right now. Besides he'll feel better after five or six hours sleep" smiled Dr. Cohen.

"Avi," said Minay, shaking his head, "you are bad. But it was a good idea. Sleep tight, Mr. President."

The night before, at the end of a long day and a tiring drive back to the safe house in Rome, Brad and Leah were exhausted and had quickly gone to their own bedrooms. But this morning, Brad had gotten up early. Walking slowly onto the deck outside the back patio doors, he squinted painfully at the horizon where the sun was just beginning to peak the crest. His sinus headache, throbbing for hours, was just starting to subside, but he still felt like he hadn't slept last night. He had, in fact, stayed up very late trying to piece together the puzzle developing before them. He had gotten out of bed at 4:00 a.m., two hours earlier.

Standing at the rail overlooking the beautiful morning view, with his white cotton robe tied at the waist, Brad reached up and rubbed his stubbled, unshaven jaw. Knowing he had to talk to Leah as soon as she was up, he decided he needed a quick shower. Just as he turned to go in, Leah was opening the sliding patio doors and stepping out. She was already groomed, dressed in a ravishing navy linen pantsuit, the collar of her crisp white blouse tucked into the lapel of her tailored jacket

"Ah, there you are. How about some coffee, Mr. Fuller?" as she offered him one of the cups she was carrying.

Though he had already had two cups, he politely took her offering. "Thank you, Miss Levy. You're up early. I trust you slept well."

"A lot better than you, I'm sure," she smiled. "I saw your light on quite late."

"Yeah, well, I'm an incurable insomniac when I'm working," he answered. "And by the way, I called Washington last night. I had a chat with Director Pratt, our CIA Chief. I told him what we found out in Flumicino, and he passed on the latest intel that's come in which, I might say, adds a strange caveat to the mix."

"Oh, yeah?" asked Leah with piqued interest. She took a seat on a bench built into the deck. "I do hope it's not just another one of those guy things that you can't tell anyone."

Brad sat down beside her, "Oh, I think you're cleared for this. You are, after all, just like one of the boys." He grinned.

"I can't tell you how refreshing it is to discover you're not nearly the chauvinistic pig you seem at first glance," she mocked.

He couldn't resist laughing, "Touché, dear. So, I'll tell you. Human resources in Zurich confirmed that intel from our new and improved Echelon system, which snatches the most interesting things out of the air, picked up a conversation between this new diplomatic wonder boy, Mr. Charon Drakon Kostos and his little buddy, Maurice Dubois, the French billionaire. As you probably know, our assets maintain non-stop surveillance on less-than-friendly heads of states and embassies around the world.

"Mr. Kostos' recent, almost too-good-to-be-true successes in the diplomatic arena had red-flagged him to my boss. He had Kostos added to our priority-one list of targets for surveillance just eight days ago."

"You Americans," sighed Leah. "Mossad's been watching that rat with a messiah complex for months."

"Well, then," Brad shot back, "maybe you should tell your super spy friends to be a bit more forthcoming with what they find.

"At any rate, it appears that Kostos and Dubois have ordered a hit on an unknown subject of some import. According to the intel, Kostos said something to the effect of, 'He's alive,' and then ordered the killing of whoever 'he' is. Then Dubois left Kostos' room and made a call from the lobby of the same hotel on an unsecured line. Big mistake. He called Rome and, after our code-breaking spooks at Langley finished untangling the verbal goobly-gook, it was clear that he gave an order for the release of a hit squad with directives to locate and eliminate the target at first opportunity."

"Could your friends tell who he called?" Leah asked with excitement.

"My dear girl, the interesting thing is not *who* he called, which is still unclear, but *where* he called," Brad said in an ominous voice.

"And?" pressed an impatient Leah, "Where did he call?"

"His call, Leah, was placed to the Vatican."

"You can't be serious!" she exclaimed. "This is getting bizarre, Brad."

Both of them were remembering the frail, elderly woman they had met the day before from the small cottages near the Flumicino beach. She boasted that she had been walking on the beach the day of the crash, and had watched in shocked horror when the missiles hit the plane. She added that she had stood in mute fear as the plane had made impact with the ocean.

Keeping their excitement hidden, they had casually asked if she had seen any boats or vessels near the crash, or had witnessed anyone swimming or moving away from the wreckage.

She startled them by revealing that a priest and nun, "such a sweet couple," had shown up at her cottage the day before asking the same questions. She remembered only the name of the nice priest, a Father Portega from the Vatican.

"The question is, *why*," Brad said, thinking out loud, "would a priest and nun be investigating the downing of Air Force One…and was the call from Dubois to the Vatican hours before they showed up at the old woman's cottage merely a coincidence?"

"Brad, do you think Kostos' talk with Dubois about killing someone was referring to President Carr? We've no evidence he's even alive, and they didn't actually say Carr's name, did they?" queried Leah.

After a moment of silence, Brad answered, "No. No one heard his name mentioned, but it's increasingly clear to me, that while there's no evidence the president is alive, there's even less that he's dead.

"But, Leah, if they were talking about killing Carr, that's a very good lead on just who's behind bringing down Air Force One."

After a moment of thoughtful silence, Brad took the last sip in his coffee cup and said, "I think it's time we go to church, my dear."

Taken aback, Leah scolded, "Say it with me Brad. Leah is Jewish. Jews do not go to church. Sometimes synagogue, but never church."

"It's not like I'm asking you to share a ham sandwich, Leah. Besides, you may find a little confession is good for your soiled soul."

"All right," surrendered Leah. "Oh, the sacrifices we make for our country."

Brad stood, "I'll go and get on my Sunday best—and it might be a good idea if you brought along your little friend, the nine-mill."

Leah jumped up and walked into the house ahead of him while speaking back over her shoulder, "You don't have to ask. I never leave home without it."

The president's secretary, 62–year-old Della, competent and always discreet, buzzed the president's intercom. "Mr. President, Mr. Kostos is here for your appointment." It was 12:30 a.m. and President Jordan Hunt had been dreading this meeting ever since he gave in to Kostos' demands to see him. He wasn't sure what the man wanted, but he knew it couldn't be good. At least Kostos had agreed to keep the meeting secret. The man had been whisked into the White House through the subterranean tunnel systems in order to keep the prying eyes of the media off his arrival.

"Della, you may show Mr. Kostos in and, short of an all-out nuclear attack, I don't want to be disturbed during this meeting."

"Yes sir, Mr. President."

Twenty seconds later, the door into the Oval Office opened. The secretary led Kostos in, and then she turned and left the room, closing the door behind her.

Kostos hadn't changed much since the president's first and only other meeting with him all those years ago. Now middle-aged, Kostos maintained his natural good looks and charming presence. His blond hair remained full and his six-foot frame carried a body that bespoke physical fitness.

The president was out of his chair and walking around his desk to greet his guest with an extended his hand in anticipation of a handshake. "Welcome to the White House."

Kostos blatantly ignored Hunt's hand, looked past him, and walked over to the massive desk. Without saying a word, he proceeded around the desk and plopped himself down in the president's chair.

President Hunt, 5'7" and very slight of build, had never been a threatening presence. To a lot of people, including those pestering political cartoonists, he brought to mind Barney Fife of the TV town Mayberry. His entire political career had been built on his backslapping, glad- handing, and back-room compromises. Even his selection as Vice President to Dillon Carr had not been the result of abilities or political prowess. He was simply the lesser of what the party considered greater evils. No one had ever suspected the man would actually some day become president.

Now, he looked on in wide-eyed disbelief as Kostos casually leaned back in the large leather chair and propped his feet up on the Chief Executive's desk. Kostos then raised him arms, interlocked his fingers behind his head in a most relaxed posture, and smiled. "Ahh. I've always wanted to do this."

Red in the face, the president's indignation exploded. "Just who in God's name do you think you are, Kostos?"

"Jordan, Jordan, Jordan," replied Kostos mockingly. "It's so unlike you to invoke the name of God. I mean, you didn't call on Him when your Russian woman turned out to be an enemy agent bent on blackmail. No, you just did as you were told and provided all kinds of classified information to her and her handlers.

"And Jordan, refresh my memory if you would, but did you or did you not call on God when your Russian mistress got greedy and wanted $1 million for herself in order to keep quiet? Wait! Now that I think about it, Jordan, you didn't call on God then either, did you? No. You called on me.

"And later, when it was about to become public that you had raided your own campaign funds in order to buy expensive baubles for your Russian lover, did you call on God then? No. You again, called on me.

"So let's leave God out of this, Jordan. He wasn't the one who saved your sorry butt.

"'Twas I!"

"Kostos," an infuriated but helpless president hissed, "let's get to the point. What is it you want?"

"Oh, I've only a very small list. I mean, for now," chuckled Kostos. "First, in a few days we'll be making an important announcement. And by *we*, I mean the IFN. In order, as you Americans would say, to build a more perfect union, we have consolidated various segments of Europe and with the cooperation of the European Union, divided the continent into 10 different confederations. The 10 shall be under the umbrella of the IFN and within a very short time we will build the greatest economic, political, and military power on earth.

"However, in order to build confidence and credibility with the World Bank, the International Monetary Systems and other critically important financial movers and shakers, it will be necessary for the United Nations to immediately recognize this new body-politic."

The president smirked, "Yeah, Kostos, like that would ever get past the U.N. Security Council."

Kostos hastily replied, "Had your predecessor President Carr lived, I'm quite certain the United States, if no one else, would have vetoed the matter. But Carr isn't president. His unfortunate demise has left you, Brother Jordan, in the driver's seat.

"You need to know, Mr. President, that after weeks of behind-closed-doors diplomacy and a bit of necessary arm-twisting, every other member of the Security Council has already agreed to vote in favor of full recognition of this new IFN consortium. With your vote, which shall be forthcoming from your new U.N. Ambassador, it will be mission accomplished."

"Kostos, you'll never pull this off. It's blackmail," spit the president.

"Mr. President, it's already, as you say, been pulled off," smiled an assured Kostos.

"Now, for the other matter with which I will need a bit of cooperation. Very soon, I shall require a squadron of your stealth bombers, fully loaded and armed to the teeth. All American markings are to be removed from the planes and replaced with Israeli markings. They will fly with their new stealth technology that hides them from radar from the American base in Ankor, Turkey."

The president laughed, "Kostos you are mad. By the way, the stealths at our base in Turkey are top secret. How do you…?"

"Mr. President," interrupted Kostos, "there are no secrets from us. Now please listen. The B-1s will fly to Bushera, Iran, where they will send a flurry of smart bombs into the bunkers of Iran's second nuclear development site. Of course, one of those bombers will also carry 100,000 leaflets that will be released over a populated area. The leaflets will implicate Israel as the attackers. It will be seen by Iran and the Arab world as an unprovoked second act of war by the Israeli Air Force. Things are just now beginning to settle down after their first strike months ago. It's time to stir the pot."

"Kostos," argued the president, "even if that insane act could be accomplished, this country would be forced to come to Israel's defense if they're attacked. Within a very short time, the whole thing would go global.

"Anyway, I'd never get away with giving an order like that. Any military officer, especially the base commander at that field, would run the order through the chain of command for confirmation. It would never work."

Kostos slowly removed his feet from the president's desk, sat up, and propped his elbows on the surface. "You, once again, Jordan, underestimate me. Your prestigious and noble Commander of that base is Lieutenant General Joel Franklin and he, my friend, is a member of the same club you are. He has a very checkered past that competes with your own in terms of stupidity. He will do as you tell him because we own him.

"The Commander's cooperation is already assured. He has, for almost two weeks, been briefing a group of your pilots with falsified, classified intelligence and those boys are gung ho, chomping at the bits, to fly into Iran. They've been told the secret mission is to help the poor Israelis, America's only friend in the Middle East. They will do it and they'll keep quiet after it's done.

"All that's necessary for you, Jordan, is to send a coded word to good Lt. Gen. Franklin to commence at the moment of my command. He will do so on your order without further confirmation."

"You've got to be kidding me, Kostos! You're irrational!" exclaimed the president.

"Irrational?" laughed Kostos. "Mr. President, you surely took philosophy while studying at Harvard. Perhaps you remember Hegel, the German philosopher—who, by the way plagiarized most of his works from the Greek philosopher, Parmenides. Both argued, what is rational is real and what is real is rational. It is such logic that governs these actions. Only by bringing things to a natural conflict can the process fully develop. It's Hegel's dialectic come to life, Mr. President. The bottom line being, the status quo remains without the imposition of conflict. Those capable of bringing a satisfactory conclusion to the conflict, via provision of advantages for all involved, find that those resolutions greatly empower the Resolver. I will be that Resolver.

"You, Jordan, will do your part to create the conflict to which I already have the resolution. Everyone comes out smiling. And the world gets a safer, happier Middle East."

"I'm beginning to understand, Kostos," the president cynically added. "And you will be hailed as the world's greatest diplomat."

"Oh, Jordan," laughed Kostos, "you are so short-sighted. I'm already hailed as that. Don't you read the papers or watch the news? Look at how the world praises my few accomplishments thus far— peace in Chechnya and Russia, in the Sudan, Darfur, in Sri Lanka, in Pakistan and in the Congo and the soon-to-be-announced new peace treaty between China and Taiwan.

"No, no, Mr. President. My goals are not nearly so modest as to become another Nobel Prize winner. Although, I will be awarded that. My aspirations are much, much higher, indeed."

Kostos then stood to his feet, "You can have your chair back, Mr. President, for now."

He walked to the door, opened it, and just before closing it, turned back. "I'll be in touch very soon. Good night, Mr. President."

ELEVEN

Vatican City, the enclave within Rome that covers 109 acres, lies within a short distance of the safe house. A bit west of the Tiber River, it is surrounded by medieval and Renaissance walls, and can be entered through any of six gates.

Brad and Leah entered the gate most commonly used by tourists, where they quickly encountered a view of Saint Peter's Basilica. Together, they walked to the center of the enormous area in front of the Basilica, Piazza San Pietro, known to westerners as St. Peter's Square.

They needed to figure out where to begin their search for the mysterious Father Portega. The Vatican's non-clerical employees all wore identity tags. They were easy to spot and seemed to be everywhere. The tourist traffic was light this early in the morning, and a number of Vatican guides were simply standing around waiting for the flood of tourists that would soon fill the enormous square. Brad asked Leah to wait for him while he approached a friendly-looking young woman wearing the identity tag of a guide.

"Excuse me, do you speak English? I'm ashamed to confess that I have yet to master the beautiful Italian language."

The pert young lady with very short dark hair and obvious absence of makeup compelled Brad to think that the girl was possibly preparing to become a nun.

The young lady answered, "That's quite all right, sir. I speak English, German and French, as well as Russian. So, I'm glad to assist you. What is it that you're looking for?"

Brad grinned and said, "I am looking for a priest."

Before he could finish, the girl smiled and said, "Well, you've certainly come to the right place. We've no shortage of priests."

Returning her smile to show he appreciated her humor, Brad added, "No, I suppose not. However, I'm looking for a particular priest, a Father Portega."

"I see," returned the guide, "I suggest you go back toward the entrance of the piazza. On your left you'll see the Palace of the Vatican. It contains over 1,000 rooms, including all the Vatican's government offices. Hundreds of priests are headquartered there. Just inside the entrance on the right is an information booth and a clergy index that lists the priests and their office locations. If your Father Portega works here, he'll be listed.

"And by the way, if this is your first visit, while you're at the Papal Palace, go look at the famous Sistine Chapel with its great ceiling frescoes, painted by Michelangelo and..."

Brad forced himself to politely listen to the girls-be-kind-to-tourists points of interest.

"...whatever else you do while you're here, do not miss the Gregorian Museum or the Vatican Library with over 900,000..."

"Do forgive, ma'am," pleaded Brad as he finally interrupted her. "You are so kind. However," Brad looked around, pointed to Leah, then whispered, "my wife there has a serious case of traveler's diarrhea and she is desperate to find a water closet. Please excuse me. Her need is, shall we say, pressing. I really must go."

Brad quickly walked the 15 meters to Leah's side, took her arm, and gently led her toward the Papal Palace.

Looking over his shoulder, he saw the young lady watching them. He mouthed the words, "Thank you," to which she nodded and smiled.

With her peripheral vision, Leah, noticing him looking back toward the girl, snickered, "Have you and the young Catholic lass got something going?"

Feigning shock, Brad said, "Do I sense a bit of jealousy?"

With that, Leah pulled away from his gentle hold on her arm and rolled her eyes. "Only in your dreams, James Bond."

After a few moments of almost comical silence, Leah asked, "Just where are we going now?"

"There," Brad pointed, "to the Papal Palace. We'll find a list of every priest at the Vatican and where he is officed."

Walking up the great stone steps to the palace entrance was a heady experience for anyone, Catholic or non-Catholic. Brad, raised in a Protestant home—Lutheran in fact, was considered by Catholics most heretical. It had been a very long time indeed since he had gone to any church but this place impressed even him. Upon reaching the top of the stone stairway, they saw the entrance where on each side stood an immaculately dressed and poised Swiss Guard. The Guards are on duty throughout Vatican City and are responsible for the Pope's protection and the internal security of the city. The guards remained stoic as the couple passed.

Just inside the doors, Brad turned right where only a few yards ahead he saw a kiosk with a sign in several languages including English that read, "Information." Several ladies manned the station. Brad and Leah, acting the part of a touring couple, walked up to the counter hand in hand. Brad spoke to a rather plump, gray-haired woman nearest to them. "Excuse me, ma'am. My wife and I are trying desperately to look up an old friend of my dear Aunt Jenny. It was her dying wish that I make this pilgrimage to the Holy City and meet her wonderful old friend, a priest who lives here. I'm praying that you are the angel who can point us in the right direction so I can keep the solemn vow I made to my old auntie."

The woman almost had tears in her little round eyes. As she reached over and patted Brad on his arm, she kindly said, "My dear young man. Your parents must be so very proud of you." Turning to look admirably at Leah, the rotund lady continued, "And your little wife here is such a pretty, isn't she? Of course I'll help. What is the name of the priest you seek?"

"His name," Brad answered, "is Father Portega. I've prayed all night that he is still here. We've come such a long way to fulfill Auntie's death-bed request."

The woman wrote down the name, looked up, and said, "You two lovebirds wait here. I'll be right back." She waddled off to a computer on the opposite side of the kiosk.

Brad glanced over at Leah, who had assumed her crossed-arm, foul-look persona.

"Is anything wrong, dear Leah?" Brad inquired.

"That old broad," Leah answered sternly, "sounds like the wicked witch of the west in your Wizard of Oz movie." Leah, imitating the old witch's voice, cackled, "and I'll get your pretty little dog, too."

Brad laughed, "My, we are in a nasty mood, aren't we?" Leah looked away and acted as though she was ignoring him.

Within minutes the little lady returned. "I've some very good news for you two sweeties. Father Portega is assigned today to an office in the Basilica. Just go in the main entrance and you'll see an information booth like this one. Ask where to find the files office for The Sacred College of Cardinals. It's on the ground floor but it's a real maze over there. They'll tell you exactly where he is."

"Ma'am, you're wonderful!" Brad gushed. "You remind me of my sweet Aunt Jenny, God rest her soul." Brad leaned over the counter and planted a kindly kiss on the woman's chubby cheek.

As the little woman blushed, Leah, now tired of the whole charade, spoke up in her best imitation of a southern belle. "Now ya gotta quit kissin' every gal that comes along, Bradford honey. Ya know Doc Baker warned ya that nasty fungus rot in yo' mouth is most contagious. Now come on, it's time for ya to gargle ya medication, hon."

So stunned by her actions was Brad, that when Leah tugged on his arm, he followed without a word.

Arriving at the bottom of the stairs outside, Brad stopped and abruptly turned to Leah, "Is that what you call 'keeping a low profile?'"

Leah burst out laughing. Before Brad could think of a comeback, the young guide who had given them directions earlier walked up behind Leah.

"Did you get to the W.C. in time, Missy?" Leah turned to face the girl and, recognizing her immediately, asked, "I beg your pardon. What did you say?"

"I'm just thinking you might want to try downing a bit of plain ol' pasta for lunch. Supposed to dry you up quick. Seems the last thing you'd want to do is hug the old toilet all day, when you could be seeing Rome. Give it a try. *Ciao!*"

The girl flashed a big smile at Brad, winked seductively, and sashayed off with a female friend.

"So much for the nun thing," Brad mused to himself.

"Whatever is she talking about?" Leah asked, looking at Brad.

It was Brad's turn to burst out laughing, which he did as he walked off toward their destination.

Leah followed but kept asking, "What Brad? You better tell me! What is she talking about, Brad?"

The long walk across the piazza gave the agents some time to compose themselves and seriously focus again upon their mission. Entering Saint Peter's Basilica, both of them were awed by the remarkable display of grandeur and wealth. Noticing that Leah was looking around with the same amazement, Brad said, "Well, I suppose it's got to be nice, if God's gonna hang here."

"I think I detect a note of cynicism," she returned. "It's gaudy and ostentatious, not to be compared to the splendor of Solomon's Temple that once stood upon Jerusalem's Temple Mount. Now that was a place God liked to hang."

"As I recall," Brad pointed out, "didn't God get quite ticked off at some of your ancestors and move back to heaven or something?"

"Brad, you're far too much of a skeptic to be taken seriously on theological matters." Pointing ahead she added, "There's the information desk. Come on."

As they approached, Leah whispered, "Now this time I'll do the talking."

Brad bowed slightly in deference, "As you wish."

Another woman kindly met them at the counter, "How may I help you folks today?"

Leah, with the shyness of a young woman who felt she may be imposing, quietly said, "Well ma'am, it's like this. My husband, Brady, here..." she held tightly to his arm and looked up at him with a bashful smile, "well, Brady and me have tried for years to track down his biological father and well, you know how they say 'all roads lead to Rome'? It seems that our quest has led us here as well. Anyway, we have finally concluded that Brady's daddy, who he's never even seen, works right here in this big ol' building. His name is Father Portega."

Before Leah could speak another word, Brad grabbed her arm, and pulling her back, spoke to the shocked woman. "I'm sorry but my wife here is just recovering from a very serious surgery and has a tendency to get confused." Brad tapped his index finger on his head and quietly said, "Tumors ya know; surely you understand. What she meant to say was my spiritual father." Leaning still closer to the little woman, even more quietly he said, "You see we're here to pray for her condition. And our parish priest back in Akron, Ohio told us that when we got here to look up his old mentor and friend, Father Portega and ask him to pray for her. Could you direct me to his place of service today?"

The woman's face bore a true look of pity as she smiled understandably. She hit a few strokes on the keyboard in front of her, looked at the screen and said, "My dear boy, Father Portega is helping work the files in the College of Cardinals' office. Go down this hall and then go right at the dead end. He'll be in the last office before the next dead end."

"Thank you so very much, ma'am." Brad then turned, took Leah by the arm, and led her away.

After moving out of hearing range, Brad said, "Has no one ever told you that Catholic priests are supposed to be celibate and that it is forbidden for them to marry?"

"Oh, my," Leah gasped "Brad, I forgot!"

"You forgot?" Brad sighed while shaking his head, "All right. It's okay. Get focused. We're about to meet Father Portega."

Leah, red faced and still trying to recover, lamented, "I can't believe I did that, Brad. I am so sorry."

"I told you it's all right. Forget it. Besides, it's a well-known fact that some of these men of the cloth have great difficulty remembering their vows. It's just that the faithful don't want to hear about it." Brad wanted her to put it behind her.

They had already made the right hand turn and were now approaching their destination. Just before they got to the right door, Brad stopped Leah.

"Are you ready for this?"

Leah grimaced and nodded her head.

"Okay," Brad continued, "then you won't mind if I do the talking?"

"After what I just did," Leah murmured, "I may never talk again."

They both turned to enter the already open door. The room, Brad guessed, was almost 200 feet long and about 50 feet wide. There were four rows of file cabinets that stretched the length of the room, with narrow aisles between them. At the front, where they entered, was a nun sitting behind a large desk. "Can I help you?" she asked.

Brad returned,. "Why yes. I'm here to see Father Portega. Where might I find him?"

The nun looked down the long center aisle of files. Leah and Brad followed her gaze.

There, about halfway down, was a sixty-ish, medium-built priest placing a folder in a file drawer. He looked up and back toward the nun and the couple just as they looked at him.

Before anyone could speak another word, the priest slammed the file drawer and took off running down the aisle in the opposite direction. Brad and Leah lost no time in sprinting after him.

As they took after the priest, they could hear the nun squawking at their backs, "You're not allowed to run in here. Stop this instant. You hear me?"

Leah was only a little behind. Brad, a bit closer to the man, saw him race through a doorway hidden behind a curtain.

Brad, followed closely by Leah, burst through the door and discovered it led into a narrow, empty hallway. Immediately, they saw the priest's back running hard away from them. Giving quick chase, they both noticed the hall was about to dead end into an archway. Approaching it carefully, they saw it was a stairway leading down.

They failed to see the tripod sign knocked out of the way by the passing priest. Had they seen it they would have read, "Entrance Forbidden. Danger. Do Not Enter!"

Brad bolted down the stone stairway knowing he would not get another chance to talk to this guy and find out his connection to the crash and aftermath of Air Force One. He could not afford to abandon the chase. Besides, the priest was running from something and Brad wanted to know what.

Finally at the bottom of what Brad thought was at least 12 flights, he came to a long hallway. Leah had just caught up and they both stood, trying to catch their breath. Brad, gulping in air, said, "Another hallway."

"This is no hallway. It's a tunnel," Leah said.

Brad nodded, "Yeah. It gets narrower as it goes deeper. These sconces along the walls every 20 or 30 feet don't give off much light, either."

Having stopped for only seconds, they could no longer see their target but they could hear him still running.

"Let's go!" They took off in pursuit.

They ran for several minutes and stopped only after they passed the last light fixture on the wall. Without light they would have to slow down, but surely the priest would as well—though he was clearly on more familiar turf than they.

Feeling their way along the damp limestone walls, they stumbled along with Brad leading the way. The tunnel progressively became narrower and both of them knew they were going deeper with each step. After 10 minutes of slowly groping along the rough stone walls, Brad suddenly stopped, causing Leah to bump into him.

"You really need to put some taillights on your posterior, Brad."

"*Sshh!* Listen!" was all Brad said.

They both heard it, maybe 100 yards ahead. A loud creaking groan that reminded Brad of giant old hinges moving under strain.

The sound stopped with a resounding *thud* of wood on wood.

"Come on, we're close," Brad said softly.

"I know," Leah whispered, "but close to what?"

They crept along, trying to visualize their surroundings, until Brad said, "Wait."

Leah answered, "Well, at least thanks for the warning this time."

"Do you smell something?" he whispered.

"In fact I do. But I know it's not me. I showered this morning," she responded.

"It's neither of us," Brad said. "The musty, damp smell at the beginning of the tunnel has faded. Now it's becoming pungent, like rotten eggs."

Leah could be heard sniffing the air. "I hate to tell you this, Brad, but that's not rotten eggs. It's like decaying flesh. Old, decaying flesh, and it gets stronger the deeper we go."

"You're right." Brad started feeling around on the walls. "Let's try to find out how much further it is to whatever made those sounds we heard. Come on."

"Lead on, Fearless One," she joked.

They covered another 70 or 80 yards, Brad figured, when his hand felt the stone wall turn into wood.

"Hey! I think I found it."

"Found what?" Leah huffed.

Quickly feeling all over the wooden surface, Brad answered, "It's a big doorway, double wide, and it's locked."

A few minutes passed while Brad continued to examine the barrier. "It has no external lock," he said. "So there's got to be a release somewhere that will unlock this. Start at the base and follow the stone where it meets the wood, all the way along the side and onto the top."

Just as he finished giving his instructions, Brad heard a loud '*clink*' followed by Leah's voice: "I think I found it. Push inward on the doors."

As he did, Brad felt the massive thick doors begin to open. As they swung open, an even stronger stench filled the air.

On the right wall a single, flickering torch lit the cave-like room. Though his vision was limited, Brad felt the room was at least 150 feet long and close to 40 feet wide. It was filled with spider webs and squeaking sounds that gave evidence to the presence of rats.

Squares, approximately two-and-a-half feet by three feet, had been deeply chiseled into the stone walls.

"Is this what I think it is?" Brad asked.

"Oh, yeah," Leah whispered. "It's a burial crypt of sorts, or some may refer to it as catacombs. Very old. I'd say around 500 B.C. to 100 A.D."

"I had no idea you were into the archaic, Leah."

"Had you done your homework as thoroughly as you pretend to, Brad, you'd know that my minor at the Hebrew University was archeology. And no one grows up in Israel without learning a lot about ancient history and archeology."

Together they moved forward to further explore their new discovery, but before either could say another word, someone behind them cleared their throat. They froze.

"Turn around very slowly and keep your hands where I can see them." The priest had been hiding behind the massive doors. As they turned to face him, he now stood 10 feet in front of them with a pistol in his hand.

"You know," Brad started, "Leah, you are right. We made a wrong turn way back there. Do forgive our intrusion, sir, but it seems we've strayed from our tour group. And our guide must be frantic with worry about us. If you'll excuse us, we really don't want to miss our tour bus."

Brad took Leah by the arm and was preparing to leave when the priest spoke again: "Shut up, Mr. Fuller. Neither of you is going anywhere. We know all about both of you and you've made a serious miscalculation by just waltzing in here. And you, Miss Levy, this really is no place for a Jewess. Surely you know that."

"I do know one thing, Father Portega," Leah answered, "if that's your real name. Innocent men don't run from authorities."

"Ha!" mocked the priest, "You two have no authority here. You're both foreign agents on the soil of a foreign sovereign state. And yes, Father Portega is my real name, and yes, I am a priest. I'm from the good ol' USA and I was invited to come here for study and service. Of course, after I arrived it was decided I'd be more useful, let's say, in other areas."

"Actually," Brad jumped in, "it's those 'other areas' that Miss Levy and I wanted to discuss with you. If you would be so kind as to put your weapon away, we can sit down, have a friendly little chat, and we'll be on our way. How's that sound?"

The priest shook his head and sneered, "You poor sap. You have no idea, do you? Well, my bosses will be delighted to discover how very ignorant you both are.

"No, Mr. Fuller, this is your last stop on the tour. And what better place to end it, huh, here in a nice burial chamber? Of course, you'll both have to share a crypt with one of our older residents. It seems all our squares are full, but I think we can squeeze you in. No pun intended." The priest laughed at his joke.

"You are very clever," Brad said, "However, our sudden disappearance would rankle some very powerful people."

"Nice try," returned the priest, "but I have it on good authority that neither of you informed your protégés where you were going this morning. Quite a breech in protocol for two super sleuths."

After another good laugh, the priest continued, "And had you lived a bit longer, which you won't, you would have discovered that your 'very powerful people' are no more than pawns. You people just don't get it. You've no idea about what kind of forces you've been messing with."

Both agents heard the click as the priest pulled back the hammer on his pistol. "I don't like you, Fuller. You're arrogant. So you die first." The priest raised his gun, pointing it at Brad's head.

A split second later, Brad heard two quick discharges. But they did not come from Father Portega's gun. In fact, the priest had just collapsed. Brad whirled toward Leah, who was standing there with her nine-millimeter still smoking in her hand.

Slowly returning the weapon to the clip on the small of her back, she said, "You'd think they'd be nicer to visitors."

Brad, still shaken from what had just happened, mumbled, "Uh, yeah...you'd think." He then walked over and knelt to look at the body of the priest. "No use in checking for a pulse. You double tapped the poor fella just above the bridge of his nose. It appears your shots are about an inch apart. Not bad."

"I'm rusty," Leah returned, "I usually put the second shot right through the first hole."

"Well," Brad said as he stood, "I'm sure your range instructor will understand. I mean, it is a bit dark in here and he was about to shoot us."

He took a deep breath, "I suppose we could stick him in with one of the current residents and then we need to get out of here."

"Yeah," Leah said dryly, "I think we can 'squeeze him in.'"

Brad just shook his head and thought to himself, "*The lady sure can be cold.*"

After disposing of the body, the pair exited the cavernous room, closed the doors and made a hasty departure. "So much for getting answers from that guy," sighed Brad.

Leah quickly spoke, "Well, I guess I could've let him shoot you."

"Oh no, no, no," Brad came back. "You did the right thing. And I thank you for saving my life. I owe you one. But I'd sure like to know what he meant by our not realizing the forces, as he said, we're messing with."

"I'm not sure. But I have a feeling that your Mr. Pratt is not being fully forthcoming with us."

They were relieved to finally reach the ground floor. Nonchalantly walking down the halls, they exited the front doors of the great Basilica, confident that no one within knew what had just occurred in the depths below.

TWELVE

WASHINGTON D.C. 3:55 A.M. THE WHITE HOUSE

They were arranged on the couches and chairs of the Oval Office, where each had a clear view of the television screen. It was on, but the sound was muted.

President Hunt, CIA Director Pratt, Secretary of State James Parlay, Secretary of Defense Carl Bates and National Security Director Carol Watts were all present.

The president cleared his throat and spoke. "I've asked you here this morning, at this ungodly hour, because I received a heads-up that the International Federation of Nations Director, Mr. Kostos, will be making an important announcement from Brussels in just a few minutes. Worldwide news is going to broadcast his speech live at 11:00 a.m. Brussels time. I thought it would be best if we all heard what he's got to say while we're together. If my intel is correct, his announcement has to do with the rapidly evolving change in the European Union."

"Sir," spoke up Secretary of State Parlay, "Kostos has been a diplomatic nightmare for the State Department. He's been acting like a mad bull in a China closet, arbitrarily rearranging international alliances, trashing trade agreements, wooing nations whose economic ties to this country are critical and, in short, wreaking havoc in our embassies all over the globe."

Almost everyone in the room shared concerns similar to Parlay's about Kostos. The president responded, "I know how you feel, Mr. Secretary. He's like the proverbial camel who got his nose under the tent and now threatens to take over the entire thing. Eventually we are going to have to deal with the man."

"Excuse me, Mr. President," injected Director Pratt, pointing at the television, "but their coverage in Brussels is beginning."

The president clicked on the sound with the remote and all heads turned toward the set. The anchor was sitting in front of a full-screen image of St. Peter's Basilica in Vatican City. As the audio came on, he was already in mid-sentence.

"...but first we've breaking news out of the Vatican. Less than 20 minutes ago, their Secretariat of State, who represents the Holy See in matters of diplomacy, released a statement. It reads...'Pope Baranoldi, Vicar of Christ, and Supreme Pontiff, was found dead in his papal apartment this morning. Though he had failed to show up at morning prayers, his assistants assumed the Pope was resting. At 11:30 a.m., after his failure to appear at an important luncheon, assistants entered his apartment to find the Pontiff deceased. He was fully dressed in his Papal prayer robes, face down on the floor, the victim of an apparent assassination. Authorities are now investigating and have assured us that more details will be released shortly.'

"And that is the end of the written statement from the Secretariat. Right now we have correspondent Harold Ford standing by at the Vatican. Harold, what's the latest?"

The television cameras at the Vatican showed the reporter standing in St. Peter's Square. "Yes, Kirk, I am standing right outside the Papal Palace where the Pope's body was discovered. The news of this tragic event is just now getting out and already, as our cameramen are now showing you, 50 to 60 thousand mourners have gathered in St. Peter's Square.

"Authorities are scrambling to prepare for hundreds of thousands. This Pope had only been the Pontiff a short 14 months, replacing his predecessor who died of natural causes over a year ago. Kirk?"

"I'm here, Harold. What are the authorities saying about possible suspects at this time?"

"As you know, it's still very early in the investigation and there are a lot of questions that need to be answered. I do, however, have it on good authority through an anonymous source that early this morning, before the rush of tourists arrived, a man and woman who were either European or Western were going from building to building asking questions about various priests and such.

"Witnesses claim the couple seemed odd. At one information booth, they told employees they were from Akron, Ohio. At another booth across the way, a couple matching the same description inquired about getting a certain priest to pray for them.

"Authorities don't know where this couple was at the time of the murder, nor do they know with any certainty that the couple had anything to do with it. The initial tip about the pair, authorities say, came anonymously. The video recordings from the security cameras are being scrutinized as we speak and I'm sure pictures of any suspects will soon be available, Kirk."

"Thank you, Harold. Keep us posted. Our network sends its condolences to the millions of Catholics the world over who are now mourning the loss of Pope Baranoldi. We will update you as details are forthcoming.

"Now, we turn to Brussels, Belgium were Chairman Kostos of the IFN has just begun what has been called by the European Union a speech of vast import."

The viewers in the Oval Office sat in stunned silence as the shock of the developments in Rome sank in. As they watched, attempting to soak up every possible morsel of information available, the scene on the TV screen went to Brussels and a close-up of a very sad Kostos, who had already begun his speech.

"...and much earlier this morning I was informed of this tragic loss. It would be most disrespectful and highly insensitive for me to proceed at this time with our announcement. The world can wait until we've all had time to process and grieve the world's loss of a very great man. I'm certain that the leaders and people of all the earth's religions join me in praying God's greatest graces upon our Catholic brothers and sisters.

"In a few days we shall return to this forum and share our intentions. Until then I know we'll all pray that the perpetrators of this heinous crime will be brought to justice."

As Kostos turned away from the camera, President Hunt clicked the television off. The room remained quiet for a few seconds.

"If any of you are Catholic, I want you to feel free to leave and be with your family, friends, or members of your parish. We can brief you later." After the president spoke, he waited a few moments.

Carol Watts, director of the NSA, stood, and wiping tears from her eyes, softly spoke. "Thank you, Mr. President." She turned and left the room.

As the door closed behind her, the president took a deep breath, "Well gentlemen, this does change the agenda. Uh...Mr. Pratt, I'm certain the CIA will get on top of this. And it should be you who contacts the Vatican investigating authorities to volunteer our full cooperation and assistance."

"Yes, sir," Pratt answered as he jotted something in his notebook.

Hunt continued, "The State Department needs to get in touch with every embassy we have in predominately Catholic countries to convey our condolences."

"Yes sir, right away," responded State.

"And I'll personally call those now in charge at the Vatican and release statements for the press. Listen, let's not waste any time in getting out in front of this. You're dismissed."

The three remaining men stood and the Secretary of Defense, Carl Bates said, to no one in particular, "You've gotta give it to Kostos. The guy is savvy enough to know that whatever he's got to say would've been trumped in the headlines by this dead Pope. I'd give Mr. Kostos an 'A-plus' in public relations."

Before anyone could respond, President Hunt shot back angrily, "Mr. Secretary, it behooves us to be more discreet when discussing statesmen of Kostos' standing. Further, I find your comment offensive and insensitive."

"Sir," stammered the embarrassed Secretary, "I...uh...I'm very sorry. I meant no disrespect. I hope you'll forgive me."

President Hunt, without responding, turned and left the office through a side door as the others moved to leave through the main entrance.

CIA Director Pratt, the last to leave, mused to himself, "All this is pretty strange. The president defending Kostos like that. And Kostos' statement of how he found out about the Pope's death earlier in the day, when the news wasn't made public but minutes before. Fortunately, I have a good man on the ground in Rome. I'll call Mr. Brad Fuller. See what he knows."

Pratt closed the door behind him, said goodbye to Della, the president's secretary, and left the White House. He was facing a very long day.

Director Pratt was driven back to his office at Langley, where CIA personnel were busy working double and triple shifts. As he walked into the outer offices, he was met by one of his best analysts, Agent Cooper.

"Mornin' Coop. Get Brad Fuller in Rome on the phone for me. Now," Pratt ordered as he kept moving toward his office.

"Sir, I've something that just came in on the wire. I think you might want to see it first," huffed the agent, trying to keep up with his boss' brisk pace.

Pratt, not happy with a delay, stopped and sighed. "In my office."

Cooper followed his boss into his office and closed the door behind him. As Pratt took off his jacket and moved to sit at his desk, Cooper tossed a stack of five-by-seven-inch photographs in front of him.

The director sat, picked up the photos, and looked through the six different shots.

"Do you recognize 'em?" inquired Cooper.

"Yeah, it's Fuller. I don't know the woman. Who is she?" asked Pratt.

"She is Leah Levy, the agent Mossad sent to assist our search for our missing president. Brad's running that op."

"Wow, even in this poor photo she's a beautiful gal," Pratt mused.

Cooper nodded in agreement. "That she is. Perhaps that's why our boy Brad is getting so careless. Sir, these pics were released just minutes ago by the Vatican and Italian authorities. These are pictures of, according to those investigating the Pope's murder, the chief suspects.

It won't be long before those two faces are plastered on every front page and news broadcast in the world."

Pratt's frustration was evident when he threw the photos back across the desk toward Cooper and barked, "Get Fuller on the phone, now. Secure line."

"Yes, sir." Cooper hurried out of the office.

Two minutes later, Pratt's phone buzzed. "Sir, Cooper here. It's 5:15 a.m. here. That makes it 12:15 p.m. in Rome. Brad and Levy are at the safe house. He'll be on line four. It's secure and he should be picking up…right about…now. Go ahead, sir."

Pratt grabbed the phone, "Fuller, are you out of your mind?"

Brad held the phone in one hand and a set of the photos in his other. He answered, "It would appear so, sir. The station chief just dropped off the snapshots you're probably calling about."

"Brad," Pratt began as he struggled to hold his temper, "before the day is over, the entire world is going to be looking at those photos. And you, along with your Israeli buddy pal, are going to be known as the prime suspects in the murder of Pope Baranoldi." Pratt, raising his volume, hollered, "Does this not bother you, Fuller? 'Cuz it sure bothers me!"

"Sir, if you'll allow me," injected Brad, "we were, indeed, at the Vatican. But we were following up on leads concerning a Father Portega, who showed up at the crash sight of Air Force One asking a lot of probing questions about our missing president. It seems that we are not alone in our suspicions about his being alive.

"We did find the priest and to make a long story short, the man tried to kill us. Only Miss Levy's marksmanship saved us from having our dead bodies stuffed in a burial crypt in the bowels of St. Peter's Basilica. As it is, the priest now holds that dubious distinction. But we had nothing to do with the Pope's demise."

Pratt snorted, "I want a detailed report of all this on my desk ASAP."

"It's already on the way, sir," Brad assured him.

"Clearly, Fuller, someone is setting you guys up. It's time for you to get out of Dodge." Pratt continued, "I met very early this morning with the president to hear Kostos' much-touted Brussels speech. As you probably know, it was upstaged by a murdered Pope. Kostos delayed his speech but he made a statement regarding the Vatican assassination. He claimed he had already been informed much earlier in the day about the death when, in fact, the Vatican had only released the information less than 20 minutes before. Things just don't add up.

"Also, while on my ride from the White House to Langley this morning, I was called by the Israelis who are working agents in a number of Arabic nations. Mossad has a double agent in Jordanian intel who's bringing out a critically important, highly-classified package. Tomorrow he'll be sneaking across no-man's-land in southern Jordan and at dark, crossing the Dead Sea into Israel."

"Excuse me, sir," Brad jumped in. "I really prefer not being briefed on somebody else's ops."

This further infuriated the director, "Fuller, will you shut up! This isn't somebody else's op!

"You and Levy will leave Rome immediately but not together. You're to use your Argentinean passport. You'll travel incognito as Manuel Benividos, the name on that passport.

"You're to catch the earliest flight available to Ben Gurion Airport in Tel Aviv. Go from there, without delay, to the King David Hotel in Jerusalem, where there'll be a room waiting.

"Levy is being told right now to catch a separate flight. She has an apartment in Jerusalem. She'll contact you, giving you instructions on where to meet her. Together you will be told where to meet our Jordanian friend. Once you receive the package from him, you'll be directed on what to do with it. Am I clear, Fuller?"

"Absolutely, sir." Brad added, in an attempt to glean a bit more info, "Do you think, sir, that you could give me one tiny, itsy, bitsy, little hint about what's in the package we're to receive? I do like to be prepared for any and all eventualities."

"Fuller, you task me," Pratt said. "Now kindly move your underworked, over-paid, bloody carcass and get out of Rome."

Brad heard his boss slam down the phone and mused, "He really needs to cut back on the caffeine." He hung up the phone.

He did realize that he and Leah were in serious danger of being busted. As soon as she emerged from her room where she had gone to shower and change, he would give her his end of the news.

Brad decided to check on flights to Jerusalem and picked up the phone, but before he could dial, Leah walked in. Holding up her cell phone, she said, “By the chastened look on your face, you must've gotten a call like the one I just received.”

“Yes, I did, Brad sighed, “I'm back in the doghouse again, it seems.”

Leah stared at him with a confused look. “Why would they put you in a dog's house?”

Laughing at her misunderstanding, Brad said, “Not a literal doghouse, Leah. It's just an American saying…never mind.”

Still not quite getting it, she shrugged her shoulders, “Well, clearly we messed up.”

“No!” Brad returned. “We're being set up, framed for the murder of Pope Baranoldi. If we messed up anywhere…” Brad stood, walked to the curtained front window and peeked out, “it was in our failure to spot those who have us under surveillance. They're good. But something's really beginning to stink around here.”

Leah came back quickly, “Well, it's not me.”

Brad cut her off before she could finish. "I know. You just showered, right?”

“You're a quick study,” Leah said as she picked up her travel bag and purse. “Now, I have a non-stop El Al flight to home sweet home. I'll see you, or so I'm told, in Jerusalem.”

“Do call, dear Leah,” Brad said teasingly, “for I shall sorely miss thee.”

“I know it.” Leah smiled as she got to doorway, “but you'll live. Shalom.” And the door closed behind her.

Director Pratt was on the phone when Agent Cooper brought it in. Rather than interrupt the boss, the agent laid it on the desk in front of him, caught his eye, pointed to the folder and left.

Continuing his casual conversation with a colleague, Pratt glanced down at the item. It had the red-striped edges and seal that identified it as Classified. The top cover sheet read: FYEO…for your eyes only. TOP SECRET. JUST IN. URGENT!!!

Seeing the import of the file, the director told his friend that something had just come up. He promised to call him back. Pratt broke the seal, removed the cover sheet, and read.

TO: Director, Central Intelligence Agency—FYEO
FROM: Station Chief Brussels, Belgium
SUBJECT: Ops…surveillance of Charon Dranko Kostos, domicile.
DATE AND TIME OF OPS: Last night/early this am—between 11:30 p.m. – 2:40 a.m.
11:30 p.m…E.U. Ambassador from Syria arrives in limo.
12:05 a.m…Syrian Ambassador departs.
12:30 a.m…Foreign Minister of Iran arrives in limo.
1:05 a.m…Foreign Minister of Iran departs.
1:20 a.m…E.U. Ambassador from Egypt arrives in limo.
1:45 a.m…Egyptian Ambassador departs.
2:00 a.m…Foreign Minister of Turkey arrives in limo.
2:40 a.m…Foreign Minister of Turkey departs.
OBSERVATION: Foreign reps in covert meetings with C.D.K.
PURPOSE: Undetermined.
SPECULATION: Possible IFN attempt to expand Euro-coalition into Middle East and Northern Africa.
RAMIFICATIONS: If successful IFN could influence Arabic nations in the Mideast and OPEC to moderate output and/or cut oil supplies to the West and to USA.
We Await Instructions.
C. Buford—Station Chief—CIA, Brussels.
Signed

After reading it, Pratt put it down on his desk and leaned back in his chair. Rubbing his tired eyes, he yawned and said to himself, "We really don't need this right now." After a good stretch, the director pushed a button and said, "Coop, try to get the president on the line. It's important."

"Right away, sir," came Cooper's reply.

Pratt stared back down at the classified memo and thought, *Too much is happening too quickly in far too many places. I have a really bad feeling about all this.*

"Director, the president is secure and on line four."

"Thank you, Coop." Pratt sat for just a moment, then picked up the phone, "Mr. President, I'm afraid we have a situation…"

THIRTEEN

Brad's fake passport and his disguise as a mustachioed, gray-haired businessman from Argentina got him on his Rome to Tel Aviv flight without incident.

Upon arriving at Tel Aviv's Ben Gurion Airport, all commercial flights, for security purposes, are de-boarded not at terminal gates but out on the tarmac. There, passengers board buses and are driven to the terminal to go through passport control and, after that, a baggage pick-up area.

Brad, as Manuel Benividos, patiently moved through the entrance procedures without incident, retrieved his bag, and exited the terminal where all arriving passengers were funneled to meet their waiting parties.

Hundreds of expectant faces searching for friends or loved ones stood just outside. The crowd was swollen by the large number of tour guides and buses awaiting tourists and by the impatient cab drivers looking for fares.

Brad waded through the frenzied crowd and at last saw a neatly dressed, 20-something man holding a small sign that read "Manuel Benividos." Brad made his way to the young man, walked up and announced, "I am Manuel Benividos. Let's go."

Without another word, he turned and followed his guide to a four-door white Mercedes Sedan. As they got in and the driver started the brand new vehicle, Brad finally spoke. "What is your name, son?"

"My real name is Clay Cameron, sir."

Brad had already surmised that his driver was a green CIA intern who had been assigned to give him a ride to Jerusalem.

"So, Mr. Cameron, just how long have you been with the company?"

Brad was somewhat amused when the intern's face took on a serious expression and he looked around as though making sure no one could hear. In a low whisper, he leaned toward Brad and said, "As you know, sir, I cannot confirm that I am actually with the company. However, between us, I have had my current assignment, which is my first since finishing training, for six months."

Brad nodded, "Yes, I know your boss. He's big on hush-hush. Tell me, does Don McGuire still smoke those smelly, cheap Coronas?"

Clay smiled, "Yes, sir, and he told me you two go way back."

"Yes," Brad smiled at the memories, "but it's been a while since I've seen him. By the way, Clay, on your way to the airport, I'm sure you checked for tails. Am I right?"

Taking on a serious tone again, while checking his rear view, Clay responded, "Absolutely, sir. Mr. McGuire says I'm green, but I'm not that green."

"I'm glad to hear that," returned Brad. "So, how far to Jerusalem, Cameron?"

Cameron explained, "Well, with this new highway, it's about a 45–minute drive. This your first trip to Israel, sir?"

Brad, who was habitually glancing at his side rear-view mirror, answered, "My first in many years. I came through on assignment over 15 years ago but hardly got out of Haifa."

For the next 15 to 20 miles, the young man droned on about his background, upbringing, family and his budding career with, as the aspiring agent called it, "a certain company whose name I am not at liberty to share."

Brad, however, while pretending profound interest in the intern's personal history, had been seriously studying the traffic on the highway behind them. Ten miles back he had picked out the dark blue, Ford Explorer hanging four or five cars behind them.

When Clay finally paused in his monologue, Brad quietly asked, "Mr. Cameron, will this car go faster than 65?"

"Oh, yes, sir. It has a high-performance engine and is built to handle the 100-mile-an-hour-plus speeds of the Autobahn. But of course, the speed limit on this stretch mandates I keep her at 65."

"Very good," Brad replied while studying the traffic behind them. "Show me how you'd drive if you were on the Autobahn."

Surprised, Cameron turned to look at Brad and finally noticed him staring out his side mirror. "Are we being followed?'

"Indeed, we are Mr. Cameron," Brad noted. "And so, let's see how much they taught you at Langley about evade and escape." Brad glanced at the intern and noticed he had broken out in a serious sweat. But without another word, he felt the sudden surge of the Mercedes press him back in his seat.

Watching the blue Ford, Brad saw that it immediately accelerated in an effort to stay up. Though the intern now had the Mercedes up to 100 miles an hour, Brad was reluctant to push him to go faster. Traffic was moderately heavy, which made it necessary for Clay to constantly bob and weave around the slower drivers.

Noticing the Ford just managing to maintain visual contact, Brad looked ahead and saw an exit off the new highway. "Where's that next exit go, Clay?"

"That'll take ya across to the old highway that this one replaced. Comes out about six miles later at the famous battlefield, Latrune."

Brad swirled around to check on the Ford and, seeing it maintaining its distance, said, "Okay, Clay, take the exit."

"Yes, sir," responded a nervous but excited intern. A quarter of a mile later, the Mercedes took a hard right off the main highway. Now heading south instead of west, Brad watched as the Ford followed their lead. There were less than three quarters of a mile between the pursued and the pursuer.

Passing a number of dirt side roads, Brad asked, "Where do the side roads go?"

Clay, still sweating, answered, "Well, the hills around here have a lot of Israeli Defense Forces outposts, and some of these roads lead to them. Tanks also train in these hills and there are lots of civilian homes and such."

"Take the next one to the left. It leads up the side of that hill...and keep your speed up." Brad added a word to encourage the very nervous intern: "And you're doing great, Clay."

As the agents approached their turn, Brad, who had not even attempted to get his weapon through Rome's airport security, said, "Son, give me your weapon!"

"What?" returned the already-shaken driver.

"Your gun! You are assigned a weapon, aren't you?"

"Uh, yes, sir. It's under my seat. It's really my backup. My primary is being worked on."

Not wanting to distract his distraught young driver as he took a hard left onto the dirt road, Brad leaned over, reached under Clay's seat, and retrieved the pistol.

Feeling the weight and seeing the size of the pistol took Brad aback. "Son, what is this?"

Glancing over, the intern responded, "It's a 357 mag, sir."

"Yes it is," Brad answered, "and it's a .357 revolver with an eight-inch barrel. Do you hunt elephants in your spare time?" Before he could answer, Brad added, "Looks like we've still got company."

"Clay, after you clear the sharp curve ahead of us, I want you to pull over quickly and jump out of the driver's seat. I'll take it from here." Brad felt the intern's relief as he answered, "Yes, sir."

Clay slowed for the hairpin turn, minimizing the slide of the automobile's rear tires as he rounded the bend. Knowing he only had seconds before the Ford came barreling around the same curve, Clay pulled over and brought the car to a sliding stop. With a speed and agility that impressed Brad, the intern came out of the driver's seat and was in the back seat in a flash. Brad jumped quickly behind the wheel.

Seconds later, the blue Ford came wheeling around the curve in a cloud of dust and dirt. It whizzed past the Mercedes. The two occupants realized only as they passed the Mercedes that they were now in front of it.

As soon as the driver of the Ford realized what had happened, he came to a sliding, hard-braking stop where the edge of the road ended and a 200-foot drop to the bottom of a deep gorge began.

Brad floored the Mercedes, pointing it right at the Ford perched on the precipice of the cliff.

"Brace yourself, Clay!" Brad yelled as he accelerated and rammed the front end of the new Mercedes into the side of the Explorer. Brad could see in the eyes of its driver a terror that indicated the guy knew he had made a big mistake. The impact at 40-plus miles an hour, though bringing the Mercedes to a jolting stop, was more than sufficient to push the Ford over the edge, where it rolled eight or nine times before coming to a dirt shrouded, upside-down stop at the bottom of the cliff.

Brad jumped out with the .357 in hand and ran to the edge to peer over at the wreckage. In seconds, an extremely white, sweat-drenched Clay was gasping at his side. Unable to see any movement below, Brad gently released the cocked hammer on the magnum and handed it, butt-first, to the intern.

"Clay, a word of advice. Get a more concealable backup."

Clay took the weapon, "Yes, sir."

Brad was already on his way back to the car. He went over, got in the passenger side, and closed the door. Walking back, Clay, still in a daze, stopped and stared at the crumpled front end of the new Mercedes. Wiping the sweat from his head with a shaky forearm, he got in the driver's seat.

"Now, if you'd be so kind, Mr. Cameron, I've got business in Jerusalem." Brad was still processing just who had been following them and to what purposes.

"Yes, sir." Clay, catching his breath, turned the Mercedes around to head back to Jerusalem. "But I need to tell you, sir, this isn't my car. All the staff cars were tied up when the time came to pick you up. So the boss, Mr. McGuire, very reluctantly tossed me the keys to this, which he just bought as his personal car. His last words to me were, 'You get one scratch on my new car, Cameron, and you'll be cleaning toilets for the rest of your career.'"

Brad smiled and replied, "Clay, I'll cover for ya. But for now, when ol' Don asks what happened, just tell him Fuller was driving and had some friends to drop off on the way to Jerusalem."

It took the rest of the trip to Jerusalem for Clay's color and breathing to return to normal.

Brad thanked Clay for the exhilarating drive as he exited the smoking Mercedes now parked in front of the King David Hotel.

Leah's departure from Rome and arrival in Tel Aviv happened without incident. She had boarded the El Al 747 as instructed and been assigned a seat in business class. She used the flight to catch up on some much-needed sleep.

Upon arrival at Ben Gurion, her credentials made it possible for her to slip right through passport control, where her small bag already awaited, along with a Mossad agent to escort her. On the way to Jerusalem, the agent informed her that Brad's plane was to arrive in two hours and that she was to contact him at the King David in four.

She was dropped off at her west Jerusalem apartment, where she cleaned up and fixed herself an omelet and warm bagels. After eating, she dressed in a well-pressed, form-fitting but comfortable tan blouse with matching pants. She looked and felt almost military.

When the time came to contact Brad, she picked up the phone and called the King David, asking for Mr. Manuel Benividos's room. After four rings, he answered.

"Hello, Mr. Fuller." she chimed, "Welcome to Jerusalem. I trust your trip was pleasant?"

Brad had jumped out of the shower to answer the phone and was now standing dripping wet, wrapped in a towel. "Yes, Miss Levy, it was very pleasant, with only minor distractions. Are you home?"

"Yes, I am. And this distraction you mentioned, was it really so minor or is it that you're just being humble, Mr. Fuller?"

Brad laughed, "Well in fact, someone had sent out a welcome wagon to greet me. So eager were they to embrace me, that they followed my driver and me on a tour of the hills near Latrune."

"Latrune?" a surprised Leah replied, "Why'd you go that far out of your way?"

"To be honest Leah, it was the hills with their winding roads and deep valleys that lured us off the beaten path."

"Ah," a sighing Leah caught on. "So you were being followed. Well what happened, if I may ask, to those who were following you?"

"Oh, them?" smiled Brad. "They decided to tarry at the bottom of one of those lovely gorges."

"Brad," Leah asked a bit more seriously, "who were they?"

"Well, I ran their plates when I got here—" Brad answered, "—the Ford Explorer belongs to a local dealer in American automobiles who has it leased to the local office of the International Federation of Nations."

After a moment of silence, Leah said, "Those guys keep showing up everywhere!"

"Yes, they do, don't they?" replied Brad. "You know, Leah, I think that they think we know something. Something to make their killing us worth the trouble."

"What's going on?"

"That's what I intend to find out," answered Brad. "In the meantime, have you received our instructions?"

"Yes, yes I have. Get a pencil. I'll tell you where to meet me in two hours, precisely."

After writing down the information, Brad added, "And be a dear, and bring your extra weapon. I had to leave mine in Rome."

"No problem. Any preferable caliber?"

Quick to reply, Brad said, "Anything but a .357 will do."

Not fully understanding the remark, Leah answered, "Okay. No .357s. So I'll see you there in two hours. Shalom."

President Carr woke up angrier than a grizzly coming out of hibernation. He had thrown the attending nurse out of the room and was demanding the presence of Dr. Cohen.

Once the good doctor had finally made it to the president's bedside, he knew the patient, at least physically, was on his way to complete recovery.

President Carr was still spitting mad and insistent that the two physicians come and immediately answer his questions. Then he had said, "I'm getting out of this zoo with or without your help!"

Dr. Cohen was finally able to settle his patient down long enough to tell him that Dr. Minay was on his way to the facility and would arrive shortly. "Mr. President," Dr. Cohen urged, "it won't be more than 20 minutes or so until Dr. Minay arrives. For your own well-being, I want you to use these few minutes to eat a bit of breakfast. It's been days since you've had solid foods, and if you plan to be up and around you'll need the nourishment."

The president, calming a bit, knowing Dr. Minay would arrive shortly, gave in. "All right, 20 minutes. Now where's this breakfast?"

Dr. Cohen smiled. "It's on its way. Eat slowly and try to relax." At that instant, a nurse arrived with breakfast, pulled the rollover tray holder into position, gave the president a warm smile, and retreated. Dr. Cohen was right behind her.

Twenty minutes later, Dr. Minay and Dr. Cohen re-entered the president's room. Dr. Cohen spoke first. "I hope your breakfast was suitable, Mr. President. Our friend Dr. Minay is here, and we are at your disposal and ready to begin."

"You can begin, doctor, by giving me my clothes and a phone."

Dr. Minay stepped out from behind Dr. Cohen, and reported, "Mr. President, with all due respect, we will honor your every wish. However, you did give us your word that first, you would hear us out."

Frustrated, the president answered, "Gentlemen, I think what we have here is a failure to communicate. So, let me try again. I am the President of the United States of America and I refuse to negotiate with criminals.

"Both of you, and all the rest of your little partners in crime in this hell hole, are guilty of any number of crimes. You're likely to spend whatever's left of your lives in solitary confinement in an American federal penitentiary. You have kidnapped a Head of State. You're holding him against his will, incommunicado, under armed guards. And I've yet to mention, you've committed the same crimes against a United States Federal Agent, Mr. Spears, who may or may not be alive.

"Furthermore, gentlemen, you've told me little to nothing about how I got to wherever it is I am. For all I know, you could be the thugs who shot down my plane and killed over a hundred innocent American citizens."

The two physicians stood patiently, allowing Carr to vent. Finally, Dr. Cohen spoke, "Mr. President, I assure you, first, that Agent Spears is vastly improved and thanks to a series of miracles, he will survive. You may visit him later today if you wish. He's conscious, partially mobile, and like you, anxious to get up.

"I also want to assure you, sir, that whether you believe it or not, you are alive because of the good people of this facility. You will realize this very soon.

"Within the hour all of your questions will be answered, then your wish is our command. A lot has happened in the last week that is radically changing the socio-political landscape of our world. You need to be fully aware of what you're facing when you leave this place. So, we've an abbreviated overview, compiled from the non-stop media coverage of events, beginning with the downing of Air Force One through this morning. It isn't long, but you must be brought up to date on these critically important events."

Dr. Minay had already gone to a far corner of the room and was wheeling a cart containing a television and DVD player into position for the president to watch.

"You're about to see everything the world has seen since your crash. After you view it, Dr. Minay and I will return and tell you the truth of what's going on behind these scenes. At first, you will find it hard to believe, but the facts we will provide will prove our claims most credible.

"Then, sir, whatever you decide to do, we pledge ourselves and the substantial resources of Sodote Shalom to help you do it."

The president, resigning himself to the situation, was now most curious about what he was being told. "Okay, Dr. Cohen, you've made your case. I'll watch your newsreel and will listen to your explanation. Then I want a telephone. Do we understand each other?"

Dr. Cohen answered, "Perfectly, sir. Now we will leave you alone for a bit. When you're finished viewing, just press the call button."

President Carr sighed deeply and said, "All right, gentlemen, roll it."

Dr. Minay took the remote from the top of the television, pushed the power on and handed the remote and a set of headphones to the president.

FOURTEEN

Just hours before President Carr had awakened and begun his conversation with his two physicians, Charon D. Kostos put in a call to the White House in Washington, D.C.

Della buzzed the Oval Office. "Mr. President, Charon Kostos is on secured line four. He says you're awaiting his call."

President Hunt grimaced, "All right, Della, I'll take it." Hunt detested Kostos but knew he had no choice but to deal with him.

"Kostos, what do you want?"

"Oh, and good day to you too, Jordan," chimed in Kostos. "Why must you always be so curt with old friends? I called for several reasons, Mr. President. First, I want to thank you for your country's U.N. vote. The Security Council approval of the IFNs new 10-state federation in Europe was unanimous."

"I'm very glad for you, Kostos," strained the president. "Now that I've done my bit, I suppose you'll not be calling me anymore."

"Oh, Jordan, Jordan, Jordan," Kostos returned, "try to remember our friendship is much more binding than that. In fact, I've some very interesting news for you but first I must ask you to call up our little puppet at the airbase in Turkey, Lt. General Franklin. You're to inform him that he is to free the stealth bombers on my command. And I'll give that command in a few days. However, it'll speed things along if you'll release the General to my discretion."

"You can't be serious about hitting that Iranian nuclear site," fumed Hunt.

"Dear Jordan, you and I both know they have at least 30 such sites for their nuclear development programs. Tragically, like Hitler, the Iranians love to put their munitions factories in the midst of population centers." Kostos laughed, "Seems they like to carry on about all the so-called collateral damage if or when their enemies bruise them."

Interrupting Kostos, the president jumped in, "We know full well that you've been secretly meeting with representatives of Syria, Turkey, Egypt, Iran and others in the Muslim community. Why hit those you're forming alliances with?"

"Mr. President, I'm not going to 'hit,' as you say, anyone. As you may recall, those bombers will bear Israeli markings, though it's doubtful anyone will ever see them. However, the leaflets we'll drop will insure the Zionists will bear the blame. So, make the call Jordan, today."

The president was over a barrel and he knew it. "Kostos, your demands must cease after this!"

"Oh, I think not," continued Kostos. "In fact I've got some fun news for you. You do remember your predecessor, President Carr? It appears that the resilient fellow is very much alive."

President Hunt turned white and stammered, "What are you talking about?"

"Well, it seems my minions missed him the first time," sighed Kostos.

"Your people brought down Air Force One?" gasped Hunt.

"Don't worry, we won't miss again. We're getting better all the time. Take poor Pope Baranoldi, another sap trying to stop progress. But not to worry. The new Pope, soon to be announced, is very much in harmony with my agenda."

Shocked at what he was hearing, Hunt came back, "You are insane! And how do you know Carr's alive?"

"It appears," Kostos explained, "that a dear old woman strolling the beach witnessed the crash. I originally sent a sweet little priest to talk to her, but she was all hush-hush. So I sent a much more persuasive fella. You know, it's simply amazing what a pair of vice grips and some white-hot screwdrivers can accomplish."

The president squirmed, "Kostos you're a sick son…"

"Uh, uh, uh, Jordan," Kostos rebuked. "Hold your dirty, little tongue or we'll have to wash your mouth out with soap. Now back to the old broad on the beach. She also saw the boat of a fisherman she'd known for years. It motored quickly to the downed plane before any rescuers arrived. He pulled two people from the wreckage and sped away. She even knew where the old goat lived and she spilled her guts, both figuratively and literally."

"I don't want to hear this," groaned Hunt.

"But you must. After further efforts that I won't bore you with, my man found the son of a Dr. Minay, who treated the president and his friend. After some serious convincing, the son told us where to find Carr. I've people this very minute about to snatch him away. Then, we'll make sure he stays dead."

The president had broken out in a cold sweat. He knew if Carr suddenly reappeared, his own reign as president would end. Worse still would be the immediate crumbling of all he had worked and fought for his entire life. His complicity with Kostos would surely be exposed, as well as his sordid past.

"Do what you've got to do," the president said firmly. "I suppose we've both got a lot at stake."

"Now, that's my boy," Kostos beamed. "I'll take care of business. So, at least for now, goodbye." The line went dead.

Drs. Cohen and Minay had gone for coffee in the commissary so Carr could watch the video they had left for him. But no sooner had they been seated than Dr. Minay was paged to receive a personal call.

After a few minutes he returned, clearly shaken. "Avi, they've butchered my oldest son. They know Carr's here, and they're coming." Then he wept.

Dr. Cohen embraced him, "Yossi, I'm so sorry…but we've not a minute to lose. Call security. Tell 'em to hurry, that we're under attack. I'll hit the alarms for immediate lockdown. Now go! Hurry!"

O'Donnell was the only name anyone had ever known him by. He had served for years as an IRA Squad Commander training fellow freedom fighters in the art of killing.

When he was younger and untainted by hatred, he had served in the British Special Forces, where he had belonged to a clandestine group of warriors who served at the pleasure of England's intelligence community. The special operations squad to which he had belonged was an elite group of commandos. Only one out of every 300 men who volunteered for the squad succeeded in passing the stringent physical, emotional and mental demands of the training. No other military group in the world, other than the American Navy Seals, even came close to the kind of demands placed on men selected for this group.

O'Donnell's father, born in London, had served all his life as a civil servant. The man had been extremely proud of his son's choice to serve in the Crown's military. He did not live long enough to see his son wash out of the elitist commando unit after only five years. The authorities, having dealt with numerous incidents of young O'Donnell's rash temper, had labeled him unfit for further service due to anger management issues. He had been labeled by military psychologists as borderline homicidal and schizophrenic.

After his discharge, he had moved to Ireland to be with his mother. That's when he discovered that all of his uncles on his mother's side had fought with the IRA all their lives. It was not long before O'Donnell had linked up with the organization himself and found an outlet for his pent-up rage and homicidal tendencies.

After years of faithful service as a commando trainer for IRA assassins, terrorists and other covert operatives, he had grown disappointed in the organization's compromising leadership. It was then that he had discovered the lucrative opportunities available to men with his skills as soldiers of fortune.

Four years prior, at the age of 43, O'Donnell, still extremely fit, at six foot, two inches and a muscular 230 pounds, had been hired by an anonymous entity to eliminate a Saudi business man. His skills and professionalism impressed the man at the helm of the organization that had hired him. After performing two more highly successful missions for the same group, he was invited to meet the man in charge.

Flown in a private corporate jet to a magnificent, mountaintop mansion, he was wined and dined for a week and then formally introduced to Charon D. Kostos. From that moment, he swore absolute allegiance to the man and became the IFN's Commander of Special Forces. Kostos liked the burly, full-bearded O'Donnell with his can-do attitude. No mission seemed too difficult or intimidating for him.

Today, after days of preparation, he and his group of 12 were poised to assault Castel Colledora, and their assignment was to kidnap a subject of great import to his boss. The security around the complex was among the best O'Donnell had ever seen. After studying the daunting layout for days, he had determined the only soft spot in the entire security network was the manned hut at the entrance gate itself. The three guards manning that position were armed with American made M-16s, as well as standard issue side arms. One of them was responsible to monitor the perimeter cameras and laser alarm components that surrounded the castle grounds. He was to immediately alert internal security forces if there were a breach of any kind.

The other two guards in the front gate security hut were not only backup to any first responders defending perimeter breaches, but they were also to deal with anyone requesting entrance to the estate. Most of their days went by unchallenged, so they busied themselves filling out reports and walking the fenced perimeter with the dogs every 90 minutes. The lack of security challenges had contributed to the lax attitude shared by the guards in the hut on this morning.

O'Donnell's two snipers were already set up in the thick brush and trees a half-mile from the front gate, and were waiting their orders to take out the guards. Two black Suburbans carried O'Donnell and nine additional soldiers of fortune he had trained and prepared for this mission. They moved slowly up the old dirt road leading to the main gate so as not to attract any attention. However, because of the winding nature of the road, their approach would not be noticed until they were a quarter of a mile from the metal gates at the entrance.

Seconds after O'Donnell gave his snipers the word to take out the three gate guards, the lead Suburban would crash the gate and, with the other following, race to the basement's exterior entrance behind overhead garage doors at the side of the castle. Once there, they would blow the doors. He would leave two of his warriors by the trucks to take out the six other guards within the castle, who would no doubt respond to the exploding ordnance. The other seven men, led by O'Donnell, would storm the medical complex where their subject was being held.

Thanks to the head of the castle's cleaning crew, whom O'Donnell had kidnapped and tortured the day before, they had the physical layout of the entire complex.

O'Donnell and one of his handpicked men would enter the private room of their subject after his team eliminated any and all armed resistance.

Only O'Donnell knew the identity of the subject. One of his men, Boyd Miller, would enter the room with him to subdue the victim and would surely recognize President Carr. On the way out of the room, however, O'Donnell had been instructed to kill Miller in order to keep the identity of the subject a secret. He would blame the guards for Miller's death as he exited with his hooded, bound prisoner.

Kostos had instructed O'Donnell to split up the group once they left Castel Colledora. He, one of his men, and the subject were to get into a different automobile and drive to an abandoned old farm only six kilometers from the scene of the kidnapping. There, on the northern end of Lago Albano, a large natural lake, was a grassy airstrip. After sundown, he and his assistant were to enter the small barn next to the old farmhouse where they would find a dozen oil lamps. They were to light and set them out along each side of the airstrip so the pilot of the small twin-engine aircraft could successfully land in the dark.

The subject was to be loaded on board still hooded, gagged and bound. O'Donnell was to kill the assistant, board the plane, and accompany the subject to another location known only to the pilot.

As the two Suburbans approached the last bend in the road just before the hut became visible, O'Donnell picked up the small comm device, keyed the mike, and said to his waiting snipers, "Now."

The three security guards in the hut were discussing the World Cup Soccer Championships. All of the men were ex-Israeli Defense Forces soldiers who now worked for Sodote Shalom.

The soldier sitting at the console monitoring perimeter cameras was the first to be hit. The only sound the other two heard was the "*plink*" of a bullet piercing the window glass, followed by a low-volume "*thump*" as a .223 caliber slug entered their comrade's head.

As the soldier slumped forward on the console, the two others were momentarily stunned. They looked first at their dead friend, then quickly at each other. Just as they realized what had happened, a second round splashed through the glass, cutting the jugular vein as it entered the second soldier's throat.

Panicked, the remaining guard reached for the phone to warn interior security of an attack. Before he could get the phone to his ear, a third bullet caught him in the right temple.

The first Suburban, at 50 miles an hour, slammed into the gate intent on smashing through. The substantial gates, however, were not constructed with the typical hollow iron bars which compromise most such structures. The gates were made of one-and-a-half-inch solid, reinforced tempered steel bars. When the SUV hit, rather than crash through, it merely pushed the gates inward, opening a four-foot gap in the center.

The Suburban came to a screeching stop, sustaining crippling damage. The front end was crumpled and the fenders on both sides were crushed backward, blowing out both front tires.

As the windshield shattered, the airbags deployed and the five occupants were shaken and bruised.

O'Donnell, behind them in the second Suburban, had seen what happened. He slammed on his brakes, sliding to a stop right behind the vehicle at the bent-up gate. He snuggled his front bumper onto the back bumper of the other. With screeching tires and burning rubber, he pushed the first Suburban on through the gates. He kept pushing until the auto was within 20 yards of the castle's front stairway leading to the main entrance. O'Donnell then pulled around the crippled SUV and raced to the side of the castle where the exterior entrance led into the basement's medical facilities.

Only seconds before the first vehicle crashed into the gates, the alarms within the castle had sounded. As soon as the first Suburban came to a stop in front of the castle, six well-armed security guards poured out the front doors, blazing away with their M-16s firing on full automatic.

The guards watched as the second Suburban pulled around to the side of the building, but were now preoccupied with gunfire erupting from within the crippled SUV. The soldiers poured unforgiving fire into and around the disabled automobile. Two of the five mercenaries inside were hit and killed. The remaining three rolled out on the opposite side, using the Suburban as cover from which to return a withering fire.

Meanwhile, O'Donnell had reached his objective, and his men were already affixing the C-4 to the overhead doors at the entrance to the basement areas. His men at the front had already taken out two of the six guards firing at them. O'Donnell's men finished placing the C-4 and ran around the corner to duck down behind the SUV with him. Seconds later, a ground-shaking explosion sent fire, smoke and debris hundreds of feet into the air.

As the smoke cleared, O'Donnell led his men into the garage-like interior. They walked in 50 feet and came to a doorway. They kicked it open and just on the other side, two more security guards were unloading their M-16s at the five intruders.

Two of O'Donnell's men fell dead as he and two others jumped back to escape the barrage. As soon as they heard the security guards reloading with fresh clips, O'Donnell and his men stepped out from behind the door jamb from which they had taken refuge and unloaded on the two guards. Both fell riddled with bullets.

O'Donnell could still hear the fire fight raging outside. He stepped over the bodies that now littered the hall and started moving down the long, sparkling clean, hospital corridor. The hall had doors on each side every eight or ten yards.

Suddenly, an elderly man in a white frock exited the room on the right just in front of them. He did not look to his left or he would have seen O'Donnell. Instead he turned and started to trot away down the hall.

O'Donnell yelled from 30 feet behind the fleeing man, "Stop or die!"

The man stopped in his tracks and with his hands up, slowly turned toward O'Donnell. He saw the terrorists with their assault rifles aimed at him.

"Walk toward me, old man." O'Donnell and his two remaining men kept their guns trained on the man as he came closer.

Only a few feet from him, O'Donnell could read his name tag.

"So, Dr. Cohen, you've got 10 seconds to take me to the room of your most distinguished guest or you will die here."

O'Donnell saw that there was no fear in the old man's eyes as he answered, "Sir, my life doesn't belong to me. If you do kill me, you are only doing the bidding of the One who does own my life. However, in hopes that you will kill no more of our unarmed personnel, the man you seek is four doors down on the right. But I warn you, be careful how you treat him or a fate far worse than death will befall you."

"Shut up you, old fool!" O'Donnell yelled. Then, with all he could put into it, he backhanded Cohen across the mouth. The blow knocked the doctor back against the wall and onto the floor. Looking down, O'Donnell sneered, stepped over him, and motioned his men to follow.

Within five steps of Carr's room, the terrorists looked up to see two more security guards burst through swinging, stainless steel doors 20 yards in front of them.

When the shooting stopped seconds later, the two guards lay dead. One of O'Donnell's men was hit and writhing on the floor in the grip of death. O'Donnell had sustained a minor flesh wound on his left shoulder. He ignored it, and turned to his remaining man. "Let's go get him, Miller."

They kicked in the door and rushed into the president's room, guns ready. They immediately saw Carr sitting up in bed, watching the television with headphones on.

Jerking off the head gear, a startled Carr demanded, "What's going on here?"

O'Donnell jerked the president out of the bed by his pajama shirt's lapel, telling Miller, "Tie his hands." As Miller complied, O'Donnell stuck his pistol under the president's chin. "Now you can go with me peaceful-like or you can die here. So what will it be?"

The president, a decorated Vietnam veteran, answered with candor, "Oh, I'd much rather go with you. I was getting rather tired of this place anyway."

Shoving the president in front of him, he noticed his man, Boyd Miller, looking in awe. "Why you're the president of the bloody United States."

O'Donnell, who had pushed by Miller, was just about to enter the hall when he stopped at the door with the president in front of him. He turned to Miller, who was two steps behind him. "Miller, you talk too much." O'Donnell shot him in the head.

He turned and pushed the stunned president into the hallway and turned right hurrying to reach the exit.

Two doors down from the president's room was the room of Agent Spears. Weapons being fired had brought him out of a drug-induced sleep only minutes earlier.

Bandaged from his armpits all the way to his waist, and with his left arm in a splint to minimize movement, he was determined to get up. Dressed only in his bandages and boxer shorts, Spears willed his body to move. With great pain, he slowly rolled himself off the bed. He walked, crouching, over to the door, slowly opened it, and focused his eyes just beyond the threshold to check the hallway. Just as he looked, he saw the president stumble out of his room, followed by a stranger with a gun at the president's head. They turned right and headed down the hallway. When the two were 30 yards down the hall, Spears pushed himself into the hallway and saw dead bodies everywhere.

Knowing nothing more than that his president was being taken at gunpoint, his powerful instinct to protect kicked in and he moved to action. Disregarding the pain, he bent down and pulled a .45 from the holster of a dead security guard. Stumbling down the hallway in pursuit, Spears heard a door open and slam in front of him further down the long corridor.

O'Donnell pushed Carr into the garage area. The Suburban was just around the corner of the garage. Looking out before heading toward his own vehicle, O'Donnell could see their other wrecked automobile. Its front end was smashed, all tires were now flat, and smoke was pouring out from under the hood. His two remaining men were still returning fire at security guards.

Arriving at his own Suburban around the corner, he pushed the president toward the passenger door just as he heard a thunderous explosion. Peeking around the corner, O'Donnell saw where his other crippled Suburban had stalled. The guards had fired a rocket-propelled grenade into the automobile and all that remained was a fiery ball of melting metal. His last two men lay dead.

O'Donnell turned around, opened the passenger door, and shoved his hostage into the cab. As he turned to run to the driver's side, he saw a limping, shirtless, bandaged man come around the corner of the garage 25 yards away. O'Donnell slowly raised his pistol, then realized that the crippled man also held a weapon.

Spears gathered all his strength, gritted his teeth and yelled, "All right, dog! Give my president back!"

O'Donnell smirked as he pulled the trigger, but his bullet missed Spears' head by an inch and hammered into the plaster covering the garage's exterior. Tiny shards peppered Spear's head and upper torso, but he fired back.

Spears then unloaded the .45 into O'Donnell's body. Not one bullet missed its mark. The terrorist fell against the side of the Suburban and slowly slid down, leaving a thick trail of blood shimmering on the metal. O'Donnell was dead.

Spears, in horrible pain, fell back against the wall of the garage, sliding to the ground and ending up in a sitting position with his back against the wall. The gun fell from his hand.

The only two survivors of O'Donnell's team were the snipers who were quickly fleeing the scene.

The president watched from the cab as O'Donnell and Spears shot it out. When Spears collapsed in exhaustion, Carr, with hands still bound in front, slowly opened the door, looked down at O'Donnell, and ran over to Spears. He squatted down next to the agent. "Spears, are you okay? You saved my life again, Agent."

Spears eyes lazily fluttered open. He nodded and with a half-smile hoarsely whispered, "Just doing my duty, sir. But do ya think you could get someone else to look after you for awhile? Maybe a nice desk job for me. I mean, if that's okay?"

Spears passed out again. The president, knowing his agent would be okay, sat down next to him with his own back to the wall. Speaking to his unconscious agent, the president murmured, "Agent Spears, you can be the Chief Justice of the Supreme Court if ya want. You're a remarkable man, Spears, a remarkable man."

FIFTEEN

Leah had instructed Brad to meet her at an entrance to the Old City of Jerusalem called the Jaffa Gate. The Old City section of Jerusalem is surrounded by a three-mile, thick, stone wall, typical of ancient cities throughout the Middle East. The 12 gates that give entrance into the interior date back to biblical days and have been rebuilt repeatedly following a multitude of wars. Some of the gates are open, while others, for one reason or another, are sealed. Within the walls of the Old City are markets, bazaars and shops of all kinds where tourists and locals go to bargain and dicker over goods and services. The area is also home to numerous, world-famous historical and religious sites sacred to Jews, Muslims and Christians.

Tourists flock to the Temple Mount, once the site of the magnificent Solomon's Temple, where now stands the Islamic shrine known as the Dome of the Rock. From there, it is less than a five-minute walk to the Western Wall, the only part of the Jewish Temple that remains standing today. Within the fortress-like walls of the Old City are features such as David's Tomb, the Church of the Sepulcher, where Catholics believe Christ was buried and rose, and the Upper Room, where Christ and His disciples took the Last Supper.

The narrow winding streets of Old Jerusalem allow no automobile traffic, and everyone must get around by walking or, in some cases, by riding a donkey. The sights, sounds and smells assault the senses of visitors, forcing them back in time thousands of years.

Brad arrived and stood in awe watching natives and tourists coming in and going out of the arched gateway. Buses and taxis crowded the area disgorging people and engulfing others. Men in turbans, Orthodox Jews dressed in their traditional black, women covered from head to toe in burkas and others in Bedouin attire were all part of a crowd that moved like ants in and out of their busy colony. Brad stood intrigued, allowing his senses to drink in the menagerie of cultures, races, sights, sounds and smells.

When Leah arrived, the traffic was very heavy so she opted to park a few blocks away and walk to find Brad. She saw him first, wearing blue jeans and a short-sleeved, light denim shirt, leaning against the stone arch supports of the gateway. Because he was totally preoccupied with the experience of the place, she quietly moved in, surprising him. "Shopping for yet another woman for your ever-expanding harem, Sultan Fuller?"

Brad turned and smiled at seeing her. Her long, black hair was loose and tumbling around her shoulders. She filled out the fashionable safari-style pants and matching top in the neutral color of desert tan. Her sunglasses were propped atop her head, and her rich dark eyes smothered him. In his dressed-down attire, he felt like a buzzard standing next to an eagle.

Brad was taken aback by how her sudden appearance had caused his heart to race. It had been a long time since he, an avowed bachelor, had felt giddy over a woman. Trying to ignore what he was feeling, he responded to her "harem" comment with a jest that sounded more sincere than he intended.

"My harem? Leah, a man who possessed one as ravishing as yourself would not need or want a harem."

Leah laughed at his ludicrous banter even though she felt for a fleeting second that she had sensed an element of sincerity in his statement. Quickly brushing it off as her imagination, she continued, "Well, if you're ready, I've parked a few blocks away." As she turned to go, he followed, quickly catching up.

She turned and said, "Don't be surprised at the logo on my car doors. It's of Caleb and Joshua carrying a large cluster of grapes on a pole, back from the Promised Land to impress Moses and the Israelites. It's there to show that I'm a licensed guide, which for the last several years, I've used as a cover while working in Israel. However, I was forced to go through the courses and the licensing procedures to guarantee legitimacy."

"Great," Brad answered. "Please feel free to educate me as we move about. Do point out any points of interest. You'll find I'm an eager student of this most remarkable place."

Realizing he was serious, she said, "The truth is, there is not a stone or patch of ground in all Israel without historical, and some believe, spiritual significance. Every grain of sand and the smallest stone have a story to tell, and for those willing to seek and listen, the story they tell leaves the hearers forever changed."

"Well then," Brad said more seriously, "I suppose the sense of awe I've experienced since arriving isn't all that unnatural."

"Not at all," returned a pleased Leah. "And today you'll see more than the city of Jerusalem. We've instructions to go to Masada, near the Dead Sea, to meet our contact. It's a bit over an hour and a half away, and as you probably know, the Dead Sea is the lowest place on earth at 1,296 feet below sea level."

Brad added, "Ah, Masada. I know the fascinating story. If I remember, Herod, the king around the time of Christ, built the massive fortress atop a tall plateau, primarily as one of his summer resorts. Right?"

"So far so good." Leah nodded, "Please continue."

"Very well," Brad answered, "It was at Masada where over 900 Jewish zealots, who were part of a Jewish revolt against Rome, ran to escape the slaughter of the legions coming to put down the revolt. The revolution was from 64–72 A.D., right?"

Leah was surprised and pleased. "Very, very good. And of course the Roman's Twelfth Legion besieged Masada for two years before they were finally able to build ramparts up to the plateau and storm the fortress."

"And," Brad interrupted, "when the Romans finally went in, they found all 900-plus men, women and children dead by their own hand, giving Rome a dubious, hollow victory."

At that, they arrived at Leah's Mercedes sedan, got in and drove out of Jerusalem into the dusty hills of the Judean Desert. On the drive into the Jordan Valley, Leah continued to point out places of interest. Forty minutes later, she stopped at a four-way intersection. She pointed down the road in front of them. "If we went straight, we would enter Jordan in a few miles, which is just the opposite side of the Jordan River. If we turn left, we'd enter the ancient city of Jericho just 10 kilometers that way. But we'll turn right and head down to the Dead Sea."

As soon as she turned, Brad noticed the military road block less than a mile in front of them. It was barricading the road with portable crossbars and strips of sharp spikes to blow the tires of those foolish enough not to stop. It was manned by Israeli Defense Force soldiers. Leah stopped, rolled down her window, and spoke to the soldiers in Hebrew as she flashed her guide's license and pointed over at Brad. The soldier at the window bent down, looked at Brad, and said something in Hebrew that caused the other four young soldiers and Leah to laugh heartily. Leah then rolled up her window and the guards lifted the pole, allowing them to pass.

"I do hope your giggling episode wasn't at my expense," quipped Brad.

With a look of mock shock, Leah returned, "Oh, no, no, no. We were discussing the hot weather, not you."

"Uh huh," murmured a disbelieving Brad. He sat back and took in the unique beauty of his surroundings.

He was amazed at the contrast of the dry desert and the orchards of date palms, citrus and other trees that sprang out of the desert floor all along their route.

Leah noticed his interest. "Everything out here used to be a salty wasteland, but when Israel re-conquered it, our scientists figured out a way to desalinate not only the water of the Dead Sea, but also the soil. The water, once useless, now irrigates this desert and we're mining minerals out of the Dead Sea found nowhere else on earth worth trillions of dollars."

Brad shook his head and softly added, "It really is a land of a million wonders."

Leah, surprising herself, was beginning to see things in Brad she had not expected. She had heard of his notorious womanizing and chauvinistic reputation before ever meeting him. Now she thought perhaps he was all those things but maybe there was more beneath that macho exterior. Not sure of what she was feeling, she decided to relax and simply enjoy the journey.

With the Dead Sea now on their left, they soon passed Qumran, the sight where the famous Dead Sea scrolls had been found. After a time of driving in silence, she spoke up. "Okay, up ahead you can see the plateau of Masada. There is a tourist area and a cable car for those anxious to explore the Roman ruins on top. But we are to meet our man in the busy little restaurant at the base. He illegally crossed the Sea from Jordan into Israel last night and is to give us the package our bosses are so anxious to get their hands on."

She brought the Mercedes to a stop in a parking area filled with tour buses and rental cars. They exited the car and entered the crowded, but thankfully, well-air-conditioned restaurant. There was a long line of tourists in front of them, so they stood waiting for their turn to be seated. Before they had waited a full five minutes, a Bedouin boy of 10 or 11 years of age tapped Leah's arm. Looking down, she saw the boy handing her a folded piece of paper. She took it and smiled. "Thank you. Now let me give you something." She dug in her small handbag and handed the boy a crisp American $5 bill, which he grabbed as he ran out the door. Leah opened the note, read it, and turned to Brad, "Come on."

As they left the restaurant, Brad inquired, "What's going on?"

Leah, moving quickly, kept walking, leading Brad around to the back of the restaurant. As they came around the corner, they saw an old, beat-up van. "He's in that," Leah said as she reached down to make sure her weapon was still inside the deep pocket of her safari pants.

"Come on," Brad said as he moved closer. He carefully looked in the window and saw a man dressed in Bedouin attire, lying down in the front bench seat.

"Get in quickly," the man whispered to Brad and Leah. They did as they were told. Once they were in the back seat, they leaned over and saw immediately the man's side was bleeding and the entire front seat of the van was stained with blood.

"Listen close. I've not time to say this twice." To Brad he said, "My name is Hussein. I am Mossad. I know who you are and why you have come. But as I was meeting a boat to come across the sea last night, I was ambushed, shot, and robbed of the microchip I was bringing out of Jordan. They left thinking I was dead. I do not know how they knew what I had, or when I was crossing, but they were waiting."

The man stopped and started coughing hard. Brad noticed a half full water bottle on the dash and reached over the seat. Leah gently tilted the man's head as Brad held the bottle so the man could drink.

"Shukran...thank you. Now I will tell you what is on the chip they took from me and you must get it to the proper authorities."

Leah, still holding the man's head up, said, "Okay, but then we are going to get you to a hospital."

"No, no," pleaded the man, grabbing Leah's lapel. "I will die here and very soon. So you must listen. Syria, Iran, Egypt, and Turkey are secretly, slowly moving thousands of tanks, hundred of thousands of troops and military convoys as close as possible to the Israeli border in the northern Golan Heights, as well as just below the Sinai in the south and into the Bekka of Lebanon."

"There's no way they could move that much firepower into any of those areas without our knowing it," Leah gasped. "You mean, they're only planning to move those resources, right?"

"No, Leah. They have done so and are continuing to add and build a massive unprecedented force. I don't know how but they've found a way to deceive our surveillance satellites, as well as our drone and aircraft overflies. I know it sounds unbelievable, but I have paid with my life to bring this news, so I do not jest or exaggerate.

"Also, Russia has pre-positioned millions of tons of munitions, rockets, launchers, artillery and aircraft at strategic locations. They have joined a coalition of predominantly Islamic nations surrounding Israel. Libya, the new Islamic government of Iraq, and most of the OPEC nations are part of it. Never in history has Israel faced such a massive invasion as the one that's planned."

"Listen, Hussein," Leah begged, "You must stay alive. We need to know more. Stay with me. What are they waiting for? When are they planning to strike?"

Gasping for air and with a stream of blood flowing from his mouth, Hussein answered in a whisper. "Very soon. Iran's nuclear sites at Bushera will be bombed. I know not how, or when, or by whom, but Israel will be blamed. That will give our enemies all the reason they need to hit us hard."

Hussein coughed hard and blood sprayed from his mouth, splattering the windshield as he gasped for air.

Leah pleaded, "Hussein, stay with us. I'm going to go get my car and we're getting you to a doctor."

"Dear Leah, no. You must listen. My life is spent. You must move quickly but carefully. Most importantly…" Hussein began gagging, trying to get a breath, but it was futile. With his last ounce of strength, he looked up at Leah.

"The IFN—" more severe coughing sprayed blood everywhere, "—check IFN they…"

Leah, with tears in her eyes, pleaded, "Hussein, what about the IFN? Tell me!"

"No time," whispered the fading Hussein. "I go now where I fear not…" Grasping Leah's bloody hand with his own, Hussein looked in her eyes, smiled faintly, and said, "Sodote Shalom."

Leah, still holding the hand of Hussein, sat for a few moments with her head bowed, ignoring Brad, who was looking on. As she finally lifted her head, Brad could see the tears rolling down her reddened face. He watched as she looked down on the body of Hussein and removed her blood-stained hand from his.

Finally, she reached up and, using her thumb and forefinger, closed his lifeless eyes. Brad heard her say something in quiet Hebrew, only discerning her last two words, "Sodote Shalom."

"Leah, we have to go now. If this guy is telling the truth, we alone carry the secrets that can stop World War III. We'll send someone back for him."

Leah sighed, "So many of our best too often end up like this. This 'guy' as you call him, was a friend of my father's and my family for more years that I can remember. He was a hero in several of our wars. But he wouldn't retire. He was the most productive Mossad agent in my lifetime."

She reached over and wiped the blood off Hussein's cheek and said, "Until then, sweet Hussein. Until then."

Wiping away tears, she said, "Let's go! This information cost a great man's life. It will get to those who know how to use it, if it's not too late."

Brad got out behind Leah and they ran to her car. He carried with him a burning curiosity about the meaning of "Sodote Shalom." He would ask later.

"Avenger arrival at PNR in four." The four B-1 Stealth bombers carried a payload of bunker-busting smart bombs with enough authority to penetrate 60 feet of steel and concrete the way a hot knife cuts butter. The ordnance would core a medium-sized mountain like an apple.

On the word of President Hunt (via authority surrendered to Charon D. Kostos and passed on to Base Commander, Lt. General Joel Franklin, at Ankor, Turkey) the bombers had been released an hour earlier at 1:00 a.m., Turkish time. All four bombers bore Israeli markings and two of them, along with their bombs, carried thousands of leaflets they were to drop after their bombing runs.

The pilots, briefed for the last month, were led to believe that they were flying a support wing for Israeli bombers also headed for Iranian nuclear development sites.

The pilots, as well as the bomber group's support personnel and ground crews, felt as though they were patriots participating in a top-secret mission, doing their part to support an American ally in its struggle for national survival.

Lead pilot, Captain William Colburn, had orders to break radio silence just prior to reaching their PNR, the point of no return. Once past that set of coordinates, the bombers were to arm their ordnance. As Captain Colburn made final contact with his base, he and his squadron were four minutes from his PNR. Seconds after the Captain called in his position, he received his reply.

"Avenger, you're good to go. The light is green. Godspeed." The Captain knew it was the exception rather than the rule that these kinds of missions were actually given the go. He felt the chill bumps ripple over his skin as he radioed his receipt of the message, "Avenger squadron copy. Lights are green. Good to go."

The Captain flashed his nav lights three times in the prearranged signal to the other bombers flying with him in a tight formation. Each in turn flashed navs twice, signaling they understood.

The four state-of-the-art stealth bombers were invisible to the most sophisticated radar in the world, but especially so to the Iranian National Defense radar detection system. As they flew past their PNR and into Iranian airspace, they were 13 minutes and 32 seconds from their target. They now had the Iranian nuclear development facility at Bushera in their crosshairs.

SIXTEEN

Director Pratt took a seat at the table in the CIA situation room located in the underground facilities at Langley. He and the other staff officers, one of which was the Assistant Director, sat in front of a console with six monitors. They were there to watch a live feed from the well hidden cameras their surveillance teams had set up in a New York hotel.

The United Nations General Assembly had been meeting all week and ended its last session the day before. Kostos, knowing most of the UN diplomats and delegations also represented their nations in his International Federation of Nations, had called for an IFN conference to be held the following day at New York's prestigious five-star hotel, The Royal Crest. This exquisite hotel was often used by international delegations and heads of state.

Kostos had not only reserved the elegant and spacious Grand Ballroom, but he had also taken over the entire top floor for him and his large staff. Kostos would be staying in the mammoth Presidential Suite.

Both areas were being swept for bugs by IFN security forces every 30 minutes in an effort to keep everything as confidential as possible. The sweeps began 24 hours before the activities were to begin. No media would be allowed anywhere near the site.

While IFN security professionals were very good at their jobs, they would fail to discover the tiny camera and mike built into the base of a coffee cup that a "waiter" would strategically place to catch the entire IFN conference. The same "waiter" acting as cleaning staff would place a similar camera and mike built into the base of a fifth of Chivas Regal whiskey on the bar in the shelves of Kostos suite.

Everything taking place in both locations would be seen and heard via a live feed into Langley's situation room. As Pratt and his staff sat down in front of the monitors, Kostos and the Russian President, Kastonof Valenko, once head of the dreaded KGB in the old USSR, were entering the sprawling living area of the suite. The first words the intelligence people heard came from Kostos. "…And I am honored, Mr. President, that you are gracing me with your presence. Please sit down. Can I get you a drink? I've some exquisite Russian vodka."

Valenko, for all practical purposes, was almost a spitting image of one of his infamous predecessors, Joseph Stalin. His cold persona reinforced the perception of their similarities. The Russian took a seat on a large sofa and grumbled in heavily accented English, "Yes, thank you. I'll accept your vodka, but I'll decide if it is exquisite or not."

As Kostos moved towards the bar to prepare drinks for both of them, the Russian continued, "First, Kostos, I want to be honest with you. I'm not so sure I like you. I've come to hear you out only because my Foreign Minister and the DUMA council suggested I accept your invitation."

Kostos handed Valenko his drink, sat in a chair opposite the sofa, and said, "It is not required that you like me, Mr. President. It is, however, important that you know, as I'm certain you do, that the ever-expanding IFN represents a very powerful coalition to the west of your country. I do want to personally assure you that the IFN has no interest in interfering in your great nation's affairs. But I do hope we can come to terms on how we can maintain that status quo."

Valenko sat up so quickly that vodka sloshed out of his small glass as he angrily responded, "Are you threatening me? Your IFN is no more than an annoyance that we could crush like the little insect it is!"

Apologetically, Kostos came back, "Do forgive me, Mr. President. No such threat is implied. I mean only to tell you that your country, as well as the IFN, has a great deal to gain if we can work together for the advancement of our common interest."

Valenko sat back and relaxed. "Other than our corporate plans to the south, what 'interests' do you refer to?"

Kostos leaned back, casually crossed his legs, and answered, "Well, for one, your nation's economy is in shambles, and your naval fleet, once the pride of the seas, has become a disastrous collection of rusting buckets. Your international credit rating is in the pits. You're mortgaged to the hilt and the world knows you can't even pay the interest on your national debt. Almost 70 percent of your GNP is being poured into your military apparatus and yet you're still slipping far behind your traditional enemies in the West...to name only a few of our corporate concerns."

Valenko scowled, "So these things bother you?"

"It bothers the world at large," Kostos added. "History proves that once powerful nations go into decline, they have a tendency, in their desperation, to lash out in all sorts of ways, often leading to their own destruction."

Impatient with the IFN chairman, Valenko interrupted, "What is your point?"

"My point, Valenko," Kostos returned, "is this. If the IFN and Russia were to join together, I have the resources, the personnel, and the raw power you need to reverse your country's misfortunes."

"And tell me, Kostos, how would you accomplish this magic trick?" smirked the Russian.

"I thought you'd never ask. First, your nation has a remarkable abundance of natural resources, some of which you are aware, most of which you are not aware.

"Your own nationalized oil company can't drill or refine your vast reserves because your technology is antiquated and your coffers are empty. Further, our people, unbeknownst to you, have found large, deep veins of the purest gold in the Ural Mountains. Additionally, in the interior of Siberia we've found massive deposits of platinum and uranium. Under that lies a stratum of geological formations that, according to our own very good geologists, in all likelihood contains the richest diamond deposits ever discovered. But all of these lie just beyond your reach."

Angry again, a red-faced Valenko raised his voice, "You've been spying on my nation. You've no right to..."

But Kostos stood and interrupted the Russian. "No right? No right to explore? No one has violated your borders, your air space or any

Russian laws. I tell you what we know and you whine about spying. And all the while you're sitting on a mountain of wealth while your incompetent state investors are losing billions of rubles to foreign markets every day. And minute by minute, your entire industrial complex is decaying from within.

"No, Mr. President, I've no right to interfere in Russia's self-destruction, but I do have a responsibility to offer you an opportunity to become the greatest hero in the history of Mother Russia."

Valenko's interest was clearly returning, "And what will all this generosity of yours cost me, Mr. Kostos?"

"Cost you?" returned Kostos. "The real question you should ask, Mr. President, is what will it cost you to ignore our offer of friendship? If you're willing to bring Russia into the International Federation of Nations as a full partner, we will provide you with the financial resources, the technical expertise, and the highly-skilled professionals needed to extract your precious metals, your diamonds, and to drill and refine your oil reserves. The economic boom you will experience will be miraculous. Further, our economists know how to rebuild your industrial complex and make you the world's number-one financier rather than its largest debtor.

"The cost, Valenko? Become our ally, our comrades in purpose. Our conference begins downstairs in the Grand Ballroom in 20 minutes. Let me announce your desire for membership in the IFN and tell them you're going to Moscow to challenge your Duma to become part of our family of nations. Then sit with me on the platform and I will share with you and the rest of the IFN delegates the great strides we've made in just the last few weeks."

Valenko threw back the remaining vodka in his glass, stood, put out his hand, and said, "I have changed my mind, Kostos. I do like you. And, yes, I will do as you ask. But you must promise to accompany me back to Moscow to make your presentation to the Duma. They will hear you.

"Just one last thing. I'm to thank you for your provision of the superior technology you've provided our armed forces as they moved toward

Iran, Iraq and Syria. We do not understand how you've done it but the West has not seen or suspected our plans for the region. It's remarkable indeed."

Kostos led Valenko to the exit. "That's what friends are for. And this is only the beginning. I will see you downstairs in 15 minutes." Kostos closed the door, and left the room.

Back at Langley's situation room, Director Pratt and his associates sat in stunned silence. Finally, the Assistant Director spoke: "Did we really hear what we just heard?"

Pratt leaned back, took a deep breath, and spoke to his men, "Yeah, we did. And if Kostos is telling the truth, the ramifications it will have on our national security, State Department and Defense Department, will be catastrophic. And something tells me that's a big part of Kostos' strategy."

The communications chief added, "And what in the Sam Hill is Russia doing moving its military assets so far south? And why aren't our, or for that matter, anyone else's, satellites picking up their movements?"

Pratt responded, "An age-old fear of the Pentagon has been that one day, one of our enemies would find a way to blind our surveillance birds. Now, what they have feared the most has come upon them.

"And the answer to your question about why Russia would be moving heavy military assets to their south can be summed up in two simple words: oil and Israel. Something big is brewing, and we better find out what that is very quickly or we're gonna be blindsided."

"So, what do we do first, boss?" asked the Assistant Director.

"Well," Pratt answered, "first, I'll quickly brief the powers that be at Defense, State, and Homeland Security. And our people in communications have less than 15 minutes to get the feed coming from that conference into the situation rooms of all those departments."

The comm chief jumped up, "I'm on it, sir." And with that the chief hastily left.

"And you," Pratt continued as he turned to his Assistant Director, "call the White House. If the president is in, he should watch as well. If he's out, be absolutely sure to get me an audience with him no later than two hours from now."

"Sir," the Assistant returned, "you are aware of how the president has been snubbing us lately. If he tells us he's 'too busy' and to 'just send a memo' or 'catch him later,' what do I say?"

"You tell him," Pratt said as he sighed, "that your boss is not asking for an audience. He is demanding it. And explain ever so briefly that he best receive me, because we are facing a very real national emergency."

"Yes, sir." The assistant jumped up. As he was going out the door, Pratt hollered, "And get back in here in 12 minutes!"

"Yes, sir," came back as the door slammed.

The Secretaries of State and Defense sat with their staffs before the monitors in their own situation rooms. Homeland Security, the National Security Agency and the Joint Chiefs of Staff were all watching in the White House situation room.

Pratt, at the CIA, was the first face that appeared on their screens. "I know this 'heads up' gave you folks very little time to get situated where you can watch this real-time surveillance of the IFN Conference in New York. In the last 10 minutes, you've all become privy to everything we know. In a few seconds, the Russian President and Kostos will appear together at the podium of the IFN Conference. Other than what you've already been told about their conversation 15 minutes ago, all we know is, Kostos told Valenko he had major announcements to make. I see they are entering the Grand Ballroom now, so we'll all hear it together."

With that said, silence dominated the atmosphere in all situation rooms, lights were dimmed, and Kostos strode to the podium among the cheers and applause of several hundred delegates. Then he began, "I want to thank all of you for being with us on this momentous occasion. Momentous, because I've several pieces of wonderful news for our IFN family.

"Today, I am announcing to the world that our scientists and computer techs have completed their project to build the first-of-a-kind Universal Software System with the computer hardware capable of retrieving, storing and processing, for whatever purposes we deem necessary, every piece of data from every single computer system on the planet." The ballroom crowd gasped in awe as one. That was followed by a corporate murmur that rippled through the crowd.

As Kostos allowed the shock of his statement to sink in, Pratt asked his comm chief, "Is he implying he can grab info off any system in the world regardless of security features or firewalls?"

The comm director, in awe as well, answered, "Yes, sir, that's what he's saying. Our own people have tried to develop such a system for 15 years, but the technology required is advancing exponentially so that by the time we could solve one problem, the techies found away to create another one.

"We'd still be on it but Congress refused to fund the continued R and D three years ago."

Kostos continued, "Fear not, friends. We've no plans to hack into, steal, or manipulate any nation's database or systems, or to exploit any confidential or sensitive information." Kostos smiled slyly, adding, "That is, at least, not yet."

Nervous laughter spread through the crowded ballroom.

"Our goal is to insure that your nation and people as members of the IFN will be looked upon with much more respect. It is a sad fact that a number of your countries and people have been forced to be the bottom feeders of the world's resources for far too long.

"Through our mutual cooperation and our new technological superiority, we will bring an end to the unjust dominance of the superpowers over the earth's abundant resources. It is time to end the disproportionate distribution of wealth where only three to five percent of the population controls 95 percent of the wealth."

Suddenly, the entire crowd within the ballroom surged to their feet in a five-minute demonstration of shouts, cheers and applause.

Kostos stood with a look of submissive humility and, as the noise subsided, he continued.

"Further, I know I speak for all IFN members just as a father speaks for his children when I say we are tired of United Nations talk and of Western handouts. We are weary of eating the scraps that fall from the tables of the world's money masters."

Cheers again erupted.

Kostos continued. "Your people deserve better and I am here to guarantee they get better. Not only do we now have the means to bring changes to the world's economic and military status quo, but thanks to the collaborative effort of IFN scientists, geneticists, and botanists, we now hold the key to the horn of plenty. We are now able to produce increased yields of virtually any and every animal and plant product on this planet, anywhere on earth, regardless of soil or environmental conditions. Your poor, your starving, your hurting people will soon be released from their stifling poverty. No longer will nations who have plenty be able to use food as a political or psychological weapon against the poor nations of the world."

Once again, the ballroom exploded into an ear-splitting cacophony of ecstatic cheering. After another four minutes they quieted.

"The time has come for people everywhere to discover the bounty we can provide, not by depending on nations whose policies and motives we all question, such as Israel's unjust treatment of the humble Palestinian people. Many nations have been fearful to speak out. Perhaps it is because for the last 20 years, Israel has subtly reminded the world that they are the only nuclear power in the region. Or perhaps it has been the constant whining of the Jews over the so-called Holocaust that has contributed much to the silence of those who have wanted to speak out.

"But no longer will we be held hostage to national policies that grieve the world, such as those of the United States. Some of you know the USA as your sustainer, that great bread basket in the sky, but that ends now!"

Once again, the delegates could not contain themselves as they erupted in cheers.

"Finally, friends, I say, within a short period of time measured only in weeks or months, IFN's technological advances will be able to provide all its members with all the oil and petroleum products your societies demand. We possess the knowledge and the technological expertise that until now, the world has only dreamed about. We can find the reserves, fields and the hidden treasures of renewable energy sources no one dared imagine even existed. But they do exist and they belong to you."

As soon as the demonstration of joy and unbridled excitement died down, Kostos wrapped up his speech with an introduction.

"Today we leave here thrilled at our achievements, but all the more so because another great nation longs to join our IFN family on our quest for world peace and prosperity. With me on the platform is President Kastonof Valenko of the Russian Empire."

Again, the crowd expressed their feelings of elation and joy, giving the Russian President a five-minute ovation.

Kostos quieted the room. "In a few minutes I will accompany President Valenko on a flight to Moscow, where he has invited me to speak as your representative to the Russian leadership. They, hopefully, will agree to be a part of our family in the International Federation of Nations.

"So, goodbye and good luck until we meet again next month in Brussels, Belgium."

The monitor screens in all the American situation rooms went black. The people occupying the chairs sat in shocked dismay over what they had just witnessed.

SEVENTEEN

Understanding the critical importance of the intelligence they had received from Hussein, Brad and Leah were speeding back toward Jerusalem across the barren, flat lands of the Jordan Valley. As they approached the Israeli roadblock that had checked their credentials on their way to Masada, they saw smoke curling into the sky.

When they were a quarter of a mile from the site, they could see the IDF Jeep ablaze and the unmoving bodies of four IDF soldiers on the ground. Neither Brad nor Leah spoke as she slowly maneuvered the Mercedes around the pieces of the shattered road block and the spike strips. She stopped a few yards past the debris and reached to see if her cell had service yet. It didn't.

Since no tour buses had passed them going the opposite direction to the Dead Sea sights, Leah figured that somewhere up ahead authorities had stopped traffic. Looking at the four young soldiers laying dead on the ground, Leah's eyes filled with tears that cascaded down her reddened cheeks.

"This is obviously the work of a Hamas terror squad."

Brad, sensing her pain over the loss of the Israeli soldiers, gently asked, "But where are they now?"

"I don't know," Leah said as she took the car out of park and put it into drive, "and I don't want to know. We've gotta get to Jerusalem quick!" She floored the accelerator and with tires screaming and rubber burning, took off.

Soon they approached the intersection where they needed to turn left to head toward Jerusalem. But as they drew closer, they saw that the intersection was blocked by an 18–wheeler and a Jeep with a heavy machine gun mounted on the back. Flying from the tall radio antenna on the Jeep was an Israeli flag. Relieved to come across friendlies, Leah surged toward the intersection, hoping to request an escort on into Jerusalem and, at the very least, use of their powerful radio.

Fifty yards from the intersection, however, Leah slammed on the brakes and screeched to a halt. Brad saw her squint her eyes and look askance at the blocked intersection. She then banged the steering wheel hard with her hand, saying, "How could I be so stupid?"

Brad looked at her and said, "Uh, I take it this is not a good thing?"

Before Leah could respond, two shots rang out from behind the big rig, blowing out both of the Mercedes' front tires. Immediately, both of the occupants ducked low as Leah spoke, "All right, you've got the Glock I loaned you." She already had her nine-millimeter in hand. "In front of you, the glove box is full of clips for that gun." She dug under her seat and pulled out a shoebox loaded with full clips for her nine-millimeter.

Simultaneously, both of them chambered a round and flipped their weapons off safety.

Brad, risking a quick look over the dash, asked, "Is there any other way back to Jerusalem?"

Leah nodded to the left, "Yeah, through those hills are a few old roads and goat trails. That's the Judean wilderness. They say Jesus lasted 40 days out there while fasting. But we don't even have a bottle of water and, Brad, you're no Jesus."

Brad faked a hurt look and asked, "Does it show?"

As soon as the words were spoken, a bullet smashed through the windshield and they ducked still lower. That was quickly followed by a hail of gunfire directed at them from behind the cover of the semi. Bullets slammed into the vehicle's front grill and into the engine block. Others continued to shatter the windshield and exit out the back window, which in seconds, was completely shattered and blown out.

Brad and Leah stayed low as the withering automatic weapons fire poured into the automobile. Smoke billowed out from under the bullet-riddled hood as the engine coughed, then died. Then the shooting suddenly stopped.

Both occupants of the smoking, disabled Mercedes peeked out over the dash. They saw a dozen Hamas Jihadists coming out from behind and under the 18–wheeler 50 yards in front of them. They all held AK-47s or other Russian assault rifles and were crouched low, walking carefully and slowly toward the car.

Pulling their heads back down, Brad and Leah's faces were only inches apart. Brad whispered, "Why is it, that ever since I set foot in your country I've been someone's target? I've been chased, run off the road, threatened, shot at, and become the object of unjustifiable hatred."

"Well," Leah answered, as she shook the pieces of shattered glass from her thick hair. "At least you've had a taste of what it's like to be an Israeli. In fact, you've just described our history."

Without responding, Brad took another quick peek over the dash. Pulling his head back down, he whispered, "They'll be in range of these pea shooters in about 40 seconds and I don't believe they know we're armed. So, I propose, at just the right moment, we throw open each of our doors, use 'em as cover, and see how many we can take out before they overrun us. You okay with that?"

Leah, who had been struggling to put her hair back in a pony tail, completed the task and answered, "Do I have a choice?"

Brad, who had been watching her, answered, "No, you don't. But why, pray tell, are you working up a new hair style now? You planning to seduce 'em to death?"

Leah, now checking her clip, testily answered, "If it's any of your business, James Bond, I can't shoot with hair in my face!"

Brad checked over the dash again and saw the terrorists were being cautious and approaching slowly. He pulled his head back down, again close to Leah and whispered, "Well it appears, dear girl, that we may never get an opportunity to explore the depths of our relationship."

Leah jerked her head toward him and with exaggerated disgust said, "Mr. Fuller, we have no relationship!"

With a look of surprise, Brad responded, "Oh, but we do. I think you really like me!"

Without warning, Brad bent close, and quickly kissed her dead on the mouth.

"Uugghh," Leah gasped as she wiped her mouth with her sleeve, "You disgust me."

"No, I don't," Brad returned, "You liked that. Now on the count of three we will both dive out and from the cover of our doors create as many martyrs for Allah as possible… one…two…three." They moved as one, flung the car doors open, jumped behind them and began unloading their clips into the terrorists, now only 25 yards in front of them.

Shocked to be suddenly under fire, several of the attackers ran back to cover behind the big rig. Four of the others were hit immediately by Brad's and Leah's fire. The remaining five dropped flat on the ground and returned their fire. Slugs were mercilessly slamming into the Mercedes' doors. The windows in each exploded, sending tiny missiles of sharp glass in all directions. The incessant fire filled the air with deadly lead.

Ducking down again behind the cover of their doors, the two agents quickly ejected their spent clips, slammed in new ones, and cranked live rounds into their weapons' chambers.

Before rising again to return fire, they caught each other's eye through the car's interior. Each noticed the other's face was drenched in sweat and already covered with the black soot from firing so rapidly. Brad nodded, indicating now was the moment to unleash fire into the enemy again. They rose and emptied their clips into the terrorists lying on the ground.

Two more terrorists were quickly put out of commission as Brad and Leah again ducked back down to reload. As Brad slammed his new clip into the Glock, he thought he heard the sound of approaching vehicles. Peering around the edge of his door, he saw two Jeeps, full of more terrorists and brimming with weapons, pull up behind the big truck.

As he saw Leah finish reloading, he said, "Looks like we got more bad guys showing up."

Before Leah could respond, the attackers unleashed a merciless barrage of lead that filled the air like a swarm of bees. Bowing low, both of them knew the inevitable ending they faced. But each of them was sorely determined to take out as many bad guys as possible before they were overrun.

As Brad was about to return fire, he heard Leah cry out. Looking across the seats, he saw her holding her leg just above the ankle. He jumped into the Mercedes, keeping his head below dash level, to crawl over and check on her. The withering fire filled the airspace in, around, and near the automobile. Before Brad could get close enough to Leah to check her wound, he was hit and fell across the seats and console on his stomach. Leah heard him cry out, "Those sorry egg-sucking dogs." She knew he had been hit as well.

His head was close to Leah just outside the driver's door as she crouched low. He watched as she groaned loudly, jumped up, and fired wildly in an attempt to slow the attacker's advance. Brad knew Leah was about to be taken down, when all at once, the shooting just stopped.

Slowly pulling himself up to look over the steering wheel, he saw a group of attackers still no more than 20 yards away yelling at each other in Arabic and pointing at the horizon toward Jerusalem. Both he and Leah followed their gaze but they heard the beating rhythm of the choppers before they saw them. Within seconds, two Israeli gunships flying in low began pouring 50-caliber machine gun rounds into the terrorists' position. The six or seven who were not immediately shredded like lettuce raced for their two Jeeps, jumped in, and attempted to speed off. But it was no contest as the lead gunship overtook and unloaded a rocket into one Jeep, exploding it upon contact and ripping the other to pieces with the 50 caliber. It overturned in a side ditch with no survivors, and then burst into flames.

Brad and Leah, wounded and exhausted, were elated as they watched a third helicopter with medic emblems and the Star of David set down close to them. Two paramedics jumped to the ground and sprinted to the couple. The first medic examined Leah's wound. The bullet had gone straight through the fleshy part of her lower calf just above her ankle.

The medic said, as he wrapped it quickly, "You're a lucky lady. Just a flesh wound. Straight in and straight out."

Leah gasped at the sting of antiseptic he poured on her leg, and then she spoke into the Mercedes where the second medic was tending to Brad. "Are you all right? Where are you hit, Brad?"

After a moment of silence, Brad spoke sourly. "Let's just say my left cheek now matches my right cheek."

Leah's pain did not stop her from bursting out laughing. "You got shot in the butt again?"

"Shut up!" Brad ordered.

But she didn't.

Both victims were loaded onto stretchers and carried to the medivac helicopter. Once they were secured, a young Israeli pilot turned in his seat and yelled to them over the noise of the choppers. "Sorry we're so late, but once our surveillance post on those hills over there got word to us, we had to fuel up again just to get here."

Brad smiled, "Your timing, my good man, was perfect." The pilot grinned and added, "We've orders to take you straight to Jerusalem's Hadassa Hospital, where doctors, along with a number of government and Mossad types, are waiting for you."

Leah murmured, "I would expect no less."

The entire firefight had lasted 17 minutes, but to Brad and Leah it seemed an eternity. As the helicopter lifted off, Brad stared silently at the carnage below and at the devastating damage that guaranteed Leah's car was a total loss. He fell back on his stretcher and whispered to himself, "I really need a vacation."

ISRAELI BOMBERS HIT IRAN
NIGHTTIME ASSAULT SHOCKS THE WORLD

"Good morning from our World News Network headquarters in New York. I'm Barry Sholes.

"Big news out of the Middle East. Late last night Israeli bombers struck what has been reported as a nuclear development sight at Bushera,

Iran. It was Israel's second such unprovoked bombing of the facility in less than 10 months. Civilian casualties are said to be high and according to Iranian officials, the damage to the facility was minimal.

"However, according to the same officials, the bombers not only struck the nuclear development sight but intentionally targeted a heavily populated, civilian center four miles away, killing up to 1,500 innocent men, woman and children.

"Iran's military personnel confirm that the Israeli bombers came in so fast and low that their radar failed to detect them. Israel, obviously anxious to let the Iranians know who did the bombing, also dropped thousands of leaflets warning the Iranian government that the State of Israel would not allow a nuclear Iran. The printed message ended with the warning that said, 'If Iran continues its nuclear research and development, the next attack would destroy more than a reactor.'

"Two hours ago, in a statement from Jerusalem, the Israeli Prime Minister, Ehud Eliad, vehemently denied that Israel had anything to do with the bombing. The Prime Minister said, 'Our enemies are conspiring to implicate Israel as a pretext to war. Perhaps the corrupt Iranian government conducted the raid and is accusing us, hoping to draw the world's sympathy in an effort to cover its own terrorist's activities.' Unquote.

"But it seems few world leaders believe the Prime Minister. The Security Council of the United Nations is already in session with hopes to avert a major eruption of hostilities in the Middle East. However, two dozen Muslim nations have already started calling up their reserves and are threatening to destroy Israel.

"In Washington, D.C., the American government, usually the first to come to Israel's defense, has balked in its support of the bombing. A statement from the White House and President Jordan Hunt was released earlier this morning. It said, and I quote, 'The United States of America has always stood by the State of Israel in their times of crisis. We believe in their right to exist in secured borders and to defend themselves. However, neither the American people nor this administration can condone Israel's unprovoked attack upon Iran and their senseless slaughter of so many innocent people. We, along with the rest of the civilized world, urge the Israeli government to immediately take full responsibility for what they've done and to make full restitution to the Iranian government and people.' Unquote.

"Later today, the Organization of Islamic Nations, consisting of 45 countries, will release their statement concerning the attack upon Iran, along with how they plan to respond.

"That concludes this special report. We will let you know if and when more details are made available. We now return you to our regular programming."

EIGHTEEN

It had been 48 hours since CIA surveillance had listened in on Kostos' meeting with the Russian President and the closed meeting of Kostos and the IFN's delegates. Since then, Director Pratt had sent multiple requests asking to meet with the president on urgent matters. Finally, after being repeatedly put off and told that the president was too busy, Pratt met with Secretary of State James Parlay, Secretary of Defense Carl Bates, National Security Advisor Carol Watts and the Chair of the Joint Chiefs of Staff, Admiral Chuck Withers.

It was only after sending a letter with each of their signatures to President Hunt insisting on an immediate conference that he finally relented. They sat in the White House situation room awaiting the arrival of the president, who was already 15 minutes late.

"Has no one informed the president of the seriousness of matters we need to discuss?" grumbled the impatient Admiral.

Before anyone could answer, the door opened and in walked President Hunt, dressed in a casual warm-up suit and carrying a golf club. He was accompanied by his Secret Service agents. Hunt laid his golf club on the table at which everyone sat, took his seat at the head, and scolded, "Gentlemen and lady, tell me what's so critically important that it was necessary for me to leave the Prime Minister of Japan standing alone on the 12th tee in order to rush here and meet with you."

Everyone in the room was stunned at the cavalier attitude of the president, but no one expressed it.

After an uncomfortable few seconds of silence, Pratt spoke, "Mr. President." He slid an intelligence dossier marked "Classified" in front of the president. "I think you will agree, sir, that the matters contained in this brief merit your immediate attention."

The president glanced down at the dossier, smirked, and pushed it back toward Pratt. "Mr. Pratt, is that the same report you sent to my residence and then again to my office with a demand—not a request, mind you, but a demand—that I read it immediately?"

Without missing a beat, Pratt answered, "Yes, sir, I do believe it is."

"Well then," the president crossed his arms with the look of a defiant child, "Mr. Pratt, for future reference, and this goes for the rest of you as well… never, I say again, never, tell me that you demand I do anything. I am the President of the United States and if there's 'demanding' to be done around here, I'll be the one doing it. Is that clear?"

Everyone around the table murmured a quiet "Yes, sir,' except Pratt, who was seething with rage at the incompetent ignorance he had been witnessing in this president.

"Sir, if I may ask," Pratt said respectfully, "did you read it?"

The president's countenance tightened and his face went red with anger as he barked at the CIA Director, "Pratt, your insolence borders on insubordination. But to answer your question, let's just say I skimmed it and for the life of me I do not understand your urgency concerning it."

Again, everyone at the table was speechless at what the president was saying. Pratt, struggling to maintain his composure, said, "Mr. President, with your permission I'd like, for the record's sake, to hit the highlights in this report."

"Pratt," returned the increasingly angry president, "you may hit your highlights. But do not drag this meeting out in an attempt to impress all of us with the CIA's sneaky little tricks. This isn't a budget hearing and I've a game of golf to finish, followed by a state dinner this evening with the new Foreign Minister of Ireland. So get on with it."

Thankful that Hunt was showing his true colors to the others present, Pratt continued, "Yes sir, Mr. President. The report details audio transcripts secretly taped at two different venues with Mr. Charon D. Kostos. The first, with Russian President Valenko, was a meeting two days ago with Kostos in New York. In the meeting, Kostos bribes Valenko by making preposterous claims about how his IFN scientists have discovered huge hidden deposits of oil, gold and diamonds in Russia. He tells Valenko that if he'll join the IFN, which by the way would consolidate Kostos' hold on Russia as well as Europe, that his organization would insure the deposits are found and mined, saving Russia's economy and making Valenko a national hero."

"Pratt," an irritated Hunt injected, "I read a bit about that in your brief. Is that all that's bothering you?"

"Sir," continued Pratt, "that's hardly all that's bothering every one of us who's asked you to this meeting.

"President Valenko then alludes to a massive movement of Russian military assets over the last two months, south to the Iranian border with Russia and beyond. He and Kostos then boast how all the intel satellites and electronic observations of the United States, Israel and NATO have been unable to detect the military maneuvers, not only of Russia, but of the entire Middle Eastern sector, where multiple nations are coalescing military assets near the Israeli border.

"Further, sir, CIA and Mossad agents within the last 12 hours barely escaped several attempts on their lives in order to get us 'eyes-on verification' that Russia, Syria, Iraq, Iran, Turkey, Egypt, Libya and Lebanon have coalition forces numbering in the hundreds of thousands, along with armor and combat aircraft, slowly making their way to Israel's borders. In fact, sir, one very brave Mossad agent did pay with his life to get us this intel."

The president, who sat drumming his fingers on the table while tolerating Pratt's briefing, spoke up. "Pratt, the nations you mention all have a right to practice military maneuvers and train with war games. Don't you think you're overreacting?"

Pratt, ignoring the president, continued, "As I'm sure you know by now, sir, we're being led to believe that last night, Israeli bombers hit Iran's nuclear site at Bushera, Iran. However, the CIA questions the accuracy of those reports. It is our opinion that a third party, masquerading as Israel, carried out that raid in an effort to frame Israel."

"Again, Mr. Pratt," said a clearly impatient president, "just before

I came in here I released a statement calling on Israel to confess their despicable behavior. I also made it clear that the United States will not support that kind of state-sponsored terrorism. It should also be clear, by our previous failed efforts, that this nation cannot police the entire world. The bombing of Iran is a Middle Eastern affair. Besides, Israel is quite capable of defending herself."

The entire room was shocked at the president's words.

"Sir, if I may," the very stunned Secretary of State added, "the United States is legally and morally bound by treaties of mutual defense with the State of Israel. Those treaties stipulate that if any nation attacks Israel, it can be considered as an act of war against this country."

The infuriated president turned quickly toward his Secretary of State, "Mr. Secretary, I am the President of the United States. As the Commander in Chief of all of our armed forces, I decide what represents a clear and present danger to our nation, not you."

In an attempt to diffuse the tension and keep the briefing focused, Pratt jumped in, "Mr. President, with your permission, there's also the very important matter of Russia joining the IFN and all the outlandish promises Kostos made to representatives at the IFN conference. Throughout his speech, Kostos alluded to and openly threatened the United States, our economy, as well as our military apparatus, and mocked America's new impotence to do anything about his plans for dominating the world. This intel, along with a plethora of supporting documents, in our opinion, represents a very serious threat to our national security."

Secretary of Defense Bates, who could not sit silent any longer, added, "Mr. President, each of us who's asked you here has access to the best minds and geopolitical analysts in the world. They all agree, after studying the facts, that Kostos is behind the chaos developing in the Middle East. For whatever reasons, the man is manipulating power structures all over the planet in order to start a war. To what end, God only knows.

"The Joint Chiefs, represented here by Admiral Withers, agrees with all of us, that we should immediately upgrade our military alerts worldwide. We further agree that the United States should immediately serve notice on the IFN, the Muslim nations, Kostos, and especially Russia, to stand down in the Middle East, warning them that the United States stands ready to defend our interest and our allies in the region. We are also recommending that you order our fleet in the Indian Ocean moved to the Mediterranean."

"Mr. Secretary," the president scolded, raising his voice, "you, sir, are way out of order! I remind you, once again, that neither the Pentagon, nor the State Department, or for that matter Central Intelligence, dictates America's foreign policy. That's my job and no such action suggested by you or anyone else at this table will be taken. In fact, I am holding a news conference later this evening to announce that I've invited Charon Kostos to meet me for talks at Camp David this weekend in an effort to reach a mutual understanding with America on the matters you've all raised today."

"Sir," jumped in Secretary of State Parlay, "please understand that inviting Kostos to talks would be considered by all of our friends around the world a retreat from our standing commitments and treaties. It would destroy our already shaky credibility in the world."

"Frankly, Mr. Secretary," sniped the president, "I don't care what others think. I care about what's right for America. And it's not right for America to be dragged into World War III, simply because the Israeli morons can't stop killing their neighbors. They've been hiding behind our flag long enough. It stops here and now."

"Mr. President," injected the shocked Chairman of Joint Chiefs, Admiral Withers, "We cannot afford to lose Israel. They are the strategic balance that holds in check hostile nations in the Middle East. If we turn our backs on Israel, we can say goodbye not only to our only foothold in the region, but to this nation's protectorates in the Persian Gulf and the entire Middle East. The flow of oil to this country will stop if Russia becomes the dominant power in the region, and that will destroy our economy."

"Admiral Withers," a condescending president answered, "Israel is quite capable of defending herself. It's not necessary to continue wasting billions of American dollars to support a state that can't get along with the rest of the world. Many people feel Israel can handle, by herself, any military challenge her neighbors make against her."

"Begging your pardon, sir," came back an astonished Admiral Withers, "if we stand by and do nothing to help Israel in the event of war, the military alliance arrayed against them right now would overrun Tel Aviv in two days.

"If Russian forces from the north are allowed to link up with the forces of their Muslim allies in the south, as it appears they're trying to do, Israel will be forced to fight on numerous fronts—one in the Sinai, one in the Golan, one further north on the Lebanese border, and one on the Jordanian border. You can add an eastern front if Russian naval forces come in from the Mediterranean.

"They'd be facing an alliance of 30 or 40 nations whose ground troops alone outnumber them 30 to one. In tanks they'd be outnumbered 40 to one and 100 to one in combat aircraft. And forget their nuclear deterrence. Russia's involvement in the equation checkmates Israel's nuclear advantage.

"Frankly, sir, if we stand down, Israel will cease to exist and if anyone is left alive in the area they'll be counting their money in Russian rubles."

Everyone around the table looked toward President Hunt to hear a response. The president spoke with noticeable contempt. "You guys at the Pentagon used to scare me. But not anymore, no sir. In the first place, such a war never has to happen. I'll be proposing at the coming Camp David meetings with Kostos that the United States seek immediate membership in the IFN. The United States should be a part of the world's problem-solving process instead of the problem makers.

"This Presidency will not go down in history as being a warmonger. I will not send American boys to die on foreign soils for the sake of a tin horn, socialistic, fly-by-night country whose sole claim to a right to exist is that they think they are God's chosen people."

The room was in awe, disbelieving what they had just heard. Simultaneously, everyone except Pratt started speaking in attempt to reason with the president.

President Hunt yelled, "That's enough! This meeting is over! Now, Mr. Secretary of State, like it or not, you will immediately get in touch with Mr. Kostos. You will invite him to attend a conference this weekend at Camp David with me as his host. If you've a problem with that, Mr. Parlay, tender your resignation and I'll find someone more supportive of their president. Am I understood?"

Secretary Parlay, white with anger, merely nodded.

"Now, I've guests waiting on the 12th tee. I suggest you all get back to work on matters relevant to the United States. Good day to all of you." The president stood and strode to the door with his agents.

Director Pratt spoke out just as Hunt reached the door. "Mr. President, there's a lot more in this report critical to national defense issues. Are you sure you can't look at it?"

President Hunt looked back at the director. "Pratt, I'm sure you folks can take it from here," he said, and slammed the door behind him.

Before anyone moved, Director Pratt spoke, "Gentlemen, and lady, something beyond our grasp is going on here. If you concur with me on that, I invite you to meet me in one hour in my office at Langley. I've some things to show you that may well shock you. If you're interested, and I do pray you are, I'll see you in one hour."

"Hello, I'm Will Cannon and this is World Network News. We're interrupting your regular programming to bring you breaking news out of the Vatican.

"Several hours ago the College of Cardinals made the decision on who is to be the new Pope. They've chosen a Cardinal Wilhelm Genavoh. The 70-year old Genavoh, born in Cherwith, Switzerland, has served the Church since he was an eight-year-old altar boy. Details concerning his theological positions on matters of import to Catholics will be released, so we're told, sometime in the next 24 hours.

"We have learned that within an hour of being named the New Pontiff, Genavoh placed a personal call to Charon Kostos, Chairman of the International Federation of Nations. The Pope invited Kostos to Rome to discuss the growing crisis in the Middle East. The Pontiff feels that Mr. Kostos has demonstrated an uncanny gift in the area of diplomacy and he hopes that together they can act as a moderating influence in the tension-filled region.

"That meeting is set to take place as soon as Mr. Kostos can make his way to the Vatican, probably within hours. We'll keep you posted on the details as they become available to us.

"Until then, I'm Will Cannon at the Vatican in Rome. We now return you to your regular programming."

Leah, with the help of a cane, was able to hobble around. Brad, whose pride was more wounded than his posterior, was agile enough but was forced to use care when sitting down. After being treated at the Jerusalem Hospital for two days, while being thoroughly debriefed by both Mossad and CIA officials, they had been released. Their orders were to return immediately to Rome.

Their flight from Tel Aviv to Rome on an El Al 767 had been comfortable, short and uneventful. Having been met at the Rome airport by the same CIA driver and car they had the last time they were there, they arrived at the same safe house as before, in short order.

Upon the late night arrival, Brad had been fully briefed in a call from Director Pratt about the strange behavior of President Hunt and his reaction to the growing crisis in the Middle East. They had also discussed the mystery surrounding President Carr and whether or not he was alive. Pratt was convinced that somehow Carr had survived the crash of Air Force One and that he was being held against his will somewhere in Italy.

The director informed Brad that just before President Carr took off on his fateful flight to Rome, he had confided to Pratt that he was privy to information concerning the IFN. Carr had told Pratt, "Something very dark, even sinister, is going on behind the IFN façade of peace and love." When asked to elaborate, the president had told Pratt, "Not yet. First, I must check it out in Rome. We'll talk when I get back."

The conversation between Brad and Pratt ended with Pratt's orders to find Carr, dead or alive.

Leah, according to Brad's boss, was still on loan to the CIA from the Mossad. She and Brad were to continue working together until the mystery was solved.

Throughout the night, Brad had been rehashing the encounter with Father Portega in the catacombs.

It was 7:00 a.m. in Rome when Leah walked out of the house onto the back deck. Brad sat at the patio table with his coffee as Leah took the seat across from him. They spent half an hour going over their assignment, and then turned their conversation to their catacombs encounter.

After a while, Leah sat back in her deck chair. Brad, sensing her concern about events in Israel, spoke, "Your country, at least, has been warned about the actions of their enemies. They're calling up their reserves and now getting on a war footing."

Leah returned, "We've been on a 'war footing' since 1948. In fact, on the very day the U.N. recognized Israel as a nation, we were attacked by five of our neighbors whose goal was to kill every Jew in the new Israel. Since then, it's been a non-stop struggle for survival, with only an occasional break from terror attacks in order to fight yet another war.

"There was the Battle for Independence of 1948, another in 1954, another in 1957, another in 1967, another in 1973. Then came Lebanon One, where we fought against Arafat and his PLO. That was followed by a Palestinian uprising called the Intifada that *still* rages. After that, we fought Lebanon Two against Syrian and Iranian terrorists called Hezbollah. All of these were just different battles in the real ongoing struggle for Israel's right to exist."

Brad listened sympathetically to Leah. "All the more reason for us to find what's behind all of this and stop the insanity."

Leah took a deep breath and responded, "Forgive my distractions. And yes, I've also been thinking a lot about our dearly departed friend, Father Portega. Do you remember him saying, 'We know all about you?' Who is the 'we' he alluded to?"

"I'm not sure," mused Brad, "but he did say his '*bosses*,' plural, had assigned him 'other areas' to work in—areas clearly outside normal priestly duties. I've got a strong feeling that all this is connected to our missing president."

Leah piped in, "You remember his reference to our ignorance and how it would surprise his bosses, whoever they are. There's no doubt, he was under the impression that we knew something. Portega was sure pleased to discover we were only fishing."

"One thing he was very clear about," Brad suddenly remembered, "was that we had been under surveillance. He knew we'd come to the Vatican that morning without informing our authorities. So not only were they very likely tapping our phones, they also had people watching us 'eyes on.' It only makes sense that they are surely still watching this house and us."

"So," Leah perked up, "if we can catch these watchers, we might be able to extract info on who's behind all of this!"

Brad interjected, "Indeed we could. So I think it's time for our morning drive to take in the beauty of Rome. What do ya say?"

"I think," Leah said as she stood to her feet, "that's an excellent idea, Mr. Fuller. If they're any good, they won't let us out of their sight. And I'll wager we're better at this game than they are. But I do have one condition that needs to be met if I'm going to cooperate."

Brad rolled his eyes, "And what would that be?"

"I," Leah said, walking toward the house, "get the first crack at interrogating them."

Brad nodded, saying, "You're on. But do try not to kill anyone."

Soon they were backing the BMW that had been left for their use out of the driveway.

NINETEEN

The attack on Castel Colledora had been a costly enterprise, not only for O'Donnell's terrorists but for Sodote Shalom as well. Besides the 10 terrorist deaths, eight security personnel had died and three others were seriously wounded. In spite of this horrific attack, because Castel Colledora's location was miles from any town or village, the intense firefight had gone unnoticed by officials of the province.

Dr. Cohen, struck in the head and face by O'Donnell's rage during the rampage, had been knocked unconscious and was laid up recovering for two days.

After the harrowing ordeal of the failed kidnapping attempt, President Carr and Agent Spears suffered minor setbacks. Each agreed to rest and recover for a couple of days while Dr. Cohen became well enough to fulfill his commitment to explain everything to President Carr.

As Drs. Cohen and Minay finally came into the president's room, Carr could see that Cohen's face was still bruised and a bit swollen. Otherwise, he seemed in good spirits.

After casual greetings and a short discussion about the recent assault, the president brought up the issue at hand.

"First, gentlemen," Carr humbly addressed the doctors, "I want to thank you both for protecting me from those butchers. At least now, you don't have to convince me that somebody wants me dead in a very bad way. After viewing the newsreel video of events after Air Force One went down and now having access to the news, I realize my skepticism about your motives was totally unwarranted. I am thoroughly convinced that the attempt on my life was part of a much larger conspiracy, part of which appears to be to place my wimpy, spineless Vice President, Jordan Hunt, into the Oval Office. Your Sodote Shalom has gone to great lengths to keep me alive, and while I am very grateful, I'm still not completely sure why, nor am I yet clear on exactly what Sodote Shalom is all about."

Dr. Minay explained, "Mr. President, if I may elaborate, Sodote Shalom is an underground group made up of scientists, doctors, rabbis, writers and various intellectuals, along with an enlightened number of discreet laypersons from many walks of life. All of us are Jewish and we have all committed ourselves to gather the resources and means to propagate a message of Messianic deliverance to the Jewish people before a series of upcoming events overtakes the world and threatens Israel's existence.

"All of us in Sodote Shalom believe in the writings of our ancient prophets. We are convinced that the God of Abraham, Isaac, and Jacob instructed them to write down the events that would come to pass in some future generation."

"Whoa, whoa, whoa," interrupted the president as he held up both hands in the sign of surrender. "You're telling me that these ancient prophets of yours, like Nostradamus and such, have told you when the world will end, and that you guys are trying to somehow save your people? I do hope there's more to your story. We've nut cases parading in front of the White House every day carrying signs saying, 'The end is near,' etc. etc. Tell me that's not your entire message."

Dr. Minay shook his head, "No, Mr. President. Our cause and our call are far more than sounding doomsday warnings. Our focus is much more redemptive and much less fatalistic, at least for those who listen. Also please understand, the prophets and their messages are not exclusively for the Jews. And it is a common mistake to classify Nostradamus as a Jew. In fact, he was not a Jew, nor is it to him that we refer."

Dr. Cohen jumped in, "Dr. Minay, if I may? Mr. President, we know your educational background and that you are a man of science, as are we. So let me begin there. There is increasing evidence which implies that this physical world and all within it is a mere image from a level of reality that is far beyond our own. The implication is that the true reality is not within this dimension but, in fact, in a different dimension altogether."

President Carr, finally interested, said, "All right, Doctor. I'm with you so far. Go ahead."

"Very well," Dr. Cohen agreed. "Of course, the supposition I'm proposing is not only a reflection of our own foundation's research. Nor did our scientists simply begin with a theory and work to find data that supported that theory. Rather, the research, whose conclusions were confirmed by our four teams of the world's greatest minds, began with no presuppositions and with the goal of following only the conclusions which the data supported."

"Which should be the goal of any valid research," the president said.

"Granted, sir," smiled the now encouraged Dr. Cohen. "The main source for this dimensional theory is one of the world's greatest and most respected scientific thinkers from the University of London. His name is David Bohm, and he's best known for his work with Albert Einstein. You may know Dr. Bohm as a highly respected quantum physicist. While he was conducting research at the Lawrence Radiation Laboratory, he noticed that gases made up of high-density electrons and positive ions had particles that stopped acting like individuals and began acting as if they were part of a larger, but well-connected whole."

"Excuse me, Doctor," put in the president. "Did their findings contradict accepted positions of the time?"

"Not really, but only because no one until then had really considered the full implications.

"Then, while Bohm was at Princeton with Einstein, they developed a supportive relationship and began to share their frustrations regarding the strange implications of what was then considered 'quantum theory.'"

Again, an intrigued President Carr interrupted. "I've read of their work, but it was while I was still a student. Didn't it have something to do with their efforts to find a common denominator between matter and non-matter?"

Nodding, Dr. Cohen responded, "That's a bit simplistic, but true. Bohm's view was all about the nature of location. He believed that quantum physics could prove that, at the sub quantum level, location ceased to exist. He felt it was meaningless to try to separate physical being from the entirety of the universal whole."

"Dr. Cohen," injected the president, "I'm sure you know that my first degree at Princeton was in physics, so I am vaguely familiar with Bohm's ideas. If I recall correctly, in the world of physics, isn't that called non-locality?"

"Very good, Mr. President," continued Dr. Cohen. "Then you should also know that Bohm's most controversial idea is that the material reality of our everyday lives is a result of a vast but more primary level of reality. It is that reality, according to him, from which all in our physical world comes. Bohm identified this lower reality as the implicate, or 'enfolded order.'"

"I follow you, Doctor," encouraged President Carr.

Pleased that he was understood, Dr. Cohen eagerly continued, "Well, strange as it may seem, there is no area of Bohm's research and subsequent conclusions that clash with a contextual biblical view of our physical world being subordinated to a spirit world in which the spiritual reality is superior to and causative of our material reality."

"Yes," the president put in, "but to the chagrin of many in the scientific community that conclusion supports 'intent and design' necessitating origin with another worldly force or God."

Dr. Minay, who had been listening patiently, spoke up. "It was a first-century Jewish scholar who wrote to his peers of the quantum reality. He wrote, 'While we look not at things which are seen, but at things which are not seen; for the things which are seen are temporal, but the things which are not seen are eternal.'"

President Carr, with a slight smile, nodded, "I am familiar as well with that man's writings."

"Then you understand," Dr. Cohen added, "that a mere secular man, whose worldview is limited by his finite capacity to reason, cannot begin to grasp the entirety of what we are about to tell you?"

"Indeed," replied the president. "Therefore, I will listen to you outside the confining box of natural reason."

"Excellent," answered Cohen. "So if you will make a maximum effort to apply your understanding of physics, while putting aside you own biases, I'm confident that you will come quickly to the conclusion that what I'm going to tell you is absolute and true."

"Okay," said the president. "Let's try to keep it simple."

"As you wish," nodded Cohen. "Brace yourself, sir. What we now tell you could be a bit destabilizing."

It had taken 15 minutes of driving out of Rome on Highway 1 before Brad and Leah were able to spot the black Mercedes following them at a half-mile distance. As soon as they spotted the vehicle, they turned north on the Coastal Expressway A12.

"Can you see how many are in the car?" Brad asked Leah as he focused on smoothly maneuvering their BMW in the moderate morning traffic. Leah studied the passenger side rearview mirror.

"Besides the driver, I can make out only one passenger."

"All right. About a quarter of a mile ahead is an exit. I'm going to take it, then turn right at the first dirt road I come to. Let's see if they'll take the bait."

"Brad," Leah moaned, "please don't do the bumper car thing again."

He grinned at the remark, "Oh, Leah, Leah, Leah. One would think by now that you'd know me and trust me."

She answered, staying focused on her rearview mirror. "Oh, I do know you, Mr. Fuller, and that's precisely why I don't trust you."

They were approaching the exit and Brad steered the car into the right lane to turn off the expressway. Upon exiting, after 500 feet they came to a stop sign at a dead end, which gave them the option of turning left or right. Brad, without fully stopping at the sign, turned right.

Leah quickly swung around, looking out the back window to see if the Mercedes would follow. "Oh, yeah," she said as the car she was watching also ignored the stop sign. "Like men the world over, they just can't resist the chase."

Brad, monitoring their pursuers through his own rearview mirror, said, "Dear girl, you couldn't be more right. Men do love the chase. What scares 'em is the catch."

"Well," Leah said as she squinted, attempting to see through the dust swirling behind them, "let's just hope the boys behind us are as dim-witted as they seem. They're now increasing their speed, and are coming up on us rather quickly."

In less than a minute the pursuers were no more than five car lengths behind them.

"It seems," Brad mused out loud, "that they are now more intent upon catching us than chasing us."

He glanced at Leah, who already had her nine-millimeter in hand and was cranking a round into the chamber.

Teasingly, Brad said, "Do try to restrain your blood lust. We need at least one of these guys alive."

Shifting her body around in the seat to get a better view out of the back window, Leah was not smiling, "Brad Fuller, do not interpret my readiness to respond to imminent threats with deadly force as something I enjoy. In fact, a little bit of me dies every time I pull this trigger. But the truth is, I've far too many colleagues lying in Israeli cemeteries whose hesitation cost 'em their lives. Mossad training is geared toward survival, not creating more dead agents."

With the BMW now clocking 80 miles an hour on the dirt and gravel road, Brad was focused on maintaining control, but did say, "I stand corrected. Forgive my insensitivity." Then, grinning, he added, "I'm just not used to dating pistol-packing mamas."

"What do you mean?" Leah shouted back. "We are not dating, you conceited moron. Furthermore, I wouldn't date you if you were the last surviving male on God's green earth. So kindly hush your senseless ramblings and pay attention to the business at hand. You are such a…"

Brad, teasing, interrupted, "No problem. I never argue with a woman holding a gun. Now, I want you to brace yourself as I am about to make a 180."

Leah quickly braced. "Brad, please don't..." Before she could complete her sentence, Brad slammed on the brakes and spun the steering wheel hard to the left. The car rapidly spun around counter-clockwise on the loose dirt and gravel, stirring up a whirlwind of dust that quickly limited the visibility to zero.

Taken completely by surprise, the driver of the Mercedes could only react instinctively by slamming on his brakes and turning hard right. He, too, found his car swinging around in a flurry of dust that left him and his passenger disoriented.

Both cars came to a stop in the cloud of disturbed debris.

The Mercedes' driver and passenger sat stunned for a few seconds, wondering what had happened and trying to see through the swirling dust storm they had stirred up. But just as the BMW they had been following became visible directly in front of them, they saw Brad and Leah standing outside each of the Mercedes' windows with guns pointing at their heads.

Both men quickly raised their hands as Brad ordered them out of the car. Very slowly, the two men opened their doors and stepped out as the agents kept their weapons locked on them.

"Whatever do you boys want?" Brad asked. "I thought surely your game was simple surveillance."

The driver, a muscular, shaved head, bulldog type, answered, "Just doing our job, boss. We had orders to take you in."

"Take us in? Where, and to whom?" Brad asked forcefully while pointing his Glock at the bald head.

"We don't know. We're supposed to call when we gotcha," growled the man Leah held in place on the other side of the vehicle.

"Why is it that I feel you are lying?" Brad murmured as he reached into his jacket's side pocket and pulled out two sets of handcuffs. He tossed one set to the bald guy, "Be a good boy and put those on."

As the man began to comply, Brad tossed the second pair of cuffs over the car's roof to Leah.

She glanced up to catch them and that gave the prisoner on her side the split second he had hoped for. He rapidly pulled out an Italian Beretta, but before he could bring the pistol up to shoot Leah, she placed a nine-millimeter slug between his eyes. As the man fell to the ground, she tossed the cuffs back to Brad. "I won't be needing those," she said.

As Leah walked around the back of the Mercedes to join Brad, the other man's face bore a look of horror.

Brad said, "Now if you're not nice, Igor, I'll turn you over to ol' blood and guts here," as he nodded toward Leah, who was not amused.

Leah walked up to their prisoner and searched him for weapons. Inside his coat, in a shoulder holster, she found his gun and tossed it off the road. She pushed the big man toward the back of their BMW, opened the back passenger door and shoved him inside. The lack of gentility prompted the man to protest, "Hey lady, take it easy."

Leah wheeled around and got in the man's face. "Sit still and shut up or we'll bleed you like the pig you are." She slammed the door and stalked to the front passenger door of the BMW.

Just before she bent down to get in, Brad teased over the top of the car, "Bleed you like a pig? Really, Leah, that's no way for a lady to talk."

"And you shut up too, Fuller," Leah shot back as she sat down in the BMW.

Once all were in, Brad jerked the Bemer into gear and, with tires spinning on the loose gravel, headed back down the road the way they had come. As they exited Expressway A-12, they were almost at the safe house when their prisoner spoke, "You know you two are dead meat, don't you? You know who you're messing with? You'll die before the sun is up."

Leah whipped around fast enough to make the prisoner jump, "You're a freak! And if you say one more word without being asked something, you'll die before 30 seconds is up."

Brad, stifling a laugh while trying to sound serious, said, "You'd better listen to the lady, my friend. She's got a nasty temper that you'll get to see a lot more of once we get you back to our love nest."

"Brad," Leah raised her voice, "you just drive, and for once keep your dirty little mouth shut. I've got more than one bullet in this gun."

Brad shrugged and looked in the rearview mirror to catch the prisoner's eye, and mouthed, "See, I told you."

Just then, they entered the long driveway leading up to the safe house. Brad stopped the car and put it in park. "Would you go in and make sure we've no uninvited guests?" he asked Leah. "I'll follow with Igor."

As she stepped out of the car, she turned and put her head back in. "Don't forget your promise. I get the first shot at this slime ball." She slammed the door.

Brad looked back at the prisoner, whose face was turning white with fear at the thought of being turned over to Leah for interrogation.

Brad caught the man's eye, smiled broadly, and said, "Man, I'm glad I'm not you. She's in an especially nasty mood today."

TWENTY

Kostos' private jet touched down at the Ciampino Airport a few miles southeast of Rome. It was just after 7:00 p.m. when the Pontiff's private helicopter picked him up and ferried him to his meeting at the Vatican with the new Pope. After a short formal reception, heavily attended by the media, Kostos and the Pope were escorted to the lavish, personal quarters of the Pontiff where they were finally left alone.

The Pope, now going by the title Pope Merciful I, turned to face Kostos. "It's been a long time coming, Charon."

As a parish priest years earlier, the new Pope, then known as Father Wilhelm Genavoh, of Cherwith, Switzerland, was in charge of the small Catholic congregation in the quiet canon. Two elderly nurses from the nearby hospital had shown up at the church very early one morning, extremely upset.

The ladies carried a newborn baby boy whose mother had died the night before during childbirth. They had thrust the baby into the hands of the priest and demanded he be given to the Catholic Orphanage in Bern. The terribly distraught nurses turned to rush out but the priest demanded more information if he was going to accept the child. Reluctantly, the women reported that no one but the doctor had been present at the child's birth the night before. They had, however, gone to the clinic very early that morning and were horrified at what they had found.

The young birth mother appeared to have been disemboweled from within. Her body lay in an unnatural position on the clinic floor and the torso cavity, where the baby would have been prior to birth, looked as if it had literally been burst open with extreme pressure from the inside.

Blood was everywhere, and there was not a shred of evidence that the old physician had attempted a C-section. There, on the floor, next to the body of the disemboweled young mother, lay a blood-smeared baby boy, very much alive.

Most disturbing to the nurses, however, was the dead body of the doctor on the floor in a sitting position, with his back against the wall. He was covered with the young woman's blood and a number of her internal organs, as if she had literally exploded. Even in death, the expression on the lifeless face of the doctor was one of sheer terror.

Both nurses were weeping hysterically, anxious to leave the church, but Father Genavoh demanded they tell him of anything else they may have seen. At that question, the women had stared at each other. One finally nodded to the other, who spoke, "Our doctor was also covered with hundreds of little bite marks over his torso, arms, neck and face. Every bite was deep and the wounds had drawn blood."

The other woman spoke up, "Show him."

At that, the senior nurse slowly reached toward the baby cradled in the priest's arms. She cautiously unfolded the blanket that covered the baby's face. With her thumb and forefinger, she gently pulled the infant's upper and lower lips back, revealing a full set of teeth. Little pieces of flesh were stuck between the teeth and the baby's lips and cheeks were smeared with dried blood.

The priest recoiled and gasped. He then made the nurses promise to return to the clinic immediately, clean up the mess, and prepare the old doctor for cremation before anyone else saw him. He promised to send a laborer by to dispose of the good doctor's body.

He told them he would accept the child for the orphanage but that they must never again speak to anyone of this incident. He added, if they disobeyed him, their penalty would be eternal damnation in the fires of hell.

However, Father Genavoh never delivered the child to the orphanage at Bern. He kept him, raising him, caring for him and educating him in the finest schools in Europe. Finally, when the boy neared manhood, the priest had secured a position of prominence for the boy in the industrial complex of the very wealthy Maurice Dubois. There, the young man had begun to understand his call. Little by little, Charon had increased his influence, developed his skills, and set out on the course that would be his destiny.

Kostos' lifelong relationship with the new Pope was known by no one outside a very tightly knit group of powerbrokers, each of them intricately involved in Kostos' rise to power.

As the Pontiff gazed admiringly at Kostos, the younger man responded, "Yes, it has been a long time coming, but now our time has arrived."

They took seats facing each other in the oversized antique chairs from the 15th century.

"Your International Federation of Nations has become a world force. I was delighted to read that the European Union has unanimously voted to consolidate their nations, their assets and resources, including economic and military, with the IFN's.

"And, Charon, your work with the Russian President Valenko, resulting in their becoming part of the IFN, was a master stroke.

"The Russians and the militant Islamic nations are poised to strike at the heart of the Zionists and soon the Jews will all be crying out for a savior."

Kostos nodded humbly, "Things indeed have gone very well, Excellency. And your predecessor has been sent on to his reward, putting you in a position of great power."

"And for that," injected the Pope, "I have you to thank. There are, however, a couple of loose ends that must be tied up soon."

Kostos stood, walked to the large window looking out over St. Peter's Square. "You speak of course, of our resilient President Carr, now being hidden by those filthy Jews."

"Yes," added the Pope, "that and the matter of those two meddlesome agents who keep interfering with our progress. You know, of course, they killed Father Portega?"

Kostos turned back to face the Pontiff. "I'm aware of that. But he was no loss. He'd served his purpose, and they just saved me the trouble of getting rid of him myself.

"However, I had hoped to frame the two spies for the murder of Pope Baranoldi. We almost succeeded, but the American CIA and the Zionist Mossad pulled strings in the Italian government and cleared them."

"And now," the Pope inquired, "you've plans to deal with both of these loose ends?"

"As for the two agents," Kostos answered, "earlier today I sent a most efficient team to pick them up. As you know they've arrived back here in Rome. They'll be taken to our people who will make short work of them. We should be hearing of their demise very soon.

"As for Carr, you're also aware that our downing of Air Force One failed to kill the fool. Once my people finally found the location where he was, I sent a team of terrorists to eliminate him but, alas, they too failed. In fact, every one of them, as far as I can tell, was killed in the effort."

"And now?" questioned the listening Pope.

"And now," Kostos continued, "he's very well protected and we'd need a full division to get to him. But very, very soon, he'll be forced to come out from under the rocks and then I will smash him like the bloody cockroach he is."

"Very good, Charon. You've always been thorough," smiled the Pope.

"Incidentally," added Kostos, "my dear Russian friends have given us a gift of 10 very powerful suitcase nuclear bombs. Thanks to our ever-fervent Jihadists, who believe they're serving Allah, each of those bombs will soon be hidden in strategic locations in 10 of America's largest cities, ready to be detonated on my command. They will light the skies from New York to Los Angeles, and from Chicago to Houston if my friend, President Hunt, fails to stop the American government from interfering with our coming conflict in the Middle East. If they take one step toward supporting Israel when everything breaks loose, I assure you, they will be so overwhelmed by the chaos I'll create within their own borders that they won't care what happens in the Middle East."

"And I understand you're going to Camp David in two days to meet our friend, President Hunt," quipped the Holy Father.

"Yes, I am, Your Excellency," returned Kostos.

"Very good my son, very good," the Pope said as he stood pointing to two large doors at the back of his residence. "Our time is short. Shall we pray our father's blessing upon our work?"

Kostos nodded agreement and followed the Pope through the doors and into the small but ornate private chapel of the Pontiff. The Pope stopped to close the large double doors and followed Kostos to a dimly lit, elegant altar. A prayer station was built into the altar with a padded kneeling cushion upon which both men knelt.

But the beautiful three-by-four-foot emerald and ruby encrusted gold crucifix that had hung above the altar for 200 years was gone.

In its place hung the horned head of a freshly slain goat, still dripping with blood.

President Carr, Dr. Cohen and Dr. Minay had moved to the modest cafeteria facilities to have coffee and continue their discussion. There was no one else in the area, so the men sat alone at a table, each with a cup of fresh coffee.

Dr. Cohen resumed the conversation. "So, Mr. President, as a physicist, you're familiar with 'thesis-antithesis,' are you not?"

"That I am, Doctor," returned Carr. "For every point there is a counterpoint or, in other words, a corresponding opposite, like cold and hot, matter and anti-matter, light and dark, and on and on. Right?"

"That is correct," the doctor answered. "Now, Mr. President, if you would extrapolate that principle into quantum terms, regarding Bohm's theory, you'll see there are point-counter points on that level as well. Negative-positive, good-bad, and, if one takes it to the extreme, which true science demands, you've God and anti-God.

"Thus woven into the human genome is the capacity to make moral judgments. Hence, we instinctively know, on a fundamental level, right from wrong. For example, we can watch the actions of Hitler and conclude he was evil. And we can conversely conclude that one who willingly sacrifices his own life that others may live is righteous, or the opposite of evil."

"So, if I'm understanding you," the president asked, "you're simply saying that the conflict in our physical world is the result of a conflict between opposing forces in the corresponding dimension of the spirit world?"

"Yes," replied Dr. Cohen, "and that fact is not something one needs to accept by faith alone. Bohm and others have proved the theory they proposed."

"I suppose that's why," shot back the president, "that long before I studied physics or ethics, I believed in absolute right and absolute wrong. As a boy stealing cookies from the cookie jar, I knew it was wrong."

"And that's because," added Dr. Minay, "a Designer encrypted into your DNA the cognitive power of discernment. Innately, honest observers understand that there is no moral relativity."

"All right," concluded the president, "so I accept the premise that there is absolute right and wrong, although, which one is which is not always easy to know in the world of politics. It can be confusing."

"But it doesn't have to be," explained Dr. Cohen. "You find it that way because the art of politics is compromise. Diplomacy, in the end, must tolerate varying shades of evil in order to secure temporary goals. But in the spiritual dimension or, if you would, the real world, truth will not compromise, under any circumstances, with evil or error. It just is and we either accept it, reject it, or in some cases, attempt to redefine it."

"Okay," the president returned, "so the bottom line is, you believe the spiritual forces behind our physical world are actively engaged in our current reality."

Dr. Cohen answered, "'Engaged' is a good description of what's happening. The two power bases at work all around us are engaged in a great warfare against each other for supremacy in our world and in the hearts and minds of humankind."

The president set his coffee cup down, leaned back, and said, "Back to these prophets you speak of. They foretold everything about this universal conflict and how it will end?"

Dr. Minay responded, "Thousands of years ago, these prophets wrote down the revelations given to them by Jehovah God. And, yes, they not only told us what would happen, but how to know when it's going to happen. And, Mr. President, our time is very short."

"And of this you're sure, I mean, according to what your prophets wrote?" Carr asked. "Surely, you know I am not a Bible scholar, nor is ancient prophecy one of my strong points. But I am convinced enough to listen to your explanation about what exactly your prophets told you is about to happen. And no more talk of quantum theory or ethical dilemmas. I want to know exactly what's going on right now. Then I'll decide whether to cast my lot with the rest of you crazies or to get the heck out of here. So, make it short."

Dr. Cohen nodded, "By necessity it will be short. We've very little time before it will be too late. So let's begin and hope that you're a very quick study, Mr. President."

Leah and Brad had interrogated the prisoner that he had tagged as Igor for nearly four hours. They were beyond shock at the information they had gleaned. Having completed the interrogation, they contacted the CIA's Rome office explaining the situation to the Chief of OPS. The CIA had picked the man up and whisked him away to his nice, new quarters in Guantanamo, Cuba.

After everyone left, Brad and Leah poured themselves a cup of coffee and wandered out the back door onto the decking, from which one could see the city lights of Rome's west side.

"So," Leah said, "Kostos' boys are the ones who tried to kill you when you arrived in Tel Aviv. Then he paid those Hamas thugs to get rid of both of us in an effort to keep poor Hussein's intel from reaching my government. And all this chaos around your President Carr's disappearance and the murder of Pope Baranoldi can be contributed solely to Kostos. It's beginning to make sense."

They stood at the deck's banister, looking out at the city of Rome, bathed in the light of a full moon and a billion twinkling stars on a cloudless night.

"It may make sense to you," Brad responded, "but I think our friend,

Igor, is nuts. He truly believes this Kostos guy is some kind of a god. He's terrified of the man. But if even a third of what Igor said turns out to be true, then Kostos' tentacles reach a lot further than anyone can imagine. I guess we're obligated to report our findings, but I'm not sure who will believe us."

Leah, staring off into the night, stood with her arms crossed, "No one…almost no one will believe us."

Brad snorted, "Hey, I'm not sure I believe it."

Leah, staring out into the night, soberly answered, "But, it's true. All of it. That and a whole lot more."

Looking over at her, Brad asked, "What?"

Quietly, Leah murmured, "It is written."

"What are you talking about?"

Tired beyond words, she yawned and simply said, "Maybe later. I'm exhausted and need to go to bed." Yawning again, she slowly walked back toward the house.

Frustrated with the conversation, Brad stopped her with his hand on her arm and turned her toward him. "Leah, if you don't mind, I'm really tired of mind games. Ya know, my whole career, in fact my whole life, has revolved around cloaks and daggers, secrets, and mystique. I've gone to bed almost every night not knowing if I'd live long enough to go back to bed the next night. I'm so very tired of this non-stop rat race.

"Ya know what I want? I want to start dealing with everyday, normal, real things, unimportant stuff. I'm tired of trying to save the world. I want to base my life on something I know to be true and on something I believe in, not what I suspect."

Leah was a bit taken aback. "Is there anything you really know and believe in?"

Gazing out at the city's sparkling night lights, Brad spoke softly. "One thing I know for a certainty, Leah, and that's for the first time in a lot of years, I've really messed up."

Leah looked over with sincere concern. "How? How did you mess up?"

He looked back at her and answered quietly, "I messed up when

I lowered my defenses and allowed my feelings for you to…to, uh.… Look, Leah…" Brad gently turned her to face him. "…I've fallen in love with you, and I'm sorry. I've no right to even tell you. I mean, we're professionals and all…but…but you're everything, and more than I've ever dreamed of…except for that blasted nine-millimeter, and I don't really expect you to return my feelings but…"

Leah's eyes were filling with tears as she reached up and placed her index finger to Brad's lips, quieting him in mid-sentence.

She then leaned forward and kissed his lips as gently as a landing butterfly that refused to linger. Then, wiping the tears from her cheeks, she spoke softly, "Some things can just never be. It doesn't matter whether I share your feelings. Some things just can't be." And she turned away from him.

But Brad very tenderly turned her back to face him, looked deep into her eyes, and asked, "Why can't it be? Is it because I'm not Jewish? Hey, I'll convert. Whatever it takes. Listen, Leah, I love you. I want to spend the rest of my life with you—and not the kind of life where we run all over the world chasing the bad guys, sometimes not even being sure who the bad guys really are. I want to settle down, get an eight-to-five, have a family, get a dog that won't fetch. I want to live like regular folks…I…"

"Brad," Leah interrupted, "it isn't because you're not Jewish. Ever since I was a little girl growing up on that kibbutz, I've dreamed dreams like yours, but we, I mean you and I…it's just not meant to be."

Brad, hurt and rejected, sighed heavily and turned back to stare at the city. "I see. So there's someone else…a man back in Israel, I suppose."

Leah turned away so Brad would not see the tears flowing down her reddened cheeks, "Yes, that's it Brad. There's another man. But it's not the way you think. It's…it's my commitment to…oh, Brad, I'm so sorry…but yes, I do belong to someone else."

Hurt and confused, Brad turned back toward the house, walked across the deck, and reached to open the door. Just before entering, he turned back and said quietly, "I know there's something you're not telling me, but that's okay. You don't owe me an explanation. I accept the fact that you've already found the man of your dreams, and I truly wish you well.

"So, I'll conduct myself professionally while we complete our mission, then we can amicably go our separate ways. And I'll never bring this up again. Good night."

Brad smiled sadly, turned and entered the house, softly closing the door behind him.

For a few minutes, Leah stood, gazing up at the blanket of stars. To her, they looked like a host of diamonds laid out on a background of black velvet.

As her tears continued their course down her cheeks, she wept and whispered, "Oh God…how I need You now."

TWENTY-ONE

The men sat in chairs in front of CIA Director Pratt's desk. Present at the briefing were Secretary of State James Parlay, Secretary of Defense Carl Bates, and Chairman of Joint Chiefs Admiral Withers. The National Security Advisor, because of previous commitments, was unable to attend.

An hour and a half earlier, they had all sat in the White House meeting with President Hunt, where they had been snubbed, rebuked and humiliated by the president who claimed he had no time to listen to the urgent CIA briefing.

"First," began Director Pratt, "welcome to Langley, and I thank you for coming. I think it's fair to say that all of us are in a state of shock over what we experienced at the White House today."

Secretary of State Parlay was beside himself, "Pratt, in my 33 years of service to this country, I've never witnessed a more irresponsible and completely insane response to a clear state of national emergency than the one we just witnessed by this president. I had our people send the invitation to Kostos to meet Hunt at Camp David. The response was an immediate acceptance. But if that meeting takes place, I will submit my resignation."

Pratt quickly responded, "James, all of us understand your anger, but I beg you to hold off on any resignation, at least until we get a grip on this thing."

"I'll tell ya one thing, Pratt," put in Admiral Withers, "not one of us wants anything to do with the policies Hunt is pursuing and unless something changes very quickly, I too, will be out of here."

"So, Pratt," asked Secretary of Defense Bates, "why'd you ask us here?"

Everyone fell silent as Pratt leaned forward. "Men, everything you hear in the next few minutes is highly classified.

"With that in mind, I want you to know that this agency has over 1,000 agents running all over Europe, Russia and the Middle East who are focused like lasers on events and persons at the center of our current concerns. Intel is now swamping our analysts, who are all working double shifts just to keep up.

"In the last 24 hours, we have uncovered a conspiracy against our nation and world unprecedented in scope and scale."

Admiral Withers injected, "Pratt, are you suggesting that there's more than what we've already heard at the White House today?"

"Admiral," answered Pratt, "the answer is yes, and as you witnessed yourself, I have repeatedly attempted to convey this intelligence to Hunt so that he could instruct the cabinet, agencies and military to take the appropriate actions. Obviously, he refuses to hear or even read the entire briefing."

"Do continue, Mr. Director," added Secretary Parlay.

"Thank you," continued Pratt. "We have indisputable proof that Charon Kostos is a conniving liar who has used deceit, personal charisma, blackmail and even murder, in order to create the most diabolic and powerful economic and military coalition in the history of the planet."

"That's quite an assertion, Pratt," jumped in Parlay, "considering the likes of Julius Caesar, Attila the Hun, Stalin and Hitler."

"Mr. Secretary," Pratt came back, "those despots pale in comparison. If you'll look at the file I left on your chairs, I'll explain."

Each cabinet member opened the folder he held, as Pratt continued.

"Kostos' IFN, which began with a small inconsequential federation of European nations, has expanded its base, borders and power structure. He's done it all while publicly preaching peace and prosperity and secretly practicing mayhem, assassinations and deceit.

"While we've been mourning the death of a president and reestablishing our government, Kostos has dismantled NATO and diplomatically overpowered the United Nations and the European Union.

"While we've been preoccupied with stabilizing our economy after Carr's demise, and restoring the nation's confidence in state and federal governments, Kostos has added the Balkans, Russia, and almost every Arabic nation on Earth, with the exception of Saudi Arabia, to his personal kingdom."

"We're aware of our miserable failings, Pratt," jumped in Secretary Bates. "Is there more?"

"Unfortunately, yes," added Pratt. "Your file will give you the details, but in short, we've got new proof that Kostos hired Islamic Jihadists to bring down Air Force One in an attempt to assassinate President Carr."

"What are you talking about, Pratt?" shouted a disbelieving Admiral.

"And that's not all," Pratt continued. "The man has been behind the deaths of 11 heads or future heads of state in the last 36 months, including the murder of Pope Baranoldi."

Pratt could tell by the expressions on the faces of the others that they were shocked at what he was telling them.

"Further, gentlemen, Kostos is a man with almost unlimited resources and remarkable—almost supernatural—diplomatic and organizational skills."

Pratt stopped, picked up another file, and handed each man a copy.

Continuing, Pratt said, "This is an addendum to the file you've already received, another the president refused to read and sent back to my office unopened, and thus not acted upon. It contains information critical to our national security and gives irrefutable evidence that we now face a very real, clear and present danger."

Secretary of State Parlay was thumbing through the file. "Is this just speculative or absolute?"

Pratt answered, "Sir, it's absolute. As you'll see upon reading it, approximately 45 days ago, behind very closed doors, Kostos' IFN with their newest member, the Russians, signed a secret defense pact with Iran, Iraq, and Syria. It radically altered the balance of power in the Middle East.

"Russia, as you all know, has been supplying the Iranians with help on their nuclear program for years, but they are now pouring technology, scientists and arms into Iran, while Syria is being flooded by Russian weapons and hundreds of Russian military advisors.

"It surprises no one that this exposes their anti-west, anti-Israel strategy. Now we've just discovered that hundreds, if not thousands, of upgraded Shehab-3 surface-to-surface missiles are being set up all along the Golan Heights that loom over the northwest borders of Israel. These missiles not only threaten Israel, but can also hit our own bases as far away as West and Eastern Europe and Central Asia.

"In short, Kostos' alliance has loaded guns now pointed at U.S. bases all over Europe as well as his own European allies just in case they waver in their commitments."

Admiral Withers was white with rage and disbelief. "This is mind-boggling. Where have our heads been?"

Pratt went on, "I think that's obvious, Admiral. Still bleaker is the fact that the president of Iran believes he has been ordained by Allah to fulfill Koranic prophecies and to start an apocalyptic war to usher in their Muslim messiah, 'Mahdia.'

"Two weeks ago, the Russians completed a project in Syria. They've installed an air defense system known as S-300 PMV-2 geared to knock down ballistic missiles fired from Israel or their allies. That system is far superior to our Patriots.

"And you're all aware that hundreds of thousands of Russian, Syrian, Iranian and other Islamic nations' troops, with all their armor, combat aircraft, and tanks are slowly moving closer to Israel's borders. That happened while something or someone figured out how to blind our spy birds."

"This is staggering, Pratt. And the president refused to even look at this? That's treasonous," roared Withers.

"Well, I have two other quick items," Pratt went on. "First, we've solid reasons to believe President Carr is still alive and is either being held hostage or is injured and can't make contact."

"Pratt, I saw the wreckage of Air Force One. No one survived that crash," Secretary Bates said, shaking his head.

"But," Pratt admonished, "we believe Carr somehow did, and I've got the best agents on the planet looking for him this minute."

"Why would Kostos want Carr dead?" asked Parlay.

"I think," answered Withers, "it's obvious. Carr wouldn't have tolerated the shenanigans Kostos has pulled. Carr would've kept NATO and the UN on their toes and cut Kostos off at the diplomatic pass long before an expanded IFN could've gotten off the ground."

"You're exactly right," agreed Pratt. "Now for the bad news. Kostos, again using terrorists, has 10 nuclear warheads with substantial yields on their way to the U.S. The plan, according to our sources, is to plant them in 10 of our largest cities to be used as blackmail to keep the USA from interfering with Kostos' Middle East plans."

"This is too much!" yelled Bates. "Where are these nukes now?"

"We believe," Pratt said, "they're coming in on oil tankers or freighters. That's the most unsecured area of our security net."

"Well, there's one good thing," Admiral Withers added. "We have six nuclear subs, including the new USS Texas that can detect radiation miles away from its source. There's not a hole deep enough to stop our new technology from sniffing those suckers out long before they reach American ports. I'll order those subs into position off our most vulnerable ports of entry."

"Excellent, Admiral," joined in the Secretary of State, "but we need you to order a new Def Con status for our military worldwide now!"

"Mr. Secretary," the Admiral responded, "that order must come from the Commander in Chief."

"Unless," Pratt jumped in, "the Commander in Chief is incapable of responding. Then, according to the Constitution, in the case of a national emergency, the Secretary of Defense can order it done."

"But the president isn't incapacitated," answered the Admiral.

"I think he is," Pratt returned. "All of you heard him. He said he had no time to deal with all this because he was 'too busy' with a head of state and then clearly told us, twice, to get back to work. It's clear that he's not got the schedule capacity to handle the situation. The last thing he said to us was to 'go back to work.' Technically, he delegated to us the job of dealing with this intel."

The men all looked at each other, nodded, and agreed that they should move in concert to protect the country.

"Before we go about the task of ruining all of our careers, Pratt," Secretary Parlay asked, "what are the odds of finding and restoring Carr to the White House before all this hits the fan?"

"I've got our best people on it and our Israeli friends have lent Mossad assets to us as well. If Carr's alive, we'll find him."

Pratt was cut off by the Admiral, "And if we don't?"

"If we don't, Admiral," answered a solemn Pratt, "then our careers will be the last thing we'll have to worry about."

The sun rose brilliantly over the City of Rome. Brad and Leah had both risen early. They were scheduled to leave at 7:00 a.m. to follow up on a lead gleaned from Leah's interrogation of Igor.

Terrified at the consequences for failing to talk, the prisoner had spilled everything he knew. Along with the additional info about Kostos' complicity in numerous terrorist acts, they also learned that very recently a Kostos mercenary named O'Donnell had led an assault somewhere in Italy on a compound in an effort to kidnap a VIP whose name Igor did not know.

He did, however, know that the assault had failed and that two snipers had escaped while the rest of the team had been killed. He knew that one of those snipers, another Irishman, ran a pub in the small village of Magilano Romano, 40 to 50 kilometers north of Rome.

After finishing with Igor and sending him off with local CIA people, they knew they had to get to Magilano Romano and find that sniper. He could tell them where Carr was being held.

At 6:00 a.m. Brad stood in the kitchen pouring himself a cup of coffee when he looked up and saw Leah entering already dressed and ready to go.

"Well, good morning, Miss Levy," Brad chirped. "Can I pour you a cup of Italy's finest?"

Leah, thankful that Brad seemed over the sting of the discussion the night before, answered, "Why, thank you. I'd love a cup."

Brad handed her the cup of coffee. "Looks like you're chomping at the bit to go out and save the world from evil."

Unable to ignore the stress she felt from their talk the night before, Leah said, "Brad, about last night. I'm very sorry about how I handled that. I was just so, surprised by what you said and I just feel like I owe you an explanation. So if..."

"Whoa, girl," Brad interrupted. "You owe me nothing. I never should have said those words. So let's make a deal. Let's play like it never happened and I promise you it will never happen again, okay?"

Again, not knowing how to respond, Leah, standing with her coffee in hand, nodded, "Okay."

"Now, since we're both already up and at 'em, I'll go get the car keys while you finish your coffee and I'll see ya at the car in, say..." Brad glanced at his watch... "10 minutes?" He smiled and turned, leaving the kitchen.

Ten minutes later they were in the Bemer fighting morning rush hour traffic as they drove north on Via Flaminio, which would shortly turn into Expressway 3. It would take them to the village they sought.

Leaving the city, they rode through the magnificent Italian countryside. The small family farms, meticulously groomed on the gently rolling hills were as beguiling as they were beautiful. The old olive tree groves and ancient landmarks, along with the nonstop idyllic scenery, provoked images of an Italy long past.

"This is one of the main routes used by Hannibal on his long march to conquer Rome," mused Leah as she drank in the scenery.

Brad quickly added, "It was also the route the mongrel Nazis used to run away from the Allied invasion to the south, in World War II. But back to Hannibal. Correct me if I'm wrong, but wasn't he the first general to bring an army over the Alps and into Italy?"

"That he was," answered Leah. "He hated Rome. And Carthage, his home country, also hated Rome. Rather than risk a frontal assault on the beaches of southern Italy, Hannibal marched his massive army over the Alps. The attempt cost him dearly. He lost 40 percent of his army and a significant number of his elephants. He used the beasts in battles and it terrified his enemies."

"And his assault on Rome?" asked Brad. "How'd it go?"

"Well," Leah returned, "for years he ran around the Italian countryside pillaging and only once approached the walls of Rome. He never did attack. The city walls were far too intimidating for him to order an attack. Eventually, Carthage ordered him home."

Brad broke in, "Our exit is coming up next. From there it's only four or five clicks to Magilano. But as soon as we're finished here, I'd like to know whatever happened to our friend Hannibal."

"Well," sighed Leah, as she checked the clip on her nine-millimeter, "Mr. Hannibal had an ignoble end to his otherwise illustrious career. Now, to the business at hand. Let's hope this guy is a true mercenary and not a bona fide believer."

Within minutes they pulled into the gravel parking area in front of a single story building on the outskirts of the village. The large sign across the top of the building read *Café de Magilano Romano*. Two other cars were in the lot.

Brad stopped the BMW, shifted it to park, and asked, "Shall we?"

Leah nodded, "Yes, but once inside, you take the lead on rousting this guy and I'll cover your back."

"All right, let's do it," Brad agreed as they stepped out of the car.

Entering the roadside pub and food establishment they saw it had a low ceiling, shuttered windows, and the feel of a business not yet open for the day's customers. A young teenage boy wearing a long white apron was sweeping between the half dozen empty tables. Two very senior gentlemen sat at the far end of a long bar, drinking coffee and reading a paper. Behind the bar, a burly man was wiping off the top of the counter area. With cropped red hair, the guy was built like a pro-wrestler.

As the agents walked in, everyone looked up momentarily to check out the couple, then simply went back to their activities. It was obvious that they were used to hungry passersby and thirsty tourists dropping in at all hours.

Leah spoke quietly. "I'm going to the ladies room. Why don't you order me a cup of tea and ask a few innocent questions?"

"Can do," Brad replied as she entered a long hallway, and he took a seat on a stool at his end of the long bar.

The big man acting as the bartender had been bantering and laughing with the two older men at the opposite end. Seeing Brad take a seat, the man tossed his rag into a sink and sauntered over. Recognizing the barkeep as the man Igor had described as the sniper, the agent was sure this was the guy they were looking for.

"What can I get you and your lady friend this morning?" the barman asked with a smile. His Irish accent was unmistakable. "Our morning cook oughta be here any minute and our menu is over there on the wall."

Brad smiled broadly. "My lady would like a cup of tea, and I'll start with some hot coffee."

"Very good, mate. Tea and coffee coming right up."

As the barkeep turned to prepare Brad's order, Leah strode up and took a seat on the stool next to Brad.

Within a minute the man returned, carrying a tray upon which sat the coffee and tea. As the man set the cups in front of them, along with cream and sugar holders, Brad asked, "And what did you say your name was, good man?"

The man behind the counter looked up into the eyes of the agent and, as a hint of suspicion swept over his face, he snarled, "I didn't."

"That's right, you didn't, did you?" Brad retorted. "It's just that my lady friend here said she thinks you're the ugliest man she's ever seen and I'd rather call you by your given name than simply hollering, 'hey ugly,' when I need a refill."

The man looked stunned by Brad's remarks, then anger overtook the shock. He reached his massive arm over the bar and grabbed Brad by the lapel of his jacket. But before he could say anything to Brad, the agent had his Glock thrust up under the man's chin.

"Now, ugly, let's walk to the corner of the bar and around the end." Brad kept his weapon hard against the man's throat as he led him around the end of the bar.

Brad stopped and turned to the shocked people in the establishment who were looking in obvious fear. "If all goes well, I'll have your friend back in time to serve your lunch. So don't do anything stupid like call the local authorities or it won't go well for you."

Brad pushed the man out the door ahead of him while Leah followed and kept an eye on the others until the door slammed behind her.

Escorting their prisoner to their car, the man growled, "Who are you people? Take the money in the register inside. That's all I got."

Leah jerked open the back passenger door and Brad pushed the man inside, then climbed in next to him while keeping the Glock pointed at the man's head.

Leah went around, jumped in behind the wheel and steered the Bemer down the road in the same direction from which they had come.

Earlier they had passed an old deserted farmhouse and barn just off the main road a couple of miles back, and had decided to take their charge there for interrogation. Leah took the dirt road leading up to the old farm and, after a mile of bumps, pulled in between the old house and barn.

Brad told his prisoner, "Get out."

Leah had already opened the back door and the man complied.

All three entered the rickety, half-open door into the barn. Two windows on each side of the barn had long since had their glass broken out. On the right were two old stalls with moldy straw covering the barn floor.

Leah looked around, found an old kitchen chair toward the back of the barn, and dragged it into the middle of the open area. She also grabbed a long, old rope hanging on the wall in one of the empty stalls.

Once the chair was in place, Brad pushed his captive toward it. "Sit."

"Look, mate, I think you're making a big mistake. I'm a simple tavern manager. You..."

Brad cut him off mid-sentence. "Shut up!"

Leah was tying the man securely to the chair, with his hands bound behind him.

Once she completed the task, Brad bent very close to the captive's face and spoke authoritatively. "Now, we're going to play a game and you should know at the outset that I'm in a big hurry and I've no time to waste. Do you understand?"

"Well sure, mate. But I..." the man began.

"Then shut up and listen to the rules of our little game. I'll ask you a question and you'll answer the question. If it's the wrong answer, then I'll shoot you in the spot of my choosing. And each question you fail to get right, I'll shoot you again, in a different spot. Understand?"

Leah leaned against the wall, curious about Brad's interrogation techniques, sure that he was only attempting to strike fear into the heart of the captive with no serious intention of shooting the guy.

"Now," Brad said as he slipped out of his light jacket and tossed it to Leah, "let's play truth or consequences."

Brad slid back the action on his gun and, with a loud click, fed a bullet into the chamber.

"What's your name?"

The man was already sweating profusely. "My name is Emil. And you must be mistaking me for..."

"Emil," Brad interrupted, "just answer the questions. Now, Emil, seven or eight days ago you were with a group of swine who attacked a site somewhere in Italy. Most of your crew, including your illustrious leader, an IRA hit man named O'Donnell, was killed. But you, Emil, and another sniper escaped the massacre."

Brad stopped, bent closer to Emil, and said, "Now is that true or false, Emil?"

"Mate, I don't have a clue what you're talking about...but if..."

Before Emil could finish his sentence, Brad pulled the trigger on his Glock and blew off the man's right ear lobe. The sound, so close to

Emil's head, also ruptured his eardrum and left powder burns on his right cheek.

Leah, as surprised as their prisoner by the shot, nearly jumped out of her skin.

Emil was screaming in fear and pain while blood dripped from his wound.

"Now, Emil, I told you if you lie I'll shoot you. The next one won't be a simple flesh wound. Are you sure you understand?"

Emil was crying and stammered, "Yeah, Yeah, I do. What do you want?"

Brad leaned close again, "What I want, Emil, is the name of the place you and the other dirt bags attacked. That's the question. Now it's your turn again. Name that place."

In spite of the fact he was scared stiff, Emil knew if word leaked that he had talked, he would be a dead man. He thought he might be able to stall.

"Look, I'm not really too sure of exactly where…"

Once again, Leah jumped as Brad's noisy gun was fired. This time the bullet tore into Emil's left kneecap, shattering the bone and cartilage and making a horrible mess of it.

Emil screamed out in pain, "Ahhh! You're out of your mind, man!"

Leah and Emil both watched as Brad slowly took aim at Emil's right kneecap.

"No, no, don't shoot! I'll tell ya, just don't shoot me again!" Emil was crying, his eyes rolling in excruciating pain.

"Emil, you're not very good at this game, are you?" asked a very calm Brad. "I keep telling you the rules and you just keep lying. So I'll give you only one more chance. Tell me the name and location of the place you attacked."

"Okay, just don't shoot again! It's an estate 40 or maybe 50 kilometers dead south of Rome. It was called Castel Colledora, I think, way out in the country. It was very well defended, something we weren't warned about."

Brad patted Emil on the head and said, "Very good, Emil. See, you can be taught. Now, who runs the place, and why'd O'Donnell hit it?"

"Mate, you gotta believe me," pleaded Emil, "they don't tell us that stuff. We only get logistics, targets and such, that's all. I swear. And as a sniper I never got closer than a quarter of a mile to the gates."

He continued, panting each word, "One of the guys did tell me O'Donnell was gonna kidnap some VIP. And he said that the place was run by a bunch of dirty Jews. I swear man, that's all I know. Honest."

Brad glanced over at Leah, who was busy studying Emil's countenance. After a moment, she turned toward the barn doors and said, "He's telling the truth. Kill the slime ball and let's get out of here." She walked out.

"Oh, my God! Oh, my God! Don't do it! Don't kill me. I told you everything," Emil begged with tears and sweat rolling down his face and neck.

Brad returned his Glock to his shoulder holster, walked over, retrieved his jacket off a nail on which Leah had hung it, and said, "Emil this is your lucky day." Brad started loosening the tight ropes. "In an hour or two, you'll be able to work yourself free. Then you can crawl down to the main road and flag down some good Samaritan. But, be warned, you better come up with a good story about all of this that doesn't include us, or I'll let my lady friend come back and take you out."

"Okay, okay. God Bless ya, mate! I'll not say a word." Emil stammered through the blood- and tear-stained face.

Brad used a short piece of rope to tie a tourniquet just above Emil's shattered knee and returned to the car where Leah sat in the passenger seat. He got in and drove out to the main highway heading back toward Rome.

After a few minutes of silence, Leah spoke. "Brad, don't ever call me blood-thirsty again. You've clearly no patience in interrogations. And next time, I'd appreciate a bit of a warning before you fire off that bazooka you carry."

Brad taunted, "Dear girl, you're the one that said, 'kill him and come on.' And you call me cold?"

Leah sighed, "Mere bravado, Brad. My father used to say, the art of manhood is knowing how to moderate the rantings of an agitated woman."

Brad laughed, "Well, obviously, I haven't yet mastered the art."

"No, you really haven't," she answered. "So, where to now?"

"We're off," Brad returned, "to try and find a place called Castel Colledora, somewhere south of Rome. O'Donnell went there under orders from Kostos to find President Carr and kill him. I only hope we're not too late, and I hope we can find this place quickly."

"Don't worry," Leah sighed. "I know exactly where it is."

Brad turned to look at her to see if she was serious. Realizing she was, he asked, "How? How could you know where it is?"

Ignoring his inquiry, she told him, "Drive straight to the city and go south on the A-90 loop until you come to the Via Appia Expressway and follow the signs to Lago Albano. It'll take us toward Castel Colledora. It's about a 90-minute drive from here."

Brad was shocked at Leah's information. "So, do I get to hear what's going on or…?"

Interrupting him, Leah quietly said, "Brad, I've got something to tell you."

TWENTY-TWO

It had been a long day for Kostos, as well as for President Hunt. In the predawn hours they had both landed in their individual planes at Andrews Air Force base in Washington, D.C. They met, shook hands, and quickly jumped aboard Marine One, the Presidential helicopter, for the short ride to Camp David.

Numerous formalities had lasted most of the morning. Kostos was then entertained over a luncheon hosted by President Hunt and the First Lady, whom Kostos found to be a boring snob. That was followed by an obligatory press conference with a select group of national correspondents. It was now late evening and a formal dinner with entertainment had finally ended.

Kostos and the president were at last left alone in the Camp David Lodge, with the exception of the Secret Service Agent posted 25 yards away at the door. The two men sat at a small table in the luxurious lodge, each with an after-dinner drink of cognac.

Kostos spoke, "Mr. President, I thank you for your hospitality. My visit to your Camp David has been a rewarding experience. But now we do have a bit of business to discuss."

As the president sipped at his drink, he nodded, "We do indeed. You should know up front that many in my cabinet and a number of my advisors think I've lost my mind by inviting you here. They feel it looks as if I condone your actions around the world."

"Oh, Jordan," cajoled Kostos, "in the short run, our relationship may cost you a few insignificant political connections, but in the long run you will be rewarded in ways far beyond your wildest dreams for your faithfulness to our cause."

"That may well be," Hunt said through a forced smile, "but what little political capital I may have had coming into this job has just about been expended. I've congressional leaders from both parties questioning my wisdom in being seen with you. It's public knowledge that the IFN has become intricately involved in Middle Eastern affairs.

"Others are grumbling about your selective globalization objectives. And no one in this country, with the exception of a few One World globalists, are happy with your bourgeoning United States of Europe or the way you've seduced most of our allies in the Persian Gulf area, which you well know are strategic to our national interest.

"And, as if that weren't enough, you're far too cozy with that Russian viper, President Valenko. Kostos, your activities haven't just interfered with our nation's interest and security concerns, you are stomping all over 'em, with seeming impunity.

"So do try, sir, to understand why I'm so sensitive about what others are saying."

Kostos answered, "Oh, in time those fat cat, self-absorbed, self-promoting politicos and idealistic bureaucrats will come around to see things our way. In fact, my people are already in touch with your Senate and House leadership on an individual basis. It's being explained in the simplest terms why it's in their best interest to support their president."

"Kostos," hissed an infuriated Hunt, "you can't blackmail all of 'em. Some are squeaky clean public servants with pure motives and impeccable backgrounds."

Kostos laughed as he set his drink back on the table. "You are so naïve, Jordan. My people are very good at what they do. And you of all people should know that every man has his Achilles' heel. Of course, it's sometimes necessary to do a bit of entrapment or setup of those Boy Scouts, but in the end, they'll all be in my pocket or they'll be completely irrelevant."

The president was fuming and visibly shaking. "Look, Kostos, I don't want to hear about that kind of stuff."

The smiling Kostos responded, "Oh, yeah, I think that's what you guys call 'maintaining deniability.'"

"All I want you to do," continued Hunt, "is tell me why we had to see each other in front of the whole world and tell me what you want."

"Mr. President," Kostos, leaning back in his chair said, "the entire world needs to know without a doubt that you are a friend rather than a foe of the IFN. We want you to be our ally, not an enemy.

"Very soon I will be the most powerful man in the world. Already my organization is on the verge of becoming the new undisputed superpower on the planet.

"Even now Jordan, we've got the technological power and resources to completely destroy your economy, devastate your nation's infrastructures and, in short, relegate the great U.S.A. into a third-world entity."

Steamed beyond anger, the president pointed his finger in the face of Kostos and hissed, "You listen to me. You're dealing with things here much bigger than me. My Secretaries of State, Defense and the NSA are on the verge of mutiny. Our intel agencies, especially Central Intelligence, are probably conspiring against me and the Joint Chiefs are going ballistic over the way military assets are being shuffled all over Europe, Asia and the Middle East. People get scared and often irrational when the status quo gets upset.

"Frankly, I don't know how much longer I can keep the lid on things. All of this could spin out of control very easily."

"You are the president," Kostos urged. "Fire 'em all if it becomes necessary. Replace them with 'yes' men, but if that's not enough, well, I'm now going to provide you with added incentive."

"What are you talking about now?" asked a leery Hunt.

"This very moment," menaced Kostos, "Islamic Jihadists, under my control, are moving 10 powerful nuclear weapons onto American soil. They're to be placed at strategic locations in 10 of your most populous cities.

"If you fail, Mr. President, to control the hot-headed, narrow-minded, nationalistic hawks in your cabinet and Congress, and if our intel or military coalition so much as senses the very slightest twitch by American forces to interfere with our efforts in the Middle East to solve the Jewish problem, then I will personally push the button to set off the nuclear device being hidden in New York City. That will signal our boys to light up your cities from sea to shining sea. Your country will face a firestorm and a nuclear holocaust that will keep you out of my affairs for decades to come."

President Hunt sat breathless in stunned silence at Kostos' words, attempting to grasp the scope of what he was saying.

"And so, Mr. President, it's advisable for you to, what's the expression? Oh yes, 'toe the line.' You just keep being a team player. Buck up, my man. Don't be cowed by lesser minds. And remember, great will be your reward in our coming conquests."

Kostos laughed heartily, and downed the last of his cognac. "Now Jordan. I've arranged for my own helicopter to be here in six or seven minutes. So, with your kind permission, I'll borrow your driver and mosey on over to the landing pad."

Kostos and Hunt both stood. The president was still speechless, realizing he was now no more than a lackey to Charon D. Kostos. They walked to the door of the lodge, but as Kostos was in the doorway, he stopped, "It's been a real honor, Mr. President. I'll be in touch. Tata."

Hunt could only watch as Kostos got in the presidential limo's back seat and closed the door. He was still in shock as the long vehicle's taillights finally disappeared in the heavy brush and trees. The president turned and ran to the nearest men's room where, sick to his stomach, he lost his dinner.

Kostos sat alone in the back of the limo on his way to the helipad. He smiled, then quietly mused, "And soon, not only you Jordan Hunt, but a whole new world will stand in awe of my genius."

Secretary of Defense Carl Bates and Chairman of Joint Chiefs Admiral Withers had left the briefing at Director Pratt's office and coordinated orders to reposition two dozen surface ships and five nuclear attack submarines. The submarines were all equipped with the latest technology to detect radiation emanating from ocean-going vessels that might be smuggling radioactive materials. The ships and submarines were stationed on sea-lanes converging on U.S. ports, in the Gulf of Mexico, the Pacific Coast and all along the Atlantic Seaboard.

The recently commissioned and newest sub in the navy, the USS Texas, was part of the East Coast contingent. It was only the second Virginia Class Sub ever built, at a cost of $2.7 billion.

The CO was a decorated combat commander with more medals than his dress blues could hold. The handsome 48–year-old Captain Bill Tucker was already graying at the temples, but worked hard to keep his 6–foot frame in excellent condition.

He sat in his Captain's quarters perusing his orders and sipping black coffee with his First Officer, Clive Garrett.

"Well, one thing for sure," growled the Captain, "this is no exercise. So, Garrett, I do not want as much as an electric eel to get by us. If it's got a signature, I want it marked and plotted. Understand?"

"Yes, sir" Garrett responded.

"What's our position right now, Clive?" asked the CO.

"Sir, we are 180 nautical miles, north northeast of Charlotte, North Carolina. I'll have latitudes and longitudes to you in a moment. Currently we're at 100 feet depth, doing a figure eight coverage of our patrol area. Each full loop has us covering a 40-mile track. We've been holding that profile for the last eight hours, sir."

"And how deep's our water?" Captain Tucker asked.

"Sir," returned Garrett, "we've 1200 feet throughout our patrol route."

"All right, Clive." The Captain stood and walked over to his bed, where he plopped down. "I know you've had a long day, but I want you to go hang out for a couple of hours in Command and Control. I haven't slept for 36 hours so I'm gonna catch a few winks. Buzz me fast if our sniffers pick up anything. You're dismissed."

"Aye, aye, sir" Garrett gave a quick salute and did an about face.

The control room on the USS Texas is a dimly lit Command Center with 70 video screens lining a spotless interior. Sonar technicians wearing headphones sit monitoring computer screens tapped into the most sophisticated sonar and radiation detection systems on the planet.

Of the two smaller but adequate side compartments, one is dedicated to five control technicians in charge of firing Tomahawk cruise missiles and torpedoes. Every weapon is launched by a simple touch on the screen.

The second small compartment holds three more officers whose sole responsibility is to monitor variables in radiation levels coming from civilian or commercial vessels. If a ship of any size passes through their patrol area carrying any kind of nuclear material, these sensors would pinpoint the ship's coordinates and heading and mark it as a contraband vessel.

This is the job the USS Texas had been built for. Their assignment is to monitor suspected terrorists transporting nuclear weapons or their components on fishing trawlers, pleasure craft, huge oil tankers and freighters.

The USS Texas' hull is covered with the same kind of skin on the body of the stealth B-1 bomber, making it completely invisible to enemy surveillance. It is only the second submarine ever built without the standard iconic periscopes with lenses and mirrors that jutted up through the hull. Instead, video cameras connected to fiber optics are mounted on a scope known as a photonic mast. They work in tandem with sonar imaging and surveillance satellites.

Helmsmen no longer steer the submarine by using a yoke pushed up or down, as in the old subs. A joystick, like on a computer game, controls the sub.

The USS Texas has a new, special decompression chamber for the compliment of nine Navy Seals to be able to do quick, underwater, covert ops.

The entire USS Texas runs on the power supplied by a nuclear reactor that will not need refueling for 40 years.

Officer Garrett had just returned to the Control Center when he was stopped at the entrance to the room that monitors radiation levels by a seaman needing his signature on a report. As Garrett signed the report, he was startled by the soft beeping from the monitoring station indicating they were detecting a strong radiation read.

"Sir," a young seaman at the monitors said over his shoulder to the First Officer, "we've got signatures."

Garrett stepped into the room and went to look over the shoulder of the young sailor, "Okay, now tell me how many hits you've got."

"Sir, the most impressive hits are coming from the northwest, at 290 degrees, 25 nautical miles out…and we're picking up multiple signatures from that vessel." The seaman continued, "And we've got another hit, a bit weaker, 15 nautical miles dead east on a 340-degree heading."

By now, all the incoming data was being fed into the sub's relative data systems and being examined by computers and analysts.

Garrett reached over the seaman and grabbed the sub's comm phone off the counter. He pushed a single red button on the phone that buzzed in the Captain's quarters. "This better be good," growled the sleepy voice of Captain Tucker.

"Sir, Garrett here. We've got multiple hits from two surface vessels. You might wanna get up here."

"Mark and chart, Garrett. I'm on my way." Tucker had not bothered to undress before falling fast asleep. He grabbed his shoes and ran out.

First Officer Garret hung up the comm and asked the seaman at the monitor, "What's your name, sailor?"

"Kramer, sir."

"All right, Mr. Kramer," Garrett said loud enough for the entire section to hear, "which of these target vessels should we pursue first?"

"Uh, sir," Kramer came back, "I'd jump on the ship closest to us. It's only 15 miles out compared to the other at 25 miles."

Garrett shook his head. "Kramer, you remind me of the drunk who lost his wallet in a dark alley. But instead of searching the alley, the drunk decides to look for it down the road by the street lamp because the light is better there." Mild laughter filtered through the section.

Garrett continued, "So, Kramer, we do not go for the easiest. We go for the most threatening. And the most threatening is the vessel showing multiple hits."

"Yes sir, sir!" Kramer responded, blushing.

Just then, the seaman to Kramer's left spoke up. "Sir, we've sat. reads on the ship with multiple hits. It's a super tanker, the Sarkosa. The second vessel will be checked out by a Navy Cruiser in that area."

"Very good, sailor," replied Garrett. "Send the Sarkosa's name to HQ and let's find out who she is, where she's been, and where she's going."

Garrett heard the ruckus caused by the CO's arrival, then he heard the CO's voice, "Nav. Put us on heading, full speed at 100 feet. Let's catch up with that bandit."

"Yes, sir," came a quick response.

Garrett spoke to the Captain in a low voice as they stood in the center surrounded by very busy sailors. "Sir, now that we found some bad guys, what are our orders?"

The Captain replied, "Board and search."

Garrett had another question. "And what if they refuse us?"

The Captain, leaning over to study the monitors, answered matter-of-factly, "Then I'll sink their sorry rear ends."

Garrett knew that was about as profane as this Captain would ever get, but he also knew the Captain would sink the tanker without blinking an eye.

"Sir, begging your pardon," another young seaman walked up and handed Garrett a memo. "It's the info on the Sarkosa you requested."

"Thank you," Garret said as he grabbed the paper and read out loud for the Captain's benefit. "So, the Sarkosa's a super-tanker. Left port in the Persian Gulf six days ago; supposedly full of Omani oil, his first destination, New York."

"And just who owns that heap of scrap?" growled the C.O.

"Sir," answered Garrett, "it's registered to and owned by Tempco Shipping, eighth largest carrier of oil in the world. But Tempco is a subsidiary of a corporation called Worldco, which, according to our sleuths, is a cover corporation for the real owners, Kostos Inc."

"They got a full crew?" inquired Captain Tucker.

"Yes, sir," answered Garrett as he looked at the bottom of the summary. "It's a mixed group of Saudis, Congolese and Omanis. The Captain is a Sudanese by the name of Hallia Alwari."

Captain Tucker rubbed sleep out of his eyes. "So nav, how long till we catch her?"

"Sir," answered a second officer leaning over a plotting chart in the middle of the control room, "if the Sarkosa maintains speed we should be on her in less than 43 minutes."

"Very good," Tucker answered. "Garrett, tell weapons to charge up and remove safeties on two forward torpedoes."

"Yes, sir," Garrett answered, but then leaned close to his CO's ear and whispered, "Sir, begging your pardon, but if they've nukes and they arm 'em, or if those guys are suicidal maniacs, they may blow 'em if we attack."

"Garrett, we all gotta die sometime. Better those suckers go off 150 miles offshore than in downtown Manhattan. Our mission is to protect the shores of the United States of America and that's exactly what were gonna do!"

The next 40 minutes was a flurry of activity on the USS Texas, as it went through preliminary tasks of battle prep.

The Captain, returning from getting a cup of coffee in the galley, walked back into Command and Control as the navigator spoke up. "Sir, in two minutes and 20 seconds we'll be 400 yards in front of her bow."

"Copy that," hollered the CO. "Prepare to surface. On your mark, nav, take her up at that position."

"Yes, sir."

The next two minutes passed in silence. Then, the command was given to surface. The USS Texas broke the gently rolling surface like the 377-foot-long sea monster she is. To any enemy, and many friends, the warlike profile of the most powerful submarine on the planet was breathtakingly intimidating.

"I want all hands to battle-stations now!" yelled Captain Tucker.

Turning to his First Officer, he added, "All right, Garrett. Send a message by radio and signal lamps. They are to immediately stop their engines and prepare to be boarded by the United States Navy. Tell 'em to have their papers ready and to open all hatches in preparation for a search."

"It's on its way over, sir," answered Garrett.

On board the Sarkosa, the helmsman, first mate, and Captain Alwari were standing on the bridge when the USS Texas broke through the surface 400 yards in front of their bow.

The three men were shocked and awed by the sight suddenly looming in front of them.

Captain Alwari shouted, "It's American! Do they think I can stop this thing on a dime? Turn 30 degrees to starboard, now!"

Sarkosa's radio man, sweating profusely and obviously frightened, ran onto the bridge, "Captain, that's the USS Texas. The Americans are ordering us to stop engines immediately and prepare to be boarded by a search party. They say any threat to the Texas or its crew will be considered a hostile act against the United States and will be responded to with deadly force."

Alwari sneered as he stared out at the massive sub. "Helmsman, cut engines and bring us to a slow stop."

The Captain spit on the floor and addressed his radio man, "Go back and answer that son of Satan. Tell him we are in international waters and he's got no legal right to stop and board us. Tell him our cargo is oil, only oil. As a gesture of international goodwill, we're asking him to trust us and let us go on to meet our crucial deadlines."

Less than two minutes later the radio man came running back onto the bridge and read Alwari the American response to his previous message.

"I am Captain William Tucker of the USS Texas, an American fast-attack nuclear submarine. In response to your request for our trust, we will trust you. However, in the spirit of the old Russian proverb, '*dover-yai-no prover-yai*', we will 'trust but verify.'

"Failure to comply immediately with our demand that you stop all engines and prepare for boarding will result in the sinking of your vessel.

"You have three minutes to shut down your engines or the next sound you hear will be an American torpedo ripping into your midsection."

After 30 seconds, Alwari smiled, spoke into the ship's intercom and ordered, "Heave rope ladders over for boarding party. Do not resist the Americans."

Twenty minutes later, a contingent of nine Navy Seals and a dozen combat-ready marines in full battle gear boarded the Sarkosa and began a sweeping stem-to-stern search of the supertanker using sensitive radiation detection devices.

An hour and 18 minutes into the search, Navy Seal, Lt. Kenny Yates radioed the USS Texas.

"What do you have, Yates?" asked Captain Tucker.

"Sir," answered the Seal, "it looks like we've got six sealed boxes of radioactive waste material from a nuclear power plant in India. It's not, I repeat, it's not weapons grade. The ship's papers, which are all in order, show that the Indian government contracted the Sarkosa to deliver it to a nuke dumpsite somewhere in Eastern Canada. That's all that's here, sir. What are your orders?"

"Pack up your boys, Yates. Thank Captain Alwari for his cooperation and get back over here."

"Yes, sir, Captain."

Garrett looked over at his Commander. "We've been had, Cap'n. The Sarkosa is just a decoy and we took the bait. The real stuff is probably on the second ship we sent that cruiser chasing."

"I'm afraid you're right, Clive." The Captain turned to speak to the navigator station, "Get that cruiser we sent chasing after the other contact on the horn for me, now! As soon as our boys are back on board, let's go after that other ship."

"Yes, sir," answered a seaman. "Uh, sir, you've already got a call coming in from a Captain Leggett on the USS Capricorn whose chasing that first contact."

"Patch him into this unit," Captain Tucker said as he reached over and picked up a receiver.

"This is Tucker. What do you have out there, Captain Leggett?" The two captains had known each other since their days at the Naval Academy.

"I oughta torpedo that tin can of a boat you call a warship, Tucker," an agitated Leggett complained.

"What's the problem, Mac?" Captain Tucker asked. "Can't you catch a rusting ol' scow?"

"Bill, we've circled and crisscrossed and run figure eights for over an hour, all over and around the coordinates you gave us. If that 'scow', as you call it, was here, it's gone now. We've plotted every possible escape route he could've taken. Our air cover, spy birds and backup can't pick up a whiff of that ship anywhere."

"Okay, Leggett," Tucker sighed. "Send an all-points ahead of you to all-ports within possible range and stand down. And Mac, thanks."

"You got it Bill, Capricorn out."

Tucker and Garrett stared at each other, perplexed. Finally, Captain Tucker spoke, "Clive, I know we're not in the Bermuda Triangle, but something unnatural is going on. Ships of that size don't just disappear."

"Captain," Garrett sighed, "it couldn't have just disappeared. In time we'll find her."

As the CO turned to go back to his quarters, he paused, looked worriedly straight into Garrett's eyes, and said, "If my bosses are right, Clive, the one thing we don't have is time."

TWENTY-THREE

Sitting down at his desk in Jerusalem, Israel's Prime Minister Ehud Eliad, reached for the telephone ringing on his desk. The call had been prearranged by the Prime Minister's staff when they were approached by an unofficial envoy from Charon Kostos requesting a moment of the Israeli leader's time.

The Prime Minister picked up the receiver. "This is Prime Minister Eliad."

The cheery voice on the other end said, "This is Charon Kostos. I thank you, Mr. Prime Minister, for accepting my call. It's an honor to speak to you."

"The feelings are mutual, I'm sure," returned Eliad. "Now, what is it I can do for you, Mr. Kostos?"

"Oh, Mr. Prime Minister, it's not what you can do for me. It's about what I can do for you." Without waiting for a response, Kostos continued, "You see, it has come to my attention that a number of regional powers who have sworn to wipe your country off the face of the planet will soon be in a position to do just that. And I know this fact hasn't eluded you or you wouldn't have already called up all your reserves and placed your IDF, Air Forces, and Navy on a war footing."

The Prime Minister was not known for his patience. "Mr. Kostos, you're telling me nothing that by now most of the world doesn't already know. Is there anything else, sir?"

Kostos responded with false humility. "I do beg your indulgence, Mr. Prime Minister, but when it occurred to me how very few friends you have left in the world at a time when your nation is facing possible extinction, I just assumed that you would welcome a hand extended in friendship. After all, it has been brought to my attention that in the last 70 hours you have personally made seven calls to the Oval Office but President Hunt has been so busy with domestic affairs that he's had no time to talk to you or to return your calls."

An irritated Prime Minister coldly responded, "The affairs of the State of Israel are really none of your concern. Now, unless you have something of value to say, Mr. Kostos, this conversation is over."

Kostos smiled to himself. "Please, Mr. Prime Minister, a bit of patience on your part. It would seem that a man who faces insurmountable odds with over a million enemy combatants closing on his borders could find a few minutes to discuss options that could well save his country from annihilation."

The very angry Prime Minister came back, "You are known to many in the international community, Mr. Kostos, as a gentle, peace-loving man with remarkable diplomatic skills. However, our government is fully aware of your involvement with those nations who now threaten our country. Perhaps you could use your influence with these aggressors by having them stand down before things spin out of control.

"Further, Mr. Kostos, you may want to remind them that the Jewish State is not impotent in its ability to defend its borders and its people. You should tell them that if the State of Israel is forced to deploy weapons of mass destruction, their use will not be restricted to the invaders but we shall rain fire and brimstone on the homelands of each of these nations. If Israelis must die, they will not die alone."

"Mr. Prime Minister," Kostos put in, "I did not call to see who could rattle his saber the loudest. But what if—and mind you, I'm only thinking out loud—but what if there was a way to avoid all this death and destruction?"

Still frustrated, a very tired Prime Minister answered, "Please, Mr. Kostos. Do not toy with me. Get to the point."

"Very well, I am a man of peace and I want that for Israel, as well as for the rest of the world. But, as a statesman you realize, Mr. Prime

Minister, that in order to achieve that lofty goal, concessions have to be made by all parties. Do you agree, sir?"

The Prime Minister sighed. "I would agree that the Jewish people, in both ancient and contemporary times, have made enough concessions."

Kostos brushed aside Eliad's remark. "But there are ways to insure that Israel does not become a nuclear wasteland. War can be avoided."

"And," inquired a guarded Eliad, "how can this war be avoided, Mr. Kostos?"

"I believe I can convince the Muslim nations and all their allies to stand down if only you could convince your people to agree to the following conditions.

"First, Israel must immediately withdraw to the 1967 green line borders and surrender the occupied territories to the Palestinians.

"Second, Israel must surrender Jerusalem to an international tribunal and allow it to become an international city.

"Third, I will volunteer my services to negotiate an agreement whereby Israel will be allowed to rebuild their ancient Temple on the Temple Mount and have unlimited access to it. This is a dream that millions of your people have longed to see for centuries."

Prime Minister Eliad had heard most of it before except the promise of a new Jewish Temple on the top of the Temple Mount. He nonchalantly asked, "And who would protect these new borders and our rights to the Old City and the Temple Mount? Those who now hold the knife to our throats would never agree to a Temple or our perpetual access to the Temple Mount."

"Mr. Prime Minister," cajoled Kostos, "the IFN, I think you'll agree, now represents a very substantial military machine throughout Europe and Asia. I can promise you, we would be honored to serve as a partner to the Israel Defense Forces in the defense and protection of your borders and we can guarantee that any forthcoming treaties would be strictly enforced."

Prime Minister Eliad slowly responded. "Mr. Kostos, I am very skeptical about your proposals. But neither does Israel long to be caught in the middle of World War III. Your proposal will sound like a surrender to many in our nation. However, I will immediately take your proposals to the Cabinet. I'll need three days for our people to discuss and debate the matter. Then we will talk again."

They both agreed to dialogue again in exactly 72 hours, and hung up.

The Prime Minister looked over at the director of Mossad, the Foreign Minister, and the Minister of Defense, who had all listened to every word of the conversation.

Prime Minister Eliad spoke first. "Gentlemen, we've grave matters to discuss. May Jehovah God grant us wisdom."

The director of Mossad spoke up. "Ehud, I for one prefer death to entering a covenant with that jackal."

The Minister of Defense said, "We must never lay down our right to self-determination or self-defense."

"At least you bought us more time to prepare our defenses," said the Foreign Minister.

The Prime Minister looked resolutely at each man and spoke. "Yes, three days. But regardless of the decision, we must never forget our vow made after Hitler's Holocaust. We swore 'never again,' and now our will is going to be tested as never before."

Doctors Cohen and Minay commanded President Carr's undivided attention and interest as they continued to explain the agenda of Sodote Shalom and their reasons for saving and guarding his life.

"I do have questions," broke in President Carr. "Twice now you've quoted passages from the New Testament. The first was regarding the Apostle Paul's confirmation of Bohm's theory. My question is, as Jews, don't you reject the message of the New Testament?"

Dr. Cohen smiled, "Mr. President, those who reject the message of the New Covenant, or as you call it, the New Testament, are without revelation."

"Then," came back Carr, "am I to suppose you are Christians?"

"Sir," answered Dr. Minay, "we are what some call Messianic Jews. We are convinced that God has already sent the Messiah. He came as a baby, born of a virgin 2,000 years ago. He came to live a righteous life without sin, and to die a substitutionary death. His blood was shed as an atonement, or payment, for our sin. He was buried, rose again on the third day, and soon He will return. His name is *Yeshua Ha Meshiach*. He is not only the King of the Jews, He is the King and Lord of the universe."

The president nodded. "Forgive my ignorance, but are not Jewish Christians a rarity?"

Dr. Cohen laughed, "Mr. President, 2,000 years ago, Gentile believers were a rarity. I put you in remembrance, sir, that both the Old Testament and New Testament were revelations sent by Jehovah, almost exclusively to Jews, by Jews, for Jews about a Jewish Messiah. The spirit of anti-Semitism that has plagued the world for all time comes from a satanic hatred for all things Jewish. And it's all because Israel was God's chosen vessel through which to send the Messiah into the world. Anti-Semitism comes in many shades and colors. Even some contemporary Christian theologians are promoting the heresy that the New Testament Church replaces Israel in God's prophetic plan and that God has rejected all Jews.

"However, even their own New Testament states in Romans 11, 'God has not cast away His people whom He foreknew.'

"At the same time, we must acknowledge that salvation, though of the Jews, is not exclusively for the Jews. In fact, your Book of Romans further states, 'he is not a Jew who is one outwardly, nor does outward circumcision make a Jew but he is a Jew who is one inwardly.' I must say, though it irks many, that true Judaism accepts all of the promises and provisions of the redemption that God extends to all humankind. God's message is not exclusive. It is inclusive to all who believe."

"Alright," continued Carr, "so you—as men of science, not conjecture—have verifiable evidence that proves these prophecies are for this day and this hour. Is that correct?"

"That, indeed, is correct, sir," returned Dr. Cohen.

"Then," Carr pressed, "if I may ask, Dr. Cohen, what is the primary sign your prophets have given you that this is truly the last generation?"

"Sir, I know you are somewhat familiar with the history of the Jewish people. The Jews had been dispersed around the world for over 2,000 years, which was in itself another fulfillment of prophecy. Yet, the Scriptures declare that the most significant sign that the world is entering the end times would be the rebirth of the nation of Israel. 1948 was the first time in 2,000 years that Israel was recognized as a sovereign state. It was the only time in the annals of human history that a nation ceased to exist and then, after thousands of years, was reborn. Biblical prophecy became reality in 1948.

President Carr jumped in, "So you're saying that the prophetic clock began its countdown on the last generation in 1948? And so you believe our generation is earth's last? But it seems I've read that a biblical generation is about 40 years?"

Dr. Minay spoke up. "Actually a generation to the Israelites could've been either a 40-year span or, in other scriptural references, 'generation' means one lifetime or three score and ten.

"Also, Mr. President, many Jewish theologians measure the true beginning of contemporary Israel not 1948 but as 1967 when Jerusalem was taken back into the nation's life after we reconquered the Old City.

"However, either way, there are dozens of other prophecies that prove we are, indeed, in the last days. We will not attempt to give dates about when anything prophesied may occur. But Yeshua told us 'the signs' would tell us when the time is near."

"I understand," Carr nodded, "but I'm sure you know as well as I, biblical prophecy is interpreted in numerous ways by different people with varying views."

"Mr. President," replied Dr. Cohen, "there is no level on which truth is subjective. Each serious student of prophecy must search the Scriptures and vigorously maintain contextual discipline rejecting the input of those who would allegorize the content. The disciple, Peter, penned the words in 2 Peter 2:20: 'no prophecy is of any private interpretation.'

"In short, sir, all prophecy is absolute, linked with corresponding prophecies, and is indisputably reliable."

"If this is so," remarked the president, "then give me an example of other prophecies that have come to pass since the rebirth of Israel. Specifics, if you please."

Dr. Cohen, smiling again, spoke, "Mr. President, I will do so, but please know, we do not rely on one, or two or even six prophecies, but the whole. Now speaking specifically, our prophets wrote that as the last days begin the Hebrew language would be reborn. Zephaniah 3:9 says, 'Then I (God) will return to the people a pure language that they may call upon the Lord with one consent.'

"You know as an educated man that for centuries the Hebrew language had been a dead language, just as Latin. Even in Yeshua's day only the Temple priests spoke Hebrew. But God promised to give back the language to the people when they returned to their land.

"In the 1800s, Eleazor Ben Yehuda began to revive the dead Hebrew language and it was reborn. Since 1948, Hebrew has been the national language of Israel and five million Jews. So exact is it to ancient Hebrew, Mr. President, that if King David walked the streets of Jerusalem today, he would understand it."

"I must confess," said an intrigued Carr, "I know of no other language that, once dead, ever made a comeback."

Dr. Minay spoke up. "Another miraculous fulfillment of prophecy in our own lifetime is the agricultural resurrection of the land. The prophets wrote that in the last days the wastelands of Israel would blossom like a rose. In the late 1800s, one of America's great writers, Mark Twain, after visiting the Holy Land, wrote the book, *The Innocents Abroad*, in which he described Israel as a vast swamp and desert. He told how he had walked from Jerusalem to Tiberias, the length of the land, and saw only one tree, one donkey and one person.

"Today, Israel is known as the oasis of the Middle East. We supply 500 million Europeans with citrus, and every morning, two 747s leave Tel Aviv for Holland to deliver planeloads of Israeli flowers to market.

Most believe those flowers are grown in Holland, but they are grown in what was once Israeli deserts. Your American Universities study our agricultural techniques and confess Israel is indeed blooming as a rose."

"I am also aware of the remarkable Israeli agricultural miracle," conceded Carr.

"But," jumped in Dr. Cohen, "let me remind you, sir, that these same prophets predicted that many of our people would reject the true Messiah, but then foretold that in the last days God would raise up a believing remnant. All over the world, Jews everywhere are discovering Yeshua. Sodote Shalom is a small part of this awakening. The secret of peace, Mr. President, is Yeshua, the Prince of Peace, be you Jewish or Gentile."

Without waiting for a response Dr. Minay came back, saying, "Mr. President, indulge us just a little longer. Numerous prophets, especially Ezekiel, told of a massive invasion that Israel's enemies will orchestrate in an effort to destroy the Jews as the end time approaches. On the brink of total annihilation, what remains of Israel will be forced into a treaty with evil itself.

"In Ezekiel, the prophet actually described and specifically named the coalitions that will invade. Today, those very nations are gathering along Israel's borders with their armies, poised to strike. This, sir, is no coincidence. And these enemies are being manipulated by a prophesied world leader of great power."

"You have alluded to this evil dictator more than once, gentlemen. It's obvious you think you know who he is."

Both physicians nodded, but Dr. Cohen responded, "Yes, Mr. President, we do know. The prophets Ezekiel, Zechariah, Daniel, and others wrote much of this evil man. He's called 'the wicked one,' 'the prince to come,' 'Antichrist.' We're told he will experience a meteoric rise to power.

"He will rule a final world empire built on a 10-nation European confederation in an effort to resurrect the former Roman Empire. His kingdom, according to Daniel 7:23, will 'devour the whole earth, trample it and break it in pieces.'

"In Daniel's eighth chapter, the prophet wrote of him, 'and in the latter time, a King shall arise, having fierce features, who understands sinister schemes, his power shall be mighty but not by his own power. He shall destroy fearfully.' His power, Mr. President, comes from Satan himself.

"Surely you know that since your near-fatal crash, Charon D. Kostos has coalesced the European nations that once made up the Roman Empire. Just days ago, the UN and EU sanctioned his 10-nation confederacy of European countries under the notorious IFN.

"It is also a fact, Mr. President, that Kostos has murdered and assassinated dozens of heads of states and potential world leaders who would have resisted his efforts, all in the last 36 months. Your Air Force One was shot down by terrorists employed by Kostos. You stood as the greatest threat to his plans."

President Carr sat stunned. "Gentlemen, I'm on sensory overload. What you're telling me is beyond bizarre. How could one man accomplish so much in so little time?"

"Sir," responded Dr. Cohen, "John wrote in Revelation 13:2, 'and the dragon gave him his power, his throne and great authority.' It's taken supernatural power to achieve his goals. The 'dragon' is Lucifer, who has taken total and absolute possession of an evil man.

"And it's Kostos who now orchestrates the actions of nations poised to invade Israel. His goal is to enter the fray after millions are killed and offer to save Israel from total annihilation. Unfortunately, Israel, desperate for peace, will at some point enter into a peace treaty that he is destined to break, ultimately positioning himself to be worshiped as the world's true Messiah."

"It's unbelievable," marveled Carr, "but it's happening, isn't it? One man is manipulating the entire world?"

"Oh, he has help in his rise to power. John also wrote in Revelation, 'then I saw another beast coming up out of the earth; and he had two horns like a lamb and he spoke like a dragon and he exercises all the authority of the first beast before him and causes the earth and them that dwell on it to worship the first beast.' This false prophet who points the world to the Antichrist is a world-renowned religious leader, head of one of the world's great religious systems, called by the prophets 'the mother of whores.'

"Mr. President, according to the prophets, this false prophet is headquartered in Rome. While you were recovering, Kostos had the Pope assassinated. He was replaced by a man who is now working hand in hand with Kostos. This new Pope, who raised and prepared Kostos to fulfill his demonic destiny, now stands by his side."

Carr was visibly shaken. "But it's all unfathomable. It's unrealistic to believe that the governments of the whole world will surrender their militaries, their economies, even their sovereignty, to a man like Kostos."

"As unlikely as it may seem, sir," answered Dr. Cohen, "it's happening this very minute. Kostos has already, through his proxies, taken control of the World Bank, The International Monetary Fund, as well as the CFR and every other power center on Earth. Only a small group of nations have thus far refused to join his IFN."

"How can he possibly control all of it?" asked Carr.

"He does it," continued Dr. Minay, "by initiating a remarkable control system to enforce his global economic policies. Only those willing to verify their allegiance to his system will be able to participate in the economy. John wrote of this in Revelation, 'And he causes all, both small and great, rich and poor, free and slave, to receive a mark on their right hand or forehead and no one can buy or sell except one who has that mark or the name of the Beast or the number of the Beast, for it is the number of the man and his number is 666.'

"Of course, Mr. President, anyone who refuses to receive this PIN number or microchip or whatever new technology it introduces, will be marked for death."

"And you believe Mr. Kostos bears the mark of 666?" asked Carr.

"If I may, sir," Dr. Cohen added, "the writer of Revelation, John, clearly spoke the language of the day, Greek. Most scholars argue that he was also familiar with Hebrew as well. Both are alphanumeric languages. In other words, every letter in their alphabets also have a numeric value, thus every Greek and Hebrew name also has a numeric value.

"We now know Kostos had a Jewish mother and that even before his birth, he had been given a name. It was the Swiss priest who raised him who gave him the Greek name, Charon Dranko Kostos. By the way, keep in mind that priest is now the apostate Pope in Rome.

"Our researchers are very busy with a code that will soon reveal Kostos' true Hebrew name. But suffice it to say, even his Greek name has shadows of 666. Charon has six letters. His middle name, Dranko, has six letters, and Kostos has six letters: 6-6-6. Further, translating his name into the Greek origins translates the name Charon into Archon, with six letters, Dranko becomes Drakon, with six letters, and Kostos becomes Skostu, also with six letters—again, 6-6-6.

"If we translate those Greek names into English, Archon is Greek for Prince, Drakon is Greek for Dragon and Skostu is Greek for Darken. Each with six letters. In English, his name translates 'Prince Dragon of the Dark.'

"So, we find the sequence of 666 repeatedly, and we've no doubt that when our analysts break the code, his original Hebrew name will have a numeric value of 666 as well."

"This is unbelievable," the president softly said, "but still, even in my absence, how could the United States ever follow this maniac?"

"Sir," answered Dr. Minay, "your country has all but signed the treaty and joined the IFN in full partnership. Kostos has blackmailed your new president over his dark past and he's now done the same to most of the leadership in your Congress."

President Carr was dumbfounded at what he was hearing. "So, if this is all prophesied, then it must happen? Can't anything be done to stop the insanity?"

"It cannot be stopped, sir," answered Dr. Cohen. "But it can be delayed. And that, Mr. President, is why so many have willingly given their lives to keep you alive. If you're willing to cooperate, Kostos can be neutralized and made to start over in his efforts. That would give Sodote Shalom time to implement our plans to forewarn and prepare our people and the world. We have the means that can guarantee millions deliverance from the deceptions of this satanic seed. It would also buy you and your country time to make some critical decisions. As of now, the world at large has no clue as to the true identity of Charon Kostos.

"By all means," urged President Carr, "tell me your plan."

"We will gladly do so. But, please remember, we must strike soon. Further, sir, we've much more to tell you about this demonic psychopath that's even more sinister than what you've already heard—and time is not on our side."

TWENTY-FOUR

After interrogating the sniper, Brad and Leah drove away from Magilano Romano. Based on the information they pulled from Emil, they knew that President Carr was being held at Castel Colledora.

Leah had shocked Brad by informing him that she knew exactly where Castel Colledora was located. Further, she had reluctantly revealed that she had something else she needed to tell him. Five minutes had passed as they drove down the two-lane country road but Leah had yet to speak. Ten more minutes went by and still she sat quietly. Brad had decided to wait patiently, knowing the deafening silence would provoke her to speak far sooner than his badgering her.

Finally, staring out her passenger side window, she spoke. "I suppose I do owe you an explanation about my knowledge of Castel Colledora."

Brad nodded. "It would be nice to be in the loop of relevant intel, since my life is also at risk on this mission."

"I'm terribly sorry that I failed to mention certain things, but until now my personal life had no bearing on our mission."

"Really, Leah, there's no need to apologize. But it would be a great help if you could just explain how you knew not only where, but what Castel Colledora is, as well as any connection you may have to it."

"Very well." Leah took a deep breath, "I know the Castel as a clandestine research and medical facility owned and operated by a very low-profile organization called Sodote Shalom."

"Aha," piped up Brad, "there it is again, that term Sodote Shalom. It just keeps popping up, doesn't it? So, what is it?"

"Sodote Shalom," Leah began, but before she could finish her sentence, her words were drowned out by the roaring engines of a very low-flying helicopter, coming from behind them and passing directly over the BMW. It cleared the top of their car by less than six feet. Jolted by the sudden, ear-splitting noise so close to them, neither Brad nor Leah spoke a word. They watched in amazement as the aircraft sped down the narrow stretch of road in front of them. They kept their eyes on it as it did a quick 180-degree about-face and slowly headed straight back at them. When the chopper was less than a half a mile in front of them, Brad slammed on the brakes, stopping the car, and studied the helicopter.

"That's what the American military calls a Firebird. It's flown by a single pilot. It's a fully armed combat gunship, typically equipped with two heavy 50-caliber machine guns in its nose. Those pods hanging down near the skids on each side of the undercarriage hold a dozen tank-busting rockets each."

"Well," Leah returned, "thanks for the education, but it doesn't have any markings. Maybe we should decide real quickly what we're gonna do."

As soon as the words fell from Leah's lips, the fierce-looking helicopter, still very slowly moving toward them at 10 feet above the road, flared and gently settled 15 yards in front of the car. It hung in midair, suspended only a foot above the highway. As it held its position, stirring up a cloud of dirt, the agents knew they were staring at a lethal killing machine capable of erasing their existence within seconds. Brad and Leah could clearly see the pilot in the cockpit wearing the menacing black helmet with the dark visor.

Brad sighed, "Perhaps we should smile and wave before Darth Vader there decides to vaporize us."

But both of them heard the approach of yet another helicopter coming from close behind them. Turning around to look out the back window, they watched as a non-military passenger helicopter softly sat down on the road 15 yards behind them.

Brad looked over at Leah and jested, "If all these guys are with traffic control, then the Italians consider speeding a very serious crime."

"You can bet they're not traffic cops," Leah countered. "Someone still wants us out of the way very badly."

Their bantering was interrupted by a voice blaring through the speaker on front of the chopper behind the BMW. "We will not ask you twice. Get out of the automobile very slowly. Carefully place your sidearms atop your car and walk toward us with your hands up. Even the slightest effort to resist will result in your immediate death. Do it now!"

Leah looked over at Brad. "What do ya think?"

"Well, mi'lady," Brad answered, "I've no desire to reenact the final scene of 'Butch Cassidy and the Sundance Kid.' We are a bit outgunned. So I say, we do as we're told, discretion being the greater part of valor and all that."

Leah nodded, "Yeah, I'm a coward too. Let's go."

Both agents stepped out of the Bemer, gently placed their weapons on the car's roof and moved toward the waiting helicopter. The downdrafts of both helicopters were whipping up a blowing sandstorm, engulfing Brad and Leah as though they were in the vortex of a small tornado. Covering their faces, with heads down, they raced toward the chopper behind them. Just as they reached the right side of the aircraft, the door slid open. They both leapt in and found themselves on a bench seat, with Leah just behind the pilot and Brad behind a skinny, long-faced man holding a gun on them. The man reminded Brad of a mortician, with a dour countenance and morbid features.

The pilot was in a military flight suit, complete with a flight helmet and the standard-issue dark visor. The civilian was holding a .40 caliber Berretta on them.

Brad saw there was another unoccupied bench seat just behind them.

As the two agents buckled in, the helicopter lifted off. Brad noticed the war bird fly off in another direction. The man holding the gun was turned halfway around in his front seat so he could keep his eye and his weapon trained on the new passengers.

"It's so kind of you two to join us on our little morning excursion," the gleeful civilian mocked.

"Well," Brad retorted, "who could resist such a compelling invitation? However, I'm sure you understand, I just hate leaving my company car out on the road like that. You won't mind if I ring up my office and tell 'em where to find it, would you?"

Smiling back, the gunman said, "Oh, I'm sure they'll find it soon enough. All they need to do is tune up the right frequency and pick up the tracking device we stuck on your car last night while you slept."

Leah spoke up, "And just who is it you're working for, Mr…what shall we call you?"

Looking over at her with a lustful sneer, the gunman answered, "You can call me Conner, lovely girl, and my employer's name is irrelevant. Suffice it to say, you've both been a real pain to some very powerful people. And so, in short, I am to eliminate you, once and for all. And I do love my job, though I might find some use for you, dear girl, before you die."

Brad broke in, "Uh, Conner, and how does your boss, Kostos, want you to dispose of us?"

Conner smiled, exposing his rotting teeth and wicked grin. "Aha, so you know the boss. No matter. He leaves the killing to my creative genius. I thought, because it's such a lovely day, that you would both enjoy a dip in the ocean this morning. So, we're going to fly 20 miles offshore and drop you off for a swim, from an altitude of 4,000 feet. Hitting the water from that altitude is like hitting a concrete wall at 120 miles an hour. I'd say you are going to make a real splash. No pun intended."

The pilot leaned over to say something to Conner. In response, the gunman bent over and picked up some nav charts off the floor. Brad saw the pilot push a button that flashed 'autopilot engaged.' He knew that would keep the chopper straight and level while maintaining the proper preset course.

Conner was about to hand the pilot the charts he had retrieved. Brad knew it might be his last opportunity to disarm him. Just as Conner was handing the pilot the nav charts, Brad kicked at Conner's gun as hard as he could.

Conner's gun hand flew up and the weapon exploded with a furious discharge. The bullet smashed into the left side of the pilot's flight helmet. The pilot immediately slumped forward.

By then, Brad had leapt to grab the gun hand of Conner, in an attempt to wrestle the weapon free. He simultaneously threw his right arm around Conner's neck and reached around to grab tightly onto his head. As soon as Brad had the necessary leverage, he used all his strength to jerk Conner's head and neck fast and hard to the right.

To Leah it sounded like a thick, dry tree branch snapped as Conner's body went completely limp and the gun fell to the floor. She reached down and picked up the Berretta as Brad fell back into his seat, gasping for air.

Without batting an eyelash, Leah gave Brad that what-you've-done-now look and said, "Do tell me, Mr. Fuller, that you can fly a helicopter."

Brad took a deep breath, "Well, no. But I do have a lot of other redeeming qualities. I do have a private pilot's license, though I don't have a clue about how to fly one of these things."

"Great. That's just great, Brad. You kill our pilot and you can't even fly this thing. What were you thinking?"

"Hey," Brad said as he leaned forward to view the cockpit gauges, "we're okay for now. He put it on autopilot just before his unfortunate demise. And, for the record, I did not kill the pilot. As you well know, Conner shot him."

"Yeah," snorted Leah, "after you kicked the pickles out of him."

Brad, ignoring her, started pulling the skinny Conner out of the right front seat. "So why not help me move our creative genius. Grab his feet and legs and let's throw him over into the empty seats behind us."

After a minute of struggling, they succeeded, and Brad twisted himself into the right front seat. He began scanning the gauges. He knew how to read the numbers for speed, altitude and attitude as well as fuel gauges.

"Brad, look ahead of us."

Hearing Leah's words, Brad looked up from studying the gauges and saw her pointing out at the approaching coastline a few miles in front of them.

He turned to Leah as he thumbed through a flight manual he had found under his seat, "Make sure he's as dead as he looks, Leah. Check his wound."

Without hesitating, Leah reached over, unbuckled the straps of the helmet and removed it from the pilot's head. She noticed on the helmet, not only the entry point of the bullet, but an exit point just inches forward. Looking quickly at the pilot she saw the bullet had only grazed the man's temple, leaving the skin torn.

"Brad, I think this guy is alive. The bullet only grazed him. Probably the impact of the hit knocked him out. Hand me that bottle of water on the floor in front of you."

Brad quickly did so and Leah, opening the plastic bottle, poured some on the wound and then splashed more on his face.

The pilot responded immediately. Shaking his head and blinking his eyes, it took him only seconds to recognize where he was. He looked at Brad confused, then saw Leah holding the gun on him.

The pilot asked, "Where's Conner?"

Brad motioned toward the back, "He's taking a long, well-deserved nap in the back. Now I want you to take this thing off autopilot and head back toward Rome. We'd like to cancel our trip to the beach."

As the autopilot was turned off, the helicopter gave a jolt and the pilot was back in control.

"Now, sir," Brad said to the pilot, "do not do anything stupid and you just may live to see tomorrow. Fly straight to Rome. Land us at Da Vinci International."

The pilot, still a bit groggy, nodded, "That'll take about 15 minutes. So what do ya intend to do with me once we arrive?"

"Fact is, my man," Brad answered, "I've no use for you. So here's the deal. You get us safely on the ground at our destination. We'll get out and you can go on your merry way."

"Very good, sir," nodded the relieved pilot, "I can do that."

The pilot executed a turn to the south and just as he did, all three on board were astonished to see two fully armed gunships, just like the one that stopped the BMW earlier, hovering 100 feet in front of them. They heard the Firebird's order to the pilot coming over the cockpit speaker.

"To pilot of helicopter 5760. You will, without delay, follow us to Rome. You will land at the Vatican, helicopter pad 3. If you fail to comply and attempt to escape, you will be blown out of the sky. Tell your passengers we would do so now, but as a chopper pilot you're an asset our boss would rather not lose."

Brad realized they had no choice but to comply. "Okay, Mr. Pilot. Do as they say."

The pilot responded to the hovering gunships. "This is heli 5760. We will do as you've instructed."

"Very good, 5760," answered the gunship. "Follow me, and remember, it'll be a fatal mistake if you forget my twin, who will be behind you. Upon reaching the Vatican landing pad, you will land first while we circle and keep an eye on you."

"Very well. This is 5760. Ready when you are." As they fell in behind the lead gunship, Brad and Leah looked at each other, knowing that their situation had suddenly gone from bad to worse, much worse.

Neither of them had any illusions about what and who awaited them at the Vatican.

After spending all night in dialogue and preparation, Doctors Minay and Cohen, two of their trusted strategists along with Agent Spears and President Carr had decided on a plan. Its objective was to maximize the impact of Carr's sudden reappearing as president, and to *hopefully* strike a major blow to Kostos' goals.

In the dead darkness of a moonless night, a private tri-engine plane with the ability to land and take off on water silently glided across the still surface of Lago Albano. The large lake was very near Castel Colledora. The plane coasted up to a single wooden pier where the passengers waited. Once secured, the plane's doors swung open, allowing the passengers to board quickly and quietly.

With the door secured behind them and the airplane already moving into position for take-off, the five passengers sat down and began buckling their seat belts. The passenger list consisted of Dr. Cohen, Agent Spears, two ex-Mossad bodyguards who were now employed by Sodote Shalom, and President Carr.

The plane flew for almost four hours across Italy and over the Italian and French Alps. They landed in southern France at a large private airstrip equipped to handle corporate jets. The airport was only a short distance from the small French town of Chambery.

The passengers were met by two men, both Sodote Shalom operatives, who whisked the group away in a Mercedes mini-bus. They were taken to a remote resort owned by still another Sodote Shalom associate. It was a short drive of less than 10 miles from the airport to the private lodge.

Upon arrival, President Carr was escorted to a beautiful private suite in the exquisite facility, and provided with a satellite phone. The call was to be made to the one man in Washington, D.C. whom Carr felt he could trust. While Agent Spears took a position just outside Carr's spacious suite, the president made his call. After one ring, a receptionist answered.

"Central Intelligence Agency. How may I direct your call?" President Carr knew full well he could not reveal his identity to the woman.

"Ah, yes. Could you put me through to Director Pratt, please?"

The weary receptionist went into the spiel she gave, at least two dozens times a day, to people wanting to talk personally to the director.

"I'm very sorry, sir, but you'll have to go through agency protocol to be able to speak to our director. He's a very busy man. I'm sure you understand. So, I can put you through to a desk agent who will judge the merit of your request and help direct your call to someone who can answer your questions."

Carr was hardly used to being denied any requests. Temporarily forgetting how tenuous was his situation, he said, "Look lady, if I wanted to talk to a clerk, I'd ask for a clerk. So put me through to the director now. I'm calling from a very long distance. I'll hold."

The short-tempered, irate receptionist, tired of fielding calls day in and day out from nut jobs, lost her cool.

"And you can 'hold' till hell freezes over, young man. Just who do you think you are, the president of the freaking United States? And I could care less if you were calling from the backside of Mars, you're still not gonna talk to the director of the CIA.

"So, buster, I'll ask you one more time: Do you want to speak to an agent, or not? If not, then get off my phone line!"

The president was aghast. No one had talked to him like that since junior high. Suddenly it dawned on him what he must sound like calling the largest, busiest intelligence agency on Earth, demanding to speak to its director.

Toning it down, the president tried again, "Dear lady, please forgive my lack of manners and sensitivity. You are absolutely right. If you don't mind, could you put me through to an analyst named Cooper? And please excuse my previous attitude."

Mollified that she had clearly won the psychological tug of war, the receptionist responded with, "*Hmmph.* Well now, that's more like it, Mister. I'll direct your call to Mr. Cooper's desk, but next time you call here you'd do well to mind your manners from the get-go."

The president demurred, "Yes ma'am, you're quite right. Thank you." It occurred to him that he ought to put the woman in charge of all treaty negotiations.

The next sound he heard was the gruff voice of Agent Cooper, one of Pratt's most valued analysts. Carr had met him only once at an Oval Office briefing.

"Cooper here. Whatcha got?"

"Yes, Mr. Cooper, I'm a friend of Director Pratt and he's repeatedly instructed me that if I had critically important information for him, that I should contact him by calling you directly. Would you be so kind to get him on the phone?"

Cooper, instinctively suspicious, pushed a button on the side of his phone that triggered a trace on the caller's line.

"Uh, yeah. Well, ya see, the director is very busy right now and asked us not to disturb him. But if I knew who was calling, maybe..."

Carr had anticipated the question. All he could think of that Pratt may or may not recognize was the very first, now obsolete, security call sign that Pratt assigned him during his campaign for the Presidency.

"Yes, if you could just tell him that Titan is on the phone for him with an urgent update."

"Titan, huh?" Cooper repeated as he jotted down the name. "All right, Mr. Titan. Hold on."

Cooper knocked on Pratt's door, waited, but received no response. So he knocked a lot more vigorously, immediately wishing he had not done so.

This time it drew the response of a very irate boss yelling through the door. "What? It better be good. Come in!"

Cooper tentatively opened the door far enough to just stick his head in and whisper, "I'm sorry, Boss, but I've got some nut on the phone. Claims he's your friend and he's demanding to speak to you. I've got a tracer on the call but thought I'd better run it by ya."

"Coop," Pratt spoke from where he stood behind his desk piled a foot high with papers, "what is it about 'do not disturb me' that you don't understand?"

"I'm sorry, Boss. I'll get rid of him." Cooper quickly ducked out and gently closed the door. As he turned to walk away, he heard his boss yell again, "Coop, get your butt back in here!"

Cooper quickly returned to the door, slowly opened it and peeked in to hear, "Did the guy say who he was, or did you forget to ask that minor detail?"

"Uh, no, sir. I mean, yes sir, I did ask his name," stammered the intimidated analyst.

"And?!" an exasperated director shouted.

"Oh, he just said to tell you it was Titan calling, sir."

"Who?" yelled Pratt again.

"Titan, sir. He said to tell you it was Titan calling."

The director fell back into his chair with a look of disbelief. He turned pasty white as the blood drained from his face and he stared through Cooper.

After a moment of silence, Cooper asked, "Sir, are you okay?"

"Yeah," Pratt answered as he struggled to regain his composure. "Uh, put the guy through. And do it on a secure line. And kill that trace now!"

"Yes, sir." Cooper rushed to do his boss' bidding.

"Titan?" Pratt said out loud to his empty office. "No, it can't be him."

Just then, his secure line lit up with a beep to signal a call was waiting. Pratt slowly reached out and picked up the phone, saying, "Hello. This is Director Pratt."

The voice he heard on the other end was unmistakable. "My gosh, Pratt. You're harder to get on the horn than the president."

"Oh my! It is you," stammered a stunned director. "I can't believe it. It's really you. Where in the Sam Hill have you been, sir? I've had our people all over the world looking for you. Are you okay? Where are you now?"

"Get hold of yourself, Will." The president needed the director to focus, "I'm fine. I got a little beat up in the crash but I'm okay now and I'm in the good hands of friendlies. I'm at a very discreet location and that's all you need to know right now. So I want you to listen to me very closely."

"Yes, sir," said a still-stunned Pratt.

"No one, and I mean absolutely no one, is to know I'm still alive. Not yet. Do you understand me, Pratt?"

"Yes, sir, no one is to know. But, Mr. President, I gotta tell ya, all hell is about to break loose here and Jordan has flipped his wig. We gotta…"

Carr interrupted him, "Listen to me, Pratt. I know all about it, and we're going to do something about it real soon. But I'm going to need you to keep your head together and help me. We've got a plan to move, but it has to be at just the right moment."

"Sir, who is 'we'?" Pratt asked.

"Don't worry about that for now. Just trust me. There's something I need you to do very quickly."

"All right, sir. I've got a pen. Go ahead."

"First," continued the president, "I want you to dispatch a company Citation, with only a pilot and co-pilot. Tell them it's a priority one, covert op, off the books. They are to fly to southeastern France to the town of Chambery. Approximately six miles south of the town is a long, privately owned airstrip. Their flight plan should identify them as a corporate jet on a business trip.

"And Pratt, they must be wheels on the ground at that location in exactly 16 hours. Right now, I'm preparing to return to U.S. soil but I can't tell you where until I get there.

"Be absolutely certain that whatever pilots you assign have the highest security clearances. Do not tell them who they are picking up or where they'll be flying once they leave France. Just brief 'em on the urgent need for secrecy."

"Yes, sir. I know just the guys we need. What else, sir?"

"Second, whoever is left in the Cabinet that you can trust with your life and the life of your country needs to be brought together in your office for a conference call as soon as I reach American soil. Do not risk bringing in anyone you even suspect could be a security risk."

Pratt continued to jot down his instructions. "I understand, sir. We've still got Admiral Withers, and also James Parlay at State and Carl Bates at Defense. All of us have already been forced to color outside the lines. But other than those three, I trust no one.

"Hunt's surrounded himself with IFN supporters, party hacks and spineless yes-men."

"Okay, Pratt," responded Carr, "it's those three and yourself. Have them all at your office in 24 hours. I'll make my call to you guys then, but remember, do not mention to them that I'm alive or that I've been in contact with you."

"I understand, Mr. President," Pratt assured him.

"By the way Will, I've been briefed on what you've had to put up with and from what I hear, you've done one heck of a job. Keep it up and we'll pull the fat out of the fire."

The director answered with tears in his voice, "Thank you, sir. And sir, you don't know how good it is to know you're getting back in the driver's seat. Welcome back to the land of the living."

"Thanks, Pratt, but we've a whole lot further to go before this insanity stops, if it can be stopped. So, go get busy and I'll be in touch."

The line went dead and a still-in-shock Pratt hung up the phone and fell back in his chair.

He knew the clock was ticking.

TWENTY-FIVE

The pilot set the helicopter down gently on Vatican helipad number three. The landing site was atop an annex building behind Saint Peter's Basilica. As the skids touched the pad, four men in dark suits came running out from under a nearby archway. Each was carrying a handgun.

Leah watched the men approach. "Here comes our greeting party, the goon squad. Gee, I do hope they're as nice as the last guy we met here, that Father Portega fella."

As she finished her sarcasm, two of the suits slid her door open while the other two stood next to the exit that Brad would use. Leah slowly climbed out and the two men took her by the arms, leading her out of the prop wash.

Brad was pushing his front passenger side door open when he felt the pilot pull on his shoulder to get his attention. "Mister, I don't know what their beef is with you, but I want you to know I appreciate...ya know...your offer to spare my life if things had gone down your way."

Brad, looking back into the young man's eyes, forced a smile. "What's your name, pal?"

"My handle was Death Star. Ex-U.S. Navy F-16 jock, retired, turned freelancer. Real name is Chuck Burns."

"Well, Chuck Burns," Brad said as he hoisted himself into the doorway, "take a word of advice. Lose this crowd and this gig before your world comes crashing down on your head. You're working for a bunch of psycho losers."

Almost out of the helicopter, Brad glanced back at the pilot, who added, "Sir, you're a gentleman, and I do believe you're right." Pilot Burns gave a crisp military salute as the other two men grabbed Brad and dragged him away.

The two agents were led through the arch into a hallway. There they came upon a bank of elevators. Their escorts pushed the "down" button and within seconds, the door on the nearest lift slid open. The entire party stepped in as the doors closed behind them. There were no numbers inside the lift to indicate floor levels, but all sensed the rush of a rapid descent. After a few long moments the elevator slowed, then stopped, and the doors again slid open.

The agents were shoved out into what appeared to be some kind of underground tunnel system. The walls and low ceilings were rough limestone. The floor was just a smoother version of the walls. The area was dimly lit, with low-wattage bulbs strung far apart, hanging on exposed wiring run along the ceiling. It reminded Brad and Leah of the long tunnels that led them to the catacombs where they had the encounter with Father Portega.

Brad sensed they were at least 15 stories below ground level.

Once everyone was out of the elevator, their escorts shoved them to the far wall and through an opening. Just a few steps further was a narrow stone staircase going down. Everyone descended. Brad and Leah both silently counted the number of steps and the approximate number of flights as they continued their descent.

At the bottom of the stairs was a large chamber with tunnels breaking off in three different directions. Brad calculated that they had descended another eight levels on the staircase. The lighting was even worse in the large chamber area, and there was no light at all coming from the triple tunnels. The damp, musky odor was very strong and the narrow tunnels would drive a claustrophobic insane.

The largest of the four men pushed Brad and Leah toward the passageway on the right, then turned to address his comrades. "Mickey and I will take 'em the rest of the way. Youse two wait here."

The greasy-looking skinny one called Mickey reached down to a pile of old torches stacked against the wall and picked one up. "Someone gotta match?"

The big fellow pulled out a lighter and held it to the blackened tip of the torch, which flamed up immediately. The smell of burning kerosene and the accompanying black smoke caused everyone a moment of sneezing and coughing.

"Get used to it," the big guy sneered to Leah as she wiped at her watering eyes. "You two losers go in first and knock all them big, furry, brown spiders and their sticky webs outta our way."

All four of their captures laughed as skinny Mickey added, "And do be careful. Them critters gotta nasty bite. Rots a hole in your flesh the size of a dinner plate."

The party of four began the journey into the dark, narrow tunnel. The deeper they went, the flickering torch revealed thicker webs and an increasing number of the huge hairy spiders. Brad, in the lead, attempted to swat down the webbing and the large, eight legged creatures that reminded him of the big jungle tarantulas he had once encountered in the Brazilian rain forest. After a 10-minute, stumbling trek, the flickering torch began to burn low, putting out only enough light to see a foot or two.

The escorts brought them to a stop in front of small, cave-like room behind steel bars. The big guy could be heard behind them pulling a jingling set of rusted skeleton keys out of a deep niche in the opposite wall. Choosing the right one, he thrust it into the old lock and with a quick twist to the right, followed by a loud click, the cell doors were unlocked. He pushed the door inward and the antiquated steel hinges screamed their rusty resistance with a bone-chilling shriek.

Greasy Mickey grinned wide, exposing his dark-stained teeth. "So how ya'll like our honeymoon suite, huh?" Both goons laughed hard at the joke.

Sighing deeply, Brad answered, "Well, one must settle for whatever one can get when traveling. But your rates are inviting."

The humor was lost on the goons. The big guy growled, "Shut up and get in."

As the two captives obliged and entered the cell, Brad turned and inquired, "And what time should we expect dinner and drinks to be served, gentlemen?"

The fading torchlight dimly illuminated the men's grinning faces as they glared at the couple through the bars. At Brad's question, both men roared with laughter. The larger one responded, "Hey, Mickey. He wants to know about dinner and drinks."

When the men's laughter subsided, the big one spoke again, "Okay, Mr. Smart Guy. First, let me inform you that your beds are already turned down. And I do hope you like a firm mattress 'cuz you'll be sleeping on gnarly, wet limestone. Ha."

The giggling Mickey chimed in, "Yeah, and if ya gets thirsty, which you will, you'll find that the limestone walls sweat. Just give 'em a good licking. And the thirstier you get, the more you'll lick and the more you lick, the quicker your tongue becomes as raw meat, swollen four times its size. But lick as you may, you just can't get enough rock sweat to quell your raging thirst."

Again, both men laughed hysterically.

"And if ya get hungry," added the joyous big guy, "as soon as we leave with this here torch, you'll find a virtual buffet crawls out and covers the floor of your new digs. You'll have your choice of delicious variety meats. You may have the very large cave rats or the huge hissing cockroaches. But the real delicacy crawls out of the cracks in the walls, which are full of a deadly species of black snakes, called 'asps.'"

They both turned to leave, still chuckling over their wit and humor. Almost out of sight, Mickey yelled back over his shoulder, "Ya'll have fun. And if you're still alive in the morning, you'll likely have a very special visitor. *If* you're still alive."

Brad and Leah stood looking out the bars into the darkness until they could no longer hear voices.

"Well, they were certainly a happy couple, weren't they?" quipped Leah.

"Yes," Brad answered. "Pity they've left. That probably ends tonight's floorshow and entertainment segment. I guess we should try to get comfortable. We may be here a while."

Leah testily replied, "I'll tell ya what. You lay down first. If you survive the rats, roaches, spiders and snakes, then perhaps I'll give it a try."

"Come now. This is an uncomfortable situation but we've been in worse."

"Oh, yeah? Is that right, Mr. Fuller? 'Cuz I sure can't remember a worse situation. And by the way, why didn't you beat those guys up and take their guns? James Bond would've taken 'em out in a heartbeat. And you call yourself a spy!"

Brad couldn't help but laugh. When Leah heard him, she, too, burst out in a giggle.

"Look," Brad said after the laughter died, "why don't we just sit down here by the bars, back-to-back, get as comfortable as possible, and try to get some rest, okay?"

He could hear Leah sigh, "Okay, you're right. Let's just hope those two jackals were exaggerating about all the other residents in here."

They both sat down, placed their backs against each other, and got quiet. After a few moments, Brad whispered, "Leah."

Feigning exasperation, she asked, "What now?"

"I just want to say, if you feel anything groping you, please know that it's not me."

"Shut up, Brad, and go to sleep!"

Kostos flew to Tel Aviv in luxury aboard the IFN's new Boeing 747. With him on the jumbo jet were various European financial barons, a number of his lieutenants, some staff and acquaintances. Landing at Ben Gurion Airport, his contingent was met by the Deputy Prime Minister of Israel, a delegation from the Knesset, Israel's parliament, and a significant number of security personnel.

Exiting his plane, Kostos shook hands with those waiting to greet him and walked straight to a podium loaded with microphones and surrounded by news crews and cameras from around the world. Stepping onto the low platform and walking straight to the podium and microphones, Kostos made a brief statement. "I thank my Israeli hosts for their gracious reception. As the Chairman of the International Federation of Nations, I have come to extend the hand of friendship and peace to the people and the government of Israel.

"As I'm sure you all know, the IFN's sole desire is to act as a bridge between foes whereby all parties can walk hand-in-hand across the abyss of chaos and into a land of peace and prosperity. The road to war and destruction is old and well traveled, but in this new world, we are blazing a trail that will lead us all to a land of promise and freedom. Later today, with the full cooperation of the leaders of Israel, I hope to bring you good news concerning the current crises along the borders of Israel. Thank you."

Kostos moved swiftly, waving at the cheering crowd as he walked to the waiting limo. The five-car convoy, flying diplomatic flags, rolled away to carry the IFN Chairman to Jerusalem for a meeting with Prime Minister Ehud Eliad.

An hour later, arriving at the Israeli Knesset, the limo was waved through a series of security gates and led to an underground entrance. Exiting the car, Kostos was met by still more security personnel, a few bureaucrats and Israeli parliament members.

After exchanging more polite formalities, the IFN Chairman was ushered inside and led to a large conference room where drinks were served, backs were slapped, and diplomatic pleasantries were exchanged with numerous ambassadors and VIPs. After a respectable amount of time, Kostos was asked to follow a contingent of security guards for the brief walk to the office of the Prime Minister.

Once there, he was ushered into a sizeable, two-room office suite. The outer was a conference room decorated with numerous Israeli antiques. Along one wall sat a long couch in front of a wall-sized satellite map of the State of Israel. On another wall were pictures of all of Israel's Prime Ministers since 1948. Near the middle of the room, it was evident that a long conference table had been removed. In its place were two, large, overstuffed chairs angled toward each other. Between them was an ornate coffee table holding a variety of non-alcoholic bottled drinks, ice in a silver bucket, several crystal glasses, and a large bowl of Israeli fruits.

As Kostos entered, the Prime Minister was just coming out of the interior second room, obviously his private office. He extended his hand, which Kostos eagerly shook. After brief, but cool casual greetings, the Prime Minister invited Kostos to sit in one of the two large chairs and he sat down in the other.

"Mr. Prime Minister," Kostos began, "you were very wise in agreeing to meet with me but I don't want to waste your time, so I'll get right to the point. I want you to know that I took the liberty of talking to the leaders of those nations whose armed forces are so rapidly closing on your borders. After extended meetings and difficult negotiations, they finally agreed, might I add very reluctantly, to withdraw their corporate military resources away from Israeli borders, if your government will simply agree to the terms I proposed to you some 72 hours ago."

Prime Minister Eliad sat patiently listening to Kostos' efforts to bend the will of the Israeli government.

"For the sake of the record, Mr. Prime Minister, allow me to ever-so-briefly repeat those few conditions. First, Israel will surrender, without delay, all occupied territories, including the entirety of the West Bank and the Golan Heights. Second, Israel will, within the next 90 days, move back behind the 1967 borders and green lines designated by the United Nations, as your legitimate borders. And, third, the State of Israel will give up its claim to the City of Jerusalem so that it can become a true international city and a protectorate of the IFN.

"As an act of goodwill on the part of those you call your enemies, Israel will be given the long-sought opportunity to construct atop the Temple Mount a restored Jewish Temple. Additionally, the new borders of Israel will be guaranteed and secured by member nations of the IFN whose combined military will soon be the strongest on the planet.

"And so, Mr. Prime Minister, I think you will agree that the conditions, terms and concessions on the part of your enemies are more than generous. I know you have used the last few days to meet and talk with your advisors and such. Now the world awaits with great anticipation your signature on this treaty." Kostos concluded by laying an official-looking set of documents on the coffee table next to Prime Minister Eliad.

The Prime Minister simply looked at the documents and, without making a move to pick them up, responded. "Mr. Kostos, what you and our enemies have concocted and now so generously offer the State of Israel amounts to the dismantling and destruction of the Jewish State and a full surrender of our sovereignty and our right to exist. Therefore, we respond to your terms with the following:

"First, the State of Israel remains open to a Palestinian state on our West Bank if they will renounce and cease all hostilities toward this nation and publicly recognize Israel's right to exist.

"Second, the borders of the Israeli State are not subject to negotiation, especially while we are under the threat of invasion by our enemies. We demand an immediate withdrawal of all armies that now threaten the security of this nation.

"And last, from the most ancient of days, the City of Jerusalem has been, and hence always shall be, the capital city of the State of Israel. It will never be surrendered or bartered away as a bargaining chip to appease those sworn to our destruction."

Kostos was secretly thrilled at the words of the Prime Minister. It was all he had hoped for. He would now have a pretext to loose the dogs of war on the filthy, Jewish State and ultimately bring them to their knees. However, he knew that he must continue with the charade of the heart-broken disappointed diplomat who had done his best to bring peace to the stubborn greedy Jews who now refused to compromise for peace.

"Further, Mr. Kostos," Prime Minister Eliad concluded, "the State of Israel is most capable and ready to defend its borders and its people.

"It is our hope, sir, that you will make it most clear to any and all aggressors that they, as well as their homelands, will feel the full wrath of this country's military might if any invasion of our land is forthcoming."

The Prime Minister had finished. Kostos sat for a moment with a forced expression of disappointment then, with faked sadness, said slowly, "Mr. Prime Minister, I am—and I'm sure the world is—deeply grieved by your intransigence. The IFN, the United Nations, even your own ally, the United States, have called upon you to be reasonable. Yet, you reject the hand of friendship and peace that the entire world extends to you. I know you are aware of the catastrophic consequences of your decision."

"Mr. Kostos," a now-irritated Prime Minister interrupted, "spare me your bleeding heart theatrics. This discussion is over."

The Israeli leader stood to his feet and added, "Sir, you know the way out."

Kostos stood as well. Neither offered to shake hands as the Israeli turned and walked back into his neighboring office.

An ecstatic Kostos left the room, worked his way through waiting crowds of reporters with cameras, all yelling their questions about the result of the meeting. However, he spoke not a word as he pushed through the crowd and worked his way to the waiting limo. Arriving, he slid into the back seat as his driver held the door open for him.

As the limo pulled away, the only other person in the back seat with him, whose identity was hidden behind the darkened windows and large sunglasses, asked, "Did things go well, Charon?"

Kostos leaned back, relaxed into the plush upholstery, and answered with a smile, "Maurice, it could not have gone better."

"So," Maurice Dubois inquired, "shall we now pull the trigger that will bring these worthless Jewish pigs to their knees?"

"Soon, Maurice, very soon. Let them stew a bit longer in their own stupidity. As the chosen of God, they certainly share His arrogance."

Dubois asked, "And what shall we do in the meantime?"

"We shall wrap up all the loose ends. I want no further complications or delays. I also want to kill that slippery scumbag, Carr. Our people have determined that he was smuggled out of Rome and we know exactly where he's headed. I've already got a surprise waiting for him."

"Which reminds me," Dubois suddenly remembered. "While you

met with the Prime Minister, I received a call from Rome. They informed me that those two irritating, troublesome agents are now in our custody, imprisoned in the miserable depths beneath the Vatican."

"Aha! More great news!" Kostos shouted, "I just happen to be on my way to Rome. It will be a great pleasure to deal with them personally upon my arrival."

"And then?" asked Maurice.

"And then, my dear friend, we shall begin to release the fury of hell."

The remote South Texas town of Laredo sits on the shallow, slow-moving, muddy waters of the Rio Grande. The river marks the dividing line between the United States and Mexico.

At 3:00 a.m., the cross border traffic had slowed to its usual, early morning trickle. The moonless night and thick cloud cover guaranteed a darkness welcomed by drug runners and the 'coyotes' who smuggle human contraband into the United States by skirting the legal entry points. Border guards on both sides of the international bridge appreciated the slower pace during this shift.

Pablo Sanchez, the 50-year-old supervisor on the Mexican side, sat in his tiny office at the checkpoint. He felt no guilt for accepting small bribes to look the other way on occasion. He had always been poor and his government salary did not come close to paying for the housing, clothing and feeding of his wife and seven children. He had no other way to enhance his income. Tonight he would be paid enough to provide for his family for many years to come. All he had to do was wave the regularly scheduled old fruit truck through without the routine inspection. The beat-up old truck crossed the border almost every morning transporting Mexican cantaloupe or other agricultural goods to markets on the American side where they brought much better prices.

On the American side of the bridge, Immigration Agent Kevin Baker, single and 32 years old, was also preparing to receive the produce truck in order to facilitate its illegal entrance into the United States. He was being paid 10 times the amount of his counterpart on the Mexican side and was planning on retiring after this one-time crime.

Baker's job was to quietly power down the radiation sensors that scanned all traffic crossing the border bridge for the almost unavoidable leakage. Following that, he was to meet the old truck and go through the motions of his job, checking papers, persons and cargo. After a less-than-thorough effort, he was to clear the truck and wave it through.

Neither Sanchez nor Baker knew what he was allowing to go across the border, and neither cared to know. Their consciences had been silenced by the sizable sum they would both receive for very little effort. They had no idea that just beneath the first layer of freshly harvested cantaloupes lay four, suitcase-sized, nuclear warheads, each with 10 times the mega tonnage of the bombs the Americans had dropped on Hiroshima and Nagasaki in World War II. Each had more than enough power to kill hundreds of thousands of people and rain horrific destruction on American cities.

Pablo Sanchez performed his duty on the produce truck, sending it on its way across the bridge. As it slowly drove off in a cloud of its own smoke, Pablo went to his little office and sent Kevin Baker a prearranged signal via an innocuous-sounding email.

Baker received the signal, then calmly walked into the secured area where the radiation detector's power supply was located. He flipped four switches that shut them down, then walked out to the truck lane of the border checkpoint and waited.

The Mexican peasant drove the truck into the well-marked area and, obeying the signs, parked and waited inspection. But the peasant was not a Mexican. He was an Egyptian and an Al Qaeda operative.

While the driver stayed in the truck, Baker walked around, took the papers handed to him through the window, and began a slow walk around the vehicle. He checked the undercarriage, then jumped up to check out the cantaloupes on top, faking a thorough inspection of the cargo. Eight minutes later, Baker signed the driver's papers and waved the vehicle onto American soil.

At two other locations along the American-Mexican border that night, similar efforts successfully carried six more identical weapons into the United States. By sun-up, the weapons were well on their way to 10 different American cities.

During the preceding week, U.S. Navy warships, working with Homeland Security, had stopped 17 ships of various sizes and origins that gave evidence of carrying radioactive material. In every case, it was discovered that the ships were transporting nuclear waste to various regulated dumpsites from nuclear power plants of American allies. All 17, the Navy now knew, were only decoys.

The Brazilian freighter, San Miguel, had two weeks earlier crossed the southern Atlantic with a load of Mediterranean bananas, dates and citrus bound for a port in Venezuela. There the fruits, along with 10 smuggled, nuclear weapons, were offloaded. The fruit went to markets and the WMDs went north out of South America through Panama, Costa Rica, Nicaragua, and eventually into Mexico until they reached the American border. There, they were successfully smuggled into the USA through South Texas, California and Arizona.

Within 36 hours after crossing the border, all 10 weapons would be securely stored in well-hidden locations in their designated cities. They were armed and waited only for the signal that would detonate each in deadly sequence.

TWENTY-SIX

Brad and Leah had been in the dark, damp cell far beneath the Vatican for almost seven miserable hours. They had very little rest, not only because they were sitting back-to-back on rough limestone, but because they had also been forced to keep busy batting away spiders and huge cockroaches, and kicking at the enormous cave rats attempting to chew on them. No snakes had yet menaced them, but both agents were tired beyond words, thirsty, hungry and worn out.

Greasy Mickey's parting words to the agents had been about a visitor coming in the morning, if they were still alive. Those words had given Brad and Leah the incentive to hope their situation would change. Morning was now upon them and they were still alive. Brad's wristwatch with an illuminated face had allowed them to keep track of time.

After an extended period of silence, Brad whispered, "Are you awake?"

Her exaggerated sigh was followed by, "Now what kind of question is that Brad Fuller? You know full well I'm awake and if I wasn't, your question would've awakened me. So, now what do you want?"

"I thought I'd let ya know that I just heard sounds way down the tunnel from the direction we came."

Leah sat up straighter. "You did? Oh, I hope you're right!"

As she quieted to listen for herself, both of them heard the distinct but distant voices of men. Within a moment, the captives saw the faint flicker of an approaching torch. It seemed to them like an eternity, but in truth it was only a few minutes before Mickey and the big fellow stepped up to their cell bars.

Grinning like Cheshire cats, the two men looked in at the prisoners. Mickey spoke up, "Hey, Tiny, they're still alive!"

The two goons laughed at the sordid appearance of the captives and mocked their situation. The big one they now knew was referred to as Tiny began to unlock the cell as Mickey held a gun on them. The cell door's rusty hinges again shrieked in protest as Tiny opened them.

"Okay, let's move it. It's ya'lls' lucky day. The head honchos are wanting to see ya. And I've got good news for ya," Tiny leered, "the boss promised that I get the lady when he's through with ya'll."

Brad, already outside the cell, quipped, "Aw, come on, Tiny. Why don't I take the lady and you can have ol' Mickey here. Whaddya say?"

Mickey, noticing Tiny was either considering the proposition or was confused about it, spoke up. "Hey Tiny. The man's a smart mouth. He's just trying to irritate ya."

Tiny looked back at Brad with a confused look. "Oh? So keep ya trap shut, wise guy, or I'll kill ya right here."

"Tiny," Brad responded, "I think Mickey's just playing hard to get."

Angered by the remark, Mickey kicked Brad hard on his thigh, pushed him against the stone wall, and got in his face. "Another asinine word from you, and your lady friend and I are gonna stop and let you watch us spend some quality time together. Now move!"

With a less-than-gentle shove, Brad was forced to walk in front as the party made the long march to the stairwell and then up to the elevators. Entering the lift, they ascended quickly, passing the ground floor and stopping on what was clearly the second story.

As they all stepped off the elevators, they were met by two well-dressed men sitting in the front seat of a large golf-cart-type vehicle. Unlike Tiny and Mickey, the two were intelligent looking, clean, and even polite. The man behind the wheel spoke first. "Mr. Fuller and Miss Levy, would you mind getting aboard for a short but pleasant ride?"

Without a word, the agents sat on the back bench seat and were driven away from Tiny and Mickey. As they moved away, Brad told Leah, "I shall miss those two delightful chaps."

Leah nodded her head, "Oh, yeah, miss 'em like a malignant tumor."

The cart traveled via long hallways and covered ramps connecting buildings until it finally stopped in front of two large, elegantly carved doors guarded by two impeccably well-tailored Swiss Guards in full regalia. The guards ignored them as the driver slid out of the cart and knocked on the doors. Within seconds, the door opened and a kind-looking elderly priest bowed to Brad and Leah, inviting them to enter the palatial chamber.

Closing the doors behind them, the priest turned to face them. "Good morning, sir, ma'am. There are separate facilities for each of you just beyond the doors to your right. You will find all of your personal effects and clothing from your previous residence. I think you call it a safe house or something like that. After you shower and change clothes, drinks and snacks await you on the table to your left. Relax and enjoy yourselves. In about an hour your hosts will join you."

The old priest bowed slightly and turned to exit, when Leah quickly called to him, "Do pardon me, sir, but we are at quite a disadvantage. Who did you say will be meeting us?"

The priest simply gave a saintly smile, turned again to the doors, and left the room.

"Sporting of the chaps to heist our things and deliver them here," Brad said softly as he let his eyes roam the room.

Leah, tired and surrendered to the situation, added, "Yeah, whatever. I'll ask questions after I've had a hot shower, clean clothes, and a bite to eat. See ya after while."

Both of them were back, clean, changed and feeling much better within 30 minutes. They walked to the table with a small, but most adequate, buffet of sandwiches, chips, breads, cheeses and various cold bottled drinks, where they settled in and enjoyed themselves. As soon as they were finished, they began to inspect the large room in which they were being held.

It was still almost 20 minutes until their so-called host was to show up. Leah walked over to an area where ceiling-to-floor curtains of lush, red velvet hung. Looking behind the curtains, she saw a set of tall French doors that opened onto a beautiful balcony overlooking St. Peter's Square. The view struck her as vaguely familiar, when it suddenly dawned on her why.

"We must be very important guests, Brad."

Brad turned and asked, "And your reason for believing that?"

"Because," Leah returned, "we're standing in the Pontiff's penthouse or, as some may call it, the Pope's digs."

Brad, now more interested, turned to look at her. "Are you serious?"

"I am absolutely serious. I'm sure you've seen pictures or videos of the Popes who stand on the high balcony outside these doors. Just below is St. Peter's Square, and this room must be the greeting room for VIPs and such."

"And," Brad added as he walked to another set of large doors at the opposite end of the room, "through these doors, very probably, is the big guy's bedroom."

Reaching the doors, Brad started to open them. "I've always had a hankering to see where the Pope sleeps and the truth is, I'll probably never get another chance."

"Brad," Leah said as she hustled across the room to his side, "do you think that's a good idea?"

Smiling, Brad answered, "I'd just never forgive myself for being this close to where God's main man sleeps and failing to take a peek."

Leah rolled her eyes. "Don't bet on that 'God's main man' thing.'"

Brad turned the knobs and pushed both doors open simultaneously.

They both looked in at an immaculate, large bedroom that spoke of royal splendor. At the far end of the room they saw a magnificent canopied bed. It was bedecked with lavender bedspreads, trimmed in gold.

The rest of the room was equally impressive, containing an ornately hand-carved sixteenth-century desk with matching chair. All along one entire wall, from the floor to the 12-foot ceiling, was an impressive library on gorgeous, antique book shelves. Tall, beautiful armoires stood majestically around the room and were filled with the priceless priestly robes and attire of the Pontiff.

The other walls were covered with original portraits by famous artists of the Popes over the centuries. Sitting upon golden pedestals and various sized tables were crystal urns and silver and gold vases all filled with fresh, colorful flowers that scented the air.

"A bit gaudy for my taste," Brad quipped.

Peering back and to her left through a darkened archway, Leah pondered out loud, "I wonder what's through there?"

Following her as she went through the arch, Brad encouraged her, "Only one way to find out."

He walked up behind her as she came to another set of large double doors. She reached down, turned the knob, and pushed both doors open at once.

They knew immediately that they were looking into the private chapel of the Pope.

From the high domed ceiling hung ornate gold and crystal chandeliers, under ancient frescos that adorned the domes interior. Several statues of saints sat around the chapel walls. To the left of the altar stood a full set of a knight's armor and on the right was a short stone statue of a gargoyle.

Four rows of wooden benches, acting as pews, sat on a smooth granite floor and added a Spartan feel to the chapel. At the very front, the altar area was surrounded by a semi-circle kneeling pad and prayer rail.

A veil hung low just above the altar, hiding whatever was behind it.

In all of the Catholic chapels Leah had ever seen, the altar was usually fronted by the Madonna and Child or a large crucifix.

Straining to see above the altar, Leah whispered nervously, "This place gives me the creeps."

Brad, already moving toward the altar, responded, "It does have an air about it."

Kneeling down, Brad's knees touched the support pad as he looked up to see what hung behind the low veil.

"My gosh," he pulled his head back in shock and disgust, "what hath hell wrought here?"

Curious more than fearful, Leah quickly dropped down on her knees next to Brad, and saw what had caused his reaction.

"Oh my..." was all she could get out before jumping up and backing away. "That's disgusting, unholy, and sick."

Brad stood to his feet and turned to Leah, "Oh, I don't know. Don't all churches have a severed goat's head covered in coagulating blood at the altar?"

Leah was about to respond when she and Brad were startled at the sound of the two giant chapel doors slamming shut behind them. Twirling around, they saw a very angry looking Charon Kostos, standing next to the Pope.

The Pope turned, and with a large skeleton key he took from the pocket of his robes, locked the massive doors. Though Brad and Leah had never seen either man in person, they recognized them from pictures in the papers and televised newscasts.

Kostos spoke. "You two have made quite a nuisance of yourselves. You've held up my progress on a number of important projects. How fitting it is to find you, once again, sticking your nose where it doesn't belong. But that's quite all right. Our altar cries out for fresh blood and you have chosen a good place to die."

Brad stepped in front of Leah and said, "Now who would've ever thought the world's most noble ambassador of peace and love and his buddy pal, Pope Fraud, are really just your everyday devil worshipers?"

In a flash, the Pope, who had finished locking the doors, swung around to face Brad with a speed that defied his advanced years. As he did, it seemed as though someone had switched on several smoke machines as smoke rose from the floor and fell from the ceiling.

The Pope's saintly look fell away as he addressed Brad. "We are far more than simple worshipers, you insignificant piece of dung."

Smoke smelling of sulfur and rotten eggs continued to billow into the small chapel, engulfing the agents, who could now see Kostos and the Pope only vaguely through the haze.

Frightened over what she sensed, Leah drew close to Brad, who kept his eye on both men.

Brad got a glimpse of the Pope's face through a brief clearing. The Pontiff's countenance was horribly contorted into hideous features worse than any horror movie's special effects could achieve. His eyes moved toward the sides of his head as his skull reshaped itself into a serpentine appearance. Through the thick haze the agents were able to perceive that both men were now literally morphing into hideous otherworldly beasts.

Leah buried her face in Brad's shoulder, trying hard not to believe what her eyes were seeing.

Brad squinted, attempting to pierce the haze and keep his eye on the two figures, not yet believing what he was watching take place in front of him.

Again, the smoke briefly cleared and Brad saw with clarity that where Kostos had stood only moments before now stood a 10-foot-tall beast. To Brad it looked like a hellish dragon. It had wings with claw-like hands on the leading edges and scaly green skin. Its reptilian head had two horns on each side and was covered with grotesque open boils, seeping a red, mucus-like substance.

The beast threw back its head and let out a bone-chilling scream, causing Leah to cling still closer to Brad.

The Pope had become a macabre creature with the body of an upright iguana and the head of a cobra. It sat on the floor in front of the roaring beast with its mouth open wide, exposing a viper's fangs and a darting forked tongue. Both creatures were terrifying to look at.

By now, Brad was convinced that the food or drinks they had consumed minutes before had been laced with drugs now causing them to hallucinate. He knew of no other logical explanation for the phenomenon.

Brad watched as the winged dragon, still making that hideous screech, slowly moved toward them through the mist. The stench emanating from the beast was repulsive. Brad struggled to control his gag reflex. Attempting to back up as the dragon drew closer, Brad continued to hold Leah, whose face was still buried in his shoulder. Sensing him step back, Leah instinctively looked up in an effort to see why Brad was moving.

She turned her head to look and at the same moment the fierce creature leapt at them, landing only two feet away. Opening its deformed jaws, the dragon revealed multiple rows of bristling sharp teeth, wickedly long. There was no doubt that the beast's intentions were to slice the agents into pieces like a shredder. Brad and Leah were now backed against the wall, unable to escape. They watched as the dragon slowly extended its neck, widening his powerful jaws, prepared to strike.

Leah again buried her face into Brad's chest as she yelled out in Hebrew, *"Ta'azor Li Yeshua! Ta'azor Li Elohenu!"* (Help me, Jesus! Help me, Lord, our God!)

Instantly, the beast staggered back as though he had been struck hard by a gigantic sledgehammer. Swaying back and forth, he bellowed so loudly that Brad thought the creature had suffered a debilitating wound. The dragon backed its way across the room to join the other creature. As it moved away, the dragon continued its terrorizing screams and kept lunging at the couple like a rabid pit bull restrained by an invisible chain. The couple watched through the haze as the two figures scampered back against the large double doors. The beasts huddled together and appeared to be communicating.

Seconds later, the ghastly dragon, in a gravelly, hoarse voice, howled, "The Jewess belongs to the Nazarene." Immediately, the smoke became so thick that it was impossible to see anything.

Standing still, Brad and Leah waited, without speaking, until they heard the distinct sound of the heavy double doors of the chapel creak open and then slam shut.

Within seconds, the smoke began to dissipate and the agents could see they were alone in the chapel.

By now, even Brad's eyes were wide, and an expression of shock shrouded his face. He glanced at Leah, who had turned white with fear. Both were drenched in sweat and physically exhausted.

Brad, cautiously glancing around the room, whispered, "We were drugged and have been hallucinating."

Leah, shaking her head in the negative, could barely find the energy to speak. "No, Brad. We were not drugged. We've just had a glimpse of things unholy behind a very dark veil—and lived to talk about it."

"I'll tell ya what," Brad said as he took Leah's hand and started toward the doors, "I'll be most happy to discuss the matter some other time. Right now, let's just get the devil out of here."

"Poor choice of words," Leah responded, "but I do agree it's time to go."

They reached the double doors and found them unlocked. They hurried through the bedchamber to the outer entrance and found the doors there wide open and the Swiss Guards gone. The agents made haste to reach an exit from the palatial building and were soon outside walking across St. Peter's Square.

On a previous visit, they had seen the area outside the gates where tour buses parked and city cabs waited for fares. Finding an empty taxi, they jumped in the back seat as Brad told the startled driver, "Take us to the Regency on the other side of the city."

The driver laid his newspaper down and, without a word, pulled away from the curb and into the flow of traffic. Leah asked, "Why the Regency?"

Brad, almost out of breath, answered, "The company keeps a room reserved there for emergencies. We can check in, recoup and call headquarters. I'm not sure, however, how much to tell them about our mind-bending, chemically-induced trip."

Leah was frustrated with Brad's doubt and denial. "I think you need to have a blood test," she said. "That's the only way to convince you that what just happened to us was not a result of LSD or acid or any other chemical."

"Leah, listen to me. The only other possible explanation would have to be that this Kostos and his phony Pope are really some kind of wicked alien creatures hiding in human bodies. I, for one, prefer the chemical explanation."

"There is another possibility. And that is, that those two men are in league with and possessed by the forces of evil itself."

"Aha," Brad returned, "now you're saying the Devil made 'em do it?"

Leah softly replied, "Don't mock me, Brad."

Feeling a bit guilty, Brad sighed, "I'm sorry, but I will concede that whatever we just experienced was not natural."

The enormous Sikorsky helicopter had been a gift from the Russians to the Syrian President in the 1980s. The Syrian generals still liked to use it to impress visiting VIPs. Thanks to a constant supply of Russian components, Syrian mechanics had kept the huge aircraft flight-worthy.

It had just flown its occupants from the Dead Sea area up the Jordan Valley and into the Syrian side of the Golan Heights. The pilots, who had been careful to keep clear of Israeli airspace, landed at a border outpost in Syria that overlooked northern Israel, toward the Sea of Galilee.

Russian General Sergy Chevsky, commander of all Russian military forces in the Middle East; Syrian General Abdulla Hofni, commander of all Syrian forces; and Commander Abrahim Hassan, the Supreme Commandant of the combined military forces of Egypt, Iran, Iraq and 12 other Muslim nations, all stepped off the Sikorsky as it touched down.

They were met by Syrian Outpost Commander Colonel Hori Kanesh and his staff. After a warm welcome and appropriate posturing and salutes, Colonel Kanesh led the group to the lookout point. He handed each a powerful set of binoculars so they could better view the no-man's-land separating Israel from Syria.

"I'm told," said Russian General Chevsky, "that this so-called no-man's-land is two kilometers wide from border to border along this stretch of your border with Israel. I can see from here that the Israelis have quite a welcoming party waiting for you. Do you have sufficient artillery on the heights to take out those defensive positions?"

Syrian General Hofni responded, "Comrade, when the order is given we will not only use our rather impressive arsenal of artillery, but that, along with your precision Russian bombers, will enable us to walk right over that position. Our prayer is that the order will soon be given."

Clearing his throat, Commander Hassan said, "It would be unwise, gentlemen, to underestimate one's enemy. I fought in the Egyptian invasion of Israel in 1973. As you know, we were allied with Syria then as well.

"Syria invaded Israel from this very spot with 1,000 tanks along this 30-mile stretch of border. However, within days, a handful of old Israeli tanks, a group of belligerent soldiers, and a few Israeli jets held up the entire invasion, giving the Israelis time to regroup and counterattack. They pushed the entirety of Syria's military all the way back to Damascus.

"Our Egyptian forces didn't fare much better. We invaded the southern Sinai, but in a very short time, the Israeli counterattack, led by then-General Ariel Sharon, pushed our forces all the way back to Cairo, surrounded the city, and had it not been for the intervention of the United States and UN, we'd all be speaking Hebrew today."

The Syrian General Hofni was embarrassed and infuriated that the well-known battles were brought up by the Egyptian. "Commander, may I remind you, this is not 1973 and this time the Americans are not backing the Jewish State?

"Further, sir, we've got 10 times the number of troops, tanks, missiles, and combat aircraft that we had in 1973. Additionally, with our new anti-missiles systems set up all along the Golan and the other border areas, the Jewish threat of nuclear assaults on our homelands is without merit. There is no way the Israelis can withstand this invasion. They will not survive."

No one else in the group responded to Hofni as they all ambled back to the huge helicopter. They took off, heading to Damascus for final consultations with their national leaders.

Colonel Kanesh stood by Major Ali, his personal aide, as the Sikorsky lifted off. "We should fear our own arrogance more than the Jews. Our pride has defeated us repeatedly."

"But Colonel," the aide responded, "our General is right, is he not? This new alliance is more powerful than anything the Israelis have ever faced."

Colonel Kanesh smiled, patted his aide on the back, and walked away saying, "Do try to remember, Major, the race is not always to the swift."

TWENTY-SEVEN

President Carr, Dr. Cohen, Agent Spears, and the two Sodote Shalom bodyguards were the only passengers on the Citation jet piloted by the two men hand-picked by Director Pratt. They had taken off from the private field in southern France 30 minutes earlier headed to a final destination in the United States. They would make only one refueling stop en route.

Only at the last minute before departure were the pilots informed about their very important passenger. Though both men had spent years flying various covert missions, it did not prepare them for the shock of seeing President Carr alive and well. They knew they would get little or no briefing on why the man was alive or what was going on. Their job was to obey orders and keep their mouths shut. That is precisely what they would do.

But they could not contain their excitement when President Carr opened the door of their cockpit and knelt down behind them. "Mr. President, sir," stammered the pilot as he managed a salute, "pardon us for not being able to stand, sir."

Carr smiled and patted the pilot on the back. "Don't worry about it, soldier."

The co-pilot chirped up. "Sir, I can't tell you how good it is to see you alive and well. The country sure needs you right about now."

"Thank you both," Carr responded, "but everyone's not going to be as glad to see me as you two. Anyway, I know we're to land and refuel at some little airport outside London. I'd like to know how long it'll take to get from there to the U.S.?"

The co-pilot acting as navigator answered. "Well, sir, if we spend no more than 20 minutes on the ground while refueling, which is our plan, our ETA to touch down on American soil will be exactly seven hours and 13 minutes."

"Very good, gentlemen." The president got to his feet, exited the cockpit, and returned to the small but luxurious cabin.

No one on the Citation knew how closely their flight was being monitored, not only by the CIA, but also by Kostos' security forces. By now Kostos' interests had gained control of all European Air Traffic Control systems and international surveillance capabilities throughout the continent of Europe and other IFN member nations. They had tracked the Citation from the moment it had left Andrews Air Force Base until it landed in southern France to pick up its passengers.

Kostos had heard a recording of only parts of the satellite phone call between Carr and Director Pratt arranging the flight, but that was all Kostos needed to lay a trap to intercept the Citation en route. As soon as the plane began its roll down the small English airstrip after the refueling stop, two French Mirage fighters were given coordinates to intercept the business jet. As the Citation reached a cruising altitude 32,000 feet, the two French war planes loaded with deadly air-to-air missiles quietly slipped into position a half a mile behind the jet. Using a secure military frequency, the lead pilot contacted his superiors. "Mirage Stalker One, in position on target and holding."

The French military command in charge of the fighters had been told by their government's leaders that the Citation was full of internationally wanted terrorists that must be eliminated.

As soon as the lead pilot of the French warplanes contacted their ground controllers, they received a reply. "Stalker One. You are cleared to destroy the target. I repeat…Stalker One destroy the target."

The well-trained French fighter pilot, glad to be part of taking out a group of international terrorists, pushed the "fire" button and the deadly missile leapt from its braces under the fighter's wing. The pilot immediately fired a second missile to insure the target's total destruction. Within seconds, the Citation turned into a blazing fireball as it exploded with a ferocity that amazed even the fighter pilots. They watched as small pieces of debris rained down into the ocean over five miles below.

The business jet and everyone on board were now only memories. As the two fighters left to return to base, they radioed their command center, "Mission accomplished. Target destroyed."

After discovering Leah was an 'untouchable,' Kostos and the Pope left the two agents in the Pontiff's chapel.

Kostos had other pressing matters to attend to and was preparing to fly to Washington D.C. for a final meeting with President Jordan Hunt. Before he left, the Pope inquired, "And what of the two diseased vermin we left in the chapel? They've now seen far too much."

"We've no choice," Kostos answered, "but to leave the Jewess alone and Fuller, that parasite, is always near her. At this point, they're little more than an inconvenient nuisance. We will proceed with our plans. No one will believe their rantings anyway."

Kostos was ready and anxious to leave Rome. He had just received confirmation that the 10 nuclear weapons were now in place in their respected cities. Now he waited for the call confirming that Carr was dead and unable to orchestrate a surprise return to power that would complicate matters.

Two hours into his flight, Kostos received a call from the President of France assuring him that the Citation business jet had been destroyed over the North Atlantic.

"I salute you, Mr. President. You've served your country and the world well by eliminating that group of terrorists. In the near future, I would like to make known to the entire world the great contribution the French military has made to the international community. However, for now, let's keep this little incident to ourselves."

The French President, humbled by Kostos' praise, quickly agreed to do as he was asked.

Six hours later, the IFN's 747 landed at Andrews Air Force Base in Washington, D.C. Following Kostos' orders, President Hunt sent a limo to bring him to the White House. Again using the underground entrances, Kostos made his way to the Oval Office. Entering the room, Kostos observed Hunt sitting nervously behind his desk. The president looked small, gaunt, and sickly sitting in the large chair that seemed to swallow him. Hunt did not stand to greet his guest.

Kostos closed the door firmly behind him. "I must say, dear Jordan, you look pitifully dour this evening. Don't you realize that we are on the verge of a great victory?"

Looking closer at the sickly president, Kostos thought the man looked emotionally exhausted, perhaps even on the verge of a nervous breakdown.

Kostos, still standing directly in front of the president's desk, waited for Hunt to speak. Finally, he did. "Kostos, I was informed, after the fact, that certain members of my cabinet, without my knowledge or consent, had ordered the U.S. Navy as well as components of Homeland Security to conduct a vigilant search for possible terrorist smugglers who may be attempting to bring nuclear weapons into this country."

Kostos chuckled at the president. "And were you also informed that your great, all- knowing, all-seeing warships were led on a wild goose chase all along your Gulf, Pacific and Atlantic coastlines?"

Hunt, remaining passive, sat solemnly and added, "Yes, I'm aware that you clearly had them chasing nuclear ghosts. And then less than 15 minutes ago, I was informed that there's a strong possibility that 36 hours ago we had a security failure along our Mexican border where it's thought that nuclear materials may well have been brought into this country."

"Yes," Kostos returned, "I heard the same rumors. It seems your border is extremely porous, Mr. President. The fact is, three shipments carrying a total of 10 nuclear bombs did enter the good ol' U.S.A. All are now safely deposited in 10 of your largest cities. But, then, I did inform you earlier of this plan—or don't you remember?"

"Oh, I remember, but somehow I believed that even you still had enough human dignity to keep you from killing millions of innocent men, women and children."

Kostos again laughed as he sat down in the chair fronting the president's desk, "Human dignity, you say? The human race has no dignity, Jordan. The entire race is scum, lower than the dirt on the bottom of my shoe. And the sooner you realize that I have no love or concern for your so-called innocent human masses, the sooner you'll see the bigger picture."

"Who are you, Charon Kostos? Perhaps I should ask, *what* are you?"

"I am your master, Jordan! Or haven't you figured that out yet? And as your master I've some new instructions for you. As you know, I originally intended to use our 10 weapons as insurance to guarantee that the American military would stand down when I initiate our invasion of Israel. However, I've decided that it'd be much better if one of our little packages went off just prior to the invasion. That would guarantee that the Americans would be focused on their own need and far too preoccupied with their own disaster to concern themselves with Israel's."

Hunt jumped to his feet. "Kostos! I cannot allow you to detonate a nuclear weapon on American soil!"

Standing quickly, Kostos answered, "Excuse me, Jordan, but did you say 'allow' me? *You* will not allow *me*? All this talk about your being the leader of the free world has gone to your head. So let me remind you: You belong to me. You sold your soul the minute you crawled on hands and knees groveling for my help over four years ago. And do I need to remind you that it is I who eliminated your predecessor, making you the president?

"I should also inform you that Carr, only hours ago, was on his way to this office to destroy you, but I had his little jet blown out of the sky. You owe me for that as well.

"So here's what's gonna happen, Jordan. Not I, nor my minions, will detonate that first bomb. You will!"

Hunt was emotionally imploding as his face turned red with rage. "You're insane! I'd never do such a thing."

"Oh, I think you will!" yelled Kostos.

Before Hunt could respond, he sensed a tightening around his neck as though a rope was closing. He grabbed at his collar in an attempt to loosen the invisible grip, but it kept squeezing tighter as though a boa constrictor were wrapped around his throat. Hunt fell to his knees while Kostos stood over him smiling and watching him suffer.

"Is there a problem, Jordan? Disobedience does bring its own rewards. If you refuse to obey, you will die. And I assure you that your fat, stupid wife and your two dopey children will suffer a fate worse than death. So, Jordan, do you think you can find it in your heart to do as you're told?"

Hunt was turning blue from lack of oxygen, and was on the verge of passing out when he forced himself to nod rapidly to Kostos.

"Very good," Kostos said as Hunt was instantly released from the invisible grip of death.

The president lay face down on the floor, coughing and gasping for air as Kostos sat back down, lit a cigarette, and waited for the man to compose himself.

Finally, Hunt struggled, first to his knees and then to his feet. Kostos watched and ordered him to sit down.

"Now, as a token of my friendship, I've a gift for you."

Kostos reached into his coat pocket, pulled out a small device and tossed it onto the desk in front of Hunt. It was shaped like a small iPod but had a single button on it lit by a small red light.

"Do be very careful with it. When I call to give you the order, you will push that single, little, red button. That will activate an electrical trigger that will detonate one of our little nukes, the one in the New York subway system just beneath Times Square.

"That single explosion will collapse your major media outlets, your East Coast communications systems, Wall Street, and billions of dollars worth of real estate, and kill hundreds of thousands of Americans. It will also create a radioactive wasteland for years to come.

"When you finish the deed, I will release on Israel the greatest invasion since D-Day, and America will be far too busy with her own disaster to care about the Jews.

"If you fail to push the button, then I'll have another in a different location that will not require your assistance to do the deed. But I will also have the other nine nukes across your fruited plains light up those cities as well. Do you understand, Jordan?"

"Kostos," gasped the hoarse president, "why? Why have me detonate the thing? You've got thousands that can do your dirty work."

"Because, Mr. President, I want you to demonstrate your loyalty. It will be the act that guarantees you a position of prominence in the New World unfolding before us. And remember, your obedience will bring you great rewards. From now on, Jordan, see yourself not as an American, but as a citizen of the New World."

Kostos stood to leave. "I'll be in touch within the next 12 to 24 hours to give you the order. Understand?"

Hunt barely managed to nod, and Kostos walked out.

The president sat motionless, appalled and terrified at what had just happened. He was convinced that Kostos possessed a power that was not of this world.

For another hour, Hunt did not move from his desk and refused all calls as he contemplated the act Kostos was demanding of him. He finally convinced himself that his destruction of New York would be similar to what Truman did when he decided to drop the atomic bombs on Nagasaki and Hiroshima, Japan in World War II. Truman did so to bring the war to a close and to save millions of American and Japanese lives. His own push of the button would guarantee that nine other American cities would be spared annihilation. He persuaded himself that he may even eventually be praised as a hero who made a difficult, but necessary, decision. He left the Oval Office and walked to his residence in the West Wing having reconciled and justified what he must do.

What he did not know, was that pushing the button would not only detonate the bomb in New York City; it would detonate all 10 bombs in 10 American cities.

Billy Dees was six years old. His mother, a working single mom, picked him up from the daycare center provided for employees of the Clauswitze Advertising Agency. Patricia Dees had worked at the agency for only six months. Her office, located just two blocks off Times Square, afforded easy access to the subway that took her to and from work.

Billy and his mother, on their way home, had arrived at the subway platform earlier than usual. Just as they decided to sit down and relax, Patricia ran into an old girlfriend from her last job. Immediately, the two women were engrossed in an exchange of gossip about their old boss and his secretary.

While his mom was preoccupied with her friend, Billy had wandered dangerously close to the edge of the platform. Looking down at the subway tracks, a shiny quarter lying between the rails caught Billy's eye. The precocious six-year-old couldn't resist the temptation to retrieve the small fortune. He looked around and saw that his mother was still talking to her friend and the few other adults standing and sitting around were either reading newspapers or dozing. No one was paying much attention to Billy.

Seizing the opportunity to become rich, Billy casually sat down on the platform's edge, dangled his feet over the side, and gently pushed himself off the three-foot-high ledge. Landing on his feet, he looked around for the shiny coin, spotted it, and bent down to pick it up. As he stooped to retrieve the quarter, he could see up under the ledge of the platform. He noticed an interesting little crawl space and decided to explore a bit further.

Drawing closer to the opening, Billy saw some blinking, green lights only a few feet further in. Crawling closer, Billy's eyes adjusted to the lack of light and he noticed the three little flashing lights were on a big suitcase, like the one his mom packed for them when they would go to Grandma's. Examining his find more closely, the boy noticed the green lights were right where the handle was on his mom's old suitcase. But this one had no handle.

The case was 34"x 26"x10", and to the six-year-old, it looked like a huge treasure chest. To Billy, it was far too valuable an item to just leave. He decided to get his mom so she could help him get it out.

Patricia, still involved in the gossip session, finally heard the subway approaching and looked around for Billy. She could not see him anywhere. The panicked mother began to yell for her son, "Billy, Billy where are you?" Immediately, a million horrible thoughts captured her imagination and panic took over her soul.

"Mom, I'm over here! I found a treasure! Come help me!" Hearing her son's voice, she turned toward the platform and saw his little blond head and excited face peeping over the platform's edge.

For a split second she froze, realizing her son was standing right on the tracks as the train was rapidly approaching.

"Billy!" she screamed and flung herself toward the platform with all the speed she could muster. Reaching him, she bent down and with strength she did not know she possessed, snatched the boy up and onto the platform just as the subway cars reached the spot where he had been standing. The cars finally rolled to a stop and the doors aligned with the platform on which she now held Billy slid open.

She grabbed Billy in a bear hug while her heart recovered. "Billy, don't you ever go off without me again. Do you understand Mommy?"

"But, Mom," Billy argued, "I found a hidden treasure and you gotta help me get it."

Ignoring his childlike pleas, his mother answered, "Come on, Billy. We'll go find a better treasure. How about an ice cream cone?"

"But, Mom." His treasure, he realized, would probably still be there tomorrow and the ice cream did sound pretty good.

Patricia hustled her son onto the subway and within seconds they were off.

Underneath the platform, the three little green lights on the nuclear bomb continued to blink off and on, warning that the weapon was armed. It waited only for President Hunt to push the button on the device now sitting on the nightstand by his bed. Once pushed, it would send a signal to a satellite transponder orbiting 25,000 miles above the Earth. Within a millisecond, the signal would be relayed to the mechanism within the suitcase and the weapon would detonate.

Times Square and everything and everyone within miles in every direction would be vaporized.

That would be followed by nine more nuclear explosions in sequential order.

As soon as the taxi dropped them off at the hotel, Leah made herself comfortable in the lobby while Brad checked in and got the key to the small suite the Agency kept on hold. The agents took the lift to the 12th floor, found the room, and entered. Brad headed straight for a chair next to the phone.

Leah asked, "Who are you calling in such a hurry?"

Brad, already completing the dialing, looked around at her. "First, I'm calling our Rome office to get them to patch me through to Langley on a secure line. Then, hopefully I'll be able to catch Pratt."

As Brad talked to his local office about arranging a secure wire, Leah fell back on the large, comfortable sofa to listen. She was curious about how he would deal with his superior concerning their unearthly experience at the chapel.

As Brad sat waiting for his call to go through, Leah asked, "Have you decided how much you're gonna tell 'em about our meeting with Kostos and the Pope?"

"At this point, everything is on a need-to-know basis and they don't need to know. At least not yet."

Brad quickly returned his attention to the phone as he heard Pratt's voice answer at the other end. "Well now, seeing that only two people on earth know this private number and that one of 'em, my mother, is away on vacation, that leaves only one other possibility. Where have you been, Fuller?"

"Yes, sir, and it's good to talk to you too, boss. And to answer your question, Miss Levy and I have been incarcerated in a dark, rat and snake-infested dungeon, kidnapped by flying gunships, almost drowned in the ocean, shot at by Mafiaso goons, held hostage by terrorists, and almost cut in tiny pieces by beastly creatures that defy description. I trust things are well with you, sir."

An impatient, very busy Pratt was anxious to focus Brad on new developments.

"Sounds like business as usual for you Fuller, so just put it all in your report. Now back here in the real world, things have not been nearly so boring. So let's start with, where are you?"

Brad was relieved that at least for now he was not being asked for details. "At the moment we, that's Miss Levy and I, just checked into Rome's Regency."

"Fuller, tell me you're not wasting taxpayers' money on another one of your 'undercover,' and the pun is intended, operations."

"Uh, no, sir. I haven't gone, as you say, 'undercover,' for a very long time."

"All right, let's cut to the chase," countered the director. "I suppose you know by now that Carr is very much alive."

"Yes, sir. We were very close to finding him when we were taken hostage by Kostos' freaks."

"And obviously," Pratt came back, "you're privy to his role in all this?"

"To some extent, sir. At least enough to know that the man is far more than he seems."

Pratt was anxious to get Brad briefed. "That's an understatement. But right now I want you to listen carefully. First, forget about rousting Carr. He's en route to the States via a company jet and should arrive in five or six hours.

"It appears our illustrious President Hunt is involved all the way up to his skivvies with Kostos, and is selling his own country down the river. As soon as Carr arrives, he'll brief me and a few other die-hard patriots on his plan to take this government out of the hands of the crazies, without tearing up the whole country."

The pause gave Brad an opening. "Well and good, sir. So does that mean I'm to head back and help pull it off?"

"Not exactly, Brad."

Brad never liked it when the boss addressed him as Brad. He only did so when about to give him a difficult or dangerous assignment.

Pratt continued, "I hold in my hand a presidential finding authorizing the neutralization of one Charon D. Kostos."

"Interesting, sir," Brad demurred, "but correct me if I'm wrong. Isn't that sort of thing against the law?"

"These are very unusual times, Brad," answered Pratt, "and as such they call for unusual measures. If any fallout came out of this, it'd not fall on you but on the president. However, I sincerely doubt that will ever happen. Someone has got to stop Kostos. He's attempting to start World War III, only for the purpose of advancing his own egomaniacal agenda to somehow rule the world. This man must be taken out with extreme prejudice. Do you follow me, Brad?"

"Yes, sir, but before you send anyone after him, perhaps I could talk to 'em. I've some rather enlightening information about the man that might be helpful."

"That's why, Mr. Fuller, I'm sending you on this mission. No one on our side knows more about him than you and your Mossad friend. Nor do we have any other assets as close to the situation as you.

"So, listen to me, Brad. We're out of time. Understand this: If this nation and much of the free world, including Israel, are going to avoid catastrophic collapse and survive Kostos' insanity, then he must be taken out as fast as possible."

"Sir," stammered a very reluctant Brad, "I agree, but this man has an impenetrable security net around him 24 hours a day, seven days a week. In addition to that, Kostos isn't, well, he's not normal, sir."

"Fuller, we've no one other than you even remotely qualified to take on this assignment." Pratt's urgency was evident in his plea. "And, if Carr's plan to recapture the government is going to work, then Kostos has to be taken out of the picture. His possible counterpunch using all the assets at his disposal would overwhelm us right now."

"Boss, I don't even know where the guy is!"

"But we do," Pratt responded. "He'll be back in Rome with you in 10 to 20 hours. That gives you and your friend time to plan your mission.

"I can't tell you how critically important it is for you to make this happen. We are dangerously close to the end of life as we know it."

Brad couldn't believe what he was being asked to do. Even more surreal were the reasons why he knew he had no choice but to try to comply.

"All right, sir," Brad sighed, "but I can't speak for whether or not Miss Levy's on board. She'll need to make up her own mind. So, here's what I'll need. I need immediate access to every piece of intel we've got on Kostos no matter how top secret. And I'll need 100 percent access to company assets. Agreed?"

Brad could hear Pratt's sigh of relief, "Agreed. I'll contact our station in Rome myself and tell 'em you've got a blank check. I don't care how much it costs or what it takes, this man must go down."

"Yes, sir, I understand. I'll be in touch."

Hanging up the phone, Brad looked over at Leah. She had fallen asleep on the sofa. Both of them had been through some harrowing experiences over the last 24 hours with hardly any sleep. He decided to let her rest while she could. He would tell her everything when she woke up and let her make up her mind about participating or not.

He dialed room service and ordered a large breakfast and a pot of coffee. Then he headed for the shower. He was not looking forward to what he knew was a real-life "mission impossible."

TWENTY-EIGHT

Two hours prior to landing to refuel at the small private airport just outside London, President Carr, Dr. Cohen, and Agent Spears had been discussing their strategy for touchdown in the States. During that discussion, Agent Spears casually inquired about the call President Carr had made on the satellite phone provided for him at their previous stop in France. His concern was for the president's safety.

Carr had remarked that he was under the impression that a satellite phone call was secure. He was shocked when Spears assured him it was not, and that any conversation on such a device, unless coded or scrambled, could easily be snatched out of the air.

They agreed that there was a possibility that Kostos' intel network could have and that Kostos would go to great lengths to insure that Carr never reached American soil.

Dr. Cohen and Spears decided, for the sake of security, to deplane the president at the refueling stop. They would then rent a car or cab to drive them to London's Heathrow Airport, where they would charter a plane for the remainder of their trip to the United States.

As the Citation landed to refuel, Carr informed the two pilots of his plans, cautioning them to change their flight plan. However, less than an hour and a half after Carr's party left them, the two pilots and the two extra bodyguards had decided it was safe to continue and they had taken off.

Catching a ride to a small village two miles from the airport, Carr and his group paid handsomely for a private cab to take them to Heathrow.

Upon arriving, with Carr in an adequate disguise, they were dropped off on the far side of the airport at a large, private charter company. After a bit of haggling, they charted a luxury G-1 business jet to fly them to the United States.

Becoming airborne, the three passengers tried to relax in the plane's spacious cabin. After a while, President Carr spoke up. "Well, that little hold up only cost us a couple of hours."

Agent Spears, sitting across the aisle from his president, added, "Yes sir, and the pilot just informed me that we'd make up a good bit of that because of strong tailwinds. We're almost back on schedule."

"That's good news. In exactly eight hours I'm to call Pratt and three of my faithful cabinet members and share the plan. That will be 8:00 a.m. U.S. time tomorrow morning. From now on, everything needs to go perfectly if this is going to work."

Dr. Cohen, sitting just behind Carr, chimed in, "Mr. President, we all know the odds are very much against us, and that in the end we're going to need divine intervention to stop Kostos. His plans are very far along."

"You're right," answered the president, "but divine intervention is a variable out of my control. The truth is, we got a late start and now we're playing a desperate game of catch up. To further complicate the matter, we're not even sure what other cards Kostos is holding—but all of us know he's resourceful enough to hedge his bets. So, first things first. We'll move as quickly as possible to regain control of our government and its resources. Only then will we know whether or not it's too late to stop war in the Middle East or to stop Kostos' insanity." With that, the conversation in the cabin quieted as the men became lost in their thoughts and struggled with their own doubts.

They had no idea that the Citation that had flown them to England had just been blown out of the sky by French fighters under Kostos' orders.

After his visit in the Oval Office with President Hunt, Kostos, aboard his IFN 747, had left Washington D.C. Excited that his plans were quickly coming together, Kostos flew to Rome for a final pre-invasion conference with the Russians.

A limo from the Russian Embassy awaited Kostos as he landed at Rome's DaVinci International. He was whisked away and driven through the heart of the city to an eighteenth-century Italian mansion that served as the Russian Embassy.

Upon arrival, he was met by Russia's ambassador and led to a large conference room for a meeting with Russian President, Valenko and the Russian General, Sergy Chevsky, who commanded the coalition forces now massing on Israel's borders.

The ambassador introduced Kostos to the General, and following casual greetings among the group, the ambassador pulled down a large wall map of Israel and its neighbors. There were bright red stars all along Israeli borders indicating where coalition forces were poised, awaiting orders to commence the invasion.

The four men stood looking at the map when President Valenko began, "Chairman Kostos, our General Chevsky has just returned from the Middle East, where he personally inspected our troop disbursements and went over battle plans with commanders of the participant armies. I have asked him to speak to his findings."

With a slight bow of acknowledgement to his president, General Chevsky addressed Kostos. "As you have been informed, Mr. Chairman, I have just completed a most thorough inspection and analysis of the international coalition now hovering on each of Israel's borders."

Reaching over to a tray on the bottom of the map, Chevsky picked up a two-foot-long pointer and continued. "From Egypt to Jordan, along the Jordan Valley to Syria, and on into Lebanon, our coalition forces have completed the encirclement of the Jewish State.

"Our combined troop strength, not including reserve units, now numbers one million men. Every battalion is accompanied by artillery units. We will go into Israel with a tank corps numbering slightly more than 10,000 tanks.

"In the Mediterranean, Israel's only other border, a fleet of Russian attack submarines, numbering 23 subs, sit three miles offshore. And 20 miles further offshore, we have 40 troop carriers with 3,500 troops each. That's 140,000 men, with armor, ready to storm the beaches of Haifa and Tel Aviv as soon as the order is given. They will be assisted by close-in air support of light bombers and fighters.

"Additionally, Mr. Chairman, our combined coalition airpower, now poised to hit Israeli targets, exceeds 3,500 fighters, 2,000 heavy bombers, and 1,800 helicopter gun ships. We also have the powerful Shehab 3 missile arsenal deployed all along the Golan Heights and the Suez Canal.

"The Israelis cannot escape the reign of terror we will soon unleash upon them. We await only your order to begin, sir."

Kostos, standing with his hands clasped behind his back, looked admirably at the map.

"General Chevsky, your reputation as one of the great military strategists of all time is obviously well deserved. I applaud your efforts and your genius. Tell your Council of Coalition Commanders in Damascus they will not have to wait much longer."

Standing proudly at attention, the General saluted the Chairman. "I will convey your message, sir, and thank you." Knowing his presentation was complete, the General left the room with the Ambassador on his heels.

As the door closed behind them, Kostos turned to address the Russian President. "Mr. President, it appears we are ready. But before we give the order to invade, I am going to lift the curtain that has, until now, blinded the prying eyes of the world. I want them to see the power we have amassed against these worthless Jews."

A confused Valenko asked, "But don't you think that would be a big mistake Mr. Chairman? It would give away our coalition's positions, expose our strategy, and hand any possible allies of Israel our battle plans."

"Trust me, Valenko," countered Kostos. "China, Great Britain, Japan, South Korea, the Saudis and a smattering of other pipsqueak nations who have yet to join our IFN family, want nothing to do with this conflict. As for the United States, they will be far too occupied with their own crises to be concerned about Israel's problems."

"I'm not sure I follow your reasoning. But," Valenko added, "if you think it's wise to lift whatever technology you've used to blind the world's radar and surveillance capabilities, then I concur. Perhaps you will soon share with us just how you accomplished such a feat."

Kostos smiled coldly. "Oh, I never give up my secrets, Valenko. But do not ever doubt my abilities. I am the prince of the air that surrounds this miserable planet."

Valenko, not sure what Kostos meant, still felt a chill sweep over him at the comment.

"And now, Mr. President, if you'll excuse me, I've a call to make."

Valenko bowed submissively, "Yes, of course, Mr. Chairman. I'm sure I'll see you later this evening at the ambassador's reception and dinner."

"Of course you will," smirked Kostos as the Russian President left the room.

Walking to the far wall, Kostos picked up the phone stationed there. "Yes, I'm ready for you to make the person-to-person call we discussed."

The voice of the Embassy operator on the other end of the line answered, "Yes, sir. Please hold."

Thirty seconds later, Kostos heard the pleasant voice of Della, the president's secretary, say, "I'll patch you through to the president."

Another 20 seconds passed before President Hunt's voice came on the line. "President Hunt here."

"Well, Mr. President," Kostos began, "since it's 4:00 p.m. here in Rome, that means it's morning time in your part of the world. I'm so glad you're already in your office this morning."

"Kostos, it's 8:00 a.m., and for your information I've been here since 5:00 a.m. fielding calls from panicked leaders all over the world who are scared stiff over the actions of your friends in the Middle East."

"Well, Jordan," Kostos cajoled, "it will all soon be over and you, my good friend, will be a hero hailed as the savior of nine great American cities."

Hunt grimaced, "Kostos, it's the City of New York that's on my mind this morning."

"Well, now, Jordan, we can't save the whole world can we? So, to the point. I want you to set your clock. In exactly 24 hours, that's 8:00 a.m. tomorrow morning Washington D.C. time, you are to push the little red button in your possession. Seconds later, the nuclear weapon in the heart of New York City will detonate. And by pushing that single button, you, Jordan, will have saved millions of lives in cities across America.

"But, do let me remind you, my friend, if for any reason whatsoever you fail to detonate that bomb on time, then my people will be forced to do so—but in addition they will also set off nukes in Atlanta, Chicago, Dallas, Houston, Denver, Los Angeles, San Francisco and Seattle. And did I fail to mention that the final bomb is well-hidden not far from where you now sit? Thus, your failure to do your duty will mean that all of those lovely people in those beautiful cities, including your own Washington D.C., will simply be vaporized.

"So, don't be late. And remember, no matter what happens, push that button at precisely 8:00 a.m. Do you understand me?"

Hunt, sitting trancelike behind his desk, robotically answered, "Yes, I understand."

Without speaking again, Kostos hung up. Jordan Hunt knew he had no choice. To fail meant millions of other lives would also be lost. He knew now he would push the button. Of that he had no doubt.

At the exact moment Kostos was placing his call from Rome to President Hunt, the British-owned G-1 jet touched down at Langley's private airstrip. It was 8:00 a.m.

President Carr had instructed CIA Director Pratt during their last conversation to have the three cabinet members he trusted in his office for a conference call this morning. Carr had no way of knowing that he would be physically present for this morning's meeting, nor did Director Pratt.

The G-1 taxied up to a small terminal where a single young Marine was on guard duty. He was used to government planes coming and going at all hours. His job was to simply check the identities of all those entering the terminal.

As the jet's door fell open and the stair steps deployed, Agent Spears bounded out and briskly approached the terminal. Spears walked directly up to the Marine who authoritatively addressed him, "Good morning, sir. May I see your ID?"

Spears, used to the routine, flashed his Secret Service badge. Upon seeing it, the young Marine came to attention, saluted and inquired, "Can I assist you in any way, sir?"

The agent smiled, "Yes, in fact you can. Are you the only one on duty this morning?"

"Yes, sir. And my shift ends in one hour. But it being Sunday and all means we don't usually see much traffic. The terminal staff is off on Sundays as well."

Spears had noticed only one old car in the small lot next to the building.

"I know you Marine guys are 'can-do' people. So, what we need is emergency transportation for a foreign VIP whom we have just flown into the country on a secret mission." Spears, in a conspiratorial tone, continued, "But before I continue, I guess I better ask you what your security rating is, Marine."

The young recruit, sensing he was being made part of something of great importance, answered, "Sir, I hold a level four security clearance."

Continuing his ruse, Spears shook his head in disappointment. "Oh, man. All this is way above your pay grade Marine. So, I guess I've no choice but to use my emergency authority. Stand at attention, son, and raise your right hand."

The green Marine instantly obeyed as Spears continued, "By the authority vested in me by the government of the United States of America, I, hereby grant you the security clearances necessary to fulfill your duties for the duration of this top-secret operation. Do you...what'd you say your name was?"

"Private Benjamin, sir."

"No kidding? Just like the movie, huh? All right, do you, Private Benjamin, swear to keep all secrets that you may become privy too during this operation?"

"I do, sir, but..."

"That's great, Benjamin. Now, is that your automobile in the lot?"

"Actually, sir, it's my girlfriend's. But it's a real pile of junk, hardly fit for a VIP."

Spears ordered, "That's okay, Benjamin. Give me the keys. I'm requisitioning the vehicle. It will be returned shortly."

"But, sir, let me call up a limo from HQ. You don't want to put a VIP in there," stammered the Marine.

"Benjamin," Spears said much more sternly, "I've no time to tell you twice. This is an emergency."

"Okay, sir." The recruit dug into his pocket, pulled out a set of keys, and handed them to the agent.

"Very good," Spears barked. "Now maintain your station and tell no one what you've seen and heard today."

The agent made his way to the parking lot and approached the dilapidated, dented Toyota. The driver's side door squeaked loudly as he began to open it, and then popped louder as he opened it wide enough to get in. The interior was a bigger mess than the outside. The upholstery was torn, old fast food containers were throughout, and a woman's dirty laundry was piled up in the passenger's seat. Throwing as much trash as he could into the car's trunk, Spears jumped back in and cranked the engine. Coming to life, the Toyota shot a large, blue-gray cloud of smoke out of the exhaust.

Knowing he had no other option than to use the junker if he was to get the president to Pratt in time, Spears cautiously pulled the beat-up Toyota close to the jet's stairway. He jumped out, ran up the short stairs, and told Dr. Cohen and the president, "Sirs, your limo awaits."

Exiting the jet behind Spears, the two men stared in disbelief at their transportation.

Dr. Cohen chuckled, "Are things so bad in the U.S.?"

Carr looked back at the doctor with a shake of his head and joked, "Doc, ya see what happens to the economy if I'm off the job for even a little while?"

Spears, somewhat embarrassed, responded, "Sorry, sir, but you did say hurry, and there's no other automobile anywhere near. So, shall we?"

Laughing at themselves, the three men crawled into the car and puttered off toward the CIA buildings only 10 minutes away.

Director Pratt, Secretary of Defense Carl Bates, Secretary of State James Parlay and Chair of Joint Chiefs Admiral Withers sat at the round table with a speaker phone terminal in the center awaiting what Pratt had convinced them was an urgent call. No one other than Pratt knew it was President Carr's call they were awaiting. All the three cabinet members knew, was that according to the director, the incoming call scheduled for 8:00 a.m., was a matter of national security.

It was now 8:15 a.m. Pratt was checking his watch again when Agent Cooper burst in. "Chief, someone in basement parking is on the intercom. Says you're expecting him. It sounds to me like the same guy that called you a few days ago, that Titan guy."

The thought that President Carr was this very moment downstairs in the parking basement stunned Pratt.

"Uh, okay. Cooper, you stay here. See if these men would like another cup of coffee or a donut or something. I'll go check it out." Pratt rushed out of the room.

The cabinet members, not understanding, just looked at each other as Agent Cooper, with a sheepish grin, asked, "Can I get you guys anything?"

Meanwhile, the elevator Pratt took to the parking area in the basement seemed to take forever to get there. Finally, the doors opened.

The first thing Pratt noticed was an old jalopy sitting in a cloud of gray smoke. Squinting his eyes, he finally saw President Carr, Agent Spears, and an older gentleman walking toward him.

"May the gods be praised!" shouted Pratt as he ran toward the threesome.

Ignoring protocol, Pratt ran and grabbed Carr in a serious bear hug.

"It's really you, sir. I can't believe you're here. I thought you were gonna call."

Regaining his composure, Pratt released the president and added, "Forgive me, Mr. President, but you can't even begin to imagine how good it is to see you. Why didn't you tell me you were coming? I would've met you."

"Wasn't enough time," Carr said turning to Dr. Cohen. "Dr. Cohen, this is Director Pratt and Pratt, you've met Agent Spears before. These two men have saved my life more than once."

Shaking hands all around, the men greeted each other.

Carr continued, "Are the men I asked you to get together all here, Pratt?"

"Indeed, they are, sir. They're waiting upstairs in my office. None of them has a clue that you're alive. And today, being Sunday, we've only got a skeleton crew working on other floors. Coop is with the men, but no one else is up there."

"Well," Carr said as he patted Pratt on the back and moved toward the elevator, "lead me to your office, Mr. Director. It's time for my resurrection."

"I sure hope that none of the men in my office have heart trouble," chuckled Pratt.

Dr. Cohen also patted Pratt on the back as they entered the elevator, saying, "Not to worry, Mr. Director. I am one of the top cardiologists in the world." Everyone on board was smiling broadly as the doors slid shut.

TWENTY-NINE

Exiting the elevator, the men were approaching the door to Pratt's office when the director stopped them in the middle of the hall. "Mr. President, with your permission, perhaps it would help soften the shock factor if I went in first and explained that you're still alive."

Carr agreed, "All right, Mr. Director, we'll just wait here for a few moments as you lay the groundwork."

As Pratt walked into his office, the three cabinet members at the conference table stopped their chatter and turned their attention toward the director. "Gentlemen," Pratt began without taking a seat, "I do apologize for my sudden exit and for the short interruption, but it seems there's a new development. As you all know, for sometime now I have suspected that President Carr was possibly still alive. Well, it seems that my suspicions have been confirmed and that, indeed, Carr is alive."

The impatient Secretary of State interrupted him, "Oh, come on, Pratt. You need to get over the loss, move on with your life. We've got big problems we must deal with now. Even if Carr was alive, he's not here now. So the ball is in our court and we best decide what to do."

Just as the Secretary finished, the office door swung open and President Mathew Dillon Carr walked into the room, followed by Dr. Cohen and Agent Spears.

"Gentlemen, good morning. In the immortal words of Mark Twain, 'the rumors of my death have been greatly exaggerated.'"

Instinctively, the cabinet members jumped to their feet with mouths open and eyes wide. They were speechless. Pratt spoke to break the silence, "Men, you're not looking at a ghost. Our president was severely injured in the crash of Air Force One. These two gentlemen with our president, Dr. Cohen and Agent Spears of the Secret Service are responsible for saving his life."

Before Pratt could continue, the stunned but elated Secretary of Defense, Carl Bates, reached over and enthusiastically shook Carr's hand, "I don't care how you got here, sir, but I for one, couldn't be happier! Welcome back, sir."

Secretary Parlay, equally stunned, added, "Sir, you've certainly chosen a most challenging moment to return to the land of the living. Welcome home, Mr. President."

Parlay was heartily shaking Carr's hand when the Admiral spoke up, "May I say, sir, you are a most pleasant sight for sore eyes as well as an answer to the prayers of millions of Americans. And by the way, Mr. President, Parlay is right. We have a situation that is almost irredeemable. I can't tell you how grateful I am to see you, sir."

After the heartfelt greetings and vigorous shaking of hands, President Carr asked them all to be seated.

"All right, gentlemen," he began, "I've been thoroughly briefed on our current situation. The first thing I need from each of you is your perspective and suggestions on the positive steps we need to take. I'll also need what you consider to be the risk level assessment of any suggestions you propose. Then, we'll establish our priorities. Lastly, we need to agree on a plan to retake the reins of this government without ushering in chaos or tearing the very sensitive fabric of the nation's psyche.

"So, let's begin."

Just five minutes into the meeting in Pratt's office, the director's intercom beeped. Agent Cooper's voice came over the speaker, "Sir, you've got a call from the president's secretary, Miss Della Stiles."

"Thank you, Coop. Tell her to hold on and I'll be with her in just a moment."

"Yes sir, Boss."

Pratt turned to President Carr, "Sir, I need to inform you that Della, your personal secretary, stayed on the job after your reported demise to serve as President Hunt's secretary."

"All right," Carr responded "…and?"

"And," Pratt continued, "as you know, your predecessor was under investigation for possible corruption. It had been decided by the previous CIA leadership to work with the FBI by setting Della Stiles up as his personal secretary. She is, or should I say, was at the time, a CIA agent of vast experience."

"You're telling me," snapped Carr, "that the CIA has been spying on me by planting that woman in my office?"

"No, sir." hurried Pratt. "When you won the election, she chose to resign from the agency because she was worn out and tired of being a field agent. She decided she enjoyed working with you in the White House and took that on full-time. However, when Hunt took over and revealed his incompetence, she agreed to be re-activated to help us monitor him."

President Carr, with a slight smile, said, "Take the call, Pratt."

"Yes, sir."

Pratt quickly picked up the phone and pushed a button. "Pratt here. Go ahead, Della."

Her voice had the sound of urgency in it, "Sir, I've some very bizarre and disturbing info."

"Go ahead, Della," Pratt prompted, "I'm listening."

"Well, as you know, we've been attempting to tap into the Oval Office security lines. Those attempts have been met with only minimal success. However, this morning, less than 30 minutes ago, via creative eavesdropping on my part, I caught parts of a call placed to Hunt from this Mr. Kostos."

"And?" Pratt coaxed.

"Again, sir, I could only catch pieces here and there but it sounded like they were discussing some nuclear devices now hidden in some American cities. I know they talked about one of them stashed somewhere in New York City. I've no idea about the others.

"But, sir, the most bizarre part of the conversation was Kostos telling Hunt that he must push a button at precisely 8:00 a.m. tomorrow morning."

"Now, listen carefully, Della. Are you absolutely sure they were talking about nuclear weapons?"

"I'm absolutely certain, but like I said, I couldn't get the entire conversation. Even though our efforts to tap those lines have only been marginally successful, I'm sure there's a whole lot more of what they said captured on that tape."

Pratt jumped in to ask, "Where is that tape now?"

"I have it in my purse. It's the only copy, and I dare not send this to you via a carrier. So, with your permission, sir, I can drive my own car and bring it out to you. I can be in your office with it in less than 40 minutes."

"Della," Pratt said excitedly, "that tape may give us the key to stop a nuclear holocaust on American soil. Are you absolutely certain that no one else knows of this tape's existence?"

"I'm absolutely sure. As soon as they hung up, I went to the hidden recorder and took it out. I've had it since."

"All right, Della, listen carefully." Pratt instructed, "Leave now. I'll dispatch a security team from here to meet you halfway. Leave the White House as nonchalantly as possible. Go directly to your car and drive straight here without stopping.

"And, please, be very, very careful. I'll be in my office waiting for you. And by the way, great job."

"Thank you, sir. I'm on my way."

And the line went dead.

Agent Cooper, just down the hall in his own small office, gently replaced the extension line he had used to listen in on the conversation between the director and Della.

He stood quickly, walked to the stairwell, jogged down to the ground floor and exited out a back door to a parking lot between the buildings. At the corner of the building, he looked around to be sure no one was watching him. Satisfied that he was out of view of all security cameras, he pulled a cell phone out of his coat pocket, pushed in a number and waited.

After only one ring, a male voice answered, "Yes?"

"Yea," Cooper whispered, "it's me. It's urgent. The White House lady is carrying a tape with the conversation between Kostos and Hunt earlier this morning. No one, including her, has heard the tape yet but she's on her way to deliver it to Director Pratt. Stop her en route. Kill her and eliminate that tape. You've got very little time."

Cooper killed the line, quickly stuffed the cell back into his pocket, and re-entered the office building.

When Pratt completed his conversation with Della, Carr continued with the meeting while they awaited her arrival.

"Okay," Carr directed, "in order to maintain the proper chain of command during this transition of power, the Secretary of State and Defense, as well as your people at the Pentagon, Admiral, must remain steadfast, focused and under a tight rein. Each of you men must be prepared to have your authority challenged. In all likelihood, many of your subordinates will be put in a position to choose whose orders they should obey. If Hunt and his cohorts contest my authority, each of you must be certain that your departments are prepared to follow your lead."

"Sir, excuse me," put in the Secretary of State, "Doesn't the same Twenty-Fifth Amendment to the constitution that put Hunt in the presidency also provide for his removal if and when the president he's replaced is capable of returning and reassuming his responsibilities?"

Director Pratt took the question, "Under normal circumstances, Mr. Secretary, that's true. But to be honest, the Twenty-Fifth Amendment addresses only two conditions for replacing a sitting president with a Vice President. The first condition addresses an incapacitated president who is unable for one reason or another to fulfill his duties. That includes impeachment, or mental and physical impairments.

"The second provision for a Vice President to be sworn in as president is in the case of a president's death.

"However, the Twenty-Fifth Amendment, technically speaking, does not directly address a scenario where a sitting president has died and then comes back to life."

"In other words," concluded Secretary Parlay, "if Hunt and his people challenge President Carr's return to power, they could create a constitutional crisis. Untangling that mess would take months. And we don't have months."

Nodding his agreement, Carr added, "Further, gentlemen, if what Della Stiles told us is confirmed on that tape she's bringing, then our deadline for success is 8 o'clock tomorrow morning. That gives us less than 24 hours to pull this off. We do not have time for a constitutional cat fight."

"So, Mr. President," Secretary Bates asked, "how do you suggest we proceed?"

"Carl, I suggest we approach Hunt directly, confront him personally, and do so without warning him."

Pratt leaned in, "You mean, just walk in and announce you're back and tell him he's out?

"Do pardon me, Mr. President," Pratt added, "but if only 10 percent of what we know about Hunt's treasonous acts is true, he should be prosecuted to the full extent of the law."

President Carr cleared his throat and responded, "Men, our first priorities should be: protect the American people, preserve the Republic and severely deal with all enemies, foreign and domestic, as quickly as possible. We don't have the luxury of knowing our adversary's game plan. As such, we must act quickly to surgically remove Hunt from power. We can deal with all his treasonous acts later. If we fail, it's all academic anyway."

The Admiral spoke up, "All right then, so each of us in the cabinet needs to secure our chain of command and prepare our staffs to stand up and fully support your immediate re-installment as president."

"That's correct Admiral, and everything must be timed like a well-orchestrated ballet." Carr continued, "The director has informed me that Chief Justice Bailey of the Supreme Court will be 100 percent supportive of our position and, fortunately, most of the other judges follow his lead. I'm told Bailey detests Hunt and his incompetence and didn't like having to give him the oath of office in the first place."

"So," Pratt added, "Agent Spears, Chief Justice Bailey, whom we'll touch base with shortly, myself and the president will make a surprise visit to Mr. Hunt either late this afternoon or tonight. The president will explain to Hunt that he's being relieved from duty and the Chief Justice will be present to confirm the legality of it. And in an effort to be graceful, you'll ask him to return to his position as Vice President. If he cooperates, the FBI will use a warrant provided by the Justice Department to snatch him and seriously interrogate him as we move to stabilize the foreign and domestic crises about to overrun us.

"Also, Mr. President, I should inform you that I've assigned a team to carry out your finding regarding Charon Kostos. They're to complete their mission within the next 24 hours."

"Very good," Carr answered. "Now, a closing word, gentlemen. All of us in this room fully realize that we may be on very shaky constitutional footing and that things could go very wrong.

"If we fail to pull this off, God only knows what Hunt and Kostos have in store for our country. Very possibly they are planning a nuclear nightmare and a hostile takeover of our government. I trust that each of you, by now, has considered your individual fates if we fail. It will not be pleasant."

"Excuse me, Mr. President," Pratt said, "but I know I speak for everyone at this table. Each of us realizes that the fate of our nation is at stake, as well as each of our lives. Still, without exception, all of us are on board with you. Sink or swim, fail or succeed, live or die, we will not fail to do our duty."

All the men around the table nodded and murmured their agreement.

"Then, gentlemen..."

Before the president could finish the sentence, Pratt's intercom beeped again, followed by Cooper's voice.

"Sir, I've got a Captain Earl Davis with the D.C. Police on the line. Says it's about a Della Stiles. I thought you'd want to take it."

A sullen quiet filled the room until Pratt finally answered.

"All right, Coop. Tell him I'll be with him in two minutes." Pratt's eyes met Carr's. Both conveyed profound concern.

Della had left the White House and made only one stop—to put gasoline in her four-year-old Tahoe. From the filling station she headed south to pick up the freeway toward Langley. Catching the red light at the corner of the last intersection prior to turning on to the freeway auxiliary road, she stopped. Traffic was light and while she waited for the light to turn green, a man approached her driver's side window. Before she had an opportunity to react, the man pointed a gun and fired two shots through the window into her head.

The assailant opened the door, leaned in, and turned off the ignition. He reached across Della's lifeless body, turned her purse upside-down, spilling the contents all over the front seat. The item he was after spilled out with the rest of her things. He reached over and retrieved the mini-cassette audiotape, slammed the door and ran.

Pratt pushed the button on the phone so everyone could listen to the conversation over the speaker.

"Pratt here. How can I help you, Captain?"

"Yes, director. About a half an hour ago, I was called to the scene of what appears to be a botched carjacking turned homicide.

"The vic, a Della Stiles, carried a CIA ID in her purse. Do you know this lady, sir?"

"Captain Davis, you haven't put any of this out on the radio yet have you?"

"No, sir, I have not."

"I'm sure you understand, Captain, that presently I can neither deny nor confirm the info you've inquired about. However, we'd like you to have her car towed out here to Langley, and her remains sent to Andrews Air Force base for an autopsy. Can you tell me how she was killed?"

"Well," Captain Davis continued, "like I said, it appears to be an attempted carjacking. Lots of these punks don't like resistance and will kill ya without blinking an eye. Your lady friend, if that's what she was, took two .38 caliber slugs in the head."

"Could robbery have been the motive?" asked Pratt.

"Well, sir, the perps emptied her purse but left a couple of hundred in cash, her credit cards, and didn't touch her jewelry. Likely they got scared and took off."

"Captain Davis," Pratt concluded, "I appreciate your cooperation on this matter and I thank you for your discretion. As you may have surmised, this is now a matter of national security and our people in cooperation with the FBI will take it from here."

"You got it, sir."

As the line went dead, a somber silence filled the room. Finally, Pratt said, "We lost a great agent in that lady. She was a class act."

"It seems, Mr. Director," Carr softly answered, "that all of those among us are not of us. There is no way anyone could've gotten to Della that quickly unless they got a warning that she was on her way here with that tape."

"You're right, sir," added Pratt, "but no one in this room has left this room since Della's call. It couldn't be any of us."

Agent Spears, quiet until now spoke up, "Who else knew about that tape?"

"Della and I were the only ones who knew she had set up the recording system. She was an electronic genius. She needed no help," answered the director.

"Then it's quite obvious, sir," returned Spears, "either someone in the White House listened in on your conversation with Della when she called here or someone in this building picked up that call. And whoever it was immediately got word to the bad guys that she needed to be killed and the tape taken from her."

"You're right, Spears," added President Carr. "Pratt, sweep this office, run a security check on all your phones and figure out who else could've possibly listened in on that call.

"In the meantime, Admiral, and Secretaries of State and Defense, go take care of business. Keep your cell phones close. I'll be in touch soon."

A corporate "yes, sir" was heard as all three Cabinet members stood to leave. As they left the room, President Carr addressed the director.

"Pratt, put the best people you most trust on this investigation. We'll take time later to properly honor Della. Right now we need you to hand over this in-house situation to your people, and then you must get over to the Court and talk to the Chief Justice. Don't tell him I'm alive yet. Tell him he must meet you about a matter concerning Hunt and national security.

"I'll call you in one hour to set up a meeting place for the three of us."

"Yes, sir, Mr. President," Pratt returned.

"And, Pratt, I'm sorry about Della. She was a friend of mine as well. Whoever did this will pay."

"Thank you, sir." The remaining men stood and filed out of the room to prepare for the confrontation that lay ahead. It was now 10:00 a.m.

Following his conversation with Director Pratt from his suite in Rome, Brad continued to let Leah sleep where she had collapsed on the couch.

After taking a hot shower and eating a room service breakfast, he decided to try and get a few hours sleep himself. He set the radio alarm clock to wake him at 6:00 p.m. It did so right on time, but with a mind-jarring, full-volume rendition of American 70s disco music. The horrendously loud music rattled Brad to partial consciousness.

With eyes still closed, the semi-comatose agent reached over to the nightstand in a desperate attempt to find an "off" button. Groping everywhere, he failed to find a way to turn off the ear-splitting noise. Finally, in an act of frustration and desperation, he got his hand around the cord, and with a violent jerk, pulled the plug from the outlet. Eyes still tightly shut, he willed himself to throw his legs over the edge of the bed and sit up.

Before he could fully wake himself, he heard Leah's sleepy voice, "Fuller, why would anyone think it's necessary to set the volume on the radio alarm on 10? Are you deaf?"

Shaking his head, with squinting eyes, he saw her standing in the doorway. He could tell by her hoarse voice, disheveled look, and wrinkled clothes that the alarm had also awakened her.

"Sorry, Miss Levy. I didn't realize the volume was cranked up so high."

As he struggled to get up out of the bed, he asked, "Why don't you go take a shower and I'll order a pot of coffee and something to eat. I've also got news from home you'll want to hear after you finish."

"All right," Leah agreed as she scratched her still sleepy head, "but don't order bacon." And with that, the shower room door slammed shut.

Twenty minutes later, Leah exited wearing a full-length bathrobe provided by the hotel, and with a towel wrapped around her just-shampooed hair.

The tantalizing aroma of fresh baked bread and hot coffee drew her into the suite's living room, where Brad stood over a cart full of breads, fruits and bagels.

"Oh, that smells good," Leah said as she moved toward him.

Turning at the sound of her voice, he saw her enter wearing the robe and with a towel-draped head. He paused to look and thought to himself, "Even just out of the shower she's exquisite."

The truth was, any man on earth would have thought the same thing. Brad walked to meet her, offering a cup of hot coffee. "Well, at least we got some well-deserved rest. I trust you found your couch comfortable."

Sipping at her coffee, Leah nodded. "I must've passed out as soon as we walked in the room. I had no idea I was so exhausted."

"Like I said," Brad replied as he poured his own cup of coffee, "it was a well-deserved rest. Everything that went on before was so surreal. It's all kind of a big blur now."

"Oh, I remember enough to know it's not something I'm eager to experience again."

"And," Brad countered, "on another note. Before I passed out, I had an interesting chat with Director Pratt in Washington, D.C."

Leah, most curious to know how the call went, took a seat on the couch. "So, what's the word on your missing president? And is your government going to do anything about the armies massing on my country's borders?"

"One thing at a time, Miss Levy," Brad sat down in the lounge chair with his coffee. "To make a very long story short, President Carr has somehow miraculously made his way to somewhere on U.S. soil. He and close confidants are preparing as we speak to retake control of the government.

"As for the armies on your borders, I'd guess they're still forming up to invade. All I know about the situation is what I heard on the WNN news earlier. They reported that your feisty Prime Minister rejected Kostos' proposals that would have, supposedly, guaranteed peace. So, I imagine that as of this moment, the war drums continue beating."

Shaking her head, Leah gazed into her cup. "Here we go again. The world sits on the sidelines as our enemies prepare to invoke the final solution, the extermination of all things Jewish."

"There is still hope, Leah. Director Pratt has a presidential finding provided by Carr."

Turning her head, Leah inquired, "What's a presidential finding?"

"Well, it's a highly classified document from a president who has determined that the nation faces a clear and present danger of major proportions. It gives an agency permission to assign an agent or agents to perform covert ops that may or may not skirt the legal boundaries of the Constitution. It also guarantees said agents full immunity from repercussions or prosecution for his actions."

"And," Leah queried, "this finding is asking you to do what, exactly?"

Brad stood up, walked to the cart, and refilled his cup with coffee. "In short, I've got orders to move with haste to assassinate Kostos."

"You've got to be kidding! I mean, it's no shock to me that a government would do something like that, but Kostos isn't just your standard, everyday, maniacal, power-hungry Hitler wannabe. The guy is…is not *human*. Did you tell 'em what we saw in that chapel?"

"No, I didn't. But even if I would have told them, and even if by some remote possibility they'd believed me, it would have only increased their desire to be rid of the monster."

"And what is it they think we can do to bring him down?"

"That's now my problem. Your involvement isn't required or requested. I want you to go home to Jerusalem. Your people will need you."

"Fuller, are you crazy? I started this op and I assure you, I will finish this op, regardless of your or anyone else's protests. Do you understand that?"

"Frankly, no. I don't understand. This isn't just another operation. It's a suicide mission. People are going to die. In all probability, I'll be one of 'em. And if I'm able to find a chink in Kostos' armor, I assure you, I'll take him with me.

"But, you, Leah, can add nothing to the success of this mission. It's senseless for you to take the risk."

Leah gasped with indignation, jumped up off the couch, and moved toward Brad. "I beg your pardon? I've covered your buns over and over again throughout this mission. I am the best that the best in the world have.

"In that firefight out in the Israeli desert, my last full clip fired into that pack of Hamas killers backed them down just long enough for our gun ships to arrive.

"And when Father Portega was about the blow your head off, I took him out and saved your hide. Over and over again, Fuller, I've done my part and more.

"So, don't you think for one minute that you can just dump me, especially when my country is at risk because of this freak Kostos. I flatly refuse to…"

Before she could finish her sentence, Brad stood up, reached out, embraced her and held her close. Without releasing her, he quietly spoke into her ear.

"Leah, listen to me, please." She quieted.

He gently broke the hug and backed up slightly with his hands on her shoulders. Gazing into her eyes, he spoke tenderly. "For once in your life, Leah Levy, just listen and do not say anything until I finish, okay?"

Sensing his urgency, she simply nodded.

Brad continued softly, "From the moment we began this mission my life has been changing. I've become a very different person than what I was before meeting you. For the first time in my life, I actually care for someone else more than I do for myself. Without even knowing it, you've taught me that life is so much more than adrenaline rushes, fast cars, faster women and thrilling ops.

"You're so different. In a thousand, thousand ways you're different from any woman I've ever met. At first, when I told you how I felt, I hated myself, but now I'm glad you know. I can no more deny my love for you than you can deny your God. And I want you to live. Go back to that lucky guy you told me about. The one who owns your heart. Marry him. Have a houseful of babies and live happily ever after.

"All I ask of you is to let me finish this job alone."

As he poured out his heart, Leah stood staring deep into Brad's eyes. She felt not only the fire of his passion, but the power of his compassion for her, her people and for his own people. She sensed the hunger in his soul for the peace and vitality he saw in her.

Leah was moved by his willingness to sacrifice himself if it meant she, whom he loved, could live. He was still speaking, but she was not listening as much to his words as she was to his heart.

Finally, Brad fully released her, and looked into her eyes. "It took me a very long time to find something worth loving and living for. But it's also worth dying for. Go home. Stay alive. Live."

Leah stepped closer, put her hands on his face, and turned him so he had to look straight into her eyes. As her own eyes filled with tears they could not contain, she spoke. "Now you listen.

"You, too, are different from any man I've ever met. You're so absolutely sure of yourself. You're not intimidated by strong women. You sense no need to try to prove your manhood. And deep down in you is a powerfully compassionate, gentle, and kind human being. You can be strong, brave, and tough but underneath all that bravado you are a tender, wonderful, loving man.

"I didn't want to fall in love with you. I've fought it every step of the way. But I've lost that battle." The tears were cascading down her reddened cheeks, but she went on. "You need to know, Brad, that the other man in my life, the one I told you about the day you said you loved me, is not just another man.

"I was referring to my Messiah, *Yeshua Ha Meschiach.* I'm totally devoted to Him. He came to me at a moment of great despair, embraced me, and changed me. I knew I had to say something to put you off that day. I can never fully give myself to any man who does not share in my relationship with my King.

"But heaven help me, I do love you, Brad Fuller. I do. And in time you will come to know Yeshua and to love Him as do I. I believe that, because I know God brought you to me. He will perform the rest of it as well.

"Now, try to understand this. Whether you realize it or not, both of us are alive today for one reason only. And that is because those beasts, Kostos and the Pope, in their altered states, recognized that I belong to Yeshua. Try to remember, how in all the confusion, evil sounds, smoke, and stench, those beastly creatures backed off and could not harm us. Why?

"They said, it was because 'the girl belongs to the Nazarene.'

"Don't you see it, Brad? For reasons you may not fully understand yet, they cannot harm me. Yeshua is that Nazarene.

"Like it or not, I'm the one real advantage you need in order to survive long enough to get close to Kostos. You must take me with you. Otherwise you will fail. And both of us will lose."

At Leah's last words, Brad sank back down into the lounge chair, silent.

After a few quiet moments he spoke.

"I had no idea you cared," he said. "But I think I'm beginning to understand why you were afraid to say you did. I had convinced myself I must go on without you. And the fact is, I'm still confused over much of what you just said. Are all men this thick?"

Leah laughingly plopped herself back down on the couch. "Finally, a man who's big enough to admit it! I know I love you now, Brad Fuller."

Brad sighed deeply. "Okay, we will deal with us later. Right now, we've some devils to take out. So, why don't you get dressed? We've got a couple of stops to make before we walk into the lion's den."

She stood up, and walking out, said, "It's all completely in His hands now. We won't be going in alone."

Hearing the door close behind her, Brad softly said to himself, "Yeah, well, alone or not, I've seen the power of Kostos and we are no match."

THIRTY

Leaving Pratt's office, President Carr, Dr. Cohen and Agent Spears decided to go to the Pentagon where Admiral Withers was to secret them into an abandoned, underground situation room. There they would continue to make the necessary preparations and contacts before confronting Hunt.

In an effort to keep a low profile and to maintain anonymity, the three men decided to make the drive in the old, beat up, smoking Toyota that belonged to the Marine's girlfriend. However, upon entering the freeway traffic, Spears could not get the old car to go faster than 40 miles an hour. To further complicate matters, the exhaust was belching an ever-growing cloud of blue smoke. Slowly puttering down the freeway, the heavy traffic swirling around them was being forced to brake hard or to swerve around the obnoxious Toyota.

Officer Tibbett, a D.C. traffic cop, sat in his squad car on a well-camouflaged off ramp with his radar gun. At first, all he saw was a huge cloud of smoke billowing over the slight rise of the freeway. As he watched it approach, the blue-gray cloud continued to grow, engulfing the traffic behind it.

When it got closer, Officer Tibbett finally saw a dilapidated, old automobile slowly moving just barely ahead of the billowing cloud. The enormous cloud, the swerving traffic, angry horns, and irate gesturing drivers forced to maneuver around the smoking car provoked the officer to turn on his emergency lights and siren, and pull out behind the Toyota as it hobbled past his position.

Through the smoke screen behind him, Spears could barely see the squad car's flashing lights in his rearview mirror.

"Uh-oh, Mr. President, we've got a cop on our tail. Normally I'd suggest evade and escape, but the odds of either in this old heap are very much against us. Perhaps if you could put your sunglasses on, pull your hat down, turn up the collar of your coat, and act like a sick ol' senior citizen, I can talk our way out of this. Just remember, sir, you are now my sick old uncle who's very ill, and I'm rushing you to the hospital."

As Carr complied and sank low in the back seat, Spears slowly pulled over to the shoulder and stopped. The police officer sat and allowed the smoke to dissipate before he got out and slowly walked up to Spear's window.

"Mister, I need to see your driver's license, registration and proof of insurance."

Spears worked to free his wallet as Officer Tibbett leaned down to look into the Toyota, where he saw Dr. Cohen's smiling face and a huddled-down, old fellow in the back seat.

"Officer," Spears said as he handed the policeman his driver's license and his Secret Service ID, "I'm off duty today visiting my only living uncle and a few minutes ago the elderly fella, who has emphysema, collapsed at his home. My car wouldn't start, so a friend lent me this one to rush him to the hospital. I apologize, but I've no clue where the registration and insurance cards are."

Maintaining his cool, unsmiling demeanor behind his dark shades, the officer said, "Sir, turn the ignition off. Stay in the automobile and I'll be right back."

As the policeman walked back to his squad car, Spears said, "This can't be good. He's gonna run these tags. Then they'll call the young lady who owns this lovely pile of junk."

President Carr and Dr. Cohen sat quietly until Spears saw the officer through his rearview mirror emerge from his car. Reaching the driver's side window, the officer bent down and handed Spears his driver's license back.

"All right, Agent Spears, we've checked with the rightful owner of this vehicle and she told us her boyfriend had borrowed it. She told my sergeant that her sweetheart is in the Service. So here's your Secret Service ID back as well. Your girlfriend also gave us her proper insurance info so you're free to go as soon as you sign this citation. I'm giving you the citation for lack of pollution control. Don't put this automobile back on the road without the proper repairs."

"Yes, sir, and thank you, officer," Spears nodded. He put the old Toyota in gear and pressed the accelerator. He drove away leaving Officer Tibbett coughing in a thick cloud of smoke.

Twenty long minutes later, the Toyota rolled up to a security gate at the Pentagon. Admiral Withers had prepared the guards for Spear's arrival. One of the uniformed officers in the security hut came out directing Spears to follow him. The man got in an army vehicle and led them to an underground entrance. They were led down until the guard stopped his car in front of a doorway marked, "No admittance, secure area."

The driver pointed at the door and drove off.

As Spears pulled the Toyota into a parking spot next to the door and turned off the ignition, the door of the building swung open. Admiral Withers stood just inside, motioning the trio to make haste and enter.

The men entered, quietly greeted by the Admiral, and followed him down a hallway, stopping in front of an elevator. Admiral Withers inserted a key into a security lock on the wall and the elevator opened.

The Admiral turned to President Carr. "Sir, 200 feet below the surface this lift will stop. That area is off-limits by my order, and is totally deserted. Once you exit the elevator, directly across the hall is a fully functional situation room, complete with all the comm devices you may need, as well as monitors connected to all media broadcasts. You'll also find a direct line to my office. Let me know if you need anything.

"There's a kitchen, fully stocked, across from the situation room. So help yourselves.

Pratt is on his way to meet the Chief Justice. He said he would contact you here when he's finished briefing him."

"You've done well, Admiral," said the president. "Thank you. I'll be in touch."

The three men stepped into the elevators and the doors shut. It was now 11:10 a.m.

Thirty minutes after pulling over the smoking Toyota, Officer Tibbett's shift was ending and he was driving the squad car back to the substation. Without warning, his onboard computer flashed that he had an updated readout available. Officer Tibbett pushed a button on his small keyboard ordering the update to come on screen.

The first thing he saw was a picture of Agent Spears.

Tibbett, following procedure, had sent Spears' drivers license and his Secret Service identification in to the police database for confirmation of the ID and to check for any outstanding warrants. It had taken Spears' information longer than usual to make its rounds through the system because of the layered bureaucracies.

Under the picture of Agent Spears, the officer read the man's accompanying short bio and history. At the bottom, in bright red letters, all in caps it read, DECEASED-KILLED IN LINE OF DUTY-ROME, ITALY, followed by the date on which Air Force One had been shot down.

"You've got to be kidding," Tibbett said out loud. He picked up his radio mike to call his captain at headquarters. He wanted to be sure that the information concerning the death of Agent Spears was corrected on the D.C. P.D. and other interagency computers. Spears, Tibbett knew, absolutely was not deceased.

He was very much alive in Washington, D.C. taking care of his invalid uncle.

"Someone," chuckled Officer Tibbett, "must be playing jokes over at the Secret Service. They're gonna get chewed out for this one."

It was noon in New York City and Patricia Dees was leaving work early to attend to some personal errands and chores. After picking up her six-year-old son, Billy, from the day care and school center provided by the company for employees' children, she went to the subway station to await their ride. Patricia took a seat on a bench on the platform and as she waited, used her cell phone to confirm her afternoon appointments. She had to get her hair done, pick up the dry cleaning, pay an overdue electricity bill, and get Billy to the dentist for a routine checkup.

While Patricia was preoccupied on her cell phone, her always-over-active son was again sneaking his way to the platform's edge. He was determined to check on the hidden treasure he had discovered only days before. The large suitcase had been underneath the overhang of the platform and Billy had been thinking of little else since he was forced to leave it.

Standing on the platform's edge, Billy took another bite of the peanut-butter-and-jelly sandwich in his hand and casually looked back at his mother to make sure she was still focused on her phone calls and not on him. She was jabbering away and jotting things down on her notepad.

Billy decided it was time. He jumped off the edge, landing three feet below on the subway tracks. Wasting no time, Billy dropped down and scampered up under the platform into the cave-like hole, a bit further back. As his eyes adjusted, he once again saw the three blinking green lights on his treasure chest. He had already decided that since the chest was too big for him to move, he would try to open it and carry its contents out a little at a time.

Crawling close to the shiny silver case, Billy noticed two clasp latches on front. Holding his sandwich in his right hand, he checked around on all sides with his left hand and discovered two more identical latches on the opposite side and one such latch on each end. The huge suitcase lay flat and Billy knew he could open it. The front two latches released without any resistance. So, he reached over, found the two latches on the back, or what would have been the bottom if the suitcase had been sitting up. They also opened at Billy's touch. He turned his attention to the snap latch on each end and they too, popped open with ease.

Pushing the top off to one side, Billy at last saw inside his treasure chest.

As he looked down on the contents, he saw that on the right side was a fat, two-foot long, silver cylinder with what seemed to Billy to be, a thousand wires all around it. Packed snugly into the center was a group of tiny flashing red and green lights sitting on top of three more fat cylinders covered with wires.

Looking to the left side, the boy saw a kind of digital read-out with five numbers. The numbers kept changing.

Just beneath the top layer of wires, lights and silver cylinders, Billy could see all kinds of mechanical and electrical gadgets and pretty little dials and switches.

The boy was totally absorbed with the menagerie of little lights and switches. But his concentration was suddenly broken when he heard the distant sound of the approaching subway.

In a hurry to exit, Billy accidentally dropped his peanut butter and jelly sandwich into the case. Moving quickly, he reached in, grabbed it and rapidly crawled out of the cubbyhole.

The first thing he heard was the frantic call of his mother. "Billy!"

He peeked up over the edge and saw his mother less than two feet away with a police officer standing next to her, trying to calm her.

Re-enacting what had happened the first time her boy had wandered off, she looked down at the tracks and saw her son. She dropped onto her knees, reached down, and plucked the boy up onto the platform, where she embraced him.

Twenty seconds later, the subway coaches rushed by on their way to a different station. Patricia held her son close, preparing once again to kiss him repeatedly before scolding him. The policeman squatted down next to them.

"Billy, you gave me and your mom here quite a scare, and she told me you had done this before. You know you're not allowed off this platform 'cause you could get hurt real bad, and then what would your mom do without you?"

"But mom," Billy excitedly protested, "I found out what's inside the treasure chest! I got it open." Used to dealing with her son's vivid imagination, Patricia let Billy out of the bear hug.

"Billy, there is no treasure down there and you must promise me you'll never, ever, go back down there, ever!"

"Mom," Billy insisted, "there is too a treasure! But it's too big for me to pull out by myself. Come look at it."

Now frustrated, Patricia scolded, "Billy Dees, you listen to me. If you ever..."

The policeman interrupted the coming lecture. "Ma'am, if I may, why don't I just go down real quick to check out the boy's story?"

"Oh, officer," she answered, "that's not necessary." But the policeman had already taken off his hat and was handing it to Billy.

"I tell you what, young fella. If I don't find any treasure down there, will you promise your mom you'll never go down there again?"

"Oh, yes, sir," a perked-up Billy answered, "and when you find it, will ya help me get 'er out?"

"You bet I will, little fella," the officer smiled, "and if I do find anything down there, you can keep my hat."

"Oh, boy!" Billy hollered. "I got a real cop's hat!"

"Not so quick, lad!" admonished the officer. "I gotta go look first."

The officer went closer to the ledge and jumped off, landing on the tracks. He bent low to look up under the platform where Billy had said the treasure was.

Billy, watching from the platform with his mother, said, "Ya gotta crawl in there a little ways."

The policeman sighed, bent lower, and as his eyes adjusted, he saw the cubbyhole. Getting on all fours, he crawled in seven or eight feet. Reaching into his shirt pocket, he retrieved a small pin flashlight and flicked it on. Immediately, he saw the large silver suitcase a few feet in front of him. The three little flashing lights on the front drew him right up to the object. He leaned over to get a closer look at whatever was inside.

Billy had left the lid off and he was able, with his little flashlight, to clearly see the contents.

It took only seconds for the officer to grow wide-eyed and start shaking.

Since 9/11, the entire NYPD had received constant training from Homeland Security on what explosive devices may look like in different kinds of packaging. He had no doubt that he was staring at a sizeable bomb of some sort. It was the complexity that shook him the most. This was no small weapon or pipe bomb.

He backed out of the hole very slowly. Once out and back on the tracks, he jumped onto the platform with a dexterity made possible only by increased adrenalin rushing through his body. White with fear, drenched in sweat, and with smudges on his frightened countenance, he looked at Patricia and tried to speak. But before he could get a word out, Billy hollered.

"See, I told ya! Now let's go get it out. And thanks for the hat." Billy bolted, to go back down but his mother caught him as the officer spoke.

"Ma'am, I must ask you to take the boy and immediately vacate this platform. Your son has discovered a powerful explosive device that could go off any minute.

"Take the boy and wait for me on ground level. I'll need to ask you a few questions. But first, I'm calling for backup and the bomb squad. And I'll need to clear this entire area. So go!"

The officer grabbed a radio mike off his shoulder and called headquarters requesting immediate emergency backup, the New York Fire Department and the bomb squad.

Patricia and Billy had just exited the subway tunnel onto ground level when a sudden rush of people shot out of the subway behind them running or walking away briskly.

She heard sirens approaching from every direction. Within two minutes, squad cars, fire trucks, ambulances and a large utility van with "NYPD Bomb Squad" written on it came screeching to a stop.

It was enough to scare her. Concerned for her own and Billy's safety, she decided to join the rest of the fleeing crowd. She grabbed Billy's hand tightly and they began to walk away. Patricia had a frightened, confused look on her face but Billy was all smiles, as he waddled along with the oversize NYPD hat bobbing on his head.

The first policemen on the scene had no way of knowing that the bomb was nuclear, or that its builders had installed a pressure sensor that would trigger a detonation if the case was even slightly moved from where it now sat.

It was 12:30 p.m. in New York.

It was 7:30 p.m. in Rome as Charon D. Kostos entered the ornate office of the Pope. Following cordial greetings, Kostos and the Pope sat in the exceptionally comfortable fifteenth-century lounge chairs arranged in front of the open French doors. Just outside was a beautiful balcony overlooking St. Peter's Square.

The sun was just slipping behind the western horizon, and dusk was slowly sneaking in for its brief visit. Soon, all Rome would again be embraced by the melancholy night.

The two men sat nursing bourbon from crystal snifters as Kostos puffed smoke from a Cuban cigar. They were confident and relaxed, especially in light of the fact that on the morrow they would unleash catastrophic death and destruction in the United States and usher in World War III in the Middle East.

"You've been a busy fellow, Charon," quipped the Pontiff as he sipped his bourbon. "Are you ready for the main show to begin?"

"Excellency," Kostos answered, "I am most ready, as well as ecstatic over the coming chaos."

"The self-absorbed Americans and the arrogant, pig-headed Jews will be humbled, or should I say humiliated, very shortly. And soon those bastardly nations will come crawling to me on their bloody hands and knees, begging for their lives."

"And I share your joy," the Pope replied. "If I may ask, what time is the show scheduled to begin?"

Kostos, with head held high, blew smoke into the air and answered, "I've already given each of the principals their instructions and timetables. I've no doubt that they will all be obeyed.

"In the morning at 8:00 a.m. New York City time, our dear President Hunt kicks off the great day by detonating a nuclear bomb now resting under Times Square. It will be during rush hour, guaranteeing a maximum number of deaths. That explosion will trigger a magnificent sequence of nine additional nuclear weapons, in nine other American cities. All this will happen at precisely 3:00 p.m. Vatican time and 4:00 p.m. Baghdad time."

"And you are absolutely certain that your puppet in the White House, this President Hunt, will do as he has been instructed?"

Kostos, relishing a sip of bourbon, smiled. "Frankly, Your Excellency, it matters not whether the little weasel pushes the button or not. We have failsafe backup that will blow the nuke even if he does not follow through. And once that bomb in New York City goes boom, it will trigger the other nine.

"The only reason we've made him part of the equation was to measure his faithfulness to our cause. Either way, as soon as he has served his purpose, he will be terminated."

"And," the Pope added, "the invasion of Israel, if I may ask, is to begin as soon as the 10 weapons are detonated in the States?"

"Actually, I just got off the phone with our Supreme Commander in Baghdad, Russian General Chevsky. The invasion will begin four hours after the nuclear weapons set America ablaze. By then, it will be noon in New York and every resource and asset America has available will be scrambling to respond to their domestic disasters.

"And when it's noon in New York City, it will just be getting dark at 8:00 p.m. in Israel. Then the fires of hell will be unleashed on the Zionist swine.

"All in all, it's going to be a glorious day."

"Indeed it will be. And where will you be during all this, Charon?"

"Your Excellency," Kostos answered as he finished the last of his drink, "with your kind permission, I will be here at the Vatican with you, relaxing in your personal quarters, watching the world burn on the telly and staying in communication with our field commanders around the world."

"That will be perfect," the Pontiff responded with exuberance. "As soon as the news breaks, we will release our mutual statement to the world expressing our shock and sorrow. Then we will call for an immediate cessation of hostilities in the Middle East."

"Which of course," Kostos added as he stood, "will be ignored, at least for the moment. Then, as the dust settles a bit, we shall initiate our next step. By then the whole planet will be begging for someone to bring order out of the global chaos.

"And who better than I to step forward and bear the burden of saving the world?"

"Charon," added the Pope as he, too, stood, "you've a long day tomorrow. I suppose you'd like to get some rest."

"Not really, but I will go spend a few hours in the chapel to refresh my vision and chill my blood."

"Very well, my Lord," answered the Pontiff. "Then I shall join you later this evening in the chapel. Until then, goodbye."

Kostos left and the Pope walked over and closed the French doors overlooking the Square.

Walking behind his massive desk, he opened another well-concealed door and entered. Inside was a small prayer cloister where an altar and kneeling pad awaited. The Pope knelt, bursting with demonic excitement in anticipation of the next day's events.

After a few moments of silence, an unearthly, diabolic roar bellowed out of the Pope's mouth. The soundproofed prayer room did little to contain the evil, satanic shrieking that continued for just under a minute.

Everyone in the Vatican proper heard the bone-chilling, demonic sounds, and paused to listen to the terrifying noise.

Then it stopped.

Those who had heard it hurriedly went about their business, too frightened to inquire about it.

Inside the little room, a sweat-drenched Pope lay unconscious, exhausted from the sinister expressions of evil.

THIRTY-ONE

The CIA Station Chief in Rome, Will Shannon, had sent a car to pick up Brad and Leah at the Regency. Director Pratt in Washington D.C. had already contacted Shannon, ordering him to provide Fuller with anything and everything he asked for, without exception.

Upon arriving at CIA headquarters in Rome, Brad and Leah exchanged greetings with Chief Shannon, then immediately got down to business.

"I do hope," Brad stated, "that you can fulfill our requests, Chief."

"Well, I can certainly try," Chief Shannon replied. "Just what is it that you need?"

"First," Brad answered, "we need you to direct us to your armory."

"No problem," answered Shannon. "We'll take this lift down to our basement. We keep a pretty well-stocked arsenal there."

In less than a minute, the agents stepped off the lift into a large basement area. There were no other exits or entrances into the secured area, which was a large and well-lit open room. Down the middle was a long row of shelves stocked with every kind of weapon imaginable. What could not be found on those shelves could be found on the wall displays around the room's perimeter, where rack after rack of weaponry hung.

As soon as the agents exited the elevator, they were met by a young man in charge of the armory. When the young man saw Brad, he did a double take. "Mr. Brad Fuller. What a surprise! How are you, sir?"

Brad, at first, could not place the young agent. Then it came to him who the guy was. He was the intern who had been appointed to pick him up at Ben Gurion Airport in Tel Aviv and drive him to Jerusalem.

"Well, well, well," Brad said as he shook the young intern's hand. "If it's not intern, Clay Cameron. How goes it with your old boss in Israel, my friend, Don McGuire?"

"Well, let's just say," Clay responded, "that he didn't take too kindly to the way we rearranged his brand new Mercedes. Not long after that, he cut me loose and I was reassigned here in Rome."

"I'm sorry about that, but it's good to see you," Brad said as he turned to Leah. "And this is my partner, Miss Levy. Leah, meet Clay Cameron."

A stammering, shy Cameron nodded, "Nice to meet you, ma'am."

The impatient Chief broke in. "Now that you boys and girls have had old home week, Mr. Fuller needs a weapon or two. So, Mr. Cameron, would you kindly help him in his selection while I get to work in my office?"

"Oh, yes, sir," Clay responded.

As the Chief turned to go, Brad added, "Oh, and there is another thing, Shannon. While we take care of business here, would you be so kind as to find a large suitcase of some sort, and then take one million in cash and put it in the suitcase?"

"Fuller," a shocked Chief snapped, "have you lost your bloody mind? We don't keep that kind of money here."

"Don't pull my strings, Shannon," Brad answered. "Now, if you'd rather I call Director Pratt and tell him of your reluctance to obey his orders..."

"No need to do that, Fuller," sighed the Chief. "I'll get it ready. But, Fuller, you're gonna have to account for every penny. I won't be responsible."

"Chill out, Chief," Brad added. "I'll take full responsibility for it and, by the way, we'll also need a car. Now, if you'll excuse us, we've got a bit of shopping to do."

Shannon shook his head in frustration, entered the lift, and returned to his office.

As the elevator closed on the Chief, Leah turned to Brad, "And why do we need a million dollars in cash? That's a lot of shekels."

Teasingly Brad answered, "One never knows when he may need a little extra pocket change.

"Now, with your permission, Agent Cameron, we'll shop around a bit and pick out our weapons of choice."

The always-eager young agent smiled, "No problem, sir. As you can see, the walls are covered with weapons of every kind and caliber, including shoulder-mounted missile launchers, small artillery pieces, body armor, optical enhancement devices, and various sorts of anti-personal mines.

"The shelves down the middle of the room hold hundreds of smaller weapons, including grenades, RPGs and hand guns. So, I'm doing inventory in my cubicle and if you need any assistance, just call me."

"Thank you, Clay," Brad returned.

As Clay turned to go back to his project, Brad and Leah started browsing through the vast armory. After 30 minutes of shopping, Brad had chosen his desired weapons. He picked out an Israeli Uzi and a .357 magnum pistol with an eight-inch barrel. Obviously, young Cameron had taken his earlier advice to get rid of the powerful but monstrous weapon. Brad, however, felt that the pistol would be a good fit for this mission. He also picked up two road flares often used by truckers when they broke down on the highways.

Leah, quite happy to rely upon her nine-millimeter, simply watched as Brad bundled up the weapons and ammunition and placed them all in a duffle bag. She somehow felt that Brad was not aware of the kind of battle they might be facing against Kostos.

Brad finished putting the weapons in the bag and turned to Leah. "Okay Leah, let's go get our money and get on with the task. And by the way, please hold on to these." He handed her two vials with protected caps on one end covering the small needles.

As soon as Brad signed out for the cash, he and Leah drove away from the place in a new Mercedes provided for their use. When only blocks away, Brad flipped open the cell phone he had picked up at the CIA office and dialed a number.

Leah's curiosity prompted her to ask, "Okay, who are you calling now?"

Keeping one hand on the steering wheel and his eyes on the road, Brad answered, "I'm calling the International Federation of Nation's Rome headquarters."

Stunned, Leah asked, "Why would you do that?"

Holding his hand up to silence her, Brad responded to the receptionist who had answered. "Yes. My name is Barry Shoals, and I work at our IFN offices in Brussels. My supervisor instructed me to contact one of our helicopter pilots in the Rome area to pick him up at Da Vinci International tomorrow morning and ferry him to a rendezvous with Mr. Kostos. Can you help me, please?"

Responding to the receptionist's inquiry, Brad answered, "Yes, I do. His full name is Chuck Burns, a.k.a. Death Star, and I'll need his personal number."

After a 15-second wait, the IFN receptionist came back online and Brad replied, "Yes, I've a pen. Go ahead…uh huh…ok…and can you tell me if he's currently on assignment? …uh huh…great! Thank you."

Brad closed the cell phone.

"Are you losing it, Brad?" Leah asked. "Isn't Chuck the name of the pilot that was flying us out to sea to kill us? Why on earth would you want to call him, and how did you know it'd be so easy to get his number?"

"First, my dear," Brad answered, "never underestimate the incompetence of those who work for a large organization like the IFN. They're taught to obey, not to question their instructions.

"Second, if we live through this suicide mission, we may need to make a very quick get-away. And I've a feeling that our little friend, Chuck Burns the chopper pilot, would love nothing better than to find honest work. If I'm right, we'll have a job for him. This cool million will add a strong incentive to help lure him from the dark side."

"And," Leah asked, "if he betrays us?"

"I'm betting both of our lives he won't," Brad answered.

"I do hope you're right, Mr. Fuller. So, now where are we headed?"

Brad made a 90-degree left-hand turn. "We're going to the Vatican to pay a visit to Pope Fraud. With a bit of luck, combined with some friendly persuasion, we can lure that spider, Kostos, back into his own web. I have a feeling the Pope will make excellent bait."

"And would you mind," Leah inquired, "telling me just how you plan to get us past the impenetrable security net surrounding the Pontiff?"

With feigned surprise, Brad shot back, "Have you forgotten, Miss Levy, that we are spies, masters of deception, trickery and manipulation? We know how to adjust and improvise. It should be no problem."

"In other words, Brad, you don't know."

"Well," Brad said as he stopped at a red light, "no, but I'm almost sure you'll think of something. And as for Kostos, the only time he's not surrounded by dozens of his security goons is when he is meeting with the Pope."

After a moment of silence, Leah spoke, "I'm not sure we have the kind of firepower we need to deal with Kostos, or for that matter, the Pope."

Brad nodded toward her, "Well, we will find out very shortly."

It was now 9:00 p.m. in Rome and 1:00 p.m. in Washington D.C. Nineteen hours remained until the nuclear bomb under Times Square was to be detonated by President Hunt.

Pratt had come up with the idea and convinced President Carr that the abandoned government warehouse six miles from the White House would be a great, out-of-the-way location to meet with Chief Justice Bailey. The warehouse had been used as a CIA storage facility for obsolete equipment and old files. Though it had been shut down for over a year, it was still under contract to the CIA and Pratt had the keys.

President Carr, Agent Spears and Dr. Cohen had left their hiding place at the Pentagon and driven to the warehouse. After quietly parking in the empty back lot, they had quickly entered the storage facilities without being seen.

Pratt had told them where the old offices inside were located. All power was off at the location, but the director assured them that the offices had high, large windows on two sides that would provide sufficient light.

As the men made their way into the office area, it was evident that no one had used it for some time. A couple of old desks and a dozen office chairs within were covered with a quarter inch of dust and spider webs. Trash of various sorts was strewn everywhere. Looking around, Agent Spears picked up an old piece of cloth and dusted off a half-dozen chairs.

After fanning the air to disperse the cloud of dust stirred up by the agent's efforts, they all sat down to await the arrival of Director Pratt and the Chief Justice.

After a few minutes of idle chatter, the men heard the opening and shutting of doors in the warehouse area. Carr and Cohen fell quiet as Spears pulled out his weapon and crept over to look through the small window in the office door.

More noises were heard, followed by footsteps approaching the office. As soon as Spears could see that it was Pratt and the Chief Justice, he put away his weapon and turned to his companions. "They're here."

Pratt had not informed Justice Bailey who they were meeting; he had only said it was urgent that the Chief Justice meet secretly with some high-ranking government officials in an effort to avert a constitutional crisis. Reluctantly, the Justice had agreed to accompany Pratt—but only because he had always had the utmost respect for the director's integrity and knew he could be trusted.

Carr, Spears and Cohen all stood as the door opened and the two men entered.

The first thing the eyes of the Chief Justice fell on was President Mathew D. Carr.

Startled at the sight, the Chief Justice quickly stepped back, bumping into Pratt behind him. The wide-eyed, unbelieving Bailey said, "Oh, my gosh. This can't be."

Turning back toward Pratt with an expression of shock, he asked, "Is this some sort of sick joke, Pratt? Where did you find such a convincing look-alike?"

"It is no joke, Chief Justice," Carr said as he stepped closer to Bailey with an extended hand. "I am very much alive and well, no thanks to your new President Hunt and friends."

Shaking Carr's hand, the Chief Justice said, "It is you. But how? I mean, you were dead."

"Almost," Carr replied, "but not quite. It seems that certain very powerful, evil people attempted to remove me from the land of the living in order to pull off an elaborate international scheme."

The elderly Dr. Cohen piped in, "And they would've succeeded had it not been for the intervention of Almighty God."

The Chief Justice turned and looked questionably at Dr. Cohen.

"Forgive my rudeness," jumped in Carr, "in failing to introduce Dr. Cohen, my physician, and Agent Spears of the Secret Service. Had it not been for the heroics of these two men, I would not be here, Chief Justice."

The Justice, though still shaken, was beginning to accept the fact that Carr was, indeed, alive and standing there in front of him.

"Justice Bailey," Pratt said, "please have a seat and we'll try to explain what's going on and why we've asked you to this unorthodox meeting."

Carr took over the conversation and started at the beginning, when Air Force One had been shot down. He told how he and Spears had been rescued by the old fisherman. He detailed events at Castel Colledora, Sodote Shalom, and of everything that Kostos had done to try to assassinate him.

He shocked his listener with descriptions of Kostos' maniacal murders of the previous Pope and other world leaders, and of his insane scheme to manipulate world powers and orchestrate World War III.

Carr left out the part about Kostos' very possible connection to biblical prophecies and the Antichrist. However, he did detail for Justice Bailey all the treacherous actions of President Hunt and of his close collaboration with Kostos. Carr also explained the very real threat of a nuclear attack on American soil, and of a possible deadline for detonation at 8:00 a.m. the next morning.

After listening to Carr's fantastic story, Justice Bailey spoke. "What you're telling me, Mr. President, is bizarre beyond belief—but I tend to believe every word of it. I've watched Hunt's irrational behavior ever since he was sworn in, and from the moment that moron took the oath of office, I've had a nagging feeling that something was just not right.

"I've watched Hunt's absurd behavior and his outlandish antics, along with the rest of Washington D.C., and I can tell you this: A whole lot of people in this town and around the country are very put out and confused by his close relationship with this Kostos fellow.

"Hunt has, in a very short period of time, attempted to reverse decades of American foreign policy and sabotaged our relations with our allies. I thought for a while that Congress would make a move to impeach him. I can only suppose that their recent reluctance to continue their resistance to his policies is because they are hesitant to drag the country through a nasty, partisan battle."

"In all due respect, your Honor," Pratt put in, "the Congressional leadership stepped back from confronting Hunt because Kostos and his goons carried out a campaign of intimidation, entrapment, and blackmail against dozens of Congressional leaders. It is fear that has paralyzed Congress, not political concerns over a confrontation."

"So," Carr added, "Justice Bailey, what we're asking of you is your full support for my reinstatement as president. I'm already aware of the parameters and limitations of the Twenty-Fifth Amendment, but surely the circumstances we face fall under the heading of constitutional intent of the founding fathers."

"Mr. President," replied the Chief Justice, "while we may be on shaky constitutional grounds, I can assure you that the majority of the court will agree with me that for the sake of the Republic, we must act to remove Hunt and put you back in the office into which the American people overwhelmingly voted you. However, I should caution you that our actions could result in months, if not years, of litigation if Hunt is bent on challenging its constitutionality."

"Future litigation," Carr answered, "is fine with me, your Honor. My term will have long since expired if it came to that. It is in the present that our nation faces possible destruction, and it is now that we must act to save it."

"Very well, Mr. President." Justice Bailey added, "So where do we go from here?"

Carr was quick to respond. "Chief Justice, I want you to accompany us later tonight when we confront Hunt in the Oval Office. The word is, he'll be working late into the night. We plan to gain access to the White House through a series of secret tunnel entrances known only to very few people, I being one of them. I can get us into the West Wing right next to the Oval Office without anyone detecting us. If we are confronted by Hunt's two or three Secret Service Agents, Spears thinks he can handle them.

"As soon as we gain access to the Oval Office, you will explain to Hunt that as Chief Justice of the United Sates Supreme Court, you and a majority of the justices agree that it is constitutionally required, since I am back and fully functional, that I should be immediately reinstated to serve out my term as President of the United States.

"We will try to keep it civil, legal and formal—even bragging, if necessary, on Hunt's great work as president. We're ready to concede his return to the position of Vice President. He won't be aware of the fact that his tenure in that office will be very short, but it may help us to use that carrot on the stick to soften the blow. Under such circumstances, we feel Hunt will refrain from cooperating with Kostos. You, then, will re-swear me in as president.

"After that, if our field agents succeed in eliminating Kostos as a threat, then we, along with our trusted Secretaries of Defense and State, along with Chairman of Joint Chiefs, will form the catalyst of a new Carr administration dedicated to restoring America to its role as a world leader and a faithful defender of our allies around the world."

"And," Bailey asked, "what do we do with Hunt?"

Carr answered, "Give the man the keys to his old office, pat him on the back, and then, after the dust settles, we'll deal with his traitorous acts. But first, we've got far bigger fish to fry."

"All right, gentlemen," the Justice sighed, "I am on board. Now, what time should we meet again to go to the dance at the White House?"

A gleeful Dr. Cohen could no longer hold his excitement, and he shouted out, "Praise be to Yeshua!"

Justice Bailey looked quizzically at the good doctor. Carr stepped in and answered the Chief Justice, "We will be in touch with you at your office sometime in the next two to three hours. We'll let you know then what time to meet us back here. From here, you, myself, Agent Spears and Director Pratt will make our way to the White House. Agreed?"

"Yes, Mr. President, agreed," answered Bailey as he stood to his feet. "And I too, say, Praise the Lord and pass the ammunition."

All five men were now standing, smiling and shaking hands.

As they split up to leave, Pratt stopped President Carr and asked if he could have a private word with him. The two men stepped away to the side and Pratt spoke, "Sir, I received word just before the Chief Justice and I arrived here that the Citation I sent to retrieve you and your party from France was shot down by a French Mirage fighter after it refueled in England. Every one on board was killed, as you would've been if you had not chosen to catch a different ride."

"I told those pilots to change their flight plans," Carr somberly replied. "Looks like they chose not to listen. But you can be sure, while it may have been a French fighter that shot those brave boys down, it was that butcher, Kostos, who ordered it. The fact is, Kostos now thinks he took me out as well, finally getting me out of the way."

"That," Pratt said, "can work to our advantage. He won't know that we're dismantling his puppet American government until it's already done."

"That's if," Carr returned, "we're successful, Pratt. Let's get outta here. We've got things to do before tonight."

"Yes, sir."

The Carr party followed Pratt to a CIA safe house just outside Washington D.C. where they would fine-tune their plan.

It was now 3:00 p.m. in Washington and 11:00 p.m. in Rome. Seventeen hours remained until the nuclear bomb under New York's Time Square would be detonated.

A mile from the main entrance to the Vatican, Brad made a sharp right onto a side street. He drove several more blocks and parallel parked in front of a small retail store.

Curious, Leah asked, "And I know you have a good reason for stopping here at this time of night?"

Brad turned off the ignition and answered, "This little tailor's shop is where everyone who's anyone in the clergy has their robes, habits and other clerical attire made. The two saintly old brothers who own and operate this place are part of the family that has catered to the Pope's wardrobe needs for the last 200 years."

"So?" Leah questioned.

"So," Brad continued, "we are going to awaken the two good brothers who live above this shop and explain to them that the Pope has sent us on a late-night, emergency errand to fetch one of the new robes they keep in stock for the Pontiff's needs. And while they prepare His Excellency's package, you and I will select, out of their well-stocked inventory, a lovely nun's habit for you, Sister Leah, and, for me, some stately priest's attire."

"And," Leah quizzed, "just what are we going to do with all this clerical paraphernalia? Start a new order?"

"Oh, no, my dear," Brad answered. "We are going to make a late-night delivery to Pope Fraud, who has demanded that his new threads be brought to him immediately."

"And you really believe this ruse will get us through the layers of security guards and into the private quarters of his royal Majesty?"

"I do," Brad answered. "Now, if you would be so kind as to reach over into the seat just behind you and bring along that small bag. It holds the few additives we'll need to complete our disguises as honored and humbled members of the clergy who are dutifully fulfilling our roles as lackeys to His Excellency, the Pope."

Brad and Leah exited the Mercedes and made their way to the little shop's entrance. There they vigorously and repeatedly rang the bell that soon roused the upstairs occupants who drowsily answered the door.

Upon the agents' departure 40 minutes later, Leah was dressed in a habit and looked the part of a frumpy, elderly nun. Brad, complete with bald head, graying beard, and wrinkled face, had been transformed into a senior priest who exuded authority.

With them, they carried two neatly wrapped packages containing the new attire that, according to them, the Pope had demanded be delivered to his personal quarters immediately.

As the Mercedes pulled away from the tailor's shop and drove toward the Vatican, it was 11:30 p.m. in Rome and 3:30 p.m. in Washington, D.C.

THIRTY-TWO

They gathered on the subway platform. There was the mayor of New York City, the Director of New York's Homeland Security, the local agents in charge of the FBI and the CIA, along with the upper echelon of officers in charge of NYPD and NYFD.

An order to evacuate a three-block perimeter around the bombsite had already been issued. To prevent a panic, authorities had released a statement for the press that a massive gas leak had been detected in the subway systems and that the evacuation was a precautionary measure until the leak was repaired.

It had taken very little time for the bomb squad experts to determine that the device under the platform was far more complex than anything they had ever come across.

A call went out to two of the nation's most knowledgeable experts in the field of nuclear weaponry. As fate would have it, the two scientists were already in New York City less than a mile from the subway station where the bomb now sat. Both were in the city to attend a symposium on the use of nuclear power for peaceful purposes.

The two experts arrived at the scene in a rapid-response, security convoy of emergency vehicles with blaring sirens and flashing lights. Dr. Shorsky Endenstein, a noted MIT nuclear physicist with expertise in weapons of mass destruction, had worked on numerous secret military projects designing master plans for nuclear weapon components. Dr. Beverly Carlyle, a professor at Cambridge with significant experience in design and construction of nuclear munitions for the U.S. government as well as specializing in triggering components for various nuclear weapons systems, joined him in examining the device in the cramped space under the platform where the weapon sat. Thirty minutes later, they crawled out and onto the platform to join the anxious authorities.

"Well," asked a very nervous mayor as the rest of the authorities listened, "what do we have?"

Dr. Beverly Carlyle took a deep breath and answered, "What we have, gentlemen, in short, is your worst nightmare."

"And what's that supposed to mean?" snapped a stressed-out, impatient FBI supervisor.

"What that means," broke in Dr. Endenstein, "is the following. This moment, less than three feet under where you stand, is a nuclear weapon far more powerful than any atomic bomb used in Japan during World War II. It has a multi-level, fail-proof triggering device that can be activated by a cell phone or a special frequency transmitter via satellite from virtually anywhere on the planet."

The nearly panicked New York Homeland Security Director gasped, "Okay, but what do we do to disarm the thing?"

Dr. Carlyle injected, "First, you should be patient enough to hear the rest of our report. This is not a little battery-operated pipe bomb that we can just unplug. The trigger has multiple backup safety features that will automatically switch to a myriad of other triggering options if the primary system is neutralized by our use of conventional technology."

The Chief of the NYPD stammered, "There's got to be some way to disarm the thing. And what about moving the monster out of the heart of the city?"

Dr. Endenstein put in, "I do not suggest attempting to move it. It is also equipped with an impressive array of very advanced sensors that will detect the slightest effort to move it from its present location. It would instantly detonate at such an attempt. The fact is, gentlemen, neither of us has ever seen a more sophisticated triggering device with as many possible backups. It's most impressive."

"So," jumped in the agitated Homeland Security Director, "what are you going to do, Doctors? Can you disarm it?"

"Sir," answered Dr. Carlyle, "with a lot of time and a lot of luck, we can possibly disarm it."

The head of the New York FBI offices hurriedly asked, "Okay, so how long would that take?"

"Well," answered Dr. Endenstein, "I think we could do that in two or three days."

"What?" screamed the Homeland Security Director. "We don't have two or three days. That digital read out, as you surely know, says the bomb will blow at 8 o'clock in the morning."

Dr. Carlyle broke in, "Sirs, you should also know that the device has a relay signaling component built into it."

The frustrated Fire Department Chief asked, "And what's a relay signaling component do?"

Carlyle answered, "It's a device triggered by the electronic pulse that sends out a signal meant to detonate additional weapons of like kind that, frankly, could be located anywhere in the U.S.A. or, for that matter, anywhere on the face of the planet."

As the crowd of authorities listened, they were overwhelmed with the scientist's reports.

The Chief of New York's Homeland Security spoke up, "Okay, everybody, listen up. Let's prepare to call a citywide evacuation—but I will not order it until Washington D.C. gives the word."

"Excuse me, Mr. Director," said the New York Chief of Police, "but this is New York City. It'll take days to evacuate this city in an orderly fashion. We're talking millions of people with a very limited transportation and road capacity. Even if we started now, the panic alone would kill thousands, to say nothing of the riots and looting it'd unleash."

"Obviously, Chief," the homeland director answered, "I don't know all the answers. But the bottom line is, this decision must be made by Washington. So, I'm going to ask Drs. Endenstein and Carlyle to begin the process of disarming the weapon. If you two need anything, anything at all, we'll get it for you. In the meantime, I'll call D.C. and return shortly with a plan to save as many lives as possible."

With that said, the two scientists returned to study the bomb and to work on defusing it.

It had just turned 4:30 p.m. in New York City and 12:30 a.m. in Rome.

Beneath the subway platform, the timer on the nuclear weapon continued to tick away the seconds, as the digital display announced that there were 15 and a half hours until detonation.

As soon as Brad and Leah left the tailor's shop, they drove straight to the Vatican, parking in a public lot adjacent to an entrance to St. Peter's Square. Brad parked the Mercedes, and as Leah sat in the car still adjusting her disguise, he got out to put their luggage into the trunk. While he waited for Leah to finish, he made a call on his cell phone. A few minutes later, Leah exited. "All right, I'm ready."

By the time they walked across the Square and approached the guarded gates of the Palace, it was well past midnight.

During Brad's latest call to the local CIA office, he had been updated with new intelligence informing him of Kostos' presence at the Vatican. According to the update, Kostos would stay for the night, probably somewhere close to the Pope's quarters. They were hoping the intel was accurate.

As the couple approached the guarded gate at the entrance onto the Palace grounds, they saw a group of Swiss Guards. Contrary to what many tourists believe, the Swiss Guards are hardly for show. They are a finely honed, well-armed security force whose job it is to enforce Vatican law and to protect the Pope. They take their work very seriously and have used deadly force on more than one occasion.

As they walked closer to the entrance, Leah struggled to adjust the weapons Brad had asked her to carry under her fat suit. Finally succeeding at gaining a measure of comfort, Leah commented, "I feel like a porker in this outfit."

Brad smiled, "And to be honest, you *look* like a porker, too."

"Why, thank you," Leah returned. "And you look like a miserable, old coot."

They both laughed as Brad added, "Well that settles it. Henceforth I'll be called Father Coots and you will be Sister Porker."

They were only 15 meters from the gate when Brad whispered, "I've been told they don't require nuns or priests to enter through the metal detectors. They are allowed to go in through that smaller entrance to the right."

As they approached, one of the guards addressed them, "Good evening, Father, and to you, Sister. Please state your business at the Palace."

Brad cleared his throat. "Yes, my son. I am Father Coots and this is Sister Porker. We have orders from the Holy Father to deliver these packages of clothing to his quarters immediately."

"Kinda late to be delivering things isn't it, Father?" asked the guard.

"It is indeed late, my son. But for those of us serving the Holy Father, our faithfulness requires 24-hour availability to his wishes. His needs are far more important than our fleshly lust for sleep."

"Very well," the guard nodded, "but because of tightened security, it will be necessary for us to open and inspect those packages. Both of you will also need to enter through our metal detectors. Another new rule, Father."

Brad, handing the two packages to the guard, replied, "Oh, that's no problem for me, young man, but…" Brad leaned close to the guard and whispered in his ear, "Sister Porker, as a result of a debilitating accident in her youth, has a metal plate in her head. Passing through such devices not only wreaks havoc on the machine but causes the sister to go into violent convulsions."

The guard looked at the frumpy old nun. "All right Father, we'll let her through the side gate just this once."

With a gentle "thank you" to the guard, Brad stepped through the metal detector and the other guard handed the two now-open packages back to him.

"May God's blessing be on you all," Brad said with a saintly smile as he and Leah proceeded.

After they had taken less than 10 steps, the guard called out, "Hold it! Wait right there!"

Brad and Leah stopped, not knowing what to expect.

The guard came running up and handed them a folded piece of paper. "If anyone else bothers you at the other checkpoints, just hand 'em this pass and tell them it's signed by the Captain of the Guard."

Both agents breathed a sign of relief as Brad bowed. "You're very kind, sir. Thank you."

As the guard walked back to the gate, Brad whispered, "That new metal detector rule almost did us in."

"I was more worried," Leah said, "about a strip search."

"Ah," Brad laughed, "that would've been interesting."

"Shut up, Fuller," Leah snapped, "or I'll have you condemned to an extra thousand years in purgatory."

By then they were approaching the building entrance manned by two more Swiss Guards. As the agents reached the guards, one of them addressed Brad, "Good evening, Father. What is the nature of your business that necessitates entry into the Palace?"

"And a good evening to you, sir," Brad bowed. "The Captain of the Guard gave us this pass. It authorizes myself and Sister Porker here to deliver these packages to His Holiness."

The expressionless guard read the note and said, "*Humph*! You should know, Father, that other than on very rare occasions, the Palace is off-limits this time of night."

"Yes, my son," replied Brad, "and please believe me, I'd much rather be in prayer and meditation right now but when His Excellency, the Pontiff, demands an immediate delivery of personal items, then ours is not to question why, ours is but to do or die."

Leah, standing with head bowed, wanted to burst out laughing at Brad's feeble attempt to sound spiritual.

The guard stood thoughtfully for a moment then answered, "All right Father. You're both permitted to enter. Inside you'll be met by a

Palace escort who will lead you to the correct area. At the entrance to the Pope's quarters, you'll encounter another set of guards. You'll need to explain to them why you're there."

"Bless you, my son," Brad said, "and may all your days bring honor to His Church."

Brad and Leah entered through the grand doorway and were immediately met by their escort. Both agents instantly recognized the old priest as the one who had greeted them in the Pope's quarters after their release from the dungeons, just prior to their horrid encounter with Kostos and the Pope in the chapel.

The arrogant escort demanded, "And you are?"

Brad spoke up, "I am Father Coots and this is Sister Porker. We've been ordered by His Holiness to bring these packages to his quarters with all haste. Here is a pass given us by the Captain of the Guard."

Studying it momentarily, the sour, old priest said, "This is quite irregular. I am His Excellency's personal aide, and I'm always informed of such matters. I have no knowledge whatsoever of this."

Brad came back, "I do apologize for the oversight but..."

The old priest cut Brad off, "And I too apologize, sir, but you'll understand my need to ring the Excellency's apartment and confirm your mission."

"Of course, Father." Brad bowed politely. When the elderly priest turned to go to a phone, Leah, without warning, struck the man hard on the back of his head with the butt of her nine-millimeter. The priest hit the floor, out cold.

Brad wasted no time in bending down to grab the man and drag him across the hall to an old stairwell. As he bound and gagged the clergyman, he said, "Sister Porker, you're a very bad girl. I'll hear your confession a bit later."

Leah, who assisted in pushing the priest further beneath the stairwell answered, "You know how it is with us nuns, always picking up bad habits."

Brad, confident that the body was well out of sight, replied, "I get it, but it's still a bad joke."

The couple then bounded up two more flights of stairs to the third floor where the Pope's quarters were located. The building at this time of night was, for the most part, empty other than the guards posted at various locations.

Stepping through the stairwell door into a dim hallway, Leah whispered, "Here is the vial of whatever drug you told me to hold onto. Take this one. I've got mine in my pocket. I suppose we'll soon need them?"

"Yes, indeed," Brad replied as he led them quietly down the long hallway. "When we are close enough to the two guards at the Pope's door, we'll stab the needle on the end of the vials into the guard nearest us. This fast-working sedative will knock these guys out for 10 or 12 hours."

At that moment, Brad and Leah could see far down the hallway where the guards stood in front of the Pope's quarters. When the agents were 50 meters away, the guards challenged their approach.

The larger of the two addressed the couple when they were within 15 feet. "State your identity and your purpose for being this close to the Pontiff's quarters."

Brad bowed low and answered, "My dear fellows, I am Father Coots, accompanied by Sister Porker on a mission assigned us by His Holiness. We were ordered to deliver these packages to the Pope immediately. They bear his personal attire."

"Step closer," demanded the guard. "This is extremely irregular. Where is your escort? You're not allowed on this floor without an accompanying escort."

"Oh," Brad offered, "you mean the nice fellow downstairs. He was busy and told us to come on up and to present you with this special pass."

Brad held out the pass as both agents stepped closer to the two guards. As soon as they were near enough to touch the two men, Leah, with amazing speed, stabbed the vial's needle into the stomach of the guard closest to her.

His body instantly fell to the floor. The other guard close to Brad was still reading the pass when he heard his partner hit the floor. He had no time to think the situation through as two seconds later Brad thrust the other needle into the man's neck and depressed the plunger. He too, fell to the floor without a sound. "That janitor's closet across the hall seems like a good place for the boys to sleep it off," Brad said as each agent began dragging a guard across the polished granite floor.

Within seconds the dispatched guards were being laid down in the closet. Brad turned to Leah. "Well, for them, it's goodnight. For us, it's show time!"

He had moved toward the door to exit the closet when Leah grabbed him, embraced him, and kissed him. Momentarily releasing him, she said, "If we don't live through this insane mission, Mr. Fuller, remember that I love you."

Astonished at her actions and words, Brad smiled, "I must say that you are beginning to pick up my nasty habits, and I'm not complaining. However, it's the first time I've ever been kissed by a fat, ugly, old nun. And honestly, it wasn't that bad."

"So," Leah chuckled, "let's go take care of business." They moved out of the closet, quietly closing the door, and tiptoed back across the hall to the big double-door entrance into the Pope's quarters.

Brad gently reached out for the door's handle and, slowly turning it, was very surprised that it was unlocked. With Leah right behind him he, as quietly as possible, pushed the door open just enough to peek inside. The room was dark and appeared to be empty.

With a growing confidence, the two moved ever so slowly into the dark room. Once inside, Brad silently closed the door behind them.

Standing side-by-side waiting for their eyes to adjust to the darkness, the only sound they could hear was the rhythmic tick-tock of the old grandfather clock across the room. Had the agents been able to see it, they would have noted it was already 1:00 a.m.

After a few more suspenseful moments, Brad let out a sigh of relief. He reached down to take Leah's hand to lead her further into the room with him. Just as he took her hand in his, a guttural, raspy voice whispered, "Come into the darkness, children. We've been waiting for you."

General Moshe Cohen, Supreme Commander of the Israeli Defense Forces, stood atop a high bunker on the Israeli-Syrian border. He peered through the high-powered binoculars across the two-kilometers-wide no-man's-land at the Syrian border.

The day before, Israel's satellite surveillance capabilities had suddenly come back online. For weeks, no nation's military drones or intelligence satellites had been able to see what was happening anywhere in the Middle East. The scientists of Israel agreed that someone had developed a technology to render aerial surveillance of the area inoperable. Hence, the full extent of the massive military buildup along all of Israel's borders had been unknown.

But now, the entire world could see the enormous Russian-Arabic coalition poised to invade and destroy the Jewish State.

While the civilian leadership of the tiny nation struggled to keep up an image of unflappable courage to the public, behind closed doors these leaders were in a panic.

General Cohen set the field glasses on the table in front of him, shook his head, and addressed his staff and the government representatives with him atop the bunker. "Never in the annals of military history, either ancient or contemporary, has a nation faced such a monumental array of armies that now threatens our homeland."

The General looked down at the most recent satellite surveillance maps spread out on the table before him. Clearly marked on the map were the positions, forces, and armaments of the armies that surrounded Israel.

"Sir," inquired the IDF Colonel acting as a liaison between the General and the Prime Minister's office, "the Prime Minister and his cabinet are anxiously awaiting your current assessment of the situation as well as your recommendations for the Ministry of Defense."

"Colonel Shinisky," answered the General, "you may tell our leadership that the Doomsday scenario long envisioned by our prognosticators has evolved from a theoretical possibility into a reality. Not one square inch of our border on any front remains free of the enemy's encroachment. They have succeeded in a total encirclement of the State of Israel. Even on our Mediterranean borders, the sea bristles with enemy nuclear submarines, warships and transports brimming with tens of thousands of troops prepared to storm the beaches of Tel Aviv, Netanya, and Haifa.

"Further, tell them that we will soon face a rapid invasion simultaneously across each of our border points with Lebanon, Syria, Jordan and Egypt. That invasion will bring a 30-nation coalition force pouring into our country.

"The ground troops will be preceded by an assault of over 3,000 combat aircraft whose mission will be to cripple and or destroy our communications network, our conventional defense forces, and our civilian and military command posts. The air assault will be followed by a ground invasion force of well over 1,250,000 troops led by a force of over 12,000 tanks."

The General fell silent as he turned again to gaze out at the Syrian border. The entourage with him nervously awaited his conclusion. After lighting a cigarette and exhaling, the General continued.

"And for this they want my recommendations? So, Colonel Shinisky, tell them, after considerable thought and counsel from senior officers in all of our military branches, that I recommend—and not lightly—an immediate preemptive strike on all fronts using tactical nuclear weapons. I and my staff have marked on this map where those weapons should be targeted. Assure them that we are fully aware of the collateral damage that will be suffered by many within this country."

The General paused and handed the Colonel a rolled-up map to give to the Prime Minister. "Remind them to review our 1997 war games scenario called Pay'ulah Esh V'Dam, Optzia Sofi.

"The plan also warns our leadership to be prepared for a possible retaliatory nuclear assault from any nuclear powers aligned with our enemies. They know the steps to take to prepare for such an eventuality.

"In conclusion, tell them that if they opt to wait for the enemy to make the first move, it will be too late to effectively deploy our nuclear arsenal. The enemy now holds a loaded gun at our head and they have just cocked the hammer. Unless we deploy, they will sweep across Israel like a swarm of locusts and we will not be able to stop them. The only viable option is Pay'ulah Esh V'Dam, Optzia Sofi."

The group of officers and VIPs atop the bunker with General Cohen were somber as he finished giving his instructions. They stood quietly for a few moments.

"What are you waiting for?" barked the General. "Get moving, Colonel! I'll await their reply here on the Golan."

"Yes, sir," the Colonel saluted and led his group to the helicopter waiting to transport them back to Jerusalem to deliver the General's message.

Only General Cohen and his personal aide remained atop the bunker. The young Lieutenant, Cohen's aide, asked, "General, correct me if I'm wrong, but the battle plan you've suggested translates into English as, 'Operation Fire and Blood, the Final Option,' does it not?"

"It does, Lieutenant," answered Cohen.

The aide responded, "Sir, it takes a great General to make such a decision, especially when knowing how many of our own may suffer."

"Son," returned the General, "Napoleon once said something to the effect of, 'many great generals exist, but they see too many things at once. I see one thing, and that is the masses of the enemy, and I seek to destroy the masses, knowing that the minor matters will take care of themselves.'

"Operation Fire and Blood is not just our final option. If Israel is to survive, it is our only option."

The aide answered, "Yes, sir. Do you have any orders for me while we await word from Jerusalem?"

The General turned to look at the young soldier, smiled, and answered, "Why, yes I do son. Go find a quiet place and pray."

THIRTY-THREE

At 6:30 p.m. in Washington D.C., darkness was just beginning to settle over the Capitol as Agent Spears drove the black Suburban with the darkened windows into downtown. In the SUV with him were President Carr, Director Pratt, and Chief Justice Bailey. Spears was driving the group to the luxury hotel, The Willard, at Fourteenth and Pennsylvania Avenue, only a few blocks from the White House.

Upon arriving, the agent turned into the six-story parking garage next to the hotel. After stopping at the automatic ticket dispenser, Spears took the first left turn that led to the basement parking. During busy daylight hours, the upper floors of the garage were packed with cars and the basement parking area was used for overflow. Tonight, however, less than a dozen cars were scattered throughout the large underground facility.

"Stop here, Agent Spears," President Carr spoke from the back seat, "and take a right into the parking space by that door marked, 'Emergency Exit Only.'"

Spears rolled the vehicle into the spot and turned off the ignition. "Now Agent," Carr continued, "that so-called emergency exit door can only be opened by entering a five-digit security code into the keypad next to the door handle. That code number is 76431. Before you open it, check out the area visually. If no one is around, open the door, go in and we'll all follow you."

"Yes, sir," Spears answered as he cautiously slid out of the SUV. He casually walked to the door, scanning the area as he proceeded. Sure that he was not being watched, he stabbed in the five numbers on the keypad. Reaching down, he turned the handle and felt the door open.

After looking around one last time, Spears motioned to the others and stepped through the door. The other three men discreetly stepped out of the vehicle and followed him, quietly closing the door behind them.

Once inside the dimly lit entrance, Carr spoke to the group. "All right gentlemen, following that hallway in front of us would lead us to a fire escape exit 200 feet from here. It comes out on the north side of the hotel. However…"

The president then turned to a door on their left and opened it. Inside was a small room for supplies and storage. Carr reached up just under a light switch and, on a keypad no bigger than that of a small cell phone, punched in another set of numbers. As soon as he entered the code, the entire wall on the left side of the closet slid open, revealing another long, dark hallway.

"Gentlemen," Carr requested, "if you'll proceed, I'll close this wall behind us."

The others entered as Carr pushed a button and the wall slid shut.

"Now, Agent Spears, we'll need the two flashlights I asked you to bring. We're going to walk a few blocks to the White House. Once we arrive at the end of this hallway, we will be close to the West Wing."

The group walked as quietly as possible, and 15 minutes later they came to what appeared to be a dead end. President Carr opened what looked like a small electrical fuse box on the wall. Inside was still another keypad, into which he entered five more numbers. The solid concrete wall in front of them silently glided open, revealing the inside of a large closet. Another door was on the opposite side of the closet. Again, Carr walked into the closet to another keypad and inserted a five-digit code, resulting in a muffled click. The president turned around, faced the group, and whispered, "Just the other side of this door is the small annex room adjacent to the Oval Office. When I open this door, we will all quietly enter the annex and walk across that small room. The door on the far side of the room is always unlocked and leads right into the presence of Hunt.

"If your spooks are right, Mr. CIA, he'll be alone catching up on legislative paperwork. His Secret Service detail will be just outside his primary office door. The Oval is well soundproofed, but if those agents hear a commotion inside, they will be there quickly. Spears, it's your job to intercept and disarm them if it becomes necessary.

"So, do all of you understand your roles?"

Each of the men nodded, "yes."

The president nodded back, "Very good. So gentlemen, let's go take our country back."

New York Governor Nathan Silverson and the Director of New York's Homeland Security, Bryan Hubbard, stood before the 20-plus officials gathered in a large suite at the posh Wyndham Hotel six blocks from the bombsite. The Governor was speaking. "Gentlemen, we're expecting a call from the president at any moment now. If everyone will just settle down and focus their attention on solutions, it'll help immensely."

"Governor," a voice from a city councilman in the back of the room inquired, "we heard that you have already called the White House several times in the last two hours, but still haven't heard from President Hunt. It that true?"

"I can take that question, Governor," put in the New York Director of Homeland Security. "Yes, we have been and we still are in an ongoing dialogue with Washington. The FBI, the National Office of Homeland Security, and the Federal Emergency Management Agency are all working with us. The FBI has just flown four additional specialists in nuclear weaponry into the city, and they are all on site working with Drs. Endenstein and Carlyle."

"But," another impatient official asked, "has the president returned your calls?"

"The president," answered the Governor, "has been briefed on the situation and has personally assigned the proper authorities to deal with our crisis. However, Washington is also dealing with a growing crisis in the Middle East. But, rest assured, everything that can be done is being done at the moment."

"Sir," asked the New York Chief of Police, "we've kept the herd of media a half-mile from the bombsite but the fact is, they don't believe our cover story about a gas leak in the subway system. It's only a matter of time until someone leaks the truth and when that happens, chaos will follow. I'm not sure we'll be able to contain the situation."

Governor Silverson answered, "Chief, I know that the situation is tenuous and your department is doing an incredible job so far. We just need all of you to help us buy a bit more time. Our experts are working as hard and fast as possible."

"Sir," asked another city official, "do we have any idea how long it's going to be until that weapon is disarmed? It's now 7:00 p.m. and only 13 hours before that thing goes off."

The Director of Homeland Security spoke up. "The scientists at work on the problem are most aware of the time constraints. And I'm absolutely certain that within the hour we'll be hearing from our president and his host of advisors. So be patient, and if you are so inclined, it might be good if you say a few prayers."

With that said, the room settled down and the men broke up into smaller groups to discuss possible options.

Governor Silverson quietly spoke to his personal aide. "Have we heard from any of those scientists on location yet?"

"Yes, sir," replied the aide. "Five minutes ago, Dr. Endenstein called to let you know that the chances of shutting the weapon down by 8:00 a.m. in the morning were slim to none."

The Governor shook his head and pushed his way through the crowd to go back across the hall to a room they had set up as a communications center. He was determined to get the president on the phone, now.

The Prime Minister of Israel sat thoughtfully in his office while his cabinet and military leadership debated the recommendation submitted by General Cohen. He flashed back to the year, 1973, when he was a fresh, young fighter pilot in the IAF, the Israeli Air Force. On that morning of the holiest day on the Jewish calendar, Yom Kippur, Israel was invaded by armies from Syria, Egypt, Iraq and a number of other Arabic nations. Their goal was the total annihilation of the State of Israel. The surprise attack caught Israel totally off guard and their enemies were achieving victory upon victory.

Israel was completely alone, without the help of even its closest allies. Desperate and on the brink of total destruction, the government ordered then-Defense Secretary, General Moshe Dyan, to order the preparation of their nuclear arsenal. It was the only time in the history of Israel that an order had been given to ready their nuclear weapons for an immediate attack. Only a last-minute arrival of American military aide and a miraculous turn of events prevented a nuclear nightmare. It had been close, very close.

The Prime Minister was jolted out of his flashback when he was buzzed by his secretary informing him that the cabinet had finished its debate and concluded the voting. It was unanimous to follow General Cohen's recommendation.

The Prime Minister entered the cabinet room, took his seat, and spoke, "As all of you know by now, *Pay'ulah Esh V'Dam, Optzia sofi* or, as the Americans call it, 'Operation Fire and Blood, The Final Option,' will have a devastating effect not only upon our enemies, but upon parts of our nation and upon many of our own people.

"However, I agree with your unanimous decision to activate the plan."

He turned to his Defense Minister, "As the Prime Minister of Israel, I release you to order the preparation of our nuclear strike force. The Israeli Air Force is to unseal our vaults, arm the weapons and load the bombers. Our silos are to activate their missile delivery systems.

"You have been given the coordinates and locations where each weapon is to be targeted. Included in those orders are the types and kilo tonnage of the nuclear weapons to be used.

"At this moment, it is now 3:00 a.m. here in Jerusalem. I plan to order the attack to begin shortly before or just after sunset. I suppose you can have everything ready by then?"

"Yes, sir," answered the Minister of Defense. "We will be ready."

"Very good," replied the somber Prime Minister. "Mr. Shalanski, as our chief diplomat, you will call our embassy in Washington D.C. 15 minutes prior to the release of our first nuclear device. You will authorize our ambassador to call the President of the United States and inform him that we are exercising our nuclear option to deal with the armies that now threaten to destroy our nation."

The Prime Minister then turned his attention to the rest of this cabinet and all the military leaders in the room. "Gentlemen, you have made a difficult decision. None of us in this room will ever face a more difficult choice than the one that we have been forced to make in this dark hour. Each of us now has much work to do in the hours just ahead. Preparations need to be made for eventual retaliation. All of you know what to do, so you are dismissed. May God be with us."

Within minutes of the meeting's adjournment, a flurry of activity began on air bases and military installations all over Israel. Silos in obscure locations along Israel's coastal plains, in the Judean wilderness, in Samaria and throughout the Golan sprang to life in preparation for the launching sequences of the missiles carrying nuclear weapons.

All systems were readied within the hour and waiting for the single word order from the Prime Minister. The time was 3:59 a.m. in Jerusalem.

As Brad and Leah entered the Pope's private quarters, the bone-chilling voice out of the pitch black darkness froze them in place.

"Come into the darkness, children. We've been waiting for you." The couple stood quietly trying to figure out where the voice had come from. After waiting for a full two minutes, Brad finally broke the silence by loudly proclaiming, "It seems to me, Miss Levy, as though our host is afraid to show himself."

Leah, not feeling nearly as emboldened as her partner, elbowed Brad in the ribs.

As the next few minutes passed without another sound, the agents quietly slipped out of their clerical disguises. Shedding her habit and fat suit, Leah, now in a black pantsuit was able to remove their weapons from her waistband and shoulder holsters.

Quietly, Leah took Brad's hand and placed the Uzi in it. He had already instructed her to put the big .357 magnum pistol into the holster clipped on his back waistband.

After another minute passed in silence, Leah leaned close to Brad's ear and whispered, "Perhaps I should set off one of these flares and shed some light on the situation."

Brad leaned in and whispered back, "That is a very good…"

Before he could complete the sentence, a glowing green mist began to spiral down from the tall ceiling, 10 feet in front of them. They watched the phenomenon as it twirled and swirled like a serpent and slowly slithered out of the main room where they stood. The misty trail wound its way through the doors that the agents knew led into the Pope's bedchamber.

Brad softly said, "I believe we are being invited to follow."

"While I tend to agree," Leah replied, "I'm not real big on accepting the invitation."

"My dear," Brad said assuringly, "what we are witnessing is nothing more than mere parlor tricks intended to frighten us. Come on."

Stepping out to follow, Leah added, "Well, if that's their intention, it's working."

The hazy, emerald substance illuminated the area just enough for them to see a few feet ahead as they followed it into the Pope's bedroom. There they watched as the serpentine ribbon slithered through the archway at the back of the bedchamber. The couple knew that through the archway was the private chapel where they had experienced the harrowing encounter with the two beasts.

Leah grabbed Brad's arm and stopped him. "Brad, I don't feel good about going in there."

Brad felt her fear. "Our hosts believe this sleight-of-hand magician's trickery will paralyze us with fear. However, why don't I go in alone and you wait for me here? I'm curious as to what kind of masquerade party they've prepared for us this time."

"Don't underestimate the power of what we are dealing with here," Leah warned. "Believe me when I tell you, the playing field in that chapel will not be level. We are dealing with supernatural forces on the other side of this door."

Again, Brad responded to her warning. "Both of us know, like it or not, I've got to go in. If Kostos isn't in there with the Pope, then the old fool can tell me where to find him. I've got no choice, but you do. Please leave now and let me do this."

Leah huffed, "Brad Fuller, you are incorrigibly stubborn. I assure you we don't have the kind of firepower for this kind of warfare."

"I'm very sorry, Brad replied, "but I'm going in. And besides, those two freaks don't have the advantage of having drugged me this time."

Leah argued, "We were not drugged last time."

"We're running out of time," Brad said as he moved toward the arches. "Please wait for me here."

"No," Leah insisted, "I'm coming too."

Following the incandescent fog trailing through the archway the agents found the large double doors already open. Entering the chapel, they saw the room was dimly lit by the greenish glow of the translucent cloud now hovering at the ceiling.

"I knew you could not resist the temptation to play hero, Fuller."

The voice dripped with an eerie wickedness and the couple scanned the room attempting to locate the source. It seemed to them the voice had come from the altar area.

Squinting their eyes to focus, both agents were amazed to see a two-and-a-half-foot-tall figure step off a pedestal next to the altar. Brad remembered having seen the stone statue on his last trip to the altar. He recalled it was the diabolic image of a gargoyle. To him, it had looked like the ugly, impish creatures that adorn the top of the Notre Dame Cathedral in Paris.

But what they saw was no statue. It had come to life, stepping off its pedestal with short fat legs, a devilish, grotesque face and dwarfed body. It moved menacingly toward them.

Brad recaptured his composure and leveled the Uzi at the wicked demon's head.

"Your weapons are of little use here, Mr. Fuller. So relax. Today is your day to die." Having said that, the vile little creature began to giggle loudly like a little girl. Ten feet away, it ceased the spine-tingling giggling, squatted down on the floor, and leered at the two agents.

Brad, believing it all to be some kind of hologram, addressed the nasty creature. "You look like a Yoda wannabe, you little freak. And yet you're a fitting spokesman for that weasel, the Pope."

That angered the demonic creature, who jumped up and yelled, "I am the Pope, you idiot."

Brad quickly responded, "All right little fella, whatever you say, but I'm looking for Sir Kostos. Why don't you tell me where I can find him."

Another bone-chilling voice behind them roared ferociously as the two large doors slammed shut. "Look no further, you foolish, foolish little man."

The couple swung around, weapons at the ready. What they saw caused their hearts to skip as they both gasped at the frightening appearance of the image before them. Standing over seven feet tall with a humanoid body in a high-collared, long, black, robe stood a wickedly vile being exuding evil.

Skeletal fingers protruded out of the black robe's sleeves. The oversized, skull-like head looked as if all the skin had been peeled off the face. Only muscle tissue and external veins covered the bone. The eyes were bulging and reptilian in appearance. The eye sockets were deep holes with a dim, red light glowing within them.

To Brad and Leah, it was terrifyingly horrendous to look at.

Brad attempted to gather his wits and rubbed his eyes with his free hand, hoping he was just seeing things. When he looked again, the horrific beast was still there. Emanating from his presence was a stifling, disgusting odor that smelled of death and putrefied raw sewage.

Before either agent could say anything, the hideous gargoyle began jumping up and down like an excited child. It was giggling hysterically and clapping its bloated little hands, saying over and over, "Kill him, kill him, kill him, kill him."

The creepy little imp ceased his death chant only when he was interrupted by the taller hellish creature. "Oh, I will kill him, indeed. But let's toy with him a bit before the *coup de grace*."

The towering monstrosity raised his right arm and extended the long, bony fingers. Immediately, Brad was picked up and suspended in the air 10 feet above the floor. Leah stood frozen with terror watching the nightmare unfold.

As Brad hung suspended in midair, the demonic, tall beast roared, "I am Destroyer, god of the world."

Having said that, the entity flexed its wrist. An invisible force grabbed Brad out of the air and threw him toward the altar. He landed hard on the two front pews, shattering one and sending the other skidding across the room.

Brad's groan of pain sickened Leah, who thought the impact might be fatal. She raced to where he lay on the floor, knelt and slowly raised his head.

"Brad, oh, Brad, can you speak?"

His difficulty in breathing instantly told her he was probably suffering from several broken ribs and possibly internal injuries. His eyes fluttered open as a stream of blood flowed from a deep gash above his left brow. Struggling to speak, he whispered, "What was that you said about needing more firepower?"

Ignoring the quip, she moved to help him as he tried to stand to his feet. As she helped him up, he leaned most of his weight on one of the pews.

As Brad tried to stand by himself, the evil one addressed Leah. "Jewess, you've no more business here. Go! Now!"

Leah, still helping Brad stand on his feet, was now more angry than scared. "We both know you can't harm me or you would've done so by now. I know who you are, Lucifer. And I am a daughter of the Light, a child of Jehovah God."

"Do not forget," the devilish creature yelled back, "you repulsive Jewish woman, that this is my time. My destiny. I will be as God. Your Nazarene will soon bow to me."

The creature moved threateningly toward Leah. In response to her defensive reflexes, she slowly reached behind Brad, slipping the .357 mag out of its holster.

Six paces away, the demonic figure said, "I will have him now. He has no shield of light. He's mine."

Desperate to stop him, Leah pulled out the big gun and leveled it at the eyes of the creature.

She cocked back the hammer and yelled, "Go to hell, Devil." But just before she could pull the trigger, the demonized dwarf, shrieked loudly, "Nooooo!" and in one leap covered the 10 yards between him and Leah. He landed on her arm that held the gun, causing the weapon to drop to the floor. The force of his landing knocked her backward toward the altar, where she fell, hitting her head hard on the granite floor. She was almost unconscious.

Brad, only partially aware of what was going on, was still gasping for air and leaning on the pew.

The ferocious evil being turned to Brad, "And now, you die, you sniveling little parasite."

Before the monstrous creature could move, the repulsive shorter demon began jumping up and down, chuckling hideously and pleading like a small child, "Let me, let me, please, let me kill him! Please, please."

"Then be done with it," the disgusting taller one roared.

The dwarfed devil looked toward the full-sized suit of armor standing next to the altar where Leah lay on the floor. She was just beginning to regain consciousness. She strained to open her eyes as she struggled up on hands and knees.

She saw the imp focused on the armor slowly lift his arm. As he did so, the long javelin held in the armor's metal hand flew into the air. She watched it fly through the chapel, make a u-turn, and speed towards Brad, who was still leaning on the seating.

"No!"

But Leah's scream did nothing to stop the flight of the javelin. Horrified, she watched as it flew into Brad's body, piercing deep into his chest. He groaned loudly as he collapsed on the floor.

Leah looked on in shock as she heard the atrocious dwarf break out in another round of hellish giggling.

Shaking her head to clear the cloudy daze, she tried to stand, but halfway to her feet, she fell right into the suit of armor and they both crashed to the floor.

Sitting dazed among the broken pieces of armor, she realized her right hand rested on the handle of the battleaxe.

Looking up, she watched as Kostos suddenly materialized from what had been the tall Luciferian being. He stood there watching her with an evil grin, "Jewess, you are finished here. Take your leave and go."

With a mocking smirk on his face, he turned around to walk out of the Chapel.

Overtaken with a rage she had never known, Leah closed her hand tight around the axe handle, jumped to her feet, and ran toward Kostos. She covered the 15 yards between them quickly. Kostos was just reaching to open the doors when he heard the Pope, now morphed from the gargoyle, scream, "Charon! Behind you!"

The warning came too late.

As Kostos started to turn, Leah was already right behind him bringing the heavy battleaxe forcefully down on his head.

The weapon's razor-sharp edge came down hard. It sliced through the bone of the skull into gray matter with ease, cutting down almost to the jaw line.

Kostos made no sound as he collapsed to the chapel floor. Leah, out of breath, stood over him looking down on the body. The axe remained imbedded.

She was shaken out of her shock by a chilling, shrill howl coming from the Pope. The animalistic cry was loud and long. As it ended, Leah watched the Pope run out of the chapel.

Leah turned and ran to Brad. He lay with the shank of the javelin sticking out of his chest. The spearhead was buried into his chest just below the shoulder, severing bone and muscle, unleashing a torrent of blood. Leah wept as she jerked the spear out, throwing it aside.

Falling down to embrace his head, she was amazed to discover he was still struggling to breathe. With tears flowing, Leah cried, "Brad, oh Brad, don't move. I'll get help." Before she could rise, she heard him weakly whisper, "Get to the Square."

Ignoring him, she pleaded, "Please don't try to speak. I'll be right back."

Again, before she could rise, he shook his head, and in a desperate whisper, strained to say, "No. Get to the Square. Chopper coming. Go!"

"Not without you, I won't." She struggled to get Brad into a sitting position, then worked her shoulder beneath his uninjured side and lifted with all her strength. After an eternity of trying, she was able, with a little help from him, to get him to his feet.

With Herculean effort, Leah began to move him out of the chapel.

THIRTY-FOUR

"One million American dollars," Chuck said to himself as he piloted the chopper closer to the Vatican. "I hope I live long enough to spend it."

Brad had called and made the offer from the Vatican parking lot while Leah was still in the car putting on her nun's habit.

Chuck was surprised to get the call from Fuller, but ever since he had met the two agents while he was working for Kostos, he had a bad feeling about continuing with the IFN.

Brad's offer of one million cash for one unorthodox mission, though probably dangerous, had sealed the deal.

Chuck had told Brad that he did not own his own helicopter. Brad had responded, "Not a problem. Steal one from the IFN fleet." Consequently, an hour ago, Chuck had made his way to the IFN's private terminal at Da Vinci International where, after knocking out and tying up two security guards, he had taken one of their small corporate choppers.

Right on schedule, Chuck flew in low just above the Basilica and the Papal Palace. At this hour, St. Peter's Square was virtually empty as he slowed and brought the helicopter to a touchdown just in front of the majestic stone stair steps leading up the Palace entrance.

Brad had instructed him to sit with the engine running for five minutes. If approached by security or the armed Swiss Guards, he was to fake an emergency, telling everyone to quickly back away from the chopper because it could explode any minute due to engine malfunctions.

For more than 90 seconds after touchdown in the Square, no one approached. However, within two minutes, a contingent of six Swiss Guards approached with pistols in hand. Five of them held their position just outside the propeller wash but a sixth, an officer, slowly came closer.

As the officer got close enough, Chuck opened his small pilot's window and yelled, "This is an emergency landing. I'm experiencing some kind of internal electrical fire. This baby could explode any minute. Now please, for the sake of your men, pull back to a safe distance."

The officer slowly retreated. Upon reaching his five men, he explained what he had been told. He quickly ordered his group to disperse and warn what few people were in the area to move far away from the troubled helicopter.

Chuck knew he was being closely watched and that the guard had alerted emergency services at the Vatican, so he began to act as though he were frantically working in the cockpit to solve the problem.

He had now been on the ground more than six minutes, a minute longer than Fuller had told him to wait. Deciding it was time to go, he was adding power to the rotors when he looked up at the building one last time. He caught sight of a woman coming out of the doors, half dragging an obviously injured man. He watched as the woman struggled to get the man down the stone steps.

Within seconds he realized the woman was Fuller's partner and the man was Fuller.

As the couple reached the bottom of the steps, they were less than 20 yards from the chopper. Chuck leaned over his seat and clicked the lever that opened the back passenger door. It slid open. He then reached across the seat next to him and opened the front passenger door.

Just as Leah got Brad to the back door, Chuck looked up at the Palace. There he saw a robed figure run out, waving frantically and pointing toward the helicopter. Looking closer, Chuck was surprised to see that it was the Pope frantically ordering the Swiss Guards to pursue Leah and Brad.

As other Guards came running back across the large Square, the officer who had lingered was jogging toward the chopper with pistol in hand, ordering the two agents, "Stop where you are or you will be shot."

Leah ignored him and was struggling to push Brad into the back seat of the helicopter.

Chuck looked toward the officer only 30 yards away and saw him level his pistol at Leah's back.

The pilot quickly reached for his own holstered Berretta nine-millimeter, pointed it out the window, and shot. The bullet struck the officer in the upper thigh, dropping him to his knees.

Chuck yelled to Leah, *"Come on lady, hurry, hurry, hurry!"* as a dozen additional Swiss Guards, all armed with assault rifles, came running at the trio from across the Square.

Finally able to get Brad's nearly limp body into the back seat of the chopper, Leah jumped into the front seat, slammed the door, and yelled, *"Go! Go! Go!"*

But Chuck was already lifting off as he saw the men on the ground beginning to fire at the helicopter. As a bullet tore through the Plexiglas window on his left, missing his head by inches, Chuck hollered, "They must know I'm not Catholic!"

As soon as the chopper cleared the tall Vatican buildings, he turned to look at a blood-soaked, exhausted Leah. "Lady, that was a little too close for comfort."

Trying hard to catch her breath, Leah just nodded.

Chuck added, "I hate to tell ya this, ma'am, but you and your friend don't look so good."

Again, Leah, still gasping for air, nodded. After a moment, she commanded Chuck, "Head south, southeast."

"And," asked Chuck as he turned the chopper 90 degrees, "where will that take us, ma'am?"

Finally catching her breath enough to talk, Leah answered, "Follow that heading for about 45 clicks. It'll take us to an old, private estate and medical facility run by some very good friends of mine. The place is called Castel Colledora. Please hurry."

Chuck, fully understanding the emergency, poured on more power and answered, "We'll be there in 12 minutes and 30 seconds. Hang on."

Leah, strapping on her seat belt, glanced at the digital clock on the control panel. It was now 2:59 a.m. in Rome.

President Carr entered the Oval Office first. He was followed by Chief Justice Bailey, Director Pratt and Agent Spears. As they stepped out of the annex room, President Hunt was intently focused on the papers on his desk.

Before any of the intruders could speak, Hunt looked up, smiled broadly, and stood to his feet. "Ah, gentlemen, you're finally here. Our sources informed us you were on your way. Come on in."

Hunt had walked out from behind his desk and was motioning toward the horseshoe arrangement of two sofas and three chairs, "Please have a seat."

The rather surprised group took a seat as Hunt had suggested and watched as he sat down with them. The four men were momentarily silenced by Hunt's nonplussed, cavalier welcome. Of all the possible scenarios they had discussed might greet their sudden appearance, this was not one of them. Hunt was greeting them as though they were old friends returning from a long trip. With a wide grin, Hunt admirably said, "Mr. Carr, you look absolutely terrific. I understand you've been through quite an ordeal."

Carr, already irritated, replied, "To you, Hunt, I am not Mr. Carr. I am President Carr. And, yes, I have been through an ordeal, all orchestrated by your good friend, Kostos."

"All right then, President Carr it is," smiled Hunt. "Let's not quibble over semantics. And as for Kostos, between you and me, at first I had no use for the man. It's just that within a very short time the persistent fellow will virtually rule the world. You wouldn't expect me to ignore such political realities would you?"

"Hunt," Carr added, "allow me to share another political reality. We're all aware of your treasonous acts in cooperation with Kostos. In spite of that, in order to expedite an orderly transfer of the presidency back into the hands of the one duly elected by the people, I will consider granting you a full pardon."

"Mr. Carr," Hunt smiled and quickly corrected himself, "I mean, Mr. President, you are a very confused fellow, indeed. I cannot allow you to just walk in here and demand that you are now President of the United States."

Chief Justice Bailey, impatient with Hunt's banter, jumped in, "You say you can't allow it! As a constitutional attorney, Mr. Hunt, I assure you that neither you nor anyone else has the power to stop it."

The entire group's attention was drawn to movement of the thick window curtains behind Hunt's desk. CIA Agent Cooper stepped out from behind them with a smile on his face and a pistol in his hand.

"Oh, but you're wrong, Your Honor." Cooper smiled, "I have the power to stop it."

CIA Director Pratt jumped to his feet, "Cooper! Are you crazy? Put that gun away, *now*!"

Cooper simply sneered at his boss, "Shut up and sit down, Pratt."

"Gentlemen," Hunt broke in as he stood, "surely you all know Agent Cooper. Each of you should congratulate him for his well-deserved promotion. Less than an hour ago, I named him as the new director of the Central Intelligence Agency."

"Well," Spears put in, "that solves the mystery of who's responsible for the murder of Della Stiles."

"Shut up, Spears, you Secret Service puke," growled Cooper. "Now be a good boy and very slowly reach in, get your weapon, and hand it to President Hunt. And don't try to play Quick Draw McGraw or I'll kill you where you sit."

Hunt walked over as Spears, using his forefinger and thumb, pulled his service revolver out of his shoulder holster and handed it to Hunt.

"Now, Spears," Cooper added, "give him your backup in the ankle holster."

Spears sighed, leaned down, pulled out his backup, and handed it to Hunt as well.

Hunt sauntered back to his desk, sat the weapons atop his desk, and said, "Well, Director Cooper, shall we proceed?"

Cooper bent down and retrieved a duffle bag from behind Hunt's desk. There were four sets of handcuffs, two rolls of heavy duct tape, and two coils of rope.

"Spears," Cooper commanded, "stand up and walk toward me backwards."

Spears obeyed, finally reaching the spot where Cooper wanted him. "Now," Cooper continued, "put your hands behind your back."

Cooper slapped on the cuffs and told Spears, "Now, lie on the floor, face down."

When Spears was down, Cooper addressed his old boss. "All right, Pratt. You're next. Stand and slowly back up to me."

Cooper repeated the drill until all four men were cuffed. He told Spears, Bailey and Pratt to get face down on the floor, but shoved Carr, pushing him down into a chair in front of Hunt's desk.

After seating Carr, Cooper got his duct tape and began to wrap it around the mouths of the others on the floor.

As Cooper was busy with that project, Carr addressed Hunt. "Hunt, you've gone mad. The whole world will find out what you've done."

"Mr. Carr," responded Hunt with a devilish grin, "don't you think calling you 'Mr. Carr' is a bit too formal? I'll just call you Matt. Now, Matt, by the time anyone finds out about me, it'll be way too late. By then, you and your friends here will be dead. And then I will be hailed as a national hero.

"As for you and Spears, everyone will still believe you died when Air Force One went down. And poor Pratt and Bailey will be assassinated by some mean ol' terrorists."

"Just answer one question for me, Hunt." Carr asked, "Why does Kostos want you to murder hundreds of thousands of American men, women and children by nuking New York City? Or have you become such a lapdog to Kostos that you didn't even ask?"

Hunt smirked and sat down behind his desk, "Matt, I never have liked you. You're such a crusader. You never understood the pragmatic approach to leadership. And, yes, I know exactly why I'll push the button to blow New York. I'll do so to save millions of others in nine other American cities."

"What are you talking about?" Carr demanded.

"I'll tell you what I'm talking about, Matt. I'm talking about nine more nukes hidden in nine other American cities, one of which is Washington D.C. Kostos' people placed 'em but he promised me once I push the button to detonate the one in New York City, he will dismantle the other nine.

"So you see, Matt, in the end I'll be regarded as a national hero. The man whose willingness to sacrifice the few in order to save the many will be praised throughout history."

Carr and the three men on the floor were stunned to hear that nine more enemy nuclear weapons existed on U.S. soil.

"Hunt," Carr inquired, "has Kostos told you why he wants you to detonate that nuke in New York City?"

"Do forgive me, Matt," Hunt answered, "but I forgot that you've been out of the loop.

"The fact is Kostos' allies have armies surrounding your precious little Jewish State. When he gives the order to invade Israel, he wants no interference from the United States military. So, to guarantee we keep our nose out of their business, he's smuggled the 10 nukes into 10 of our largest cities as leverage to insure that we sit this one out.

"However, as I just informed you, he's agreed to dismantle the other nine if I will faithfully detonate the one in New York as the invasion of Israel begins."

Carr was having trouble believing Hunt. "You mean to tell me that you're willing to kill hundreds of thousands of people to help Kostos start World War III? I must ask, why are you doing this?"

"Oh, Matt," Hunt groaned as he rolled his eyes, "you are so myopic. Wake up, man. It's a new world and Kostos is ushering in the new world order. And guess who will sit next to the throne at his right hand?"

Carr, shaking his head, countered, "You really believe Kostos is going to share his power with you? Hunt, you're a sniveling little parasite and a bigger fool than I thought. You're nothing but a pawn, a useful idiot, and a deluded maniac."

Hunt, now infuriated, grabbed one of the pistols off his desk and yelled, "Shut up, Carr, or I'll kill you myself!"

Cooper, having just finished gagging and tying up the three men on the floor, stood. "Mr. President, you promised me the privilege of killing these morons.

"As soon as I gag and tie up Carr, I'll stash 'em all in the annex room. And in the morning, after you blow New York, while everyone's preoccupied, I'll finish 'em off and dispose of their bodies. No one will ever know they were here."

As Cooper moved toward Carr with the duct tape, President Carr pleaded, "Listen to me, Hunt! It's not too late to stop this insanity. You can't just kill all those innocent people."

Cooper pulled his gun out of his waistband and struck Carr hard on the head with the butt of the pistol. Carr fell to the floor unconscious.

Kneeling down to tie and gag Carr, Cooper said, "All right, Mr. President, I'll stick 'em in the back room. Right now it's getting close to 8:00 p.m. That'll give 'em about 12 hours to contemplate their fate."

"Just hurry up, Cooper," returned Hunt, "I've got a lot to do."

The intercom on Hunt's desk beeped. Pushing a button, Hunt asked his new secretary, "What is it?"

"Sir," she answered, "I've New York Governor Silverson on the line demanding to speak to you. He's called at least a dozen times in the last hour. Your Chief of Staff handled the other calls, but the Governor insists on talking to you."

"Very well," Hunt replied, "tell him I promise I'll return his call in 15 minutes."

"Yes, sir, Mr. President."

As Cooper began to drag the bound and gagged men into the annex room, Hunt sat back down and glanced at his watch. "Twelve more hours," he thought to himself. "In 12 hours I will save millions of lives all over the United States and prevent billions of dollars worth of properties from being destroyed. New York City will be devastated, but as

Kostos said, we can't save the world. Still, I will be hailed as a national hero for making history's most difficult, but boldest decision. Just 12 more hours."

As Cooper dragged Carr, the last of the group, out of the room and into the annex, Hunt reached into his pocket and brought out the small triggering device and looked at it admirably.

"Mr. President," Cooper said as he walked out of the annex and closed the door behind him, "they're all tied up nice and tight. They won't be giving us any more trouble. I look forward to disposing of 'em."

"Very good, Cooper." Hunt nodded, "Fix yourself a drink." Hunt pushed a button paging his secretary, who promptly responded, "Yes, Mr. President."

"Get Governor Silverson on the line."

"Right away, sir."

Chuck had set the chopper down at the Castel Colledora helipad located just behind the castle. Leah jumped out and ran inside. Within seconds, she led medics and nurses pushing a gurney to retrieve Brad.

He was rushed into an operating room while Leah met up with the elderly Dr. Minay, embraced him, and briefly explained Brad's wounds. She wept throughout the update. "Now, now child," a sympathetic Dr. Minay assured, "I need to go see if I can assist in helping your friend. You can tell me the whole story afterwards. For now, you go to our waiting room and as soon as we know something I'll come out and tell you."

Wiping tears from her eyes, Leah nodded, "Please help him, Doctor. Don't let him die."

As Dr. Minay walked back to the operating room, Leah turned to go to the waiting area. Chuck, whom she had almost forgotten about, walked up to her, "Did we make it in time?"

Leah, still weeping, nodded, "I pray we did. We'll know soon. Come with me and we can wait down the hall."

As soon as the couple sat down in the waiting room, Chuck fell asleep in his chair.

Two hours passed before Dr. Minay, still in his surgical attire, entered the waiting area. Leah jumped up and ran to the doctor. "Is he still alive? Will he be all right?"

Embracing her, the old doctor patted her on the back.

"Sit, sit, Leah, and I'll tell you all about it."

The two took a seat next to each other as Chuck continued snoring across the room. Dr. Minay began, "Your friend came in on a day when we were being visited by Dr. Menoha, the best trauma surgeon on the continent. He didn't hesitate to scrub in and lead the surgical team."

"And," Leah anxiously interrupted, "will Brad be okay?"

"I want to be honest with you, my dear," the kindly doctor explained. "His injuries are very serious. We don't know if he'll survive them until after a 24-hour period. If he's still alive tomorrow, his chances will increase dramatically. Your friend was only minutes from death when he was rolled into our operating room. The right side of his chest cavity was partially crushed by the large spear. It severely damaged his right lung and severed muscles, tendons and arteries. Permanent paralysis of his right shoulder and arm is very possible. His loss of blood alone was almost fatal.

"Additionally, on the left side of his chest he had four broken ribs, one of which had punctured his lung. His left arm was broken just above the elbow. And the deep gash above his brow took 38 stitches to close. Fortunately, there was no fracture of the skull.

"If he survives, my dear, it will be a long recovery followed by extensive rehab."

Leah, listening intently, asked, "Is he conscious, Doctor?"

"No, Leah, and he won't be for the next 24 hours. We're keeping him sedated to restrict his movement."

Leah's clothes and person were still covered with Brad's blood.

A nurse walked into the waiting room and addressed Leah. "Ma'am we have prepared a private guest room for you and another for your sleepy friend over there. You'll be able to clean up, rest, and eat something—or whatever you choose. If you'll follow me, I'll take you both to your quarters."

Leah thanked the nurse as the woman woke Chuck and explained to him that a room awaited. The still-sleepy pilot got up and followed the nurse out, but Leah remained seated with Dr. Minay.

"Doctor," Leah continued, "before I go to my room, I must inform you about what happened at the Vatican."

The doctor gently patted her hand, "If you're up to it, I'll gladly listen."

She began by telling of Brad's mission to assassinate Kostos and of their entrance into the Pope's quarters. She also related everything about their first supernatural encounter with Kostos and the Pope within the chapel.

She continued by explaining how, on this second visit, the Pope had taken on the persona of what had been a statue of a gargoyle and Kostos had morphed into a Luciferian beast. Leah explained how Brad had been tossed around in the air like a rag doll and then pierced by the javelin manipulated by the smaller being.

Dr. Minay responded, "While some may have great difficulty believing you, I believe you completely. I know that you and your friend were dealing with satanic forces."

Leah, still shaken, added, "I know it, and I tried to warn Brad but he believed it was all a magician's sleight-of-hand. At least until he was thrown through the air."

She continued describing the horror of the battle in the chapel, explaining everything up to the point where she found herself laying on the floor amidst the pieces of armor. "And then, Doctor, I looked up just as the tall satanic figure turned back into Kostos before my eyes. He just stood there grinning at me with this demonic look in his eyes.

"By then I was enraged over what had just happened to Brad. I picked up a heavy antique battle axe off the floor and rushed toward Kostos, who was leaving the chapel."

"Didn't he attempt to stop you?" the doctor asked.

"He didn't have time," Leah answered. "I came up quickly behind him and split his skull with the axe before he even realized I was there."

"You say you split open his head?" the amazed Dr. Minay gasped.

"Yes," Leah repeated, "I killed him. He crashed to the floor with the axe still deeply imbedded in his head."

"This is extraordinary, child," the doctor marveled. "And you've no doubt that he was dead?"

Leah answered, "Dr. Minay, unfortunately in my business I've seen a lot of dead people. Kostos was dead, of that you can be sure."

"Oh, my," the astonished doctor stood up, "this is incredible news. I must leave you, Leah. It's most urgent that I get this information to others. Please go and clean up and rest."

"Dr. Minay," asked Leah as she stood, "Kostos' death, was it a bad thing?"

"Oh, no, my dear Leah," the doctor answered. "It means a lot of hellish plans may suffer a setback, at least for a while."

Leah did not understand his statement. "What do you mean, 'setback for a while'?"

Dr. Minay answered, "Dear girl, the prophets foretold that at one point the Antichrist would be killed by a fatal head wound, but they go on to tell of a diabolic miracle that follows his death."

"I'm not sure I understand, Doctor," Leah added.

"I'll explain later," Minay hurriedly replied, "but for now I must make some extremely urgent calls. I'll see you in an hour or so. You need to go now, Leah." Dr. Minay turned, hurriedly walking away and thinking to himself, *The girl doesn't have a clue about the historic and prophetic significance of her actions.*

"May Jehovah help us, now."

THIRTY-FIVE

New York Governor Silverson had waited by the phone in his New York City command center, hoping that President Hunt would keep his promise and return his call. He was not disappointed when the phone rang moments later.

"Yes, Mr. President," a relieved Governor answered, "thank God you called, sir. I'm sure you know that we face a rather desperate situation here. The nuclear scientists have tirelessly worked but, at last report, they're still very negative."

"Governor Silverson," the president calmly assured, "I am fully aware of your status. However, I want you to listen very closely to what I've got to tell you."

The Governor was anxious for any word of hope or direction the president could offer. "Yes, sir, I'm listening."

Hunt continued, "I am going to share a top secret, highly classified piece of information with you."

"Uh, yes, sir," the Governor replied. "I assure you, your confidence is well placed, sir."

"Very well," the president continued with his lie, "and do remember, Governor, this is for your ears only. You must tell no one until I release you to do so. With that said, I want you to know that we have developed a top-secret method to neutralize any and all nuclear devices. The bomb in your subway will not, I repeat, it will not explode. Our new technology renders it impotent.

"Now, try to understand that we cannot release the news about this new technology just yet. We are convinced our enemies who placed that device will soon show their hand if they remain convinced their bomb will actually work. But, I assure you, Governor, it will not.

"Now, I can promise you this. By tomorrow's 8:00 a.m. deadline that the bomb is set to go off, we will have the sorry terrorists who planted that weapon in custody. Then, and only then, can you inform your people of our technological victory."

"Mr. President," the Governor gushed, "that's the greatest news I've ever heard. And trust me, sir, I'll not say a word until you release me to do so.

"Uh, by the way, sir, and I'm sure you already know, but Dr. Endenstein has told me that the device in the subway has a trigger relay of some sort. He believes that when the bomb is detonated, it will send a signal to one or more other nuclear weapons, causing them to detonate as well. So, I'm just wondering, Mr. President, if you can tell me, if our government is aware of any other such weapons on American soil?"

For a moment, Hunt was stunned into silence and had to shake himself in order to respond, "Uh, no, Governor, rest assured there are no more such devices in the U.S.A."

"Thank you, sir," the Governor sighed in relief. "That's great to know."

"All right, Governor," Hunt returned, "I've other matters that demand my attention. I must go now."

Hunt hung up and sat thoughtfully processing what the Governor had said about other bombs that may detonate. Hunt pushed the intercom button, paging his secretary.

"Yes, sir, Mr. President."

"Call the Vatican in Rome and get Charon Kostos on the phone for me. He should be there somewhere. And tell 'em it's urgent. Do it now!"

"Yes, sir."

Hunt glanced again at his watch. It was 8:40 p.m. and less than 10 and a half hours until detonation.

Governor Silverson was elated and sat basking in the news Hunt had shared with him when Dr. Endenstein entered.

"Governor, forgive my intrusion, but I must advise you once more. We've virtually no chance of preventing that bomb from going off. I counsel you to evacuate the city."

"Dr. Endenstein," a smiling Governor answered, "please sit down a moment. I really shouldn't tell you this, but I trust you can keep it to yourself. It's very highly classified, and you must not tell anyone."

As the eminent scientist listened, the Governor gleefully related to him everything the president had said about the brand-new technology that neutralized nuclear weapons.

When he was finished, Dr. Endenstein shook his head and replied, "Please believe me, Governor, as the head of the government's Nuclear Research and Development Agency, privy to more classified information concerning our nuclear capabilities than the president, I can absolutely assure you, there is no technology in existence that is capable of doing what Hunt has told you.

"For whatever reason, the President of the United States is not telling the truth!"

It was 5:00 a.m. as General Chevsky, Commander of the coalition invasion forces poised on all of Israel's borders, sat deep within the bunker overlooking the Golan Heights. He took a seat at his desk to receive a call from Russian President Valenko in Moscow.

"Yes, Mr. President, this is General Chevsky."

"Ah, General," the president replied, "it is good to hear your voice. I have only two questions, General. The first is, have you heard from Kostos in the last few hours? And second, has the time been absolutely set for the invasion to commence?"

"Mr. President," Chevsky answered, "I have not talked to Kostos since late yesterday, when he gave us the precise time we are to launch the invasion. We are to attack Israel in approximately 15 hours, according to him, whether we hear from him or not.

"Kostos has assured us that four hours prior to the invasion, the United States will be suffering its own national crisis and far too occupied to be concerned with Israel. So, Mr. President, once again, unless we hear from Kostos himself ordering us to stand down, nothing will stop our forces from commencing the invasion of the Jewish State on schedule."

"General," replied Valenko, "we trust you will award the Motherland with a great victory. I will look forward to your report."

"Yes, sir, Mr. President. It won't be long now. Goodbye."

WORLD NEWS NETWORK
LIVE AT THE VATICAN IN ROME—8:00 A.M.

"I'm Ron Blevins coming to you live from the Vatican with this Special News Bulletin. The man heralded as the greatest diplomat and peacemaker in human history is dead. The body of Charon D. Kostos was discovered this morning in the guest quarters of the Papal Palace. Investigating authorities are reporting that he was assassinated.

"I repeat, Charon Kostos, President of the International Federation of Nations, and often referred to as the Prince of Peace for his remarkable successes in international diplomacy, has been assassinated.

"At the moment, we do not know much about what's going on behind the walls here at Vatican City. However, I was just handed a statement being released by the Pontiff. So I'll read it to you as-is, and I quote…

"'Charon D. Kostos, loved by millions of people the world over as the greatest humanitarian and peacemaker in all of human history, has been murdered. Mr. Kostos was left alone in his private suite at 11:00 p.m. last evening. This morning at 5:30 a.m., Vatican personnel delivering his breakfast discovered his body.

"'According to witnesses, Mr. Kostos suffered a fatal head wound inflicted by unknown assailants who had somehow managed to breach the heavy network of security surrounding his quarters. An international manhunt is already underway for the perpetrators of this brutal and heinous act.

"'As the Vicar of Christ and the Head of the Church, it was my privilege to be a counsel and friend of Charon Kostos. It may be fitting that Charon leaves behind no living relatives, for he was a man who belonged to each of us within the human family who also seek peace, equality and prosperity for all.

"'We will honor Charon Kostos' life and legacy as he lies in state inside St. Peter's Basilica. Such an honor is usually reserved for Popes, God's representatives on Earth. However, to people all over the world, this man was a saint and shall be honored as such.

"'Kostos' achievements rival the great works of our Lord Jesus.

"'I, as Pope, will grieve with the entire civilized world, the loss of this one man who could have led us all into a Universal Kingdom of Peace and Prosperity.

"'Today, I urge people of all faiths and religions to join together in praying that this selfish act by hate-filled people will not end the glorious vision of Charon Kostos.

"'We must also pray that the Almighty would yet smile upon all humankind and grant us another chance to realize the dream of Charon Kostos.'

"And, friends, that ends the Pope's latest press release.

"Again, I repeat, Charon D. Kostos has been assassinated while he was an overnight guest at the Vatican.

"No group or individuals have thus far claimed responsibility and, according to what the Pontiff just said, a worldwide hunt for the assassins is now underway.

"WNN will be on location throughout the day to bring you up-to-the-minute coverage of this tragic event. This is Ron Blevins reporting from the Vatican in Rome."

The news of Kostos' death swept around the globe with remarkable speed.

In areas where it was still dark, cities and villages were awakened by sirens or church bells. In neighborhoods where most residents had gone to bed, people who heard the report of the tragedy knocked on doors waking people to share the news. It was not long until literally millions of people all over the world were jamming phone lines, sending e-mails and clogging up cell phone traffic as they, too, spread the news.

Within a very short time, people all over the planet wept and mourned the death of Kostos. Heads of state across Europe, Asia, Africa and the other continents declared the day a national day of mourning and remembrance. Cities spontaneously organized prayer vigils, memorial rallies and massive candlelight services in honor of Charon Kostos.

It was midnight on America's East Coast and 9:00 p.m. on the West Coast when the WNN live newscast hit the airways. It was early enough in most of the United States for massive sections of the population to hear about it.

Newspapers being readied for the morning editions stopped the presses and reworked headlines. Networks went to work immediately throwing together television specials for the morning shows. Radio stations and news channels replayed the Pope's press release over and over.

The news hit Washington D.C. at midnight as well. Officials all over the area rushed to the Capitol. The lights in the White House burned bright and the nation's leaders hurried to their offices.

President Hunt, whose secretary had failed earlier to get Kostos on the line, had gone to rest in his quarters. Upon hearing the WNN report he, too, ran back to his office. When he arrived, a long line of Congressional leaders, Cabinet members, and various department heads waited to see him.

Hunt, however, refused to see anyone, with the exception of Agent Cooper, who had remained in the Oval Office to keep an eye on the captives in the annex.

Hunt ordered his Chief of Staff to inform all visitors that he was busy handling a series of crises and would not be able to see anyone until mid-morning. The president sat at his desk in a state of shock and despair, paralyzed by the news of Kostos' sudden death.

Hunt was remembering what Kostos had said to him about pushing the button to detonate the subway bomb in New York. Kostos had repeatedly warned him that no matter what happened, he must push that button at 8:00 a.m. sharp. If he failed to do so, Kostos had assured him that others who worked for him would explode the bomb, adding that they would also detonate the other nine bombs hidden in American cities.

Hunt had just received the latest intelligence from the Middle East and Kostos' armies were still preparing to invade Israel. Everything seemed to be on schedule—everything except Kostos.

Hunt addressed Agent Cooper, also one of Kostos' lackeys, who sat on the sofa in front of the president. "Maybe this is just another one of Kostos' ways of testing our faithfulness. If it is, I must prove myself worthy."

Agent Cooper replied, "And if he really is dead, would it change what you're going to do?"

Hunt shook his head and stoically replied, "No, I've still got no choice but to push the button to blow New York. If I don't, then his minions will certainly detonate the others, as well as the one in New York City. So, nothing's changed. I must follow through. If Kostos is truly dead, I'll still be hailed as a national hero for saving the other nine cities."

"And," Cooper asked, "what about the so-called trigger relay on the subway nuke?"

"I only know," Hunt answered, "that Kostos promised me he wouldn't allow any other nuclear device to explode if I obeyed. I trust him and I will obey."

President Carr, Director Pratt, Justice Bailey and Agent Spears were all still bound and gagged in the annex room next to the Oval Office. They knew something important was going on because of all the sirens, noise, and traffic sounds they were hearing.

All of the group, with the exception of Agent Spears, had given up trying to wiggle free. But Spears was a trained and skilled ex-Navy Seal and special agent. He did not give up, ever. Additionally, he was a lot more physically equipped to meet such a challenge than his three friends.

As they all quietly listened to murmurs in the Oval Office, Spears, still struggling, suddenly felt his wrist ropes slip just a little. If he could loosen the ropes, he knew he could handle the cuffs. He and his Seal buddies used to see who could break free of handcuffs the fastest. Spears never lost one of those matches.

While the other bound and gagged men in the annex slept and things outside the room became somewhat calmer, Agent Spears continued to strain, twist, and pull until finally the ropes released their grip on his wrist.

Shaking the ropes off—and with his hands still cuffed behind him—Spears, using brute strength snapped the chain holding his wrist together. With his hands free, he reached for the ropes on his legs and feet, quickly untying them. He stood up, jerked the heavy duct tape off his mouth, and took a deep breath. Glancing at his watch, he saw it was already 6:45 a.m.

Shuffling quietly to the small desk on the other side of the room, he found a paper clip, tiptoed over to Carr, and woke him. Carr looked startled, but only for a second, as Spears untied the ropes and removed his gag.

"Be very still, sir," Spears whispered, "and I'll get those cuffs off." Spears proceeded to pick the cuff's lock using the paper clip.

Ten minutes later, the other two men were also free of their restraints and the four men huddled in a corner discussing what to do next.

As the huddle broke, Spears sneaked to the door leading into the Oval Office and slowly opened it just enough to see the room was empty except for Agent Cooper, who was asleep on the sofa.

Moving like a jungle cat sneaking up on an unsuspecting gazelle, Spears crept over to where Cooper lay sleeping. He moved with speed to put a sleeper hold on the agent and, within seconds, Cooper was out cold. Spears dragged the man into the annex and tied him up.

A few minutes later, Cooper came to, looking down the barrel of his own gun. Spears pressed it hard on the man's nose. "You up to answering some questions? If not, I'll kill you now. It'll save me the trouble of doing it later."

Cooper's eyes were wide with fear. "Okay. Whatever you want, you got it. Just be careful with that gun, Spears. It's got a hair trigger, please."

Carr stepped forward, "All right, Coop. What was all the fuss about a few hours ago?"

"Sir, Kostos was assassinated by someone in Rome. News said they know little else about it. Then the Pope sent out a release that said a bunch of nice things about the guy. That's all, I swear."

"And," Carr continued, "where's Hunt now?"

"He went back to his quarters about an hour and a half ago. Said he'd be back around 7:30 a.m."

Carr, rubbing on his wrist trying to get his circulation moving again, addressed Spears. "Gag him good, Agent Spears."

Carr and the three others settled down in the annex to wait for Hunt to return to the Oval Office. While they waited, Carr took Cooper's cell phone and called Admiral Withers, Chair of the Joint Chiefs, and Secretary of Defense Carl Bates to tell them everything that had happened since he'd left, and to give them instructions. He followed up by calling Secretary of State Parlay to update him.

By the time he finished his calls, it was already 7:25 a.m. The men sat quietly and waited.

Behind schedule, at 7:49 a.m., a very unstable-looking Hunt reentered his office. Carr watched him through a small crack in the door and was amazed to see how unkempt and out of it Hunt appeared. His suit was badly wrinkled and his tie loose. It was clear that he had not bothered to shave, and the dark shadow of his stubble gave the man a slovenly look. Worst of all, Carr thought, was the dazed, distant look in his eyes.

As soon as Hunt plopped down behind his desk, Carr and the others quickly entered the room.

Hunt simply looked up at them and sneered. "You again? I ordered Cooper to kill you people before 7:30 a.m."

Carr sat down in the chair in front of Hunt's desk, "I'm sorry, Hunt, but both of us know how hard it is to find good help.

"Now, I have some orders for you. You are going to write up a short letter of resignation as president and give it to our Chief Justice. If you refuse to do so, you will be immediately placed under arrest and hauled out of here for the world to see."

Hunt reached to open his desk drawer as though he was getting some paper but when his hand came out it was holding one of Spears' weapons secured from him earlier. Pointing the pistol at Carr's head, Hunt spoke to Spears, "Put the gun you took from Cooper on the floor or I'll blow your president's head off."

Spears slowly reached inside his coat and did as he was told.

Holding the gun on those in the office, Hunt addressed them, "In less than five minutes my legacy will be eternally established. I will be hailed as the greatest president in American history who acted to save millions by bravely choosing to sacrifice the few."

Hunt reached into his suit pocket with his left hand and pulled out the small trigger device he would use to detonate the bomb in New York City.

"Hunt," Carr addressed the man as though he were the psycho he appeared to be, "you don't need to resign at all if you'll just hand me that detonator. If you'll do so, I'll get up and my friends and I will leave and disappear forever. What do you say?"

Hunt sneered at Carr with a delirious expression. "Oh, it's far too late for that. It's time to prove my worth and to show the world I am strong, decisive and unafraid to make the hard choices."

Hunt looked at the digital clock on his desk. It read 8:00 a.m. He then raised the device, pointing it like a remote at Carr, smiled wickedly and pushed the button to trigger the nuclear bomb.

"*Aha,* now it's done. You'll see, you'll all see. I'll be enshrined on the heart of every American. And now, it's time to say, goodbye."

Hunt then raised the pistol still pointing it at Carr, but when he got the gun level with Carr's head, Hunt turned it toward himself, stuck the barrel into his mouth, and pulled the trigger.

Two minutes before Hunt pushed the button on the triggering device, the two scientists working to disarm the bomb were still beneath the subway platform hovering over the device.

New York Governor Silverson, who chose to believe President Hunt's lie that the bomb had been neutralized by American technology, had refused to leave the command post close to the bombsite. He had told all the other officials with him, "I've got it on good authority the bomb will not explode. We are safe." To a man, they had believed the Governor and remained with him.

Now, with only 20 seconds left on the countdown mechanism, Dr. Endenstein turned to Dr. Carlyle. "Professor, I am sorry to say it but we have failed."

Both scientists looked down at the timer as the final five seconds expired, 5-4-3-2-1.

As the timer clicked over to zero time left until detonation, the two scientists, already resigned to their fate, watched as the device seemed to come to life. They saw a series of red flashing lights turn to green flashing lights and listened as a high-pitched whine resonated from deep inside the weapon. They were braced for the explosion that would end their lives, but instead of an explosion, they heard a muffled 'pop,' as though a small light bulb had blown out.

As they stared in wonder at the weapon, they heard three more such pops. The pops were followed by the release of three thin trails of smoke rising from within the device and one such wisp of smoke coming from the trigger mechanism that sat atop the metal cylinder.

Both doctors were drenched in perspiration and in a state of shock as Dr. Endenstein quietly spoke, "Those popping noises sounded like electrical shorts."

Dr. Carlyle added, "And the smoke trails must be the circuits burning up.

"Did we cause that?"

Dr. Endenstein looked closely at the one-inch by half-inch trigger mechanism atop the device. He picked up a powerful magnifying glass from his tool bag, intently studying the tiny device. After a moment, he reached again into his bag, pulled out a small plastic probe that looked like a long, very thin toothpick, and gently worked it in and out of the trigger housing.

Dr. Carlyle, watching in curious amazement, whispered, "What is it?"

Dr. Endenstein, now examining a small bit of something stuck on the tiny tip of the probe answered, "It's a wee remnant of some sort of substance. It was stuck between the firing points of the trigger mechanism, preventing it from completing the electronic cycle. The points cannot fuse if even microscopic particles work their way between those hyper-sensitive points."

"That's why," Dr. Carlyle added, "we construct such devices in bio-sterile environments."

Dr. Endenstein was again gently running the probe into the trigger device in an attempt to pick up more of the foreign substance. He withdrew the probe and once again studied the small sample through his magnifying glass.

Finally, he set his magnifier down and touched the end of the probe to his tongue to taste it.

"What is it?" an anxious Dr. Carlyle asked.

Thoughtfully savoring the taste a second time, an astonished Dr. Endenstein turned to his associate, "Peanut butter. It's peanut butter with a hint of grape jelly!"

A very amazed Dr. Carlyle replied, "You've got to be kidding. Peanut butter and jelly? But how..."

Interrupting her, Dr. Endenstein, equally mystified, answered, "I've not the slightest idea. But it miraculously gummed up and then shorted the relays. So much for our nuclear engineering geniuses."

"But," Carlyle mused out loud, "if we had attempted to interrupt those circuits ourselves, without doubt, we would've caused an immediate detonation. It had to have been a one-in-a-million freak accident, wouldn't it?"

Scratching his head, Dr. Endenstein thought out loud, "Peanut butter and jelly? If I remember correctly, it seems that someone mentioned to me upon my arrival that a small boy was the first to discover this weapon while he played under this platform. I wonder..."

"If so," Dr. Carlyle jumped in, "civilization, as we know it, may have just been saved by a boy with a peanut butter and jelly sandwich. Poetic justice is sweet."

Dr. Endenstein leaned back and sighed, "Extraordinary. Simply amazing."

The sound of gunfire in the Oval Office brought the two Secret Service agents outside the main doors running in with weapons drawn. Barging through the door, the first thing the agents saw was the body of President Hunt on the floor. Thinking the worst, the agents spun to face the others in the office, ready to shoot to kill. It took the two men only seconds to recognize President Carr, Director Pratt, Chief Justice Bailey and their old friend, Mark Spears.

Before they could ask anything, Carr spoke. "Gentlemen, Mr. Hunt just committed suicide. You'll find the weapon under his body."

Justice Bailey pushed his way forward to stand in front of the president and addressed the group, "You two agents, Director Pratt, and you, Spears, will now witness the constitutional swearing in of President Carr."

Bailey then faced Carr, who raised his right hand as the Justice administered the oath of office. When he finished, Carr turned to address the two still-shocked agents. "Men, what you've been witnessing is the tragic end to a failed coup by former President Hunt and various foreign enemies of the United States.

"As president, I'm ordering you to say nothing to anyone about the events that just took place in this office until we have released proper statements to the press."

One of the agents answered, "Mr. President, neither one of us is sure of what's happening here. You were dead and now you're standing here alive. But everyone around Washington knows Hunt has been doing some very strange things lately. So, we will honor your orders. By the way, sir, White House employees who work in this wing of the mansion are just coming to work, so I'm sure no one else heard the gunfire."

"Thank you, gentlemen," Carr replied. "Now would you two please retake your post just outside the door?"

"Yes, sir." The agents agreed and left the room.

Before another word could be spoken, the intercom beeped, followed by the voice of the new secretary. "President Hunt, the Governor of New York called and left a message saying how grateful he was for the information you shared respecting the subway bomb. And he says that the bomb did, indeed, fail to explode."

"Thank you," answered Carr as he and the others shared quizzical looks.

"How about that, sir?" piped up Pratt.

"Great news, indeed!" Carr replied. "When we get some time we'll look into what caused that miracle but for now, Pratt, I need you to call Admiral Withers and the Secretary of Defense. Tell 'em to release their prepared statement now.

"Among other issues, those statements will tell the press and the world that Agent Spears and I have been found on a small island off the Italian coast, where we were nursed back to health after severe injuries as a result of Air Force One's crash."

Chief Justice Bailey spoke up. "That'll open a Pandora's box of questions."

Carr smiled, "It's okay. Everyone is to claim ignorance of any further details, for now.

"And Justice Bailey, prepare a document explaining how you, among others, were witness to Hunt's suicide. Tell them he was obviously a stressed-out, exhausted man who was overwhelmed by the pressures of the office.

"Also, include how you reinstated me as president."

"Yes, sir," agreed Bailey as he turned to leave.

"Now," continued Carr, "Spears, contact the Press Secretary, whoever he is, and explain to him very briefly that I am back and that I will go live to the nation in 20 minutes. That will be 8:35 a.m. D.C. time. I want all networks airing it."

"Yes, sir, I'm on it," and Spears ducked out.

Before the door could shut, one of the agents guarding it stuck his head in. "Excuse me Mr. President, but Chief Withers is here with the Secretary of Defense."

"Thank you, send them in," Carr answered as he walked around and sat down at the desk.

The two men entered as the Secretary of Defense began. "It's sure good to see you in that chair, sir. But I've a bit of rain to pour on your parade.

"As the whole world knows, the Russian-Arabic coalition sits on Israel's borders with over a million troops and 3,000 war planes. They, according to our latest intel, are only hours from invading."

"Your suggestions, gentlemen," replied Carr.

"We advise," spoke up Admiral Withers, "an immediate, very stern, personal call from you to President Valenko in Moscow. Tell him, for starters, the United States will no longer ignore their aggression the Middle East. Explain to him that we have three large aircraft carrier battle groups about to enter the Mediterranean. And that we've got a massive fleet of Stealth B1 bombers full of nukes in the air, headed for the region. Further, you may want to remind him of the 20,000 ICBMs we have pointed at his head.

"You also need to inform the national leaders of the other armies in the coalition that if they put one foot on Israeli soil, they'll be committing suicide."

"And," the Secretary of Defense added, "we suggest, sir, that you make those calls immediately, before you go live on the air, so you can tell the American people what's going on in the Middle East.

"And, one other thing, Mr. President," added the Admiral, "please call Prime Minister Ehud in Israel and explain to him that we're standing with him. Try to convince him not to move against the coalition preemptively until we've had a chance to try to get his enemies to withdraw peacefully."

President Carr answered, "I'll move on your suggestions immediately, but get me some help to track down all these heads of state and get 'em on the line for me."

"Yes, sir," saluted the Admiral as he and the Secretary of Defense hurried out of the room.

Americans and citizens of the world were about to be shocked by the startling turn of events unfolding in Washington D.C. and the very real possibility of World War III about to break out in the Middle East.

THIRTY-SIX

Hello, I'm Bryan Hister with this WNN Special Report from Washington D.C.

"The American Capitol is reeling this morning after a shocking turn of events overnight.

"We've been informed in just the last few minutes that President Mathew Dillon Carr, once thought to have been killed during the crash of Air Force One, has been found alive. The word is that, until very recently, he had been recuperating from injuries sustained in that crash on a remote island off the Italian coast where there were no means of communication with the outside world.

"That's all we know about his sudden reappearance at the moment.

"But, in another rather stunning turn of events, according to our sources, the current American President, Jordan Hunt, has just died of a self-inflicted gunshot.

"Shortly after that incident occurred, the Chief Justice of the Supreme Court, Justice Bailey, swore Carr back into office as the duly elected President of the United States of America.

"President Carr is about to address the nation and the world from the Oval Office."

THE WHITE HOUSE

Cameras panned in on President Carr sitting at his desk in the Oval Office.

"My fellow Americans, I only wish that I was returning to office during a more positive set of circumstances. As you have probably heard by now, my Vice President Jordan Hunt, who assumed the office of the Presidency after my supposed demise, is dead by his own hand. The details and all related information regarding the death of President Jordan will be shared with the world in the next few days.

"As for me and a very special Secret Service agent, Mark Spears, both of us are alive today because an elderly fisherman and his grandson near the crash site of Air Force One picked us up as the lone survivors. They whisked us away to an isolated island with no access to newspapers, radio or television well before search-and-rescue teams appeared on the scene.

"In fact, there was not even electricity in the tiny hut where we were cared for and nursed back to health, and the kind fisherman and his grandson had no idea who we were. We will soon give a detailed account of that ordeal to you, the American people.

"I must also inform you that since I have been reinstated as your president, I have learned that Russia and a number of Middle Eastern Nations have massive armies on the verge of invading the State of Israel.

"The Israeli people and their nation are long-time allies of the United States, so I have sent three aircraft carrier groups into the Mediterranean Sea and have ordered several American squadrons of B1 Stealth bombers into the skies over Israel. The remainder of our military structure is on a def-com emergency stand-by prepared to respond if needed.

"Further, I just got off the phone with Russian President Valenko and the leaders of the other nations involved, warning them to order an immediate withdrawal of all their military forces or to face the wrath of the American war machine.

"I'm asking Americans everywhere to pray that we can avoid war, but let there be no mistake, America will not tolerate an invasion of Israel.

"Now, I must close and give my complete attention to resolving this crisis, but please know I will, within days, come before you again and answer all your questions. Until then, I say, may God bless you and may God bless America.

9:00 a.m. Washington D.C.…5:00 p.m. in Syria…Invasion of Israel, to commence in two hours.

From past experience, Russian President Valenko knew President Carr never bluffed. After the American President's call and warning, the Russian leadership had scrambled and ultimately ordered President Valenko to call off the Russian-led coalition's invasion of Israel.

Valenko put in an urgent call to General Chevsky, commander of the armies poised on Israeli borders. The General took his president's call in his command bunker on the Golan Heights.

"General Chevsky, this is President Valenko. Can you hear me?"

"Yes, Mr. President, I hear you. I assume you're calling about the bizarre events taking place in the United States. We have been following the updates from here."

"Then, General Chevsky," returned Valenko, "you are aware of the assassination of Charon Kostos and also of the return to power of President Carr. Carr has issued an ultimatum demanding our coalition stand down and begin an immediate withdrawal of all forces from Israel's borders. The Duma and I have decided to stand down for now and to postpone the invasion."

"I am most aware, President Valenko, of America's saber rattling, big talk and this so-called ultimatum. However, I am sure you know we are well past the point of no return. The orders are already out, our armies are this minute moving into position, and I've 3,000 warplanes sitting on tarmacs with engines running. Very shortly, we will launch an invasion that will sweep Israel off the map and bring Russia a glorious victory."

Valenko was shocked at General Chevsky's audacious resistance to Kremlin orders.

"Let me make this clear, Chevsky. You are ordered by the leaders of Russia and the Duma to call off the invasion and to begin an orderly withdrawal of coalition forces. And General Chevsky, we are not asking for your assessment, your political opinions or your advice. We are ordering you to stand down and withdraw now. Do you understand, General?"

"With all due respect, Mr. President," Chevsky growled through gritted teeth, "no, I do not understand. It is time for the Motherland to stand up to these American cowards. I am perfectly capable of dealing with them and these Jewish maggots!"

"General Chevsky," Valenko angrily roared, "the matter is not open for debate. The decision is made, and if you resist further, you will return to face a firing squad for treason. Am I clear?"

General Chevsky laughed into the phone. "You and the rest of the old fools in the Duma are cowards who have outlived your usefulness. It is I who command this coalition and, in fact, I who control the Russian military. I will not obey your orders nor will I grovel like a whipped pup at the feet of the American threats.

"The invasion will go on as scheduled and we shall prevail. Good bye, Mr. President."

Infuriated, Valenko yelled into the phone, "Chevsky don't you hang up on me, you imbecile! You are a fool!"

Realizing the line was dead, the president slammed down the phone.

The 12-man council from the Duma in his office had heard every word.

They watched the red-faced Valenko put his face in his hands, then lean back in his chair. After a solemn moment of silence, the president turned to his aide. "Major Kostalov, get me the American President on the phone and hurry."

All Israel had watched the news broadcast from Washington D.C and heard President Carr's warning and ultimatum to their enemies. Prime Minister Ehud gladly took the call from President Carr.

"President Carr, we are most thankful for your timely return from the grave, and for your country's support in our time of need."

"Thank you, Prime Minister," replied Carr. "However, I'm calling to inform you that General Chevsky, commander of the Coalition forces now on your borders, categorically refuses to obey the Kremlin's orders to withdraw. He is planning to proceed with the invasion."

"Mr. President," the Prime Minister answered, "we are most grateful for your generous offer of support. However, I must inform you that a unanimous decision has been made by our Cabinet to resort to our nuclear option and a preemptive strike within the hour."

"Mr. Prime Minister, I implore you to reconsider," pleaded Carr. "Give us a little more time to resolve this situation. This very minute, our Secretary of State is talking to the Middle Eastern Heads of State whose armies are in the Russian Coalition. He is making it very clear that if they follow General Chevsky's orders, they will be committing national suicide.

"If you resort to a nuclear strike, you're inviting a rain of nuclear missiles on Israel from the Russians."

"Please, Mr. President," put in the Prime Minister, "do not lecture us like we are children. We did not make our decisions lightly, and surely your own intelligence has informed you of our ability to shoot down most, if not all, nuclear missiles long before they hit Israel."

"However," Carr argued, "it doesn't have to come to that.

"All I'm asking, Mr. Prime Minister, is that you rescind your order for deployment for one more hour. That'll give us time to finish negotiations with the Middle Eastern forces, and hopefully, to talk to General Chevsky. If we fail, then the United States will support any actions you choose to take."

After a few seconds of silence, the Prime Minister answered, "Very well. We will wait one more hour. If we do not receive a favorable report, evidenced by the beginning of a withdrawing of enemy combatants from our borders, we will strike."

"Thank you, Mr. Prime Minister," Carr gratefully replied. "I'll be back in touch with you shortly."

Leaders of the Middle Eastern nations within the Coalition were gathered in Damascus, Syria, where, in a videoconference with America's Secretary of State, and after heated exchanges, they voted to order their troops to stand down and begin to withdraw. However, their combined forces, poised on Israeli borders with Egypt, Lebanon and Jordan, amounted to only 30 percent of the Coalition's total firepower.

The vast majority of the military assets belonged to Russia and were controlled by the rebellious General Chevsky, who sat on the Syrian borders with Israel. When the Middle Eastern leaders informed Chevsky of their decision to withdraw, he went ballistic, vowing that with or without them he would invade.

President Carr was quickly informed by Secretary of State, James Parlay. Carr immediately placed another call to Prime Minister Ehud in Jerusalem.

The Israeli Prime Minister answered the phone.

"Yes, Mr. President. Thank you for calling, but there is no need for you to go into a long explanation of what has transpired in Damascus or in the conversation between General Chevsky and the other leaders in his coalition. Our intelligence network allowed us to hear every word of all exchanges.

"We are now re-targeting our nuclear strike zone away from all the cooperating armies and focusing them exclusively on the Russian positions on our border with Syria as well as their naval forces in the Mediterranean."

"Mr. Prime Minister," injected Carr, "would you kindly hear me out first? I have just issued orders for a squadron of Stealth B-1 bombers to eliminate the Syrian command bunker where General Chevsky is currently located. Our bombers will be over the target in twenty-two minutes with very powerful bunker-busting smart bombs that will make a valley of that mountain in short order. I'm asking that you grant us that 22 minutes to complete that mission and take out the bunker and General Chevsky."

"Mr. President, our country is facing annihilation. Nevertheless, you have your 22 minutes to launch your assault. But if you fail to destroy this madman Chevsky, we will have no choice but to go nuclear."

"Agreed, Prime Minister," the grateful president exclaimed. "We will not fail."

WNN SPECIAL REPORT

"I'm Bryan Hister reporting from Jerusalem, and we have just been informed that the Coalition forces of Russia and numerous Middle Eastern nations set to invade Israel have begun to withdraw military assets from the border areas.

"The withdrawal is proceeding thus far without a clash of arms between Israel and Coalition forces. However, only minutes ago, we were told that a massive series of explosions occurred on the Syrian-Israeli border. Sources near the incident are saying that the explosion has literally leveled a large mountain along the Golan Heights, leaving a huge crater where the mountain used to be.

"American satellite surveillance is now confirming that a large detonation of some kind did in fact occur, and they have concluded that in all likelihood, the site was a Coalition arms storage facility containing not only multiple types of bombs and ammunition stores, but millions of gallons of fuel as well. The explosion is said to be accidental and for now we do not know how many casualties there are.

"Again, the main story is, the Russian and Middle Eastern invasion forces on the Israeli border are in a full withdrawal.

"The American State Department announced that all parties have agreed to meet next month in Washington D.C. for peace talks.

"This is Bryan Hister from Jerusalem. WNN now returns you to your regular programming."

Drs. Cohen and Minay sat drinking coffee at a table in the nearly deserted cafeteria of Castel Colledora.

"God has answered our prayer, Yossi," smiled Dr. Minay.

"Yes, He has," responded Dr. Cohen.

"I was pleased with our council's report," replied Minay. "Already our missionaries, excuse me, I mean, our representatives, report that they are finding fertile ground in Israel as well as in America. They tell us of a bountiful harvest.

"Also, our workers in Petra have completed their mission. Thankfully, the prophets foretold that during the fierce judgment to come, the Jewish remnant will flee to Petra. Now, when they arrive, they will find the writings that can save them.

"And," Cohen came back, "with Kostos and his henchmen out of the way, our people in Europe are free to work in the open."

"So, how much time," inquired Minay, "do you think we have before that vile fellow returns and the final, seven, horrid years of judgment begins?"

"I do not know, my friend," answered Cohen. "I don't think anyone other than God knows. I do know we must redeem every moment to reach as many as possible."

Dr. Minay slowly sipped from his cup. "The next time that devil brings those armies to the land of Israel, he will not be stopped until most of those left alive bow their knee to him. Then he will begin to show his fangs and the world will start to understand who he really is.

"May the grace of God help us, as you say, reach as many as possible with His Truth, before Yeshua appears in the clouds to remove the righteous from the judgment to come. And thanks be to the Lord, we will not be around when those seven years of hell on earth come."

"He has given us this short season," nodded Cohen, "before that secret taking away of His own, and we must now pull out all the stops to share His message of redemption with the Jewish people and to every Gentile who will listen."

"I know," Minay replied, "the prophecies are clear. It can't be much longer until you and I, my friend, will be carried away with the rest of His saints. And as for me, my brother, I am most ready. I think we'll finish well."

"Yes, I agree," smiled Cohen. "And how I long to see Yeshua, who paid such a high price to save us from the wrath to come. But there is no doubt about it. We will, indeed, be on the last ship out of port before a new kind of darkness descends upon this world."

"Yes, hallelujah!" grinned old Dr. Minay. "I say with John the Revelator, 'even so, come Yeshua Ha'Meshiach' and Maranatha.'"

Every day, Leah spent hours in Brad's hospital room at Castel Colledora. She watched his rapid improvements and even assisted the physical therapist in his rehab sessions.

She told Brad of her call to Director Pratt, as well as to the Mossad, giving them a complete rundown of Kostos' death and of Brad's wounds and current condition.

When he was able to be pushed in a wheelchair, Leah wheeled him out to the castle gardens, where they enjoyed long talks. It was in the garden where Brad began to ask more about her affiliation with Sodote Shalom and Yeshua.

It was a particularly beautiful, sunny day as the two of them sat again in the resplendent gardens, now in full bloom. Brad cleared his throat and tentatively asked, "I don't mean to impose on your personal matters, Leah, but you told me Dr. Cohen told you of Yeshua at a critical moment in your life. What had happened to bring you to that point?"

"Well," Leah sighed, "since you've asked, I will tell you. Nine years ago, when I was 21, I joined the Israeli army because, as you know, in my country it's compulsory that men and women serve two years in the IDF. I joined the same week with three of my dearest friends.

"Rachael, Benjamin, Avi and I had grown up together on the same kibbutz, gone through school together and, after basic training, we were all assigned to the same unit in the south. Rachael and I were like sisters, and Ben and Avi were truly like our big brothers. There was no romance, but a very close bond between the four of us.

One morning, we were all sent out in a Jeep to look into a possible terrorist's incursion near Gaza. We walked right into a trap and were ambushed by a group from Hamas. There was a fierce firefight. When it was over, the five Hamas gunmen were dead but so were my three closest friends."

"That had to be a horrible blow. I am so sorry," Brad put in.

"I thought I'd never recover." Leah, wiping away a tear, continued, "After a few weeks of leave, I received orders to report to an office in Tel

Aviv. I was met by two men who I later came to find out were Mossad. They offered a fresh start and I accepted."

"I hope you took a bit more time off before you jumped out of the pan and into that fire," Brad added.

"No, I didn't. I dove in, and after training, became consumed by the work until a few months later when I met 29–year-old Lt. Col. Nathan Levy, a deliciously handsome officer who swept me off my feet. We fell in love and four months later we had a beautiful wedding atop Mt. Carmel overlooking Hiafa and the Med."

"I had no idea you'd been married. Why didn't you tell me?"

"You never asked," Leah smilingly replied, "and besides, I hadn't planned on falling in love with you.

"Anyway, just a couple of hours before our wedding, Nathan received orders to report immediately to the Lebanese border. So, five minutes after we said our vows, he jumped in a waiting helicopter and headed north. We'd tearfully agreed to go on our honeymoon when he returned.

"But, he never returned. He was sent into Lebanon to check out the location of a Hezbollah camp. His Jeep hit a road mine and the next time I saw him, he was in a coffin draped with an Israeli flag."

"I can't tell you how deeply sorry I am," Brad said softly. "You lost your three best friends and a husband within six months."

"The truth is, I never got to know Nathan as a husband. We never even consummated our vows.

"After Nathan was killed, once again I was given leave and that is when I met sweet Dr. Cohen. We were both at a beachfront concert in Netanya and the group singing and dancing to Jewish folk music was a Messianic group of believers in Yeshua.

"Most Israelis shun such groups because of our people's history with Christianity. The Inquisition led by the Catholic Church, and of course, the early Crusades centuries ago left dead Jews all over Europe and the Middle East, all in the name of Christianity. And during World War II, so-called Christian Germans under Hitler called us 'Christ Killers' as they threw six million of us into ovens. Very few Jewish people realize that all those atrocities were perpetrated by those pretending to be Christians. True believers are, in fact, Israel's greatest friends and supporters.

"But that night on the beach I sat down next to Dr. Cohen, and after a while, we began to talk.

"Until then, I had always had this big void in my life, an emptiness that nothing could fill. I was a hurting, lonely, bitter person. And, I was so hungry for love—not the romantic kind, but real, unconditional, dependable love that couldn't be snatched away by bombs or bullets."

"Your search for that is not unique," Brad tenderly put in. "I think we're all searching for that something to complete us."

"I know that now," Leah nodded, "but that's when Dr. Cohen told me about Yeshua—not the Catholic or historical Yeshua, but the Son of God, the Messiah. He lovingly explained that the emptiness in our lives is the result of our rebellion, our sin, against Jehovah. Our rebellion has murdered our spirit and because of that we are cut off from God.

"And then, he told me the most beautiful story I'd ever heard about how God loves us so that He sent His Son to die and shed His blood to pay for our sins. He said that if I would receive Yeshua as my Messiah, He would fill my life with His joy and peace, and that I'd receive eternal life.

"So right there on that beach, Dr. Cohen and I knelt together in the sand and I asked God to forgive me and to let me know His Son, Yeshua.

"And, boy, did it ever change my life. I later became a part of Sodote Shalom. You already know that is Hebrew for the Secrets of Peace. That secret to peace is Yeshua. He is the Prince of Peace.

"As I've tried to tell you before, Sodote Shalom is a low-profile, widespread group of Jewish professionals from every field: doctors, attorneys, entrepreneurs, army personnel, business people, and even a few Mossad agents like myself who have accepted Yeshua as Messiah.

"Our goal, among other things, is to reach out mostly to Jews around the world and to share with them the message of the prophets about the Messiah. We have no doubt but that soon horrible judgment will fall upon this earth led by one the Scriptures allude to as the Antichrist. As

I recently learned, the prophets foretold how this Satan-possessed man will literally take over the world, but that he also will suffer a fatal head wound and then somehow return to complete his quest until Yeshua destroys him."

"Kostos! The devil incarnate!" Brad gasped. "That explains a lot. So, you were right. We weren't drugged or crazy. We really saw what we saw!"

"You are beginning to understand," smiled Leah. "And now God has given us time. We can't be sure of how much time, but we shall use what we have to share the great news of Yeshua and to warn our people about this soon coming false Messiah. His seven-year reign of terror will end when our true Messiah, Yeshua, returns to destroy the rule of Satan and establish the glorious Kingdom of God on the earth.

Brad had listened to her story in a most introspective way. Now he looked her in the eye and softly said, "I would like to know more about this Messiah, Yeshua."

A few days later, Brad's doctor told him he could be released from the hospital the coming week, but only if he promised to continue his rehab from wherever he went. The same day, Director Pratt ordered him to take six months off to heal up.

Leah had also asked for an extended leave, which had been granted.

The next morning, she entered Brad's room full of cheer, and sat down to talk to him.

"My family owns two bungalows on the north end of the Sea of Galilee, and I'm asking you to come to Israel while you've got some time off.

"I'll stay with my still very much alive mother in one of the bungalows, and you can stay in the other one, I mean, until you're better and ready to go back to work."

"Oh, I don't know," Brad answered. "I don't want to be a burden on you or your family, and I'm really not sure about ever going back to work with the CIA."

"Don't be silly," Leah laughed. "You're no burden. But you do need some serious rest time. We can eat like horses, boat, swim, fish, and beat up beach bullies. Hey, it'll be fun! And then you can decide about your future. It'll also give me time to answer all your questions about Yeshua. What do ya say?"

"I say," Brad smiled broadly, "it's not only the best offer I've had, but it's the only offer I've had! So, yes, besides, I do need to talk to you about the future as well. Let's do it!"

Five days later, flying on a private jet owned by one of the businessmen who belonged to Sodote Shalom, Brad and Leah left Rome's DaVinci International Airport.

They landed in Tel Aviv at Ben Gurion Airport and drove to the Galilee in Leah's brand new Mercedes, bought for her by the Mossad to replace the one destroyed when she and Brad were almost killed in the Judean wilderness.

For both of them, life was good again—at least for now.

VATICAN CITY, ROME

Charon D. Kostos' body lay in state, enclosed in the hermetically sealed glass casket resting on the altar of St. Peter's Basilica. Every day, tens of thousands of mourners filed by to pay their respects.

After 21 days, the Holy Father ordered the casket removed and secretly taken to his private chapel, where it rested on the altar beneath a freshly severed goat's head.

Three times a day the Pope quietly entered the chapel to stand silently over the casket and look intently down at Kostos' body.

It was now midnight as he made his final visit of the day.

The Pontiff prayerfully approached the casket-laden altar. He came to a stop and again looked into the face of Kostos' corpse and quietly spoke.

"Soon, Master, we shall complete that which we started and the world will bow their knees and worship you as God."

As the Pope was about to leave, he turned to look one more time at the countenance of Kostos. A sense of destiny swept over the Pontiff as he watched a faint smile momentarily creep to life on the dead man's face and then slowly fade away.

The Pope nodded his head and whispered, "Soon, very soon." He turned and left the chapel.

...and I stood upon the sand of the sea and saw a beast rise up out of the sea, having seven heads and ten horns, and upon his horns ten crowns, and upon his heads the name of blasphemy.

And the beast I saw was like a leopard, and his feet were like the feet of a bear, and his mouth like the mouth of a lion; and the dragon gave him his power, and his throne and his great authority.

And I saw one of his heads as though it were wounded to death and his deadly wound was healed, and all the world wondered after the beast.

And they worshipped the dragon who gave power unto the beast; and they worshipped the beast, saying, Who is like the beast? Who is able to make war with him?

And all that dwell upon the earth shall worship him, whose names are not written in the Book of Life of the Lamb slain from the foundation of the world.

If any man have an ear, let him hear. (Revelation 13:1–4, 8–9; KJV)

The End...Perhaps.

FREE CD

Purchasers of the *The Man Who Would Be God* may receive a free CD entitled The Antichrist is Alive and Well from Phil Arms' popular series *Prophecy—The Last Generation.*

Simply fill out the form below with your name and mailing address, and you will receive your copy within two to three weeks.

For more information on the 11-part series *Prophecy—The Last Generation* by Phil Arms, or to find a complete list of resources by Phil Arms, visit LifeReachMinistries.com or call 1-800-829-9673.

Name____

Mailing Address__________________________________

City________________State______Zip code____________